MOONSTONE OBSESSION
BY
ELIZABETH ELLEN CARTER

ACKNOWLEDGEMENTS

Thank you to editor Kyle A Lewis, who believed in this story.
Thank you too to my darling husband.

TITLES BY
ELIZABETH ELLEN CARTER

The Moonstone Romances
Moonstone Obsession
Moonstone Conspiracy
Moonstone Promise

Warrior's Surrender

Dark Heart

Heart of the Corsairs Trilogy
Captive of the Corsairs
Revenge of the Corsairs
Shadow of the Corsairs

The King's Rogues Series
Live and Let Spy
Spyfall
Spy Another Day
Father's Day

Nocturne

The Thief of Hearts

The deWolfe of Wharf Street

The Promise of the Bells

LEARN MORE AT EECARTER.COM
OR SEARCH 'ELIZABETH ELLEN CARTER' ON
AMAZON

DEDICATION

To my mother, Elizabeth Ann, who spent a lifetime loving books
and who taught me to do the same.

TABLE OF CONTENTS

PROLOGUE

Captain Francis Armsden stood erect, hands behind his back, legs braced. The rocking movement of the two-masted brigantine grew more violent as the storm built up over the Celtic Sea.

He was proud of his ship, the *Pandora*, which was filled with the best of English manufactured goods—dinner services from the Staffordshire potteries, bolts of the finest wool, copper, iron and brass tools, and engines.

A commercial treasure created by the Industrial Revolution, en route to the New World.

Captain Armsden watched his men tighten the rigging, giving the square-rigged vessel stability in the rising wind and seas. With quick, economical movements, they worked to maintain control of the vessel as it battled the rising swell and blustering gale. February in Cornwall was for sailors, a savage time of year in a savage part of England. Miscalculations saw many a ship run aground on the rocky coast, with cargo and lives lost by the score.

Snatches of conversation were ripped away by the wind as the sailors responded to barked commands of officers to steady the course—far enough away from the coast to avoid the rocks, but close enough to watch for the beacons that stood high on the cliffs.

The captain yelled to one of the officers for his telescope.

Stepping closer to a lantern, Armsden checked his pocket watch, a bright shining piece, a marvel of engineering precision, and a gift from his wife of thirty years. Three hours out of the safe harbor of Bristol, by his estimation. They should be sighting the lighthouse near the mouth of the River Camel at Padstow in the next short while.

Pulling his telescope to full extension, the captain scanned the coast.

There on the headland, rather fainter than he had expected, a light.

"About! Fifteen degrees starboard," he called. The cry carried forward to the helmsman to make adjustment to their course.

Armsden frowned as the falling rain became torrential, obscuring the light. Murmuring thunder increased in volume. The veteran sailor wasn't afraid of much, but he'd long learned to trust his instincts, and tonight they told him something was wrong.

A gale force gust hit the brigantine broadside, pushing it closer to the coast. At that moment, lightning momentarily revealed the scene before the *Pandora*—rocks directly in front of her, all glossy black with pallid sea foam slithering back down their length.

The captain's command of *hard to port* was lost in the lightning's accompanying thunderclap, but by then it was too late; a noise louder still ripped through the howling gale and pounding surf as the *Pandora*'s hull breached.

The sailors frantically adjusted the rigging, trying to pull the vessel away before further damage could be done. Then another gust, followed by a powerful wave, dashed the ship, causing it to tilt on a sickening angle from which it failed to return fully upright.

Armsden did not need to consider his next command. "Abandon ship!"

Members of the crew dropped into the water, struggling to dodge broken timbers, tangled rigging, and containers of merchandise that would now never see their intended homes.

A wave sweeping across the deck cast Armsden into the water. He pulled himself to the surface, fought quickly out of the heavy coat that would drag him down, and, with powerful strokes, headed toward shore.

Eventually, the waves churned him onto the beach.

Battered and cut by the rocks, wounds stinging from the brine, the captain forced frigid, wet air into his lungs and scrambled onto the shingle, a mean piece of land edged by tall, precipitous cliffs. Turning to the sound of footfalls, he heard screams cut short.

In a nightmarish scene lit now by almost constant flashes of lightning, Armsden saw the cause of their misfortune—wreckers! Some were already pulling wave-swept cargo to shore; others used knives and swords to slay the defenseless crew.

A man stepped in front of the captain. He was dressed roughly but efficiently for the weather in a long, dark oilskin coat. His upturned collar and broad-brimmed hat obscured his features. In his hand, a pistol.

The powder flash was the last thing Francis Armsden saw. His watch being removed from his waistcoat pocket was the last thing he felt.

CHAPTER ONE

London

12 May 1790

Every window of Chesterfield House in London's fashionable Mayfair was ablaze with light. The strains of orchestra music wafting through the open windows welcomed those fortunate enough to be attending the ball thrown by the Viscount of Chesterfield for his good family friend James Mitchell, Lord Penventen.

Or, rather, hosted by the Countess of Chesterfield for her good friend Lady Christina of Penventen to mark her only child's return from the Americas.

Ladies in expensive silks and frothy laces stepped sideways to accommodate their wide skirts designed to emphasize tightly corseted waists and draw attention up to the display of cleavage that for many young, and not so young, women threatened to spill over the low-cut, square necklines.

Men in fitted breeches, elaborately designed waistcoats, and jackets added further to a riot of color among the fabrics.

Outside, Selina Rosewall steadied herself as the carriage rolled to a stop under the portico of the grand townhouse. Feeling the gaze of her brother William beside her, the young woman turned to face his amused look. Brunette ringlets tickled her ears as she turned, and the weight of drop earrings—sapphire-and-diamond ear bobs, a wedding gift from her father to her mother—swung pendulously with the movement.

"Close your mouth, dear sister. How on earth will you attract a husband if you look like a frog trying to attract flies?" teased William.

At once Selina's expression turned serious.

"I know how important tonight is to you, Bill. I promise not to be an embarrassment."

"You could never be an embarrassment, Selina, I was only teasing," he said, giving her hand a reassuring squeeze. "You look beautiful. Maman would be proud."

Selina blushed. Her brother smiled in return.

Although she would have been loath to hear it, most of all from her brother, Selina was a strikingly pretty young woman. When she smiled, her sparkling blue eyes held people in thrall.

At twenty-one years, she ought to have been married, perhaps to a sea captain like her brother or late father, perhaps to a well-to-do merchant, or, *dammit*, as her brother was fond of saying, at the very least have a gaggle of suitors from which to choose. But while other girls at the age of sixteen were being courted, Selina had been nursing their widowed and ailing father as William spent months at a time at sea, trying to hold the family business together.

She knew her brother's teasing words were lighthearted and made in jest, but there was truth behind them. With her sister-in-law expecting another baby—her fifth—finances were tight, and William could not be expected to support a spinster sister as well as his own expanding family.

Selina straightened in her seat. Tonight was an important opportunity for William to establish business relationships and perhaps receive some aristocratic patronage. Her role was to portray her brother in the best possible light.

She would not disappoint him.

A footman opened the carriage door, offering a white gloved hand to aid Selina from the conveyance. She took one last look down at her gown. It was a much narrower silhouette than those worn by many of the other fashionable women this night.

The fact was Selina's dress was adapted from a ball gown belonging to her sister-in-law, Sarah, that had been purchased in the first year of her marriage to William. Selina had owned no dress suitable for an occasion befitting royal patronage. Everything she had was practical clothing for running her father's house or her recently worn mourning clothes following his death.

William had kindly offered to buy his sister a new gown, but she could not justify the purchase and agreed instead to try on Sarah's old dress.

The dress was fashioned in shimmering sky-blue silk, and pink satin ribbon roses trimmed the edge of the festooned overskirt that had been raised to reveal the buttermilk cream lace that decorated the petticoats. The same lace adorned the sleeves at the elbows and the neckline to lend an illusion of modesty to the low-cut bodice.

The gown had been altered to fit Selina, and the only concession to the current fashion was the addition of a moderate amount of padding to the seat and hips to aid the spread of the cascading skirt. Only the truly wealthy wore the elaborate bustles that made the wearer appear nearly as broad as she was tall.

Selina had been dismayed when she tried the refitted gown on a few weeks earlier.

After turning this way and that to examine its fall in the mirror, she had eyed her sister-in-law's reflection askance.

"What?" Sarah Rosewall had responded from her chair in the drawing room. "You look beautiful! No man will be able to keep his eyes off you."

"Well," Selina replied, "if my conversation is lacking, perhaps my bosom will provide sufficient entertainment." She looked down at herself ruefully. When she walked, she feared exposing her breasts altogether.

"Perhaps I should add a kerchief," she mused, tugging the neck once again.

"You will do no such thing!" Sarah scolded. "You're a beautiful young woman. Show off your figure, flirt, and enjoy the attentions of young men. You're too young to dedicate yourself to spinsterhood."

Selina watched her sister-in-law nursing her youngest child, a girl. Sarah's peaches-and-cream complexion matched her sweet nature. She was only four years older than Selina, utterly in love with her husband, and more than content with her role as wife and mother.

"Perhaps that's not the life for me," she said, hating the wistfulness she heard in her voice, "but I have to be practical. I've imposed on you and William long enough. At the end of this summer I will apply for a position."

Sarah merely nodded and rolled her eyes. The discussion was a familiar one, and one topic Selina could not be dissuaded from. She had only agreed to go to the Penventen ball in the first place at the insistence of her brother.

So tonight, in London, far from the family home in Bristol, Selina stood and resisted the urge to tug at the dress.

"Ready?" William asked, offering his arm.

Selina took it and gave a smile, not quite her full generous smile, but William accepted it, allowing for her nervousness. Together they approached the luxurious townhouse filled with the treasures of Philip Stanhope, Viscount of Chesterfield.

The viscount was a gentleman not given to philanthropic works, instead dedicated to decorating his own life. Nonetheless, so far as Selina could see, Stanhope was a man of exquisite taste.

They walked to the gallery along imported Indian carpets hand-knotted in jewel-colored wool and stopped at the prize of the home— an intricately carved curved staircase complete with cast bronze balustrade that had been bought at auction following the death of the Duke of Chandos.

William paused at the centre of the balcony. Like the experienced sea captain he was, he took the time to survey the scene before him. He drew Selina's attention to a gaggle of young women elegantly coiffed with white wigs twelve inches tall, sporting elaborately colored and styled gowns with skirts many times the size of the wearer.

"In the purple is Charlotte, the Princess Royal. Over to your right"—he nodded to two men in powdered wigs—"is the Prime Minister, Mr. Pitt, talking with our host Philip Stanhope, Viscount of Chesterfield. The man with his back to us is, I believe, James Mitchell, Lord Penventen of Cornwall."

"And the man about to join them?" asked Selina, nodding at a distinguished but wan-looking gentlemen in his thirties now including himself in the group's conversation.

"That is the Member for Yorkshire, Mr. Wilberforce."

"The abolitionist William Wilberforce?"

"The very same."

Selina allowed herself a smile. Despite her nervousness, she was now looking forward to the evening.

"Well, one can be certain that conversation at supper won't be dull," she murmured.

Oh, to speak with these interesting men, if only for a moment, she thought.

* * *

At one end of the ballroom, Lady Christina Mitchell sat with her contemporaries, the dowagers and society matrons, watching the younger guests dance.

She gave a sidelong glance at her son.

He'd grown into a handsome man of twenty-eight years, so much like his father in looks, but his five years in Pennsylvania away from polite society had coarsened him, and he had returned with a certain eccentricity in his thinking she no doubt found somewhat alarming.

Tonight though, Lord Penventen appeared to be on his best behavior. He was dressed immaculately in tan breeches, an azure watered silk waistcoat lightly embroidered with silver thread, a crisp white shirt with fewer ruffles than was fashionable, and a fitted jacket in a slightly darker blue than the waistcoat.

His hair, a rich dark brown the same color of his eyes, was tied with a black velvet ribbon. For the life of her, Lady Mitchell could not persuade her son to wear a wig.

James had returned to England following his father's death a little over a year ago, but since had steadfastly refused to take his place at the family estate in Cornwall, instead preferring to manage his business interests from London.

It was time he wed, his mother had decided, and tonight she was pressing the claim of the usefully connected Abigail, Lady Houghall, lady-in-waiting to Charlotte, the Princess Royal.

But James Mitchell had a keen ability to read people—a handy skill in both cards and business negotiation—and knew that a sop to convention, such as agreeing to attend this ball tonight, would go a long way to appeasing his mother. Her harping was becoming a distraction he could ill afford; much better to mollify the woman, even if only momentarily, he decided.

Still, events such as these bored him, no matter how necessary, and being bored put him in a mischievous mood. James sipped his champagne and watched as the elaborate and mannered baroque dance came to an end.

"Lady Abigail appears free," he heard his mother whisper.

Yes, he could see that. He sipped from the flute again as the young woman with the alarmingly high white pompadour curtsied to her dance partner, all the while regarding him through lowered lashes.

Lady Abigail was the accomplished coquette. Her curtsy was low enough to give her dance partner a generous view, but nothing to suggest impropriety. James knew this lady was aware she was being observed, and not just by his devilishly handsome self.

She wore a gown that was the height of fashion, newly imported from Paris from the same couturier as the princess royal. Her pink, cream, and mauve striped gown was trimmed in gold satin bows that embellished the bodice from bust to waist. When she moved, smaller bows in the same color fluttered and danced like butterflies across the expanse of pleated fabric on the skirt.

Abigail's parted lips were daubed carmine, a vivid slash of color on a white-painted face. Her grey-green eyes made larger with expertly applied smoky eye shadow and eyebrow pencil.

James decided now was the time to make his escape.

"Perhaps the next dance, Mother. I've just spotted someone I need to speak to."

It was a lie and they both knew it, but as James moved out of Lady Abigail's orbit to seek an object for his excuse, his excuse found him.

"Lord Penventen…"

With an overly bright smile, James turned and exclaimed, "There you are, my good chap! I've been trying to catch you all evening. Where have you been keeping yourself?"

William Rosewall frowned, his confusion apparent. James had said no more than a few words to the man since arriving, and now he treated him like a long lost friend.

James ignored Rosewall's bemusement as his eyes lit on the young woman next to him.

"And pray tell where have you been keeping this gorgeous creature?"

Selina's eyebrow rose at the hyperbolic greeting, and she nudged her brother.

"Forgive me, Sir James, I wish to introduce my sister, Miss Selina Rosewall."

With eyes twinkling, James bowed low, sweeping Selina's hand up with his and presenting the back of her wrist with a theatrical kiss.

"Shall I compare thee to a summer's day? Thou art more lovely and more temperate."

Expecting the confused giggles he had received from the other women on whom he'd used this greeting, he was surprised by a light and genuine musical laugh.

"That man that hath a tongue, I say is no man, if with his tongue he cannot win a woman," she responded.

James blinked in surprise at her Shakespearean touché.

He drew himself to his full height of six feet and looked at her properly for the first time.

Selina Rosewall's sparkling blue eyes gave him pause. She was a pretty little thing. Unlike the garishly painted creatures at the ball tonight, she was fresh faced apart from a little color on her lips and the heightened color of her cheeks, which he suspected was natural.

And, rather than looking back at him in that obvious way most husband-hungry young women did, she met his gaze directly and with a great deal of amusement.

"Teach not thy lip such scorn, for it was made for kissing, lady, not for such contempt," he batted back.

* * *

Selina felt William shift on his feet beside her. Oh dear, as much as she loved her brother, he could be sometimes overbearingly protective. It was time to bring this harmless diversion to a close.

"Well said—that was laid on with a trowel."

It was James's turn to laugh.

"You *do* know your Shakespeare."

She smiled in acknowledgment.

Lord Penventen was one of the most handsome men Selina had ever seen. His elegant evening attire was expensive and fashionable but not foppish. And it was clear that he was an accomplished flirt; his dark eyes held dangerous mischief.

"Lord Penventen," she said, "my brother, Captain Rosewall, tells me you have interests in a colliery in Pennsylvania and engage in trade with the New World. Might I be so bold as to suggest that you and he might actually have some business interests in common to discuss?"

James accepted the opening and addressed William directly.

"Where's your fleet based, Captain?"

"Bristol, sir. I own one ship and have use of two more which I hope to own should trade be favorable."

"Triangle Trade?"

Selina saw her brother's mouth form a tight, stiff line. She knew that many of William's contemporaries made considerable fortunes by sailing goods to Africa, then transporting Negro slaves to Jamaica and making the trip back to England with rum and sugar.

William refused to take part, and she admired him beyond measure for it. He had told her briefly of serving as a young able seaman on a slave ship, and he vowed to never be a part of that accursed trade as master and commander of his own ship.

"No, sir. Straight trade to America and the Continent. It's a decent enough living for honest men."

* * *

James smiled and nodded in agreement as he glanced about the room. "Dangerous, nonetheless," he said absently, catching sight of Abigail slowly making her way through the crowd toward him.

"Sir?"

"Oh, nothing especial. I was merely recalling a vessel lost out of your home port recently. Taken by wreckers I understand."

"Ah. The *Pandora*. I knew its captain, Francis Armsden, if only by reputation. One or two of his former crew sail with me. Losing an experienced seaman is always a cause for regret. His death at the hands of wreckers is unconscionable."

James was no longer listening. Abigail was getting too close for comfort. He reached into his waistcoat pocket for a card, which he deftly handed to William.

"Do call on me early in the next week, Rosewall."

"I will, sir. Thank you."

"Oh, and one more imposition…your sister's hand?"

William gave a worthy impression of a freshly caught North Sea cod. The Captain's eyes bulged; his mouth opened and closed several times without issuing a sound. James observed Selina struggling to keep her composure at her brother's incredulous expression. Fortunately she took pity when his face turned an alarming shade of puce.

"He means for a dance, brother," she answered with unfeigned amusement. She turned to him and curtsied.

"He is at a loss for words, Lord Penventen, which does not happen often. So might I be so forward as to accept your offer…to dance, that is?"

CHAPTER TWO

The evening had passed pleasantly, and now, just after eleven o'clock, many of the elderly guests had left or retired, leaving the young and the drunk to further drink and dance until midnight or so, when supper would be served in the banquet hall.

Selina was happy to sit out this set. It had been more than an hour since she had seen William, and she hoped that opportunities to talk business were fruitful.

Her feet were sore from the long evening and the inattention of a couple of clumsy dance partners. Furthermore, Selina suspected the fruit punch that several young men had gallantly procured for her was more than liberally laced with alcohol despite their protestations to the contrary.

James Mitchell caught her eye again from twelve feet away, and he raised his glass of what appeared to be whiskey. She nodded and raised her half-full glass of champagne, one she had nursed for an hour, in response.

The man had claimed a further three dances in two hours, not excessive but enough to pique the curiosity of some of the guests, some of whom also claimed a dance, such as Geoffrey Dobell, Viscount Canalissy, son of the Earl Canalissy, who was, as it turned out, a neighbor of Lord Penventen's from Cornwall.

Other interested parties, such as Lady Abigail and the coterie of ladies-in-waiting, openly speculated about Selina behind their fans but, as they had done all evening, made no effort to speak to her themselves.

Instead they sent a volley of their swains to ask her to dance and fish for information—an action Selina considered the world's most laughable attempt at an interrogation. Those women would have learned she was no threat to their beaux if they'd simply engaged her in conversation.

Let them gossip, she thought. It's not like she was ever going to see them again after tonight. Just six more weeks in London and she would return home to Bristol to plan her new life as some family's governess.

Waiting on her writing bureau in Bristol was a newspaper advertisement she had written.

Position of governess or lady's companion wanted for young lady of quality. Accomplished in all the feminine arts. Literate, numerate, fluent speaker of French. Character references available.

Perhaps she could find employment attached to a nice middle class family, she thought. One of this new generation of self-made gentry, for whom hard work and merit mattered more than a fortunate birth.

The popular country dance ended and the floor cleared, gentlemen taking a bow, ladies a quick curtsy, and lovers retreating into the shadows and out to the garden for fresh air.

Heavy lead crystals in suspended chandeliers, lit by hundreds of candles, caused prisms of light to dance on the empty parquet floor as the orchestra sounded the first few bars of a new piece, one that was all the rage on the Continent. The waltz.

A murmur ran through the crowd along with titters of amusement. Those men who had not selected partners for the next dance quickly pressed their claim with their favorites.

"Shocking! I'm surprised the Duke of Chesterfield allows such indecency," Selina overheard an elderly dowager seated behind her harrumph to her companion. "Have you ever seen a waltz? Pressing bodies together so barely a kerchief passes between."

Although growing in popularity at the most fashionable soirees, waltzing was highly risqué. Selina had only ever danced it with one of

William's twin boys on her hip as a dance partner. She smiled at the memory while she watched couples move out onto the dance floor.

"Do you wish to scandalize the Countess of Harrogate?" James spoke close to her ear.

She jumped, but not before a delicious shiver ran down her spine.

Selina's first thought was to demur, but the promise she made to her sister-in-law weeks ago to flirt and enjoy asserted itself, so she gifted James with a dazzling smile.

Reacting to her changing expression with a knowing look of his own, James bowed formally, taking a proffered hand to escort her to the floor.

Selina was surprised at how smoothly she and James moved together. In contrast to the other dances this evening, with their highly rehearsed steps, the waltz simply required the couple to move in harmony.

Encircled by James's right arm at her waist, his left hand holding her right, Selina was more than aware of his masculinity as they moved around the floor. Unlike some of the other men she had danced with this evening, men whose overly liberal scent of cologne nearly made her gag, James smelled of crisp pine and rich, fresh tobacco.

She looked up to find him regarding her equally thoughtfully. It was disconcerting, so she spoke.

"My Lord, do you feel a sharp pain in your back?"

He frowned, confused.

"I fear the daggers being cast in your direction by the Lady Abigail must surely be drawing blood."

"Ah, so that's what it was I felt." He grinned before leaning in to whisper, "I thought the ill will was from the Viscount Canalissy for dancing with the most intriguing woman here."

A sudden rush of heat bloomed through her, and with that, every coherent thought fled. If not for James's firm hold and skilful movement, Selina was sure that she would have tripped over her own feet.

"Oh, now I know you're having fun at my expense," she said breathlessly.

"Are you sure?" He grinned.

She looked him full in the face and arched an eyebrow.

James's smile broadened as Selina recovered her poise.

"You don't believe me?"

She gave a long slow smile and shook her head in response.

Seeing the challenge, he leaned in. "Let's go see," he whispered, and changed direction suddenly, pulling her close so her body molded to his as he deftly pivoted midstep.

As the dance continued, he challenged her—a chasse to promenade, a reverse turn step—until the waltz came to an end and the audience applauded, distracted by the wafting scent of hot food being brought into the adjoining banquet hall. The band leader announced one more dance before a break and the final set dances of the night.

Selina felt her hand snared before she noticed Viscount Canalissy beside her.

"Miss Rosewall, I couldn't help but notice you on the dance floor. You are Terpsichore, the Muse of Dance brought to life," he said breathlessly. "Would you do me the honor of sharing your gift?"

The viscount wasn't a bad-looking man in his own right. He was equally as tall as James but leaner. His periwig was the height of fashion. His gold-trimmed olive waistcoat matched smartly with the breeches and coat. But his pale grey eyes ringed with dark lashes gave him a look of intensity that Selina found disconcerting. And where James's hyperbolic speech was humorously ironic in nature, the viscount's sounded a parody, like false flattery or a pretty tune played off-key.

She hesitated in her reply, hoping that James would come to her rescue. She glanced in his direction to find him distracted by Lady Abigail and swallowed a measure of disappointment.

It didn't go unnoticed by Sir Geoffrey, and she sought to mollify him.

"You flatter me more than you ought, my Lord, but alas, I must go in search of my brother before supper is announced."

Selina smiled what she hoped appeared a genuinely regretful smile, but, as she moved to pull her hand away, Lord Geoffrey's grip tightened.

"Then allow me to assist. I believe I saw the Captain in discussions in the billiard room where some of the men are playing cards."

She doubted it. William never gambled. But perhaps, as an ice breaker for business discussions, he'd made an exception?

Against her better judgment she allowed the viscount to escort her from the throng in the ballroom, along a long hallway where she heard the sounds of masculine discussion and laughter just ahead of the pungent odor of tobacco, whiskey, and sweat.

Selina stood in the doorway of the billiard room where, through the blue-grey smoke of pipes and cigars, she could see tables of men in groups of four and eight, gaming with cards or dice.

A large billiard table dominated the room and here two men with long, tapered cues circled the rectangular table with all the concentration of two men stalking game.

"He doesn't seem to be here, Miss Rosewall," said Lord Geoffrey, stating the obvious.

"Indeed not." Selina swallowed her irritation, suspecting that she'd been deliberately misled. "Perhaps I'd better return to the ballroom. I'm sure that is where William will expect to find me."

Her movement back toward the hall was halted by Lord Geoffrey's restraining hand around her wrist. She tugged futilely and glared at him. His expression was impassive, and a trickle of unease worked its way up her neck.

She looked into the billiard room; no one had noticed them, the men completely absorbed in their gaming.

Lord Geoffrey was six inches taller and a good deal stronger. He could easily overpower her and pull her into one of the empty connecting rooms off the hall before she could mouth a protest. Apart from the activity in the billiard room, they were alone in a quiet part of the house. What would it do to her reputation if she looked for sanctuary in a room full of men? Would it hurt her brother's cause to make a scene?

For the first time in her life, Selina felt vulnerable.

A burst of laughter from a gaming table broke the spell. At the distraction, she yanked her arm free and moved as fast as her skirts would allow down the hall, turning right along another passage, which opened outside onto the colonnade.

There she heard the sound of the orchestra and could see, some yards distant, light and people spilling from the wide-open ballroom doors.

Thanks to her pulse thudding in her ears, she had no idea whether Lord Geoffrey followed or not. Selina slowed from the brisk walk, her corset preventing the full measure of air that her lungs demanded.

Just a yard or two away from the ballroom, close enough to rejoin company if she needed to, Selina leaned against a column to gather her breath, the stone cool to her heated cheeks.

Stupid, stupid girl, she chided herself.

"Selina?"

Jumping at the voice, Selina turned to its owner wide-eyed and mute.

* * *

James inspected the clearly frightened woman. Her gown appeared intact although her elaborately curled hair had started to come adrift of its pinning. Her face was flushed. Had she just come from an assignation? For some reason the thought didn't sit well with him.

"Wait here," he demanded.

Moments later James returned with a glass of unadulterated punch in one hand, and with the other led her to a low stone bench within sight of the ballroom but mercifully cast in shadows by a boxwood hedge.

Now seated, Selina accepted the glass, turning it in her hands, grateful for the distraction and the anonymity of the shadows and obviously thankful not to be on the receiving end of an interrogation as she would receive if her brother had found her first.

James waited patiently for her to speak, and for a few long moments they sat in silence.

"Thank you," she offered. James nodded and it was understood that she meant for more than the glass of punch.

"I'm sure I have inconvenienced you horribly," she added softly.

He shook his head, even though she could not see the gesture.

"Selina, look at me…please."

She did and the light from a garden lantern revealed she was blinking back tears.

His heart softened. If it was any other woman, he'd see her safely back to her escort and consider his work done, but he sensed Selina was different—needed something different from him.

He met her gaze.

"Will you tell me what happened?" he asked.

She shook her head before looking back at her glass.

James shifted in his seat to look back down the colonnade in the direction he was sure she had come from. As he did so, a movement in the shadows caught his eye.

Was someone listening in on them? Who?

He turned back to his companion, whose composure was returning.

"In that case, will you assure me that you are unharmed?" he murmured low.

"I am."

Silence.

Selina raised her head and looked at James fully in the face.

"Truly, I am unharmed." She nodded. "All except, I think, for my dignity, because you have been more than kind and you are far too important to have your time monopolized by me."

James gave a half smile.

The tension and fear that had radiated from her when he first found her had dissipated. All she had needed was time, not a big scene, which would have only embarrassed her further.

He decided to test the mood.

"And what if I told you that you are the only woman here whom I wouldn't mind being monopolized by?"

Selina genuinely laughed. "Then I'd say you are a most notorious scoundrel and breaker of women's hearts and I shouldn't believe a word you tell me."

James laughed at the spirited rejoinder.

She stood, placing one of her hands in his and giving it a squeeze.

"Thank you." She smiled down at him.

He stood also, his eyes capturing hers. His hand returned the pressure before lifting her hand to his lips for a kiss that lasted a few moments longer than it needed to.

"I want to see you again, Selina."

Chapter Three

Lady Christina Mitchell cringed as her son engaged in the vulgar activity of whistling as he entered the sunlit drawing room where she elected to have breakfast this morning.

"Good morning, Mother," he said, greeting her with a kiss on the cheek.

Although it was just two of them for breakfast, the little table was set immaculately with pressed linens and dominated by a glittering gilt tray holding silver tea, coffee, and chocolate pots.

He took his seat at the opposite end of the small oak table and allowed his valet, Jackson, to pour him a cup of strong black coffee. Lady Christina raised a cup of tea to her lips and the sleeve of her pale pink morning robe drifted down her arm and away from the dish of preserves at her elbow.

James was dressed for business. Dark grey wool breeches tucked into polished black riding boots. A narrow-cut frock coat in matching wool was relieved by a crisp white linen shirt and a lightly patterned maroon cravat.

James knew his mother rarely rose before eleven o'clock any morning, and since the Christmas season, he'd only ever seen her at the evening meal.

The fact that his mother had arisen and dressed before ten in the morning meant that the Lady wished to have "a word."

"Did you rest well?" he enquired.

He waited. This could be interesting.

"James," she began, "it may surprise you to learn that I am not a young woman any longer and that I know it would be your father's wish to see our estate's future secured."

James ignored her sarcasm. He deliberately sipped his coffee and waited for her to continue.

"And by secured, I mean a legitimate heir with someone of quality and respectability, not a by-blow with a sailor's daughter or some scullery maid."

"Has some young woman approached you to say that she is carrying my child?" he asked, his voice low and cold.

Lady Christina matched her son's serious look.

"Your reputation as one who enjoys feminine company has reached even my ears. Surely it wouldn't be too much to ask you to choose one to take as a wife."

"Like Lady Abigail you mean?"

"Lady Abigail would be ideal, with her direct connection to the crown. But if not her, then there is Lady Catherine or Lady Alexandra, both of whom are…"

Enough, James vowed, before she rattled off the names of all the eligible women of the ton.

"Why the sudden interest in my matrimonial state, Mother?"

"I already told you."

No, there was more to it than that, he knew. More like looking for a protégé to train in the art of brow-beating, nagging, and scolding of the type that sent his father to an early, miserable grave.

James was sure the old lord died just to get some peace and quiet.

He mentally saluted his sire before returning his attention to his mother. She stared at him, expecting an answer to a question he didn't remember being asked.

How to salvage the morning before his mother decided to have one of her tempers? James could happily spend all day, and all night, away from the house, but the servants could not, and he felt he owed them a debt.

To this day he still carried a pang of guilt at a boyhood prank he played on his mother involving a tree frog and an expensive teacup. The son of one of the gardeners had been blamed and was roundly thrashed in James's stead for furnishing the amphibian.

From that day on, James vowed to own his mistakes.

And allowing this conversation to continue was shaping up to be another one. He decided to launch a diversion.

"Mother, could I impose on your impeccable social skills to assist me to prepare a house party at Penventen this summer?"

To the casual observer it would have seemed that the woman's expression had not altered a jot, but James saw the signs—the slight widening of the eyes, a tic in a cheek muscle. He hid a slight smile behind another sip of coffee.

"If you insist," she answered cautiously.

James granted her a full grin before rising from the table.

"Then that's settled. Ten guests for a month at Penventen Hall ahead of Pitt's masquerade ball. There's one or two names I'll want to add, so I'll be back at supper to approve the list."

* * *

Selina fixed her gaze down the sweep of lawn toward the lake that was the centerpiece of St James Park. Created by Charles II, the parkland and lake were London's answer to the beautiful palace gardens of France.

Bounded by three palaces—St James, Buckingham, and the ancient Westminster—the gardens had seen their share of romantic assignations of both royalty and commoners alike, many such captured in bawdy verse by Charles II's favorite, John Wilmot, the second Viscount of Rochester.

Today, under the mild sun and blue skies of spring, the park was innocence itself. Tall boulevards of trees offered shade; hedgerows offered privacy. Willows by the water became hideouts and haunts for playing children, while fallen petals from the cascading clumps of wisteria laid a carpet of mauve flowers for couples who walked arm in arm.

Among them, Members of Parliament, their staff, messengers, and lobbyists crisscrossed the park either on foot or horseback, headed to meetings of varying import.

Dressed in a simple pale green walking dress with practical elbow-length sleeves for painting, Selina had been seated on a bench with her portable easel for about an hour, making the occasional stroke on the paper with a charcoal but mostly distracted by the antics of her three nephews—six-year-old twins Timothy and Richard and three-year-old George—who had turned a willow tree into a fort to be playfully defended from other boys.

Her sister-in-law had finally settled her youngest child, twelve-month-old Charlotte, the very picture of her mother, to sleep on a picnic blanket and turned to examine the sketch at length.

"It's a fine piece of work but it looks nothing like the scene in front of us," she remarked in a warm, teasing voice.

It was a sketch of James as she recalled him from the ball several nights before—handsome, confident, charming, with a knowing lift to his mouth and his intense and intelligent dark eyes.

"I thought if I came down to the park and sketched something else I might be able to get thoughts of him out of my head," Selina admitted. "But then I realized that if I didn't put down his likeness, I wouldn't be able to draw anything else."

"Are you in love with him?"

Selina was scandalized. "Sarah! I only met the man the once."

Sarah shrugged, nonplussed.

"I knew I was in love with your brother the moment I saw him."

"That's different!" Selina busied herself by putting the finished sketch in her leather portfolio before readying another paper on the easel and opening a tin box of watercolor paints.

"He's a peer of the realm. He'll be expected to marry a Lady of court and, if I believe what I saw, there's one particular Lady who is waiting on more than just the Princess Royal."

Sarah laughed at the description of Lady Abigail, whom Selina had briefly described the morning after the ball following Sarah's insistence that she share every detail of the evening.

"William tells me that Lord Penventen wasn't the only eligible young man vying for a dance. In fact, you were so engaged he didn't get to dance with you at all."

Selina laughed. "And aren't my toes glad! When it comes to dancing, your husband has two left feet and the grace of an ox."

"Don't I know it! Why do you think I insisted you go in my stead? I need my feet to keep up with these four!"

The two women dissolved in a fit of giggles before Selina turned her hand back to capturing the landscape in front of her, deftly re-creating the tapestry of richly colored flowers of red, yellow, and purple in garden beds, the line of trees, the sweep of the lake, and the pair of water fowl swimming toward the aptly named Duck Island.

After a period of companionable silence, Sarah brushed Selina's elbow and nodded at a tall man in a top hat who started toward them, having come from the Horse Guards Parade entrance.

Selina had noticed him earlier. He spent several long minutes in deep conversation with another man who, before leaving, had been handed what appeared to be a dispatch box. Strange, but she supposed not so very unusual around the Parliament.

Sarah's eyes twinkled with mischief. "Could this be your Lord Penventen, coming to call?"

"He's not my Lord anything," Selina hissed, instead focusing her attention on the watercolor.

"By night a skilled dancer and now I learn you are a gifted painter. My dear Miss Rosewall, dare I say you are the very embodiment of all the muses?"

Selina's eyes widened to hear the voice of Viscount Canalissy, who now stood at her shoulder, fingering his hat. Between Sarah at her right, the bench at her back, and the easel in front, Selina was trapped.

She strained her neck to look up at the viscount, who regarded her with the same odd expression he wore outside the billiard room last night.

"My Lord Canalissy, what an unexpected surprise."

Well that much she could say in all truth. What she really wanted to say was that someone as finely educated as he ought to know that the Greeks had no muse for painting.

"May I introduce my sister-in-law, Mrs. William Rosewall?"

Viscount Canalissy bowed and greeted the other woman although his eyes never left Selina's. Tension thrummed through her once again until it was broken by a cry from young Richard, who had tumbled and grazed his knee.

Sarah went to see to the child, and Geoffrey took advantage of the vacant seat. Although there was ample space between them, Selina still felt stifled.

"How do we deserve the honor of your company today, my Lord?" she asked, risking a snub by refusing to look at him, instead putting her attention to cleaning her brushes.

"It must be fate, Miss Rosewall. I've found that you've occupied my thoughts since the ball, and now, as if I had conjured you up, here you are."

"Such regard is an honor most undeserved," she remarked.

Canalissy laughed, taking her words as flattering, no doubt.

"Not at all. I'm sure that you've occupied the thoughts of many others after watching you dance so intimately with Penventen."

That was a pointed statement.

"Well then, my Lord, they wonder in vain." Selina spared him a glance before laying down the paintbrush and wiping her hands on a rag with sharp, efficient movements. Anger had given her a measure of boldness.

"By the end of next week they will have found someone else to gossip about. Besides, my family and I return to Bristol at the end of the month, and it is likely to be a very long time before I shall see London again and receive the attention of such distinguished company."

"I've offended you," he said. It was a statement, not an apology.

"Truth plainly spoken is never offensive. May I be so bold as to ask why you've elected to take such an interest?"

"Not at all. Lady Abigail is a second cousin, but she will break her heart waiting on Penventen to make good his promise of marriage."

"And what has this to do with me?"

"You may feel I speak out of turn, but I have high regard for James as well. We grew up side by side in Cornwall, but he's a restless man given to throwing himself headlong into any cause that captures his attention.

"I saw the especial regard he paid you. In fact, who could not? It would be remiss of me not to take the initiative in preventing at least one more heart being broken, so I was only too willing when Lady Abigail asked me to draw your attention while she spoke to her intended."

Selina listened silently, cursing herself as her stomach turned to lead. The viscount made perfect sense. Could she have misjudged him? Perhaps he had no intention of doing anything improper outside the billiard room, only intending to delay her return to the ballroom for Lady Abigail's sake.

She recalled her final conversation with James, when she accused him of being a scoundrel and a "breaker of women's hearts."

James had laughed. He hadn't protested the description, and why should he? He was just being kind to a silly young provincial woman at her first royal ball.

Selina used the movement of packing away her easel to gather her thoughts before turning to Viscount Canalissy. He looked at her with that same neutral expression, and she began to wonder if it was part of his usual countenance.

She surprised herself by speaking evenly.

"Thank you very much for taking the time to explain this delicate situation to me. It is certainly not my intent to be the cause of anyone's discomfort."

A slow smile split Canalissy's over-full lips.

"You are a young woman of rare quality, Miss Rosewall, and I say so most sincerely. For the short time while you are in London, and I hope for some time after that, I would have the honor of being considered a friend."

"Thank you, my Lord. You honor me indeed."

Sarah and the boys approached and, oblivious to the serious conversation in her absence, Sarah schooled the children in giving a little bow to the viscount, which he acknowledged with a smile and a nod.

"Help your Aunt Selina with her things, boys, while I pick up little Charlotte."

"Madam, allow me." Sir Geoffrey bent and swiftly lifted the still-sleeping girl into his arms. "I have my carriage at the entrance to the park. It is at your disposal to take your party home."

Sarah curtsied. "Thank you, my Lord, your kindness is welcome."

Excited by the unexpected adventure of riding in a viscount's carriage, Richard's small injury was forgotten, and he, along with his twin and young George, were on their best behavior while the carriage's horses clip-clopped their way through cobbled streets.

Charlotte sucked her thumb sleepily while on her mother's lap, watching her Aunt Selina and her new friend.

"Then I'd say you are a most notorious scoundrel and breaker of women's hearts and I shouldn't believe a word you tell me."

Selina replayed the conversation in her head and now cringed with embarrassment. How could she have been so naïve as to believe she could flirt without consequences? Why should she think he was being anything other than polite when he said he wanted to see her again?

Not that she should ever expect to see him again, she thought ruefully.

Selina considered burning the sketch that lay in her portfolio but decided against it. She would keep it as a reminder of what happened when one let one's guard down. Selina would not let herself be as foolish again. She would post her advertisement to the newspaper tomorrow.

At their destination, the townhouse William had rented for the season in Soho, the viscount's carriage drew in behind another coach. Selina assumed it belonged to a business acquaintance of her brother.

Geoffrey assisted her from the vehicle while Selina in turn held out her arms for Charlotte, allowing her sister-in-law to gather her children. Geoffrey escorted them to the door and into the black-and-white-tiled foyer.

As the viscount was about to leave, the study door opened on Selina's left, and she turned to find herself face-to-face with the man she had been convinced she would never see again.

CHAPTER FOUR

James recovered from his surprise faster than Selina did hers. Surveying her, he determined that, even dressed in an ordinary green walking dress with her hair loosely pinned, Selina was still one of the prettiest women he'd ever seen.

He gave her a warm smile, then acknowledged the introduction of Sarah and the children before the mother bundled her brood out of the room. James then turned his attention to the other party. Viscount Canalissy didn't appear to be pleased to see him here.

Good.

"Why, Geoffrey," he said mildly, "even in a city as large as London, we do seem to be crossing paths more and more."

Canalissy grinned, but the effect was rather cold.

"Some of us are here to be of service, and, with my mission now complete, I bid everyone adieu."

Canalissy turned to Selina, taking her hand and pressing it urgently to his lips.

"Thank you for the pleasure of your company this afternoon. Perhaps you will allow me to call again?"

Surprise and confusion clouded her features, but Selina curtsied, out of habit it seemed.

"If that is your wish, my Lord."

Geoffrey released her hand and turned toward the door before taking a last triumphant look at James.

"And I'm sure our paths will cross at the opera tonight. Lady Abigail tells me she's looking forward to your company this evening."

"No doubt," James agreed.

Then a quick bow and nod to William, and the viscount departed.

To his disappointment, Selina refused to look at him after Geoffrey's words and simply addressed her brother.

"Attend your guest, William. I'll go and assist Sarah with the children."

* * *

It was unlikely that William and Sarah had noticed that Selina was more quiet than usual at the dinner table that night. The lively chatter of the three boys coupled with toothy squawks of agreement from Charlotte meant that she wasn't required to contribute much to the conversation.

Once the children were in custody of the housekeeper for cleaning and putting to bed, the three adults moved to the parlor.

"It was a pleasant surprise to see Sir James Mitchell here this afternoon. I know that he had promised an appointment, but I never expected him to make a call," observed Sarah, accepting the glass of sherry William had just poured.

"No more surprised than I," said William, handing a glass to Selina, who was seated in a wingback chair close to the window. She had determined to take advantage of the twilight to complete her watercolor from the day.

"It seems that he is very agreeable to the idea of a business partnership," said William, taking a seat next to his wife and sipping from his own sherry glass.

"He tells me the coal deposits around the city of Pittsburgh are huge, larger than Yorkshire, and then there is the trade that services the south. Transportation by ship and smaller boats are sorely needed there.

"He has proposed that he purchase the remaining leasehold on the *Andorra* and the *Diamond*." William paused significantly until all eyes were on him. "And in exchange for a half share in the *Marguerite*, he will fund an agent in Pittsburgh."

Selina started in surprise. The three-masted barque, the *Marguerite*, had been their father's ship, named for their mother.

The ship was his pride and that, too, of his son.

"That's an extraordinarily generous arrangement, brother," piped up Selina. "But to sell a share in the *Marguerite*…"

"I know and I'm not taking the offer at face value," he replied. "We have a broad agreement and that is all. There will be at least another month of negotiation before we agree to sign contracts."

William paused and sipped his sherry for a moment. He seemed to be choosing his words carefully.

"It was a very pleasant surprise to see the Viscount Canalissy this afternoon," he sounded out.

"Yes, very pleasant," Selina replied levelly. She waited to see the direction this conversation was heading in, all the while with a horrible feeling that it would be the same old discussion regarding her marital state.

"Perhaps you should encourage him to call."

"I shouldn't get your hopes up William. Viscount Canalissy was simply being kind," she said, hating the way she allowed her ruefulness to color her words. "Besides, he was putting on an act to teach your new business partner a lesson."

Now she had the attention of both William and Sarah and she knew neither would let the matter drop before she explained.

Deciding on her words cautiously, she told of Canalissy's diversion at the ball and his warning regarding Sir James's relationship with Lady Abigail.

Seeing her brother's darkening countenance, Selina realized she hadn't been cautious enough.

"Let me explain again," she continued. "Lord Penventen did nothing untoward at the ball. He was pleasant and amusing. It was me. I was the one at fault. And the viscount knew that Lord Penventen's…" She struggled for the right word "…*vivaciousness* might be misunderstood by someone who's…inexperienced."

William settled somewhat and now it was Selina's turn to grow red. "I'm sorry, Will."

"For what, darling?" her sister-in-law soothed. "You're a beautiful, intelligent young woman, and it should be no surprise that men would be hovering around like mayflies. Just know that not every man has the most honorable intentions, is all."

"This summer cannot end quickly enough," Selina muttered, mostly to herself.

"Well, don't be in too much of a hurry to rush off into service. There's plenty of time for a husband to sweep you off your feet," Sarah advised.

* * *

James cast a glance back at Abigail, dressed flawlessly in a gold-and-coral brocade gown, less wide than her royal ball gown but still at the very height of fashion, with sleeves that puffed slightly at the shoulder and fitted tightly at the elbow.

Satisfied that she was preoccupied with the attentions of a gaggle of admirers and friends, her escort disappeared down a passageway leading to the opera boxes on the far side of the house.

He had less than ten minutes during this intermission to attend his meeting.

Counting down until he found the right box, he silently slipped into a seat beside a man who remained in a shadowed corner.

"Enjoying the performance?" James greeted.

"Not particularly," the man chuffed, and then went on. "You knew that idiot Charles Fox has thrown his hat in with the Revolutionary Society?"

Ah yes, the Leader of the Opposition and thorn in the side of the Prime Minister for nearly ten years.

Fox was not a man who liked to be humiliated, but he certainly had been when he and his coalition partner, then Prime Minister Lord Frederick North, had been defeated in a vote of no confidence in 1783. He'd spent every moment of the intervening years trying to undermine Pitt's government.

James nodded. "I heard Fox was at the event to commemorate William of Orange's landing at Torbay. If he thinks the revolution in France is going to be as glorious as that in America, he has another think coming."

The shadow nodded in agreement before addressing his chief concern.

"There are fears that the King's madness is making another appearance."

James's heart sank. George III's illness resulted in a constitutional crisis just eighteen months ago, with Fox leading the call to install the Prince of Wales, George's weak-willed, profligate heir, with all the powers of sovereign.

In response, William Pitt the Younger, the thirty-year-old Prime Minister of England, had successfully pushed the Regency Bill through the House of Commons to limit the powers of the Regent. The need for Royal Assent to the legislation was bypassed when Pitt invoked the authority held to reside in the Great Seal.

It was a risky move with no guarantees that the bill would pass the House of Lords, as it seemed the King had made a recovery last March; the legislation was not put to the test.

News of the King's derangement reasserting itself was grim indeed, James mused. There was no chance of Pitt's slick political maneuvering working a second time.

The man in the shadows cleared his throat before continuing.

"Also, I have recently discovered that revenues at the Treasury do not tally. The difference in gold has been being spirited out of the Exchequer for the last three years.

"Of course, we all know the Foxites are supplying private funds to support the revolutionaries in France. But they may also be behind the Treasury's losses to the same end. And if they learn the King is unstable again, they won't support the Prince of Wales this time, they'll openly throw their lot in with Jacobites, and that will mean war in England."

The man shifted in his seat.

"James, losing the American colonies has cost us dearly, not only in prestige but also revenue, not to mention the cost of the war itself."

"We're back in trade with the Americas, surely…"

"It takes time," the man added impatiently. "We're not in position to fight a war on our doorstep and certainly not against revolutionaries within our own borders.

"We need time to replenish the Treasury, even raise an income tax if needed, then stamp out corruption and institute real electoral reforms. I know people want change, but the godless radicalism that has taken root in France is not going to bring liberty; it's going to bring bloodshed."

The man quieted his impassioned speech and added, "France is also bankrupt, which means she is desperate. With Louis under house arrest, I doubt he will keep his grip on power for much longer, even with promises of constitutional reform, so the last thing we need is stolen gold leaving our shores to have it return in the form of cannonballs and musket shot.

"It is vital we find if it is the Foxites who are behind the fraud and also how the gold is being smuggled out. It's why I called on our friendship to bring you back from Pennsylvania. You're one of the few I can trust to be effective and discreet."

Voices and foot traffic increased as the opera-goers started back to their places for the third act.

The man handed over a sealed envelope which James placed in his inside coat pocket.

"There's a list of dates and approximate amounts of gold lost from the Exchequer, names of people we suspect are involved, and the name of the man who will be your contact. It would not be wise to meet too frequently. Anything Fox can do to discredit me, he'll use, including my friends."

The men stood and shook hands.

"Don't worry," said James. "I'll be careful."

He moved to the door and glanced back with an afterthought.

"Needless to say, you have my vote in the upcoming election. I wish you the best in the rest of the counties."

William Pitt the Younger loomed out of the shadows momentarily, a sardonic smile on his lips.

"The best of luck to you too, James," he said.

James slipped from the Prime Minister's opera box without detection and returned to Lady Abigail armed with two glasses of champagne. If she had noticed that his absence was over long, she didn't remark, accepting the glass and threading her arm through his. The full skirt of her gown swished as they made their way back to their box.

"Do not think that seats at the opera and my acceptance of your company for the evening mean I have forgiven you," she spoke under her breath as she smiled and nodded to an acquaintance.

"For which of my many sins do I need your absolution, my dear?" he asked, distracted by thoughts of his meeting with Pitt.

"You know very well I'm talking about the ball. You make us both a laughingstock by leaving me like a wallflower most of the evening while you try to make an easy conquest of some silly country girl."

He bristled at her unflattering description of Selina.

"You never want for masculine company, Abigail, not on that night or any other. I wouldn't have thought you'd notice the absence of one."

She took her seat and deliberately positioned her body away, ignoring him and speaking animatedly to Comte Alexandre and his escort, Lady Olivia, as well as the Earl and Countess of Cambridge, whose box they shared.

James knew that Abigail would expect a fulsome apology and a declaration of devotion by the end of the evening. Spending four weeks with that woman at a house party would be a chore, but it was a concession that he was willing to make to ensure his guest list included an invitation to Selina.

As curtains rose on the opera's final act, James sat back, deep in his own thoughts.

Had his interest in the pretty little brunette been so obvious? James thought back over the ball. Perhaps it was.

The memory of her light laugh, her intelligent conservation, the feel of her in his arms as they danced stirred something in him.

Lust most likely, he supposed.

Then he recalled discovering Selina frightened and out of breath by the columns.

The thought of someone touching her made him angry and brought out protective feelings that didn't quite sit well with him.

The idea that the Viscount Canalissy was also paying her attention irritated him even more. What the hell was he up to? As neighbors they had virtually grown up together, but that's where the familiarity ended. As they grew to manhood, their interests differed, and by the time James had achieved his majority, he was off and making his own way in the world, encouraged by his father.

James hadn't needed a second encouragement. He reasoned that it was much easier to avoid emotional entanglements and devote his energy to creating independent wealth instead of working his way through his inheritance as others of his class had done.

Not that he had gone without feminine company. The cities and towns he'd visited had their share of disorderly houses, although he had always been careful. In his travels he'd seen enough of the ravages of venereal disease, although judicious consorting with the occasional prostitute seemed preferable to the weighted shackles of marriage as modeled by his parents.

He'd seen his father turn into a husk of a man at the hands of his poisonous mother, and the "eligible" women he'd met since his return to England appeared to have been cut from the same cloth.

That is until two weeks ago, when he first spoke to Selina Rosewall.

Furthermore, he was becoming more and more disposed to believing in God's benevolence after today's fruitful meeting with Captain William Rosewall.

The business transaction was straightforward as these things go—there was a lot of money to be made in transportation as there was in manufacturing goods and extracting resources—but it remained to be seen if Rosewall could be trusted with the news he had sealed in the envelope in his pocket.

He needed allies to help the government, and the only way he could be certain that he could trust William and Selina Rosewall was to keep them close at hand.

And the idea of being under the same roof for four weeks with Miss Selina Rosewall was very appealing. At that he smiled broadly and genuinely for the first time this evening.

James turned to Abigail, who had since lost interest in the opera and instead was using her mother-of-pearl opera glasses to spy on the occupants of the other boxes. Rather on one location in particular, where an indiscreet couple alone in their box were fondling each other quite openly.

He leaned in close to her ear. "I see you like to watch."

James grinned as she jumped, squeaking in surprise. The clatter of her glasses was just audible over the aria on stage.

Abigail turned to give James the full heat of her glare, her anger made worse by his indolent smirk.

"I hate you," she hissed.

James grinned even wider.

CHAPTER FIVE

27 June 1790

St Mary Woolnoth was the most unusual church Selina had ever seen. Instead of lofty conical spires or the castellated square towers of Norman churches, it was in the high English Baroque style for which its architect, Nicholas Hawksmoor, was renowned.

On a site that had been a place of worship since the Romans and not completed until 1716, the church had no cross and no spire. Instead it featured two small flat-topped columned turrets that housed the bells that had survived the Great Fire of London in 1666.

In turn, the turrets rested on six Corinthian columns behind which a squat block tower sat. It was relieved of its starkness by three full-length rusticated niches supported by a beveled pedestal into which three square windows were placed evenly along its length.

The bottom third of the building was the most fascinating architectural feature of all, with walls of horizontally grooved stone bands. They drew Selina and her family toward its distinctive entrance, an inset, forward-curving pediment that rested on skewed columns.

If the outside of St Mary's was stark and imposing, the inside was a revelation of color.

The large spacious nave was painted white. Geometric tiles gave color to the floors. Wooden pews, altar, and wainscoting around the walls added warmth.

It was an unusual church for an unusual clergyman, the Reverend John Newton.

His history as a hard-drinking, slave-trading gambler was widely known, as was the fact he had undergone a most remarkable religious conversion. His subsequent reputation as a vocal abolitionist, hymnist, and confidante to some of the most important people in England made his parish the most popular in London and Newton himself arguably the city's most popular preacher.

William and Sarah's boys were herded to the pews, their eyes following the heavenward trajectory of the columns that supported the vaulted ceiling. The family took its seat.

The invitation to worship at St Mary Woolnoth's was an unexpected one. While the church was open to all, its proximity to Westminster, England's, seat of wealth and power meant the Sunday services were attended by many leading figures.

On this day, William Wilberforce was in attendance, looking much healthier than at the ball, and Selina wondered whether he would be singing in the full rich baritone that had captivated many in society, including, it was rumored, the Prince of Wales himself.

The Rosewalls had received their invitation to join Lord Penventen and his mother, Lady Christina, at St Mary's—followed by luncheon at James's townhouse in Mayfair—just two days ago. It was the continuation of several invitations by James to the family over the past six weeks that included trips to Hyde Park and tours of the Houses of Parliament and Tower Bridge.

Just as the service was about to begin, the Rosewalls were joined by James and his mother.

It was clear to Selina that William was delighted by the opportunity to meet with James again. Her brother had spent several days planning new trade routes for the *Marguerite*, the *Andorra*, and the *Diamond* and was looking forward to discussing them with his new business partner.

She was absolutely earnest in her advice to William. Before committing a great deal of time and money to this venture, he ought to satisfy himself of his partner's scruples.

But whether or not her advice had been heeded, Selina had taken the liberty of making enquiries herself. As mistress of her father's house, she had learned that the richest source of information was the servants' network, and her very first enquiry found gold. The upstairs maid revealed that Winifred, the housekeeper's daughter, was sweet on Penventen's groom, and the young man was equally besotted.

Winifred was old enough to be observant but young enough not to know when to guard her mouth. Opening it took just a paper bag filled with chocolates and the promise not to reveal why her errands from the house took twice as long as they needed to, for Selina to get the full story one afternoon in a sunny corner of the back garden.

It seemed the Mitchell family did not want for money, but it was generally accepted that it was the success of the young Lord's business ventures that paid most of the bills. Wages had improved when Sir James returned to England about a year ago.

Winifred's beau had complained that Lady Christina had a temper but was nonetheless tolerated well enough by the servants. She regularly entertained her contemporaries, but the widowed Duke of Canalissy had started making weekly calls in the past three months, and it had been noticed that his visits were most often when his Lordship was not at home.

Winifred had stuffed another chocolate into her mouth as Selina crafted her next enquiry.

She decided to be to the point. "And what of Sir James?"

"Oooh…'e is 'andsome, miss, ain't he?" Winifred sighed.

Selina leaned in slyly in an exaggeratedly conspiratorial manner. "Is he really such a rake as they tell?"

The teenager giggled. "Ain't they all, miss? Becky—she's the upstairs maid—said sometimes the master is out all night unexpected. He don't come home an' his bed's not been slept in.

"But give 'im 'is due. Becky said he's never once behaved improper toward any of the maids. Oh…begging your pardon, miss!"

Selina smiled and urged the girl to continue.

"Well," said the girl, "Becky's sister works for the Duke of Ashgrove and she's said his youngest 'arrasses her and the other girls something terrible, pinchin' bottoms and tryin' to steal kisses."

Winifred popped another chocolate between her lips and looked sideways at Selina, as if adjudging the extent to which she might be familiar with her temporary comistress. She apparently judged herself on safe ground. "Ooh, but it would be nice to be kissed by someone of quality like 'im, wouldn't it? Lord Penventen, I mean. There's got to be somethin' being kissed by a real gentleman. Don't you reckon, miss?"

"I suppose there must be, yes," replied Selina.

Then Mrs. Stout, Winifred's mother, brought the interview to an end by calling out for the girl in a frustrated tone.

Alone in the garden, Selina reflected on what she'd just learned. It was little beyond a common decency of not preying on the female servants and that he occasionally stayed out at night.

Selina was no closer to confirming what kind of relationship James had with Lady Abigail. His bed was unslept in. Where did he spend his nights? With her?

As the congregation stood and opened their hymnals, she noticed that James had cast a sidelong look in her direction. She decided to pay him no heed for the duration of the service. Instead, Selina turned her attention to the pulpit from which the Reverend Newton was soon reading.

"From the book of Deuteronomy, chapter four, verse nine, 'Only take heed to thyself, and keep thy soul diligently, lest thou forget the things which thine eyes have seen, and lest they depart from thy heart all the days of thy life, but teach them thy sons, and thy sons' sons.'"

John Newton raised his eyes from the Bible and looked directly at the congregation, scanning the faces as if acknowledging each and every one.

"Who would have thought it needful to caution remembrance of such great things as they had seen? But the Lord knew and experience had already proved, that their hearts were forgetful, evil, and perverse. But the exhortation is to us likewise," he explained.

"Believers have seen great things, which if duly remembered would powerfully constrain, preserve, and animate them in the Lord's way. Such things as none can see but themselves, because they only have eyes to see. The Lord works wonderfully, but how can the blind see?"

He shifted at the lectern and considered his next thought before speaking.

"You have seen the evil of sin. Sufficient it should seem to make it hateful forever. You have seen it as the cause of all misery, of the death of Jesus. You have seen and felt it, in its bitterness and danger in your own souls, in conviction and backsliding.

"You have seen the love of Christ. Many hear of it, but to you it has been revealed. How seasonable and welcome its first discovery. Perhaps you then thought it impossible to forget what you saw. You have seen it since, in secret and public. It has refreshed your heart, healed your wounds, lightened your burdens, and comforted you under sorrows.

"You have seen the Lord's faithfulness to his promises. Could you not say 'my heart has trusted and I have been helped?'"

Newton paused, a moment's reflection, then continued. "You have seen the wisdom and goodness of God in his providence, how he manages and overrules, causes light to shine out of darkness, and brings good out of seeming evil.

"You have seen the importance and reality of the great things within the veil…"

Leaving the church took twice as long as it did to enter, as members of the congregation stopped for a word or Newton himself enquired after their well-being. Although round of cheek and of belly, he was no less imposing up close than he was when standing in the pulpit.

After greeting Lady Christina, Newton turned to James.

"You're looking very well my boy, much happier than when I saw you last." He turned to Selina and shook her hand. "Could this young lady be the cause?"

Selina blushed but said nothing.

"Reverend Newton, I'd like to introduce you to Selina Rosewall. She is here with her brother Captain William Rosewall and his family for the Season."

"I thought the name was familiar. I knew of your father, sir, although we never served on the same vessel," said Newton, now shaking William's hand and lowering his voice to a more confidential level before concluding, "He did not approve of the trade and I believe he saw the light before I did."

"I'm proud to keep his legacy," replied William. "There's no slave trade on my ships."

Newton smiled before reaching into the pocket of his vestments and crouching down to be eye to eye with Timothy and Richard. In each of the boys' hands he pressed what appeared to be a coin about the size of a penny.

"Perhaps your boys will follow in your father's footsteps," he smiled.

Outside the church, the boys examined the gift—a medallion of white jasper made by Josiah Wedgewood's pottery firm. In black relief, the figure of a chained man half kneeling, bound hand and leg in chain, arms raised in a plea.

Timothy turned the disc in the sunlight to better make out the figure and the inscription on the edge.

"What does it say?" prompted his father.

Timothy read the words in the halting manner of a child, "Am I Not a Man and a Brother?"

William nodded in agreement at both the twins. "Never forget that boys. And take good care of those gifts from Reverend Newton. They're precious."

* * *

Lunch had been a surprisingly enjoyable affair.

Selina had been uncertain what to expect from luncheon at the Penventen family townhouse, but any uncomfortable moments there might have been between families of different social standings evaporated with the inclusion of Colonel and Lady Butterworth.

And now seated in the drawing room, Selina sipped tea from a fine bone china cup, content to retreat into the background as she watched the others in conversation in the absence of their hosts.

A scant five minutes later they returned, and from beneath her lashes Selina appraised mother and son.

It was clear that a discussion had taken place that may not have been altogether pleasant.

James caught Selina's eye for the barest moment before begging the colonel's pardon to further a business discussion with William.

The portly colonel stood and patted his girth, asking his Ladyship's indulgence to take a short turn about the garden.

Lady Butterworth and Sarah returned to their conversation about raising children.

The coolness Selina had initially felt directed toward her from James's mother appeared to melt completely into a puddle of benign pity when the older woman asked of her prospects.

"A governess!" exclaimed Lady Christina over the rim of her teacup. "It's a wise young woman who makes her mind up early about eschewing matrimony."

A twinkle in the older woman's eye announced that dig was most certainly intended. "Yes, it's very enterprising of you. You must be very accomplished."

Selina smiled wanly but decided to say nothing.

"Do you speak a language?" asked Lady Christina.

"I speak French, ma'am. My mother's family were Huguenots who fled persecution in France. She taught my brother and me to speak and write fluently."

"Do play an instrument and sing?"

"The piano a little, though I prefer the guitar, but I do not sing well at all."

"What about painting?" enquired Lady Christina, simultaneously proffering the teapot.

Selina politely shook her head at the offer of a refilled cup and smiled. "Drawing and painting are my great interests, Lady Christina. I've been told that I have some skills in that regard. Landscapes are nice, but I do prefer portraits."

"Then it is settled," the older woman announced. "You would make a suitable temporary lady's companion to Lady Margaret Westmacott, James's grandmother, who has decided to grace us with her presence at Penventen Hall in Cornwall next month.

"It's always important to have accomplished young women about to ensure the guests are well entertained."

Selina sat back, surprised both by the offer and the obvious tone of dislike for Lady Margaret.

"I'm honored but I'm not sure I—"

"It's all settled Selina," interjected William, who had returned to the room with James.

"Sarah and the children travel with you to Bristol, and you will travel with Lady Margaret from Bristol to Padstow.

"When the *Diamond* returns to London from its run to Newcastle, I'll captain her to Newquay. That's only ten miles away from you. It will also give the crew time to ensure she's shipshape for the Atlantic crossing. We're planning to relocate her to Pittsburgh before the winter.

"Then I'll join you at the end of July in Padstow to finalize arrangements with Lord Penventen."

Selina slid a look to Sarah, who smiled mildly and nodded her head in approval. It would seem there was no support to be had there.

Anger simmered in her breast. How dare William plan her life like this? How dare he treat her as one of his children? At twenty-one, she had attained her majority, and it was her right to determine her life as she chose.

Admittedly, she had promised both William and Sarah to wait until the end of this summer before making up her mind about going into paid employment, and a letter of recommendation from Lady Margaret would be most advantageous.

They, the poor things, held out some hope of her marriageability, but considering she had been so inept at her flirtation with James, Selina was becoming more and more convinced that love and romance were far too nuanced and subtle for her to master.

Besides, she believed true love came only to a select few such as her parents and, indeed, William and Sarah.

More fuel was added to stoke the anger building beneath her calm expression when she met James's intense brown eyes considering her. How he must be secretly laughing at this silly, naïve girl, she fumed silently. How amusing she must be. Oh, how James and Lady Abigail must laugh, along with Lord Geoffrey!

Better to give up this folly right now before she became one of these pathetically desperate spinsters grateful to accept the attentions of any man.

With all eyes on her, she mustered a smile and accepted with a gracious thank-you, but not before a brief but pointed look at her brother.

CHAPTER SIX

Now the whole world was conspiring against her. What else could explain how she was now walking home from Mayfair to Soho on a fine summer afternoon with James while the rest of her family was invited to ride in Colonel and Lady Butterworth's carriage?

Yet Selina was thankful for the exertion. She still fumed at her brother, and the first five minutes of the walk took place at a fast clip without conversation.

James kept pace with her effortlessly, then finally spoke. "I know my mother can be tiresome, but does the idea of spending the rest of summer at Penventen Hall disgust you so much?"

Selina slowed her pace, shamefaced.

"I'm sorry. I must appear so ungrateful," she started. "Your mother's invitation is very generous, and I'm honored to accept it. And while I know they mean well, I'm just so angry at my brother and his wife for trying to determine the course of my life. They've been doing it constantly. Especially since the death of Papa."

They walked in silence again for a few seconds.

"Perhaps they recognize that it's time for you to start living," James offered.

Before she could vocalize a protest, he continued. "Five years running a household alone and caring for an ailing father, your sister-in-law, and her children while your brother battled to keep the family business from bankruptcy? I'm sure it must have been demanding and hard work, but it was also predictable and safe. The only world you've known. Now you want to control your new circumstances by exchanging one form of service for another.

"You're using your brother's responsibilities as an excuse to run away from the world."

Selina stopped. His words shocked her and then caused heat to rise up her face as its truth resonated. Her eyes dropped to her feet while she composed herself.

"That makes me sound self-pitying," she said finally.

"Only if you allow yourself to shut the door on possibilities," he added softly. "Don't do that, Selina."

She looked up into James's eyes to see if pity colored them. Instead he met hers steadily and without reservation.

"That is a blunt assessment from someone who hasn't known me long," she said.

"Nonetheless it's true," said James. "And, if I'm honest, I also speak to remind myself."

He paused, seeming uncomfortable with the self-reflection. He continued.

"I've come to believe, Selina, that you're a person who appreciates honesty over empty flattery. Am I wrong?"

"No, you're not wrong. I'm just not used to anyone speaking with such candor."

"Are we still friends?"

Selina allowed herself a long sigh before accepting his arm. The walk continued at a more moderate pace.

"I have some questions for you," Selina announced after a few moments.

"I'd be surprised if you didn't," James observed mildly.

Broaching the matters Selina had pondered for the past few weeks was more difficult than she thought.

"You've offered a very generous partnership with my brother…" she ventured.

James nodded. "Let me see if I can anticipate your questions.

"Yes, I can afford to fund my half of the partnership, although it will mean a mortgage on the coal mine in Pennsylvania. My debts in England are modest and easily covered by the trust left to me by my father.

"My mother does spend more than her allowance and my business interests in America subsidize her.

"Our family is well off but not wealthy. Penventen Hall has been neglected for three generations, but over the past ten years my father, and most recently myself, has spent a small fortune to bring at least half the hall back to its former glory."

James looked down at her.

"How am I doing?"

In spite of herself Selina smiled. "Very well indeed. Please, continue."

"As you've gathered, my relationship with my mother works best when we don't spend time in each other's company, but that could be easily remedied if she'd find herself a charity to occupy herself rather than fretting about my matrimonial state," he finished.

"Is your curiosity satisfied, Miss Rosewall?" he asked in a low voice intended only for her ears.

The man was deliberately teasing her, and Selina was helpless not to respond in kind.

No, one part of her mind answered, *not nearly enough satisfied,* and she wondered what it would feel like to have him hold her again as he did during that waltz, the memory of which had lived on unbidden late at night, leaving her restless these past weeks.

She slid a long sideways look up from his feet, his strong legs, his trim and tapered waist that broadened from his torso to his chest, before her eyes reached his face.

But alas, he was not for her, although she was thrilled to find her scrutiny did not leave him unaffected.

"Satisfied for now," she replied huskily, "but you have only confirmed everything I already know."

"I don't believe so," he contradicted.

She raised an eyebrow.

"I think you'd like to know me better; perhaps ask about Lady Abigail?"

"That's none of my business," she answered hastily.

"I'm making it your business," he stated firmly, the teasing tone vanishing from his voice. "On the day Canalissy brought you and your sister-in-law home, I saw your face when he mentioned Lady Abigail and the opera."

Selina was chagrined. "My Lord," she said, her glance away from him a pretence of casualness, "Lord Geoffrey was simply good enough to explain the nature of your relationship with Lady Abigail, and that made me realize his actions that night at the ball were…"

Selina's voice trailed off as she looked back toward James and saw his expression changing like a landscape swept by a cloud's shadow on a sunny day.

Selina saw the unverbalized turn of emotions—surprise, disgust, and even anger—pass quickly across James's unguarded face before he schooled his temper, though it still colored his voice.

"Selina, if you never promise me anything else, promise me this. Do not ever believe a word that man says. Do not trust a thing he does."

Selina was surprised by the vehemence in his tone.

She considered that, over the past few weeks, Lord Geoffrey had called on her several times, and they had walked in Hyde Park. His manner was slightly supercilious though pleasant enough, but occasionally his pontificating on the ills of society left Selina with the impression he was rehearsing a speech for a Parliamentary career rather than revealing any significant social or political insight.

And though he flattered her often and shamelessly, there was nothing in his words or his regard that stirred her as James did.

"As you wish," Selina agreed, and shrugged as though the matter was of no importance, though she wondered about the history between the two men. Now was not the time to ask.

They crossed a street that marked the boundary of Mayfair with other less affluent areas of London such as near neighbor Soho.

Now dominated by displaced Huguenots, the borough was a cosmopolitan affair with French-style coffeehouses and shops, although its glory days as a respectable part of the city were now beginning to fade against the bloom of lower rent accommodation and the bohemian social scene that was beginning to infuse the district.

A few moments further into the walk, Selina laughed. "I've just realized that I've demanded a thorough interview, and you hardly know anything about me or my family at all."

"Not so," replied James. "Your brother has been most forthcoming about his business and finances. I know fortunes have been thin since the loss of your father's second ship, the *Prospect,* two years ago. He adores his wife and sister"—Selina smiled at this—"and he knows that his future lies with the American trade.

"The fact that he refuses to have anything to do with the slave trade further marks him as an honorable man.

"I also know that you are the youngest child and that three siblings between yourself and your brother did not survive beyond infancy."

Selina was surprised by her brother's candor. James continued.

"In addition to being a very good painter, you're also an avid reader. Unlike many other ladies, your tastes extend to political tracts and business newsletters.

"You have the works of Alexander Pope and Jonathan Swift by your bedside but are currently reading Burke's *Reflections on the Revolution in France,* which, incidentally, you must lend me when you've finished. I've not yet managed to get a copy."

Through the last, Selina's sapphire-blue eyes widened. "You know what I have by my bed?"

James continued as if she had not spoken. "Also, despite your otherwise sweet nature, your irrationally stubborn insistence in refusing a modest allowance from your brother to replenish your wardrobe here in London has been the cause of a small friction."

She halted. "How…my brother never would…" The words died in her mouth as she saw James extract a small paper bag of chocolates from his coat pocket.

"I have some of the same sources as you, my dear." He grinned.

And, with a shake, he proffered the bag, one from the very same shop from where Selina had procured the treats for Winifred.

She shook her head to decline and watched as he popped a chocolate past his sensual lips.

Unconsciously she licked hers and briefly wondered what it would be like to kiss him. James watched her reaction closely.

"But your sister-in-law was right to insist that you wear her dress to the ball because no man could keep his eyes off you."

"You shouldn't say such things to me," she said breathily. "I might start believing you."

"Would that be so bad?" he asked, his tone matching hers.

"I don't know, I haven't decided."

To her relief, James steered the conversation to safer ground—politics—and Selina was delighted to find a ready listening ear to her thoughts on Burke's political treatise.

The conversation lasted several blocks until something tickled at the edge of her consciousness.

It had taken a few more turnings across several streets before Selina was convinced that she and James were being followed.

She looked up at him, brows slightly furrowed. As she was drawing breath to express her observation, James, without warning, pulled her around a corner and into a small alley and then engulfed her in his arms.

Her mouth opened again, this time with another question on her lips. He shook his head and gently placed one finger to her lips to ask for silence while they waited for their pursuer.

The smell of him was an intoxicating mix of leather, musk, and pine. She pressed herself to him as if driven by instinct. James shielded her view of the street, and she realized his cloak largely hid her and her lavender sprigged muslin gown from passersby.

Within moments, the sound of not one but two pairs of running feet rounded the corner.

"Go down there," the first voice commanded. "They must be only just out of sight."

The sound of the second pair of feet faded into the late afternoon.

Still shielded by James, Selina could hear the owner of the first set of feet slow to a walk and head farther down the street, before stopping and turning back toward them.

* * *

James pushed Selina away and in a swift, sure motion, he stepped out of the alley and grabbed the arm of their shadow. The man swung and landed a lucky strike on James's cheek.

James reeled from the blow but kept his feet and used the momentum to deftly firm his grasp on the assailant's arm, twist it behind his back, and shove the man bodily against the opposite redbrick wall of the alley.

"Who do you work for?" James demanded.

The man, unremarkably dressed, was a lean, tallish individual with narrow-set eyes and a thin, almost emaciated face. He did not respond, only grunted in discomfort. James shoved the man's arm farther up his back.

"Reynold is telling you leave matters alone, Penventen," he finally gasped.

"And yet he's too much of a coward to deliver his own message. Tell him that from me."

The man smirked and cast a glance at Selina, who stood a few yards away watching with alarm.

"Pretty girl you've got there," he grunted as James tightened his grip, causing the man pain.

James leaned in menacingly. "If Miss Rosewall and her family are harassed in any way, there will be no place on Earth that you will be safe from me."

He pulled the man away from the wall and shoved him toward the cross street, where the rat-faced man half walked and half staggered over the cobbles to his companion, who waited on the corner. He was about the same build as his friend, but his features were obscured by a tricorn hat and high-collared jacket.

With one long last look at James and Selina, the two disappeared around the next building.

Satisfied that they had gone, James dabbed the back of his hand at his cheek where a small cut had opened from the initial punch. He glanced at Selina, who, instead of cowering in fright as he had expected, appeared to be furious.

And she appeared to be furious at him.

"You let that man go! Why, James?"

"He didn't do anything wrong."

"He hit you!"

James merely shrugged in response. Selina gave a long-suffering sigh as she opened her drawstring purse, withdrawing a handkerchief and wetting it with a small amount of her perfume before handing the linen to him.

He accepted the kerchief with its scent of bergamot and lavender and winced as he put it to his left cheek.

"The alcohol in it will help clean the cut," she explained, annoyance still plain in her voice.

"He was just an opportunistic bag snatcher," James offered.

She raised an eyebrow waiting for James to account for himself.

James sighed, knowing that Selina would not accept anything but the truth. The problem was he didn't know the truth for himself, although he was going to get to the bottom of this tonight.

"What if I tell you that it's the best explanation I have for now?"

"Then I suppose that is satisfactory…for now."

"You're a jewel." He grinned and quickly kissed Selina on the cheek, taking delight in watching the color rise to her cheeks.

The rest of the walk was, thankfully, uneventful, and, as if to persuade each other that they really did think nothing of the startling event with their pursuer, they settled into a comfortable, companionable amble and discussed mutual interests, which, to James's delight, were many.

* * *

As they walked, twilight cast long shadows through the street and painted the sky in pastel hues of rose, apricot, and lilac as the sun disappeared over the tallest of London's buildings.

Ahead of them, bright pinpoints of light burst into life in the hands of the shadowed figures of servants tasked with the job of lighting the front of their masters' residences before full night fell.

The front of the Rosewalls' townhouse was shrouded in shadow. It seemed Selina's brother was not yet home and the servants were still busy in other areas of the house. James stopped Selina's hand as she reached for the elaborate brass door knocker. She looked at him questioningly.

"Before you go in…"

James drew her farther into the shadow of the porch and snaked his hands around her waist, drawing her to him. With certainty, Selina knew he was going to kiss her. She watched his eyes before being drawn to his lips, moving ever closer to hers.

The first contact was exquisite, soft and gentle—quite at odds with the firm, muscled shoulders she found herself holding on to.

The pressure of their kiss deepened, his mouth encouraging hers to open for languorous exploration.

A restless yearning only hinted at the ball ignited in Selina full force, and the feeling that she recognized in herself as arousal was given its moment in the pressure of his lips, the feel of his tongue, and the rasp of late-day stubble as it grazed her cheek.

Tentatively at first, she used her own tongue to explore the contours of his mouth, eliciting from him a groan that only fuelled her own desire.

But it was James who first pulled away.

At first Selina thought she had done something wrong, but seeing in his eyes a naked desire, she knew it was not that. With both hands he touched her cheeks, stroking them gently.

"I've wanted to do that since the night of the ball," he confessed.

Selina blushed and cast her face downward. An insistent finger under her chin forced her to raise her eyes to his.

"You're beautiful, Selina."

The sound of footsteps in the foyer indicated that a servant would soon appear at the front door. He leaned in to quickly but thoroughly kiss her on the lips before rapping on the front door in strong, confident strokes.

The door opened, and Selina left the dimly lit porch reluctantly.

She turned back to find James standing there, watching her with the same intense regard that stirred her at the ball.

"Good night," she whispered, desperate to prolong the mood, but unsure how.

"Good night, Selina." James smiled in response. "Don't forget."

Selina's brow wrinkled, not understanding.

"Don't shut the door on possibilities."

Selina watched as James turned to leave. He raised his hand in a quick salute before disappearing into the dim London night.

"Miss?"

Selina knew from Winifred's expression that it wasn't the first time the maid had tried to attract her attention.

"The Captain an' Mrs. Rosewall have accepted Colonel Butterworth's invitation to dinner. The children have 'ad their supper and are in bed, Miss."

Selina nodded distractedly.

The taste of his lips still lingered, and a yearning welled up in her, all the stronger for his absence.

She watched Winifred close the door, and at the sound of the bolt being thrown, James's last words resonated with her.

What might be if she were open to possibilities? The prospect both thrilled and frightened her.

CHAPTER SEVEN

The Black Boar Arms on the Isle of Dogs marked the start of the shipbuilding district of London. It had a permanent acrid smell of smoke, stale beer, unwashed bodies, and piss.

In the back corner, two men, both dressed in cheap, shabby clothing like the rest of the patrons in the pub, sat hunched over their pints of ale, seemingly disinterested in everyone and everything apart from their drinking. Despite this, their tankards emptied slowly. Not so slowly as to attract the notice of the two harried barmaids, but not so quickly as to make these two patrons drunk.

Somewhere, as a clock struck the tenth hour of the evening, one of the men shifted in his seat.

"Perhaps something has happened to him, James. Or perhaps he was warned off like you were…" Jackson remarked in a low voice to avoid being overheard.

"Maybe," muttered James into his tankard.

Since arriving in England, Jackson had performed the role of valet to the Lord of Penventen assiduously and with all the deference the position entailed, at least in front of others. He even frowned if James lapsed before his mother into the informality with Jackson that he'd been used to in the United States. No wonder Lady Christina adored him, much to the annoyance of his employer.

In reality, James Mitchell and Toby Jackson were two men as close as brothers, with Jackson having full authority as manager of James's business interests.

While the men were same age and build, there were differences. Where James had dark hair and eyes, Jackson's hair was fair and his eyes blue. Jackson was American born, and he missed the clean country air. London was loud, crowded, dirty, and dank—only little better than the air in this pub—but he took his role as James's friend and confidante seriously.

Ten minutes later a rotund, grey-haired man entered and rolled up to the bar as if he'd been thrown out of his first three. His dress gave the impression of a gentleman who once had a fortune but had lost it. The man slid a coin across the bar in exchange for a tankard and started looking for a spare seat. Veering across the room, he adroitly sidestepped other drunken patrons to avoid spilling his ale.

At this, Jackson nudged James and inclined his head in the man's direction.

"The drunk is not a drunk."

James raised his eyes and watched as the man came closer to their table.

"Seat taken?"

And without waiting for the answer, the old man sat heavily across from them.

"What news have you?" he asked without preamble.

"Tell our friend that his suspicions are well founded," murmured James. "We tracked a shipment of Exchequer gold to the *Pandora* that went aground in February.

"But we won't be able to confirm whether the cache has been dispersed in the locality or whether it has been moved on until we get to Cornwall. If it is being shipped as a single cargo, it narrows down the number of people who have cause and means."

The man snorted through a mouthful of ale. "That explains the interesting guests expected at Pitt's masquerade ball."

"Yes," agreed James. "You can thank our friend for the guest list." He took another sip from the glass. "That, and my business venture with William Rosewall gives me a good excuse to be seen places and ask questions."

"Can Rosewall be trusted?"

James nodded almost imperceptibly. "I believe so, but I plan to get to know the family better."

The old man smirked. "Yes, so I believe," he responded. He drained his beer and belched loudly.

"Apparently Abigail is making everyone's life a misery over it, so you'd better sort this quick before the woman thinks you're serious about Rosewall's sister. You do know Earl Canalissy's son has taken a shine to her, don't you?"

James shifted uncomfortably in his seat. Jackson hid a smile but said nothing.

The old man glanced from the young Lord to his friend and back. "If that's all, I'll leave you gentlemen tonight."

But before the man could rise, James snagged the arm of one of the passing barmaids and with a friendly leer, said, "'Ere darlin', three more o''em." He slipped coins into her hand and slapped her on the bottom to send her on her way.

When she had gone, he turned to his contact.

"Our mission's been compromised."

The man's eyes sharpened in concern and surprise, then impatience as the young Lord made him wait until after the arrival of the beer to tell the story of being followed and the message he'd been given.

"Reynold is not a name I know," said the man at last, "but I'll ask around. Probably not the one pulling the strings."

James and Jackson both nodded in agreement. It was a conclusion they had already come to.

The man looked thoughtful. "Did the Rosewall girl buy your story?"

"No, she's too bright for that," James admitted.

"That's not good," the old man grunted. "Even if she couldn't identify them, they've been keeping you under observation, so they know who she is. If they suspect you've developed an attachment for the girl, they will use it against you."

James thought back to their kiss earlier that evening and wondered if they were being watched then. If so, there would be no doubt of his "attachment."

Oh, he wondered, what had he gotten Selina into?

* * *

The couple were intertwined, the passion of their stolen kisses heightened by the urgency of their secret tryst. Her eyes were closed in ecstasy, and her head tossed back to give her dark-haired lover access to her neck.

She clung to him as if this moment might be all that they would ever have.

Night was closing in and the shadows in the landscape portended dread. With the last of the light, the wind had picked up, blowing a lock of softly curled hair away from the woman's face, while the hem of her lover's jacket reached toward her as if it wished to be part of the embrace.

"Oh, Selina! It's beautiful. I'm in love with them already," her sister-in-law exclaimed. "I want the painting when you're done. It will be a masterpiece!"

The compliment might have been a little overdone, but even Selina had to concede that the canvas was one of her best.

She had been up most of the night unable to sleep, reliving the day and James's kiss many times before deciding rest was impossible, and reached for a couple of oil lamps and a sketch pad to capture what she felt.

As the sun rose, Selina completed not only the sketch on which her new oil painting would be based, but also sketches of the faces of the two men who had accosted her and James. Those she kept hidden, along with the story of the afternoon's drama.

"There's something compelling, almost tragic about them," Sarah continued, "as though they were expecting her overly dutiful but lovingly heroic brother to chase him off with a sword."

Selina turned, bemused, but Sarah's eyes twinkled in mischief.

"You can tell me…before Will comes in, James did kiss you last night, didn't he?"

The younger woman was mortified and flushed bright pink in response.

"He did! Oh, I know he did, I can see it in your face. I could tell over lunch, that he wanted to, the way he kept looking at you."

"I don't think it's any of your business, Sarah," Selina snapped.

Sarah was immediately apologetic. "Oh, sweetheart, I'm sorry I embarrassed you, but you deserve some romance and I'm glad it's him."

"It was one kiss, Sarah, not a declaration of love and a proposal of marriage."

Oh dear, there was that twinkle in Sarah's eye again, and Selina rued opening her mouth at all.

"One kiss is usually how it starts," Sarah retorted.

Selina threw her arms in the air. "I give up! You and Will are absolutely impossible! You engineer my walk with James and practically forced his mother to invite me to Cornwall. You've done just about everything but put a sign around my neck saying 'Free to good home'!"

She pouted as she looked back at her painting. "James's attention could very well be just politeness to the sister of his new business partner. He could easily offer for Lady Abigail by the end of the summer or decide to be off and marry some American woman he's met.

"You're making too much out of one afternoon walk and one kiss. Stop meddling in my life!"

Selina halted her tirade as she turned and saw the dismay in Sarah's face and the possibility of tears blooming. She had forgotten that her sister-in-law was prone to crying at little provocation at various times in her pregnancy.

She left her seat and rushed over to hug her.

"Oh darling, I'm sorry. I didn't mean to make you cry, and I didn't mean to sound ungrateful. You and Will want the best for me, I know that."

Sarah nodded and dabbed at her eyes and tried a watery smile. Selina gave her another squeeze and sat on the footstool in front of her.

"I made a promise yesterday to be open to possibilities," she began. "So I accept there is a possibility that James might hold me in some regard. I accept the possibility that I might have a pleasant summer at Penventen Hall, and I also accept the possibility of having such a pleasant summer that I won't miss you and the children too desperately.

"And I accept the possibility that you truly love my artwork."

Sarah reached out to hold her hand and smiled. "Open to possibilities…that's all Will and I want for you."

William, dressed for business, walked into the drawing room reading a news sheet, oblivious to the previous tension in the room, but his expression turned suspicious when he saw the two women sitting so closely together and smiling conspiratorially.

He dropped the hand holding the paper and regarded the two women.

"Is this something I'm going to regret?" he asked.

"Not at all Bill, it's just that Selina has something to ask you," answered Sarah, giving Selina's hand a quick squeeze of encouragement.

William focused his attention on his sister. Selina stood. "Bill, does the offer of shopping in Cheapside and the Strand still stand?"

Selina knew that would surprise him. Over the past month, she had rebuffed—sometimes rudely—every offer to spend money on herself.

She grinned at his expression. He assented but no doubt wondered when the other shoe would drop and the inevitable argument would begin. To relieve him of such angst, Selina walked over to him and kissed him on the cheek.

"Thank you, brother." She smiled and giggled. "You may close your mouth now; otherwise someone might mistake you for a frog trying to catch flies."

Over her shoulder to Sarah, Selina called, "I'm just going to get dressed."

William watched his sister leave the room before turning to his wife.

"Would you mind explaining to me what just happened?" he asked.

Sarah stood and gave William an enthusiastic hug.

"I think your sister might be remembering how to live again."

* * *

After spending a pleasant hour viewing the displays of domestic goods as well as exotic merchandise from across the empire, Selina noted that her young companion was becoming restless.

"Is something amiss, Winifred?"

"No, miss," she said with a pout. "Although I do wish you would buy something already."

"Shall we stop for a cup of tea and cake and perhaps chocolates for afters in the next little while?"

Selina smiled as the expression on Winfred's face changed from dismay to delight.

But the shopping proved to be more time consuming, and expensive, than Selina had thought. But still, her purchases were worthwhile—a new walking dress in forest green, fashionably ankle-length, with a slim silhouette and a scoop neck emphasized by a short bodice in ecru that tied high on the waist, and, although Selina hardly rode at all, she treated herself to a riding habit in deep rose pink with a built-in jacket under which was a cream blouse with a high neckline, trimmed in stripes of plaited gold brocade.

A formal gown was ordered to be delivered to the Rosewall townhouse, a shimmering silvery-white gown in satin over which an aqua and silvery-white redingote was fitted under the shoulders, sculpted and falling to a short train at the back.

The modiste insisted it was a style favored by Marie Antoinette herself. Initially, Selina blanched at the price, remarking that she finally understood why France was broke, but she bought it anyway.

Two more high-waisted embroidered day dresses in teal and sky blue joined the order, and dancing slippers to match the ball gown and sturdy riding boots to go with the riding habit completed what Selina considered the essentials.

It had all taken too long for Winifred, however. Despite a reviving cup of tea and a cinnamon tea cake, the youngster had gone from willing assistant to tired, bored, and not at all interested by the time she slowed to look into a jewelry shop window.

The late afternoon sun sparkled on the precious and semi-precious stones in settings of gold and silver.

Although the rubies and emeralds held their own appeal, Selina found herself fascinated by iridescent moonstones that flashed lights of pink and blue. They were set off to their most beautiful in a display of earrings and pendants.

"Are you tempted by anything Miss Rosewall?"

Startled, Selina looked up.

Viscount Canalissy's reflection manifested itself in the shop window. He stood at her shoulder, a little too close for propriety. A half turn sideways resulted in her shoulder's brushing against his chest.

Once again the feeling of being trapped surged in Selina, and a quick scan of the street told her that Winifred had well and truly disappeared.

Damn that girl!

Selina collected herself. "There's plenty to be tempted by, my Lord, but nothing I can afford."

"I've had quite a good run at cards." Canalissy smiled rather too smoothly in Selina's opinion. "So I'm feeling particularly generous. Is there anything you'd like as a gift? Those sapphires that so match the color of your eyes, perhaps? I would give you those, and plenty more, if you'd let me."

James's warning of yesterday filled her ears, and she tried to calm her speeding pulse with the thought that, viscount or not, he could hardly molest her in the street. She was safe enough in full view of passers-by.

"That's a generous offer. I couldn't possibly accept, and it's most improper of you to make it," she told him. Annoyance gave her a feeling of control over her unease.

Lord Geoffrey's lips thinned.

"No matter how honorable my intentions, my words seem to have the opposite effect on you." His voice was controlled but angry. "Any other young woman might have made her refusal more prettily or accepted the gift as a token of esteem, but not you."

Canalissy eyed her up and down.

"I take the time to stop you making a social faux pas at the ball, I educate you about the relationship between Penventen and Lady Abigail, graciously offer you friendship and my valuable time, yet you run away from me, ignore my warnings about engaging with Penventen, and then you kiss him in public like a common street whore."

Selina's unease turned to trepidation and then full anger. He had spied on them? Selina fretted, glancing quickly about, but help was nowhere to be seen.

"I think that's enough, my Lord. I must be going," she told Canalissy, and pressed her lips firmly together for fear of saying much worse. Then she propelled away from the shop window and down the High Street.

* * *

She did not see the round-bodied older man with grey hair pass her, lightly brushing against Canalissy as he dipped his hand into the viscount's pocket.

The aging thief rounded a corner and stopped to open the billfold he had secreted in his sleeve. He ignored the bank and promissory notes. A list of names and numbers caught his attention.

He slipped the piece of paper into his own pocket and emerged from the alley to shuffle quickly after the Viscount Canalissy, who indeed appeared to be following, at a distance, Sir James's young lady friend.

"My Lord, my Lord!" He affected a wheeze and a huff that belied his true physical condition.

"Yours, I believe," he said as Canalissy finally stopped. The wallet was proffered with a flourish.

The young man patted his pockets to confirm the loss. "Empty no doubt," he grumbled, accepting the wallet.

"Not at my hand, my Lord, I'm as honest as the day is long."

Canalissy grunted and quickly scanned the contents. The notes were there.

"I s'pose you expect a reward, old man."

"Why, that would be most generous, my Lord."

The old man found a sixpence in his hand. Adopting his most humble expression, he tugged his forelock and backed away. "Most gracious, good sir. Most gracious…"

The viscount turned and stalked off, visibly annoyed that he had lost his quarry and yet unaware he was being watched by the old man, who now stood fully upright, unconsciously stretching and feeling his vertebrae pop.

"Interesting. Interesting indeed," he mused, flipping the coin in his hand and, in his mind, already composing the note he would send by messenger to Penventen.

CHAPTER EIGHT

5 July 1790

Selina glanced at her fellow passengers. In front of her, Lady Margaret Westmacott was asleep, as was the aged Captain Mainwaring, who sat beside her, both completely set at ease by the swaying carriage and the regular pounding of hooves.

Sharing Selina's red leather bench was the middle-aged spinster Miss Rosalie Gray, who was engrossed in the latest gothic romance novel. Sitting on the far side of the carriage, Miss Gray's equally bookish brother John was reading about ancient Rome.

As she had done frequently on this journey, Selina fixed her gaze out the window, pretending to take an interest in the passing scenery.

The five-day journey by carriage from London to the port city of Bristol, and now on to the seaside town of Padstow in Cornwall—home to the Mitchell family pile, Penventen Hall—left Selina with plenty of time to think about the eventful week just passed.

She had returned home from her encounter with Viscount Canalissy more shaken then she had wanted to admit.

How had Canalissy known about her and James? Had he spied on them? Or had he sent others? Were the men who followed them on that Sunday sent by the viscount?

Learning that Winifred had arrived home, Selina summoned her immediately. The youngster supposed Selina's thunderous mood was entirely her fault for wandering off, and Selina used the girl's apprehension to her advantage.

She ordered Winifred to take a note to Lord Penventen, to go straight there and speak to no one on pain of being punished severely for her disappearance. Even now, Selina felt a twinge of guilt about threatening to tell Mrs. Stout about Winifred's tarrying with Angus the groomsman if she failed to deliver the message.

Then, for the sake of her family, Selina had forced herself to pretend that nothing was amiss and put on such an act of carefree gaiety that Sarah was convinced that she was madly in love—a notion particularly reinforced at her relief at the news that Sir James was joining them for dinner the next evening.

That day had been spent packing for the journey, and the indoor activity suited Selina well. She'd had enough of London…

The next day Winifred bobbed in a correct but unexpected curtsey. "Excuse me, miss." Selina must have put the fear of God into the child the previous afternoon.

The maid had a large bouquet of flowers in her arms. The elaborate display of lilies, roses, and peonies were a riot of color, and Selina had a sinking feeling that she knew the new owner of the hugely vulgar display.

"They're for me?" She hoped for a moment that her brother, in a fit of ardor for his wife, had a momentary lapse of taste and judgment so as to waste a good deal of money on the arrangement.

"Yes, miss, and there's a card."

"From whom, Winifred?" asked Sarah, who had just walked into the parlor.

"A footman from Earl Canalissy delivered them for Miss Selina, ma'am."

Sarah instructed Winifred to place the flowers in the dining room. When the girl had left, Sarah hugged Selina and laughed.

"Two of the most eligible men in England are paying you attention, and here we were concerned that you'd end up a spinster governess or lady's companion. Your brother and I needn't have worried," she teased.

"What am I to do, Sarah? I don't want Lord Geoffrey to pay me attention," she begged, giving voice to her discomfort for the first time.

"Well you're going to have to let him down gently," Sarah advised. "What if he should show up as a guest at Penventen Hall? The Earl is a good friend of Sir James's mother."

Selina grimaced by way of reply.

"Then make him understand that you can only accept friendship from him since your affections are attached elsewhere," counseled Sarah.

"And that would be entirely his point," answered Selina, exasperated. "Any affection I have is misplaced because it is fully expected that James will be contracted to marry Lady Abigail by the end of the summer. I'm sure she will be a guest at the house party too."

"And if it were true? Would you accept Lord Geoffrey's pursuit, keeping in mind that James will still be your brother's business partner even after the summer is over?"

Selina shook her head. "I couldn't be so dishonest as to keep any man on a string. And while the viscount's regard was flattering at first, there's something about him that makes me feel uncomfortable and inadequate."

It was the truth, although somewhat diluted.

Thus Selina's mind was somewhat at rest when James arrived the following night.

He brought gifts—a small pull-along horse for Charlotte, painted wooden soldiers for the boys, a bouquet of elegant yellow carnations for Sarah, and a bottle of Kentucky bourbon for William.

With a twinkle of mischief in his eyes, he presented Selina a box of chocolates.

"I'm given to understand that chocolate is a popular gift, Miss Selina," he teased.

She noted the momentary distraction of William and Sarah with the children and smiled. "In our case, it appears to be the currency of spies," she said softly.

He returned the smile and lowered his voice. "We'll talk soon…"

Selina wondered how James would make an opportunity to talk with her alone. First, it was the boys insisting that he direct one more battle with them, then William who wanted more details about safe harbors in New York.

But finally, she gratefully leapt on Sarah's suggestion that she might like to take James for a stroll in the back garden while she and William bade the children good night.

Selina and James sat on a garden swing, close enough to the house to be seen but not overheard.

He reached for her hand and held it, his thumb stroking her hand. She found it comforting.

"It will be all right, Selina, just tell me what your note was about," he prompted

"The Viscount Canalissy. He knows about us, James. The kiss…"

She ventured a glance at him but instead of anger or surprise, she found that he was studying her intently.

"You're not surprised," she said. Then realization dawned. "You already knew?"

He shrugged. His lack of reaction puzzled her.

"It means he was spying on us or had spies watching us," she said, "perhaps even those men who followed us. Does it not concern you?" she asked irritably.

James shook his head.

"I see I've been mistaken about a few things," she said abruptly and stood. "Good night, Lord Penventen."

Instead of letting go of her hand he tugged it.

"Sit back down, Selina. There are a few things I need to tell you," he instructed quietly.

This was it, Selina thought, and a lump the size of a grape formed in her throat.

A dozen scenes played themselves in the time it took for Selina to reclaim her seat. They all ended with her heart being broken. She raised her face to his. The warmth was there but so was wariness.

"I received another message just before your note. It was from a… friend…who had observed you and Canalissy on the street," he started cautiously as if gauging her reaction. "He said you looked angry but before he could intervene, you had walked away."

"I *was* angry," she averred. "He told me that he knew we had kissed…and then called me a common street whore."

James closed his eyes and expelled a deep breath.

"He's jealous."

"Yes, I realize that," responded Selina sharply. "He said as much in a note that accompanied some flowers today."

She pulled the note from a pocket in her skirt and handed it to him.

"I haven't dared show Will, otherwise he'd be challenging the viscount to a duel within the hour."

James read the note.

> *My darling Selina,*
>
> *I have no right to your forgiveness but I beg it anyway. Your beauty drives me to such distraction that I cannot think of anything else. I find myself insane with jealousy at the thought of Penventen touching you as I yearn to and my heart broken that you would prefer his caress despite (perhaps even because?) of his attached state. The fact that it can only end in your being hurt rends my conscience and I feel it a duty to save you from this folly. My courting of you has been clumsy, I know, and if you would but show me the smallest piece of kindness, I would spend the rest of my life as your most obedient servant. I wish to plead my case to you in person and would consider it an honor if you were to suffer my presence once more.*
>
> *Most humbly, sincerely and most devoted,*
>
> *G*

Selina chuckled at James's bilious expression. Canalissy's florid and hypocritical words could have that effect.

"I have to confess to the same reaction as yours," she said.

"Did you respond?"

"I had to. I sent a reply that he need not trouble himself with a personal call, that the flowers and the note were apology enough and I had already forgiven him as an act of Christian charity."

James gave her hand a comforting squeeze before releasing it. "Selina, I need to explain about myself and Abigail."

Unconsciously, Selina licked her lips.

"Canalissy is not wrong when he suggests that there has been an understanding between Abigail and me."

Selina fixed her eyes on a spot in the lawn. If she looked at him she'd burst into tears, and she wouldn't allow him the satisfaction. She waited without comment for him to continue.

"Six years ago I met Abigail at a ball here in London. At nineteen she was the most beautiful woman I had ever seen.

"We became lovers over that summer, and I had decided to ask her to marry me."

Selina's eyes watered and she closed them. She wondered miserably if this could get any worse.

"There was a ball hosted by the Canalissys to mark the end of the Season, and at supper I intended to ask her father for permission to officially court her and for us to be wed at Michaelmas.

"First I thought I would surprise Abigail with a betrothal ring before I spoke to her father, so I went looking for her. She wasn't in the ballroom, and she wasn't in the ladies' drawing room."

James's voice hardened.

"I found her in the garden with another man between her legs."

Selina gasped in shock and turned sharply, eyes wide. James was looking straight ahead, his face in part shadow, his posture slightly bent, and his arms resting on his knees.

"Far from being in a distressed state, she was encouraging the man's attentions in language I've only since heard in a brothel."

"What did you do?" she whispered.

"I walked away and got drunk. I have no memory of the three days afterward.

"When I sobered up, I told my father that I intended to leave England and planned never to return. I expected him to be furious, but he patted me on the back, told me that I was making the wisest decision a man could ever make, and gave me a letter of credit for five thousand pounds."

A short bitter laugh ended the telling.

"It was the last time I saw him," James added as an afterthought.

Selina forced a swallow past the lump in her throat. "But you returned."

"My father's death and some business brought me back."

"Then, at Christmas, Abigail learned I had returned, most likely from my mother, and begged an audience with me. She told me that she bitterly regretted her actions that night and that she'd remained unmarried in the hope that I'd return.

"And, yes. I have been her escort at a number of events this season and she's made plain her renewed interest in me. And about three months ago, I started to entertain once more the thought of offering for her."

"Oh…" murmured Selina. To her horror, she couldn't think of anything else to say, nor make her body get up and walk away as her mind screamed at her to do.

"But I won't, not now," said James.

"Why? Who's there to stop you?" asked Selina in a voice no more than a whisper.

James turned to look at her and drank in Selina's features like a thirsty man. "You are."

Selina's eyes widened, allowing a tear to roll down each cheek. Pulling a linen from his waistcoat, James reached forward to wipe them away.

"I found myself pulled into the merry-go-round of lying, cheating, and debauchery that passes as entertainment in these circles," he confessed. "I allowed myself to entertain my mother's notion that a politically advantageous but hollow marriage with Abigail could be acceptable and profitable. Despite my best intentions, I was about to make the same mistake as my father.

"Frankly, I didn't like what that said about the man I had become."

James looked down to find that her hands had somehow become intertwined with his own.

"I don't understand what that has to do with me," she whispered.

James smiled softly.

"At the ball I realized that I couldn't go through with the charade. And then I met you…"

Selina frowned. James touched a finger to her lips, begging for silence.

"You were a genuine rose amongst gilded lilies that night. So bright, so fresh, so honest. I knew you felt out of place, I could see it, and I was suddenly reminded what it was like to be beholden to no one but one's own conscience.

"I still recall the love and admiration in your eyes for your brother when he told me he'd have no part in the slave trade, and I remember thinking what it would be like to have someone—*you*—look at me that way."

* * *

The carriage jounced suddenly and Selina blinked away the tears she felt in reliving the memory of that night. Her focus returned to the present and she found she was the subject of Lady Margaret's considering gaze.

The carriage crossed the small stone bridge on Melingey Turn at Little Petherick, over the brook that fed into the River Camel, just four miles from their destination.

Finding comfort in habits of the past week on the road, Selina glanced around the carriage to identify property that might belong to Lady Margaret or herself.

Before they'd reached another milestone, all loose items had been packed away and hand luggage placed by the door and she had reread the instructions for meeting the Penventen carriage that would take them to the hall.

Satisfied with her preparations, Selina took advantage of her window seat to take in the view of Padstow for the first time.

Bathed in sunshine, the village hugged the hill that led down to the River Camel.

From the top of the High Street, Selina could see the sunlight play on the water, tipping small waves in liquid gold against the azure blue of the deeper water, driven by the light breeze across to the verdant green of the opposite banks before the carriage dropped down along the narrow street, past little whitewashed three-story terrace rows.

Her initial misgivings about the trip, and her trepidation about meeting the redoubtable Lady Margaret, were now giving way to anticipation.

One way or another, this place would mark the beginning of a new future.

Chapter Nine

Padstow was a bustling fishing town, the main trade of which was now being supplemented by arrival of timber from Canada's rugged east coast.

Despite the fact that the weekly Wednesday markets were still two days away, the sounds of fish sellers and grocers hawking their wares in Market Square competed with the squawks of seagulls. The sharp tang of the salt-water air emanating from the harbor, which fed directly into the Celtic Sea, also carried with it the warmth of summer.

With an efficient confidence borne out of running her father's household, Selina had arranged for refreshment for herself and Lady Margaret at the tea house, and for a messenger from the post office to be sent up the mile long road to Penventen Hall to call for the carriage.

Selina couldn't help but feel her every action over the past three days was being evaluated by her elderly employer. Over tea, while the lady continued a letter she had started that morning, Selina took up her own scrutiny of James's grandmother once more.

The only concession to Lady Margaret's seventy-five years was her use of an exotic bamboo walking cane with a delicately carved ivory handle. Her hair, the color of steel, matched her personality, and she was the type of woman who always wore black, not because she was still in mourning, but because the color looked magnificent on her.

Her sharp brown eyes missed nothing. Her age and status afforded her deference from others that she wasn't above exploiting, as Selina had discovered when accommodations and food at Exeter was not to her Ladyship's standard.

Those who experienced her displeasure were left in no doubt of their error, and Selina considered herself fortunate not to have been one of them.

Along the way, Lady Margaret insisted on hearing everything about Selina and her family background. There wasn't much to tell, so that line of conversation lasted just half of the first day.

The second full day was spent discussing the merits of the works of Hester Chapone and, to Selina's surprise, new writer Mary Wollstonecraft on the subject of female equality and education.

Lady Margaret offered a quote from Wollstonecraft: "Taught from infancy that beauty is woman's scepter, the mind shapes itself to the body, and roaming round its gilt cage, only seeks to adorn its prison." She then wryly suggested it described Lady Christina rather aptly.

"I've shocked you dear." She had grinned, seeing Selina's expression.

"Don't be. It's quite admirable to have such a close bond with your brother and his family. Not everyone is as fortunate.

"I can understand why you're quite drawn to Wollstonecraft's writings though. To be able to be mistress of one's own destiny is very appealing. Our age appears to be one of revolution, perhaps there will be one between the sexes too."

"I believe that to be so, Lady Margaret," Selina had answered, "but while revolutions may begin with high-minded ideals, they can also end in animosity, acrimony, and violence.

"Ideology, when not tempered with a proper fear of the rights of the Creator, can only lead to the worst elements of human nature being allowed to prosper unchecked—'all human laws are, properly speaking, only declaratory; they have no power over the substance of original justice.'"

Lady Margaret looked at Selina. "I see you side more with Edmund Burke than Thomas Paine," she observed.

"I do."

"Then, to quote Wollstonecraft again, 'Strengthen the female mind by enlarging it, and there will be an end to blind obedience.' I believe

I shall take great delight in scandalizing our traveling companions tomorrow by discussing politics from Launceston to Padstow."

Despite Lady Margaret's apparently ferocious nature, Selina found herself growing rather fond of James's grandmother.

* * *

Penventen Hall sat in an elevated position over Padstow but was protected from the worst of the weather that beats against the steep and rugged coastline by a gentle elevation. Woodlands surrounded the property on three sides and, beyond them, farm and sheep lands spread in a multicolored patchwork over the countryside.

First built during the reign of Queen Elizabeth, Penventen Hall could best be described as a castle in miniature. Every wall of the two-story manor was topped with battlements.

Eschewing the Georgian trend for Greek and Roman Revivalism, and the slavish need for symmetry in building design, the Mitchell family continued the gothic revival style made popular by Horace Walpole's Strawberry Hill House forty years earlier.

At Penventen Hall's eastern corner, stone stairs led up to enormous arched windows, a feature that would not have been out of place in a cathedral, above the entrance.

Further along, a round tower thrust outward with its arched double-height doors facing onto the wide lawn. From the top of the entrance stairs, the sparkling waters of the River Camel were clearly in view beyond the spacious, manicured grounds.

As footmen took their luggage, Lady Margaret and Selina were greeted by Mrs. White, the housekeeper, who preceded them through the vaulted foyer and into the light and airy drawing room located on the ground floor of what turned out to be the round tower.

Primrose-yellow jacquard wall paper and mint-green curtains with matching ornamental swags added to the spring-like freshness, aided by the exquisitely detailed carved Queen Anne furniture in upholstered pastel hues. The sweet scent of fresh lily of the valley in voluminous round glass bowls added to the feminine charm of the room.

The housekeeper departed to supervise the finalizing of their accommodation. The two women were left to themselves with Selina quietly surprised that Lady Christina wasn't present to greet her mother-in-law.

She waited for Lady Margaret to sit on an apricot velvet settee before she took a place for herself on a balloon-back chair opposite.

Minutes went by with only the occasional muffled sound of servants at work in other areas of the house, and the rhythmic *tap-tap-tap* of Lady Margaret's bamboo walking stick keeping time with the clock on the mantelpiece.

The rapping of her cane was a sure sign of the older woman's displeasure. Catching Selina's eye, she observed, "The manners of the lady of the house haven't improved since my last visit."

Selina was about to reply, at first thinking to suggest some innocent reason for their hostess's tardiness, but the look on Lady Margaret's face told her she was in no mood for excuses.

More minutes passed before the housekeeper, a brisk, efficient woman who wore her grey hair in a tight bun at the top of her head, returned to show them to their rooms, located on the second floor.

Whatever propriety Lady Christina lacked so far was in part made up for by the quality of Lady Margaret's room.

It was a large, well appointed chamber with two sizeable casement windows letting in an abundance of light.

A superbly embroidered Chinese bedspread and matching bed curtain were the centerpieces of the room. On the textiles, exotic birds in iridescent colors of sapphire, ruby, emerald, and amethyst swooped, perched, and warbled on a jade green background.

It was the most beautiful piece of fabric Selina had ever seen. She stood at the threshold of the room waiting for Lady Margaret's reaction.

"It is satisfactory," the old lady pronounced.

The housekeeper continued along the hall, turning left, and Selina followed. From the doors that were ajar, she could see that while the other guest rooms were freshly and cleanly presented, none were as exquisitely appointed as the one afforded to Lady Margaret.

Another slight turn and Selina noted that they had entered an older part of the house. The walls were not oak panel and wallpaper lined; instead they were daubed creamy grey; still immaculately clean, but clearly part of the house that had not yet been renovated.

Mrs. White stopped at the end of the hall and stepped aside from the last door to allow a housemaid to bustle past with an armful of linen. En route, the girl stopped, hurriedly curtsied to the two women, and continued on her way.

The housekeeper turned to Selina. "Forgive me, miss, it's been some years since we've prepared the house for so many guests," she explained. "This part is usually closed off. I'm afraid there was insufficient time to finish preparing all the bedrooms."

Selina entered the room. It was narrow, just wide enough for a passage between a single bed and the armoire. Her luggage—one medium-size trunk; a smaller trunk; two portmanteaux; and a leather hold-all containing art paper, brushes, and paints—was piled under the single window.

Selina smiled graciously and assured Mrs. White that the room was just fine. The housekeeper thanked her and left.

The room was small, certainly, but it wasn't that much smaller than the one she had in London, and it was certainly preferable to sharing with another guest.

The bed was in good order and the mattress new; the sheets were crisply clean and the woolen blankets atop in a basic red and green plaid pattern were soft—actually much better than some of the coaching inns she had stayed in.

The dressing table was not only an adequate size for toiletries, but could also double as a writing surface.

Beside the window, with her luggage stacked alongside, stood the final piece of furniture the room could comfortably contain, a corner washstand holding a blue-and-white Delft bowl and jug.

Knowing she had a few hours to spare before she needed to wash and dress for dinner, Selina set about unpacking, only to be interrupted after thirty or so minutes by the young housemaid who she'd earlier seen with Mrs. White.

The girl, who introduced herself as Bridget handed Selina a large package and told her that it had arrived for her a few days earlier.

It was surprisingly heavy, so Selina set it on the dressing table to unwrap it. Beneath the paper and string was a plain burl walnut box, the color of honey and featuring no other especial adornment to detract from the beauty of the wood.

On top of the box, which stood twelve inches wide and six inches tall, was a plain white envelope which held the small brass key.

It was an extravagant gift with as yet no clue to its giver. Certainly her brother wouldn't spend such a large sum of money on an extravagance except for a major birthday.

She opened the lid, revealing a peacock blue watered silk lining with a scooped envelope pocket.

Selina withdrew a second envelope from the pocket and set it aside, momentarily distracted by the etched silver-topped glass bottles in their fitted slots. In each back corner, two shallow cut-glass bottles were filled with vivid blue ink. Two of the bottles beside these were empty, but a third was filled with a pale yellow liquid. When the lid was opened, the vessel bloomed with the scent of her favorite perfume—a blend of lavender and bergamot.

Filling a further space were two oblong glass boxes, designed to hold pins and combs but currently empty.

At the front was a wooden pen recess that tipped up to reveal a storage place for pens and a cardboard box of nibs; another cardboard box announced that it held drawing charcoal.

In the centre of the box in the same peacock blue silk, a shallow padded compartment with lid revealed a lady's silk kerchief edged with lace and embroidered with the initials SA. Her initials, Selina Ann.

And as she looked further she realized the monogram was replicated again and again on the silver lids of the bottles and boxes.

The intriguing, delightful box was not simply a gift for her, but one that had been specifically customized.

She glanced hesitantly at the unopened envelope then back at the box.

Near the brass hinges in the box itself, two latches caught Selina's eye. She released them in turn. The one on the left discharged a front drawer containing a hinged writing slope. The embossed blue leather surface covered a shallow tray with plain white writing paper and envelopes.

Releasing the right-hand latch caused a small and shallow drawer to spring out from the side. It was lined with silk and designed to secrete jewelry or billets-doux.

Her examination of the writing and dressing table box complete, Selina turned her attention to the envelope and sighed. She feared the gift was from Viscount Canalissy.

Oh dear. She adored the box and would hate to have to return it.

She opened the envelope. The letter inside was in James's confident hand.

> *Dear Selina,*
>
> *I neglected to return your handkerchief; I hope you consider this an adequate compensation.*
>
> *Don't let my mother or anyone else intimidate you or make you feel less than who you are. You are their equal and more.*
>
> *I hope to be with you in Cornwall within a fortnight, my business here all being well.*
>
> *Love,*
> *James*

Smiling, Selina reread the letter, then replaced it in the lid pocket and drew her fingertips across the beautiful bottles and silk.

The gift was perfect. It was beautiful, practical, and elegant, the type of thing she would have chosen for herself had money been no object. She was touched. No other man knew her as well as James did.

She had forgotten about the kerchief although she well remembered the night of their first kiss and the night two days later following James's revelation about he and Abigail.

James had stood and held his hand out for her. Their way lit by moonlight, they walked to the far end of the garden, away from the windows and the light from the house, where he turned her into his arms and kissed her.

Quick to capitalize on her newfound experience, Selina parted her lips readily to his and allowed her tongue to follow his lead, exploring his mouth as thoroughly as he explored hers.

His embrace tightened and, as he held her body closer, she was aware of his growing hardness. Selina responded instinctively by pushing closer still, her whole body now pressed against his.

James's hands swept up her back to her neck, fingers tangling in her hair. With a moan, Selina threw her head back and he took advantage of the action by trailing hungry kisses across her cheek to her neck.

The sensation was intense, almost overwhelming, and she reached to twine her own fingers in the lush, dark hair at his nape.

A restlessness suffused Selina's body, causing her breasts to ache and warmth to bloom between her legs.

James's lips left her neck and returned to her mouth for a long, slow teasing kiss while his fingers trailed down her sides to her waist, fleetingly brushing the side of her breasts.

She wanted more. She shifted to encourage his hands to touch her. He teased the neckline of her dress with his fingertip, reveling in Selina's instinctive sensuality as, in a whispered moan, she gave voice to her pleasure.

The sound of a window closing brought Selina back to herself. She looked up to James watching her attentively.

"What are we going to do?" she whispered.

James responded by giving her a soft warm kiss and stroking her hair. Selina pressed her cheek to his shoulder.

"I'll break things off with Abigail as soon as I'm able," he said, nuzzling the top of her head with his cheek. "But unfortunately that's not going to be until after she arrives at Padstow. The Prince of Wales took a party to Brighton last week and instead of returning to London, she's planning to travel from there to Cornwall. And I can't leave London for another week."

James moved to face her and placed her hands in his.

"I need you to listen to me, Selina."

Selina looked at him, surprised by the urgency in his voice.

"There's more to my business here than just Pennsylvania and my partnership with William, and I can tell by the look in your eyes that you've already guessed that," he whispered.

"Certain events do make more sense that way," she answered with a wry smile. James matched it and kissed her forehead with affection.

"I can't tell you more, I wish I could. My life is more complicated than it ought to be and because of it I'm not certain what the future holds or what I can promise you.

"The one thing I am certain of is I want you, Selina. However—"

She silenced him with a kiss.

"I'm attached as your grandmother's companion until the end of the summer. You'll be host and I'll be a minor guest amongst your titled company," she began. "You might feel differently about me before the summer is over."

James shook his head and drew breath to speak. Selina touched his lips to still them.

"You make this harder than it need be," she complained hoarsely as he kissed her fingers and played his tongue over them.

James stopped his tease and enfolded her into his arms.

"Let's agree not to talk of any future between us until then." She nodded, to convince herself as well as him. "And if we still do not see how there might be a future for us by the end of summer, then we agree to go our separate ways for good."

"Selina…" He groaned.

"It's the only promise I'll make you," she warned.

"Then it will have to do," James reluctantly agreed.

CHAPTER TEN

Jackson followed James into the Marylebone Club just after half past nine in the evening. It was certainly a league or two above the Black Boar Arms, several leagues in fact, and if a group of spies were to have clandestine meetings, then this was a much better location.

This night, the two were dressed as respectable young men about town. They were shown to a curtained-off room with a decent-sized green baize table. The cards and counters were already in place for the card games that were to be the cover for the meeting.

The gathering had been called by Prime Minister William Pitt, but this time he would not be attending in person. He had arranged to send a trusted secretary, Sir Percy Blakeney, in his stead.

In all, over the next ten minutes, three additional men joined them at the table. As much for enjoyment, as to establish their cover, the game began. One chair was left empty for Sir Percy's arrival.

Sir Percy's entry some thirty minutes later was heralded by the sound of a man loudly greeting other patrons as he approached. Then the curtain swept aside and his first impression was of a vibrant silk frock coat of duck-egg blue, a caramel-and-cream striped satin waistcoat, and a white shirt with frothy lace protruding from the cuffs and collar.

Blakeney did not so much walk as glide into the room before collapsing indolently into his chair.

He was no older than thirty, tall and slender, with a sparkling wit and a handsome face that had attracted many in court over the past ten years. Despite his widely vaunted success with some of the bored married court ladies, unkind and unwarranted gossip suggested that he relished his unattached state rather too much and preferred the company of men. Pitt in particular.

So there had been eyebrows raised when, in a whirlwind romance of just a few months, Sir Percy had married the celebrated French actress Marguerite St Just who had sought asylum in England rather than return to troubled Paris with her company.

"So, so glad you didn't wait the game on my account, dear chaps," Sir Percy announced loudly to the table.

James was the first to stand and shake the hand of their tardy guest.

"I'm looking forward to replenishing my purse before I leave for Cornwall, Percy."

"Aha! You might find that easier said than done, James. I don't recall losing last time we played! It's good to see you again."

Percy lifted one eyebrow almost imperceptibly at the last of his greeting to James, a subtle acknowledgement of a change in their relationship as occasional fellow gamblers from overlapping social circles to newly identified co-conspirators.

Sir Percy was, without a doubt, the contact in the envelope of information given James by Pitt at the opera.

The dandy acknowledged the other men at the table with a nod and, with a flourish of his wrist, he summoned the footman waiting patiently by the curtain and ordered champagne for all.

After the sixth round of cards, the footman had been instructed to refill glasses, refresh napkins, and replenish the whisky decanter, and his further services were dismissed. Another round was dealt.

Then, during a quiet moment, and as if sensing the impatience of the American seated to his right, Sir Percy suddenly dropped the affected voice of the dandy and addressed the group in a low voice designed to carry no farther than the table.

"William sends his regrets," he said as he shuffled the deck and dealt. "He's playing Rumplestiltskin and trying to turn straw into gold."

The joke met with a sardonic chuckle from the men.

"The situation, as it stands, gentlemen, is this. His Majesty's illness appears to have grown no worse, thank God, but he has become fixated on financing the court of Louis to the tune of £700,000 in gold."

Sir Andrew ffoulkes snorted softly. "Pitt had better start spinning that straw then," he said, rolling one of his counters between his fingers. "Between paying off the debts of the Prince of Wales, the gold the Foxites are filching, and now this mad scheme, the nation will be bankrupt before this year's elections are over."

"It would teach Charles Fox right if he opens the cupboards of the Exchequer and finds them bare," remarked Sir Philip Glynde.

"Nevertheless," interrupted Sir Percy, "His Majesty appears to believe the answer to the stolen gold financing the revolutionaries is to send more gold to the Royalists. The first consignment of £50,000 is leaving in six weeks' time and, to confound any Frenchie spies here in London, it'll be going from Bristol.

"The shipment will go to Gibraltar, where Louis's royalists will secure the gold and deliver it to Tuileries Palace, where he is being held with Marie Antoinette and the dauphin.

"That this mission is a success is imperative, gentlemen. This is, perhaps, a last opportunity to stabilize France and forestall war. It is also gold we can ill afford to lose or, worse still, see fund the revolutionaries abroad and at home."

Blakeney slugged back a mouthful of whisky with the ease of a hardened drinker and cleared his throat.

"Under the napkins by your drinks," said Sir Percy, "each of you will find an envelope with an assignment. Read it, learn it, destroy it."

* * *

10 July

Selena studied the view across Padstow Strand and added sharp grey lines to her painting, copying the sweep of the stone wall that marked the small town's harbor. Then she began sketching in the people. Before her there was a man pushing a cart, a young courting couple walking along the promenade, two soldiers in full uniform, and a group of fisherman sitting cross-legged in a group, mending their nets.

The role as a lady's companion was far easier than Selina had imagined. Lady Margaret appeared a rather independent woman and, with the arrival four days earlier of Lady Mary with her granddaughter, the honorable Edith Waldren, Selina found herself at leisure most days.

The first day had been spent in part with Lady Margaret and another of the guests at Penventen Hall, Comte Alexandre Charlemont, a suave man of about thirty and a recent arrival from France who had befriended Lady Christina during the London Season.

In the morning the three walked the grounds. They explored the gardens, the hedge maze, and the bordering woodlands, and ventured to a lookout at the edge of the property that boasted a magnificent view down to the river.

Selina found she enjoyed the older woman's company, but it was an awkward lunch during which Lady Christina, though polite, seemed cool and distant. Shortly afterward, Lady Margaret announced that she was still tired from her journey and would rest for the afternoon.

The second day marked the arrival of Edith and her grandmother. Edith was a pretty little thing, a good three inches shorter than Selina, with porcelain skin, exquisite blonde hair, and vivid green eyes. Selina was pleased to find that, unlike some of the other well-to-do young women she had met in London, Edith wasn't a snob.

In fact, if Edith had a fault at all it was that she seemed much younger than her nineteen years and was a hopelessly naïve romantic. No wonder the grandmother kept a close eye on the girl, Selina thought.

Now, as Selina sketched, she spotted Edith having managed to evade her chaperone. The girl was a vision in a pale tangerine dress trimmed in caramel-colored ribbons, holding earnest conversation with a uniformed officer who didn't seem much older than the girl herself.

Then she spotted Selina and rushed to her with the young man trailing along behind.

"Oh! You're an artist! I should have guessed you were very clever," she gushed. "I never had any such skill. My cows look like boxes with horns and my sheep look like clouds with legs. Let me take a look. You don't mind, do you? They say artists hate anyone looking at their work until it's complete, but you're not like that are you?"

Selina stifled a grin and shook her head in response as Edith skipped around the easel to stand at her shoulder.

"Oh that's marvelous!" Edith enthused. "I know you're not finished yet, but I can see it's going to be wonderful." She turned to the patient young soldier. "Come over here and see what a gifted artist Miss Selina is."

The young man—tall, broad shouldered, and a lieutenant by the decoration on his uniform—dutifully complied.

"It's a very nice painting, miss," he agreed.

"Oh!" said Edith. So much of what she said began with that single exclamation. "How rude of me! Miss Selina Rosewall, please allow me to introduce Lieutenant Roger Walsh."

"At your service." He saluted.

"A pleasure to meet you, Lieutenant," acknowledged Selina. "Are you based in Padstow?"

"Temporarily, miss. I'm with a platoon based in Newquay, but my squad is in Padstow until the end of the summer on official business."

Roger looked at Edith and his tone softened.

"I really have to go Miss Edith. I'm still on duty."

"Oh Roger, I will see you again, won't I? My heart will be broken if I do not."

Before the young man could address the issue of Edith's potential distress, a voice called from across the square so sharply that it captured the attention of a number of passersby.

"Lieutenant!"

Walsh snapped to attention as a colonel strode toward them. He was an imposing man whose dark brown hair was peppered with grey at the temples. Selina guessed that he was in his early forties.

"Sir!"

"Your duties, Lieutenant," he warned. His no-nonsense voice was tempered, nonetheless, with an edge of amusement.

"Sir, yes, sir!"

Lieutenant Walsh saluted, hastily bowed to the two ladies, and marched off along the Strand before disappearing around the corner into Mill Road.

The man bowed to the ladies and introduced himself as Colonel Martin Pickering, at their service, before he followed in the direction of his lieutenant.

Edith offered a huge sigh and collapsed to sit on the stone wall beside Selina.

"I believe I'm in love," the girl said wistfully.

"With someone you've known for five minutes?" Selina enquired, quite amused.

"With some people you know immediately," she avowed. "I shall be Mrs. Robert Walsh by the end of the summer."

"*Roger*," said Selina.

Edith peered at her questioningly.

"Pardon?"

"His name is Lieutenant *Roger* Walsh," said Selina.

* * *

After the promising start to the week, it was fitting that it rained, Selina decided, coinciding as it did with the arrival of Lady Abigail and her friend Lady Catherine, and that of Edgar Elkerton, the second son of a wealthy industrialist who was developing some small renown as a geologist and naturalist.

With their arrival, a depressing drizzle settled in that was to last three days, and with it, the atmosphere at Penventen Hall changed.

What had been a comfortable camaraderie between the guests earlier in the week turned grim.

The already cool relationship between Lady Margaret and Lady Christina was now an ill-disguised hostility made all the more shocking to Selina when she learned that Lady Margaret was actually Lady Christina's mother. Lady Mary had the good sense to make herself scarce when the two women started launching barbs at one another.

Edith's lovelorn sighs and hand-wringing were not at all helped by Comte Alexandre encouraging the matter by reading the already tragic mademoiselle pages and pages of French romantic poetry.

Selina's initial delight in having someone to speak French with had now settled into an unshakable ennui, birthed by her inability to finish her painting of the Padstow quayside and exacerbated by the awful characters behaving horridly to each other in a novel the Comte had thought she might enjoy, *Les Liaisons Dangereux*.

On the second day of rain, Selina abandoned the book and gave in to Edith's cajoling to paint her portrait as a gift for Lieutenant Walsh.

After spending an hour with Edith—the most time the flighty girl could be persuaded to sit—Selina spent the rest of the morning walking up and down the hundred-foot-long gallery and conservatory. After nearly a mile of such walking and watching the unrelenting rain from the windows, Selina sensed that she was no longer alone in the room.

"Miss Rosewall, I wonder if I might have a moment of your time?"

Lady Abigail stood in the doorway, elegantly dressed for a day at home in a fashionable bed jacket of mulberry-colored silk over lighter red skirts.

In her own grey dress, Selina felt as drab as a pigeon might next to a robin.

"By all means Lady Abigail," she answered, making her way to one of the wicker armchairs and inviting the other woman to join her.

Lady Abigail glided across the room, a cloud of jasmine and gardenia perfume following in her wake, as did a housemaid with a tray of tea with two cups.

Selina was put on her guard. This meeting wasn't by happenstance; it was engineered, which could only mean that Lady Abigail believed she had the upper hand.

"I understand you consider yourself to have a connection with Sir James," she announced once the maid had left.

"My connection is a matter of fact, my Lady. Sir James and my brother are now business partners, and James"—Selina deliberately dropped his title and watched Lady Abigail's expression change—"and I have become close friends."

"I'm glad you've not decided to act the ingénue, Miss Rosewall. It is so much better to speak plainly of these matters," Lady Abigail responded. "It is your friendship that I wish to talk to you about."

"Since we've agreed to speak bluntly, I have to ask what interest our friendship is to you?" Selina replied.

Lady Abigail smiled confidently. "As you're new to London and doubtless unaccustomed to society, it would be unreasonable to expect you to know there is to be an announcement of my engagement to James by the end of summer."

Selina forced herself not to react to the barb in the preface to Lady Abigail's statement. Instead, she watched the woman sit back and regard her. That was it? Selina realized that Lady Abigail had played her trump, so she continued with renewed confidence.

"I've heard the rumors, Lady Abigail, but I have to say that when James and I have been together, your betrothal is not something which has crossed his lips," she said, allowing the underlying meaning of her words to filter through.

It had the desired reaction. Lady Abigail's eyes narrowed and a slow rise of heat flushed her cheeks. Selina knew her actions were uncharitable but couldn't help herself.

Then Lady Abigail's expression turned shrewd.

"I've underestimated you, Miss Rosewall. It is a mistake that I shan't make again, but I ask as a courtesy that you do not underestimate me either," she said. "My determination to my course of action was set in motion long before your arrival. Despite James's wavering over the past two months, there is too much momentum to prevent there being an announcement."

"Engagements are broken all the time, Lady Abigail," Selina observed. "And while it is true that you have known James longer, I believe I am well enough acquainted with him to be confident in his ability to steer his own course in life."

Lady Abigail flushed fully. Pressing her advantage, Selina stood and walked out of the room, only to be met immediately outside by Lady Margaret, who motioned with a nod of her head to follow her. She led the way to the library down the hall.

Nausea effervesced in Selina's stomach. How long had Lady Margaret been standing there? How much had she heard? What would she think of a mere commoner hinting at intimacies with her grandson?

Once alone Selina faced Lady Margaret with as brave a face as she could muster.

"Bravo, Selina," approved Lady Margaret. "It's about time someone stood up to that little harlot. And don't look so shocked, dear. I might be old, but I still remember a thing or two about sex and how it can completely addle the mind of the male of the species. James is making the right choice in you."

Selina was stunned for a moment before finally finding her voice. "I'm not sure what you m-mean," she stammered.

"Now don't do that. I'm just beginning to like you. Don't spoil it by being conventional," Lady Margaret chided. "I'd like to know how you came to be in love with my grandson."

CHAPTER ELEVEN

14 July

As if to make up for the previous days of bad weather, Wednesday dawned bright, clear, and warm. Over breakfast, Edgar, a thoughtful but rather quiet man in his early thirties, announced his intention to go down to Padstow and spend the day walking along the wide sandy beaches of the River Camel to the cliff at the river mouth. Accordingly, he was dressed in sensible attire for the task.

"Do tell us more about your interest in the local cliffs, Mr. Elkerton," enquired Lady Catherine.

"This is a fascinating part of England, Lady Catherine," he answered. "The north Cornwall coast sees so much adverse weather and the strata in the rocks are most interesting. The folded and contorted stratification of shale and sandstone is unique in southern England. I've spent some time looking at Culm Measures and the folding rocks at Millook Haven about thirty miles from here. Being in Padstow for this summer allows me to compare the features of the natural harbor at Bude, which is where I had the opportunity to explore during the spring."

Lady Christina regarded him with an indulgent smile.

"We must have the Rector of St Petroc's over for tea," she announced. "He's an amateur geologist. I believe he has some fascinating collections, although I must confess to not holding so much of an interest in rocks myself."

"I'd enjoy that very much, Lady Christina," Elkerton replied. "It's good of you to advance the interests of science. Indeed, it would be wonderful if the Rector could be persuaded to host a walking tour of the area. I'm sure he'd be a wealth of knowledge."

Edgar leaned forward conspiratorially. "Not only of geology, but perhaps he can tell us tales of pirates and smugglers!"

"That would very interesting indeed, Mr. Elkerton. I believe we'd all agree it would be a marvelous diversion," Lady Catherine answered, to nods of agreement around the table.

Selina glanced at Lady Abigail and suspected that the woman wasn't so impressed that she was included in such a sweeping invitation.

She wondered about the nature of the friendship between Abigail and Catherine.

Both beautiful, pampered, and spoiled by doting parents and the flattering of numerous admirers, the pair behaved like sisters, and it would be easy to confuse them for such from their similar fashionable figures, grey-green eyes, and peaches-and-cream complexions. The main attribute that set them apart was their hair color. Lady Abigail's was as white as freshly laid snow, while Lady Catherine's was a light brown.

They claimed to share a deep and adoring friendship, but in reality there was a rivalry between the two of them that had manifested itself particularly during the confinement of the past few days.

Regarding them both at the table, Selina decided that Lady Catherine was the more pleasant of the two; then, a thought occurring to her, she turned to Edgar Elkerton.

"Might I impose on going into town with you, Mr. Elkerton?" asked Selina. "I have some errands to run for Lady Margaret and would love to finish my painting before the afternoon."

"Of course, Miss Rosewall, but I must leave in ten minutes. I want to catch the outgoing tide."

A few moments later as Selina came down with her artist's accoutrements, the letters to be sent, and orders from various shopkeepers to be placed on Lady Margaret's behalf, she met Abigail and Catherine at the foot of the stairs.

"There you are, Miss Rosewall!" Lady Catherine exclaimed. "We're so glad to have caught you before you left."

"Yes, we are," purred Lady Abigail. "You wouldn't mind running a few errands for us too? There's a good girl."

Selina fought to keep her expression neutral. Nothing like a little reminder of where one stood in the social order, she thought bitterly.

Selina squared her shoulders and gave the pair a smile—a smile that only her brother would know meant trouble.

"More than happy to oblige," Selina replied evenly, and took possession of a small bundle of letters to post.

Lady Catherine thanked her and walked away, but Lady Abigail stood, blocking her path.

"Was there anything further, my Lady?" Selina asked, raising an eyebrow.

"Just remember where you are and who you are. And what you are not."

* * *

Lady Abigail's attempts to put Selina in her place were quickly forgotten, and the errands in town were quickly completed.

Once again Selina took position on the Strand and continued her painting, pausing every now and again to sketch the faces of various passersby while she let the paint dry on her watercolor.

Wednesday being market day meant the streets were busier than they had been the previous Saturday. People jostled to examine the wares, traders called, voices chattered. Finding herself distracted by the crowds, Selina packed her gear and moved down North Quay Parade, then marched a little way up the hill above the street until she was satisfied with her elevation and quieter position.

She pulled out her sketch pad and started on a new scene—one that captured the boats in the little harbor in the foreground.

A soldier's bright red jacket caught her attention, and along with it a bloom of rose pink swishing alongside. It appeared Edith had found

Lieutenant Walsh. The couple were at the end of the harbor arm and were walking back to the Strand.

The voice nearby startled Selina. "Are you enjoying the day, Miss Rosewall?"

She looked round to find Lieutenant Walsh's commanding officer, Colonel Martin Pickering, beside her. He stood smartly beside the low fence that separated the path from the four-foot drop to the road.

"I am," said Selina in reply to his enquiry. "It's lovely to see the sun out."

"Indeed," he replied personably. He smiled and there was a moment's silence that threatened to become awkward.

"Such a coincidence to see you again, Colonel," said Selina, filling the void.

"Oh? How so?"

"I'm not the only one enjoying the day."

She gestured with her pencil in the direction of Lieutenant Walsh and Edith.

"Ah…yes. The lieutenant does appear to have taken a shine to Miss Edith." The colonel smiled indulgently. "He's a good officer, quite sensible."

"Excellent, he's the type of man Edith needs," blurted out Selina.

The colonel laughed and Selina blushed.

"Oh dear, that was rather indiscreet of me. Edith is a lovely girl…"

Colonel Pickering held his hand up to silence her.

"No need to speak further, miss. I believe I fully understand."

* * *

The sun lay poised on the edge of the cliff, its long beams promising a fine late afternoon and extended twilight.

Before the Penventen carriage rolled to a complete stop, James threw open the door and alit. Jackson jumped out behind him. James waved the driver on through to the coach house, telling him to bring their luggage after the horses had been attended to.

"Looking forward to being home, James?" asked Jackson as they climbed the stairs to the cathedral-like doors.

"I feel like I'm exchanging one nest of vipers for another, but these ones are in much closer quarters," James responded as he dusted down his coat and rapped on the door.

"That's hardly the way to speak of your friends," joked the young American.

"Friends?" James grunted, unimpressed. "I don't know half of 'em, and those I do I don't trust."

"And what of Selina Rosewall?" Jackson grinned.

"Who knows? She may no longer be here. A week with my mother might have her bags packed back to Bristol already," James grumbled.

"Or your Lady Abigail may have devoured her whole," Jackson suggested.

Ha, ha, James silently mocked.

The door opened and the footman stepped aside. Lady Christina stood inside.

"My darling son, you've arrived!" she cried. James responded dutifully.

"Excuse me, sir, I'll go see to your luggage," Jackson the valet announced with merriment twinkling in his eyes.

James turned with a nod and mouthed *Coward!* at him.

"Come along, dear, you must be tired from your journey," twittered Lady Christina, threading her arm through James's. "Your guests have all arrived and most of them are in the drawing room."

Indeed they were. He could see for himself, but his mother introduced everyone anyway — his grandmother, whose cheek he kissed; Lady Mary, whose cheek he didn't. He shook hands with Comte Alexandre and with Edgar Elkerton, who his mother informed James was a geologist of some note.

He greeted Lady Catherine with a bow over her hand, and then moved on to look Abigail in the eye. He bent his head over her hand but barely touched it with his lips.

He knew she felt the slight.

"I've missed you, James," she chided. James nodded once to acknowledge that he'd heard her.

"Now then, we're all here. It's such a nice evening, I've arranged to have dinner in the conservatory tonight," Lady Christina announced.

"Christina, we should wait for Miss Rosewall and Miss Waldren," interjected Lady Margaret.

"Well, if those two girls are going to do me the discourtesy of being late, then I…"

The end of Lady Christina's sentence was lost with the sound of four people entering the house—Selina and Edith along with Colonel Pickering and Lieutenant Walsh.

"…and that's how Dame Archibald's washing got full of musket shot," concluded Colonel Pickering.

The end of the tale was met with laughter from the two ladies and Lieutenant Walsh.

Lady Christina greeted them in the hallway and allowed Edith to introduce the two men. The colonel apologized for the interruption, explained they were merely escorting the ladies home and would now bid them good-bye. Lady Christina's response was to insist on introducing them to the other guests.

As introductions were made, James caught Selina's eye. She gave him a heartwarming smile, which he returned, although he didn't move from where he stood next to Lady Abigail.

Selina was forced to own that the two of them looked very fine standing next to each other.

"I apologize for disrupting your timetable," said Colonel Pickering to Lady Christina. "The day was too lovely not to take full advantage, and I confess that I encouraged my lieutenant in monopolizing the time of these two charming young ladies."

Lady Christina, seeing an opportunity to add other suitors to the party, gave an expansive approbation and extended an offer for the men to dine with them later in the week.

"Forgive me for keeping everyone waiting," Selina added with a curtsy, giving Edith, who was staring at the retreating back of the lieutenant, a nudge.

Edith offered a halfhearted apology and followed Selina out of the room.

* * *

"I was beginning to think I'd never get you alone, darling," Lady Abigail purred, leaning closer to press her breasts against James's arm as they strolled through the hedge maze after dinner.

"You seemed somewhat distracted by your new little friend over these past couple of months; I had rather thought that you'd forgotten our arrangement, though it's usually customary for the husband to wait until after marriage before taking a mistress."

James found Abigail's touch increasingly irritating and shook her off.

"There's not going to be a wedding, Abigail," he said.

She looked at him icily. "Are you against marriage in principle or are you just choosing not to marry me?"

"At the moment no one is getting married."

Abigail deftly batted her fan to stir a small breeze in the still night.

"Does your sweet miss know about this? She doesn't seem the type to lift her skirts without a promise."

James's expression hardened.

"Whereas your legs have opened more times than Parliament— and to as many men."

The sound of the slap may have been heard many feet away.

James rubbed his cheek. The heat of the blow lingered.

"Is that the best of your argument, Abigail?" he muttered.

"We have an arrangement, James, and I'm not going to allow you to back out of it now," she hissed angrily.

"There is no arrangement. Only that which you and my mother have concocted together; now I'm telling you we are through and once this summer is over we will never see each other again," said James firmly, then added more gently, "I'm sorry I've gone along with this during the past year. That was an error of judgment on my part."

"The only error is the one you're making now," Abigail tried reasonably. "I can see why you're infatuated with her. She's a pretty girl, probably with a very sweet and docile nature. But you have an adventurous, wanderlust spirit. You'll get tired of her sooner or later and she doesn't strike me as being the type of woman who would kindly overlook her husband's 'side pursuits.' Neither would her brother, come to think of it."

James said nothing, so she continued.

"Just get this business deal done with William Rosewall and if that includes romancing his spinster sister for the summer, then so be it. But don't you forget," she added, laying a hand across his arm, "Your future lies with me, and the sooner you make that clear by announcing our engagement, the better it will be. The masquerade ball in a fortnight's time will be ideal."

She turned to walk away from him.

James was unable to hide his irritation.

"Are you dense, woman? I will not wed you under any circumstances."

"I beg to disagree," said Lady Abigail. She turned back and regarded him with a languorous smile. James had once thought that smile breathtakingly beautiful but was now aware of the treachery it revealed.

"One word from me to the right ears in court," she said, "and I can have your beloved's brother so tied up in legal injunctions that he would be broke by winter. And another word could have him up on charges of treason."

Abigail saw the sneer of disbelief on James's face.

"You might scoff my love, but as mad as King George is, he knows there is gold missing from the Treasury and all it will take is the suggestion that Rosewall is in league with Charles Fox to defraud the Crown and he'll be swinging from the gibbet."

James was stunned. Not by the threat against Selina's brother, which he would gamble would be an empty one, but by the fact that the missing gold was now court gossip.

Sir Percy needed to know of this and so did William. Selina's face came to him briefly, and he silently groaned. She would hate him if she knew any of this.

"How do you know of this matter?" he asked.

Abigail shrugged. "You'd be surprised by the things men will reveal to women between the sheets."

She gave James a long, appreciative look.

"But then, perhaps not," she added.

"So which of your many lovers has been blessed with such a vivid imagination?" James demanded, hoping to goad her into revealing how widespread knowledge of the missing gold had become.

"Not a word from my lips, but suffice to say that my source takes a very keen interest in the subject, and he is very heavily reliant on there being plenty of gold in the Exchequer."

James inwardly groaned. That narrowed it down some—just most of the House of Lords, the House of Commons, and the members of the Royal Family...

Abigail stood and sashayed toward the hedge row corner before halting to look back.

"We have an understanding after all, don't we lover?"

Chapter Twelve

Selina waited as the harried maid placed the ewer of steaming hot water on the washstand. "I'll bring some cloths shortly, miss. I have to finish attending to Lady Catherine's bath, and then Lady Abigail has to have her bed warmed, then Miss Edith wants..."

Selina rubbed her eyes. "That's fine, Bridget, just come back with the towels. I can take care of the rest myself."

The maid showed her relief, curtsied, and moved out of the room at speed.

Selina was quite used to undressing herself. It had actually felt quite odd to have someone to unfasten her laces and brush out her hair over the past week.

She removed her day dress and corset, electing to remain in her linen shift as she brushed the hair that tumbled down her back. Lamplight in the room highlighted red and gold in her brunette locks.

She glanced at her reflection and pulled a face. Putting up with Lady Abigail on her own with her snide comments and condescension was bad enough, but she could ignore it. Lady Christina acted as though she didn't exist, and she could live with that as well.

But now with James here, she could only imagine how much worse it would be with Lady Abigail marking her territory like a tom cat, egged on by his mother.

She smiled wistfully; it was wonderful to see James again.

Selina had to confess that she missed him. Seeing him again in the flesh and the smile he greeted her with made her relive their last evening together with the feel of his lips on hers.

She missed him terribly in fact, but over the past two weeks, he had somehow become somewhat less real, more a romantic notion or a work of fiction—simply a lovely memory she would take with her at the end of the summer to sustain her in quiet moments in whatever employment she found.

Selina looked at her reflection. It was flushed. She closed her eyes.

Stop it! she admonished herself.

It was too awful that James's grandmother knew her secret.

Lady Margaret saw more than she disclosed, but were she to react like little lovesick Edith every time he entered the room, then not only would it put James in an invidious position, but it would also give Lady Abigail and Lady Christina all the more ammunition to make her life a true misery.

Perhaps it was a good thing that James took Abigail out for a walk around the hedge maze. Spending time with her alone might make him realize that someone from his own society would make him a much better match. If the woman didn't truly care for James, why would she have waited six years for him to return, and why would she try to warn off a potential rival?

Hating the direction of her thoughts, Selina put her hairbrush down and loosened the neck of her shift, letting it fall to her waist. By now the hot water must have cooled enough to wash. She drew the sponge across her neck, her arms, and her breasts.

Again unbidden, the remembrance of James and the way he had allowed his fingers to brush against the top of her breasts aroused her as she washed. Oh, she despaired, life was so unfair she could almost cry.

So caught up in her thoughts, she almost missed the soft knock at the door.

"Come in, Bridget," she answered, not turning to the door. "I take it Lady Catherine wasn't so demanding tonight? You can leave the towel on the bed."

Selina continued to wash herself when it occurred to her that she didn't hear the girl leave.

"Was there something else, Bridget?"

No reply. She turned and was startled by the sight of James standing there. He looked at her with a hunger she had never before seen. Belatedly, she drew her chemise over her breasts.

Selina's mouth dried. She couldn't form the words to tell him to leave. And she should be outraged.

If it had been any other man, she'd be screaming the house down, but seeing his hooded look, she swallowed and glanced at the bed.

What would it be like if he were to take her now? Fresh arousal filled her.

"If you look at me like that again, I won't be able to stop myself, Selina," he said huskily, as though reading her thoughts.

She blushed and retied the neck of her slip.

There was a new knock on the door.

"I have your drying cloths, Miss," called Bridget. The knob turned and the door started to open.

A short, sharp shove from James closed it.

Bridget responded from outside with a squeak of surprise. Selina also jumped, eyes wide in shock.

Bridget knocked again. "Miss?" she asked uncertainly.

Shaking herself, Selina dragged her eyes from James and addressed the door. "I'm not dressed!"

Selina grimaced at her flimsy excuse and shaky voice.

James simply grinned, earning him a scowl.

"I'm sorry, Bridget," she called out, "just…just leave them by the door, please."

There was a moment's hesitation on the other side of the door, then, "Yes, miss."

Selina sighed quietly in relief. She listened as the maid's footsteps retreated down the hall and out of earshot, then marched to where James stood in front of the door. After pushing his shoulder firmly to make him step aside, Selina opened the door cautiously, picking up the towels and peering down the corridor.

It was empty.

She closed the door and threw the locking catch to prevent any further close calls, before turning on James, who now stood farther inside the room, a look of amusement on his face.

"Are you intent on fully ruining my reputation?" she demanded in an angry low voice. "What if Bridget had seen you in here with me undressed? The gossip would be through the house before the hour was out and then what would your mother say? It's bad enough that your grandmother knows I'm in love with you, but how am I to make a decent employment if on my very first post I'm seen seducing the master of the house?"

The amused expression evaporated from James's face.

"What did you just say?"

"I said how am I to make a decent living when—"

"Before that."

Embarrassment flushed Selina's cheeks.

"Your grandmother knows that I'm in love with you," she whispered.

James grinned once more.

"You find that amusing?" demanded Selina.

"Come here," he said, holding out his hand. "Perhaps I haven't been clear in expressing how I feel about you, so I'll have to show you instead."

He led her to the end of the room in front of the washstand.

"Do you trust me, Selina?"

Selina was frozen on the spot, mesmerized and fascinated by his eyes, which appeared to have darkened to the color of coal. Without hesitation she nodded, despite her earlier anger.

Holding her hand, he turned her away from him to face the washstand and loosened the ribbons around the neck of her chemise, allowing the loose fabric to slide across the heightened sensitivity of her skin. A soft sigh left her lips.

The soft linen fell to her waist as it had done a few moments before.

James reached past her and picked up the sponge, dipped it in the warm water, and squeezed it to remove the excess.

"I see you and my spine reacts like this." He drew the sponge slowly up and down Selina's back.

The feel of the warm water and the sensation of the sponge caused her to gasp. Even within Selina's limited experience, she knew not all the goose bumps that prickled her skin were to do with the sensation of the wash.

James turned her to face him again. With unhurried purpose, he bent to kiss her and her mouth opened for him, but after one thorough kiss, he ended the contact with a gentle peck on each cheek.

He dipped the sponge in the water again.

"My arms remember what it was like to hold you while we danced," he spoke, drawing the sponge up and down each arm in turn, then dipping his head to plant kisses down each side of her neck and across each shoulder.

A whimper left Selina's lips, and James bent to whisper in her ear.

"Let yourself go, my love, experience just this."

Selina shivered again.

For a third time, the sponge emerged from the warm wash bowl to wash across her neck, the top of her chest, and down across each breast. Selina's nipples puckered.

With eyes closed, she heard James inhale deeply to steady himself.

The flickering lamplight highlighted her firm round breasts, which sat high on her chest. He sank onto the bed and pulled her toward him, standing her between his spread legs.

"I've spent nights recalling the feel of you against my chest..." He captured one of her rosy pink nipples with his lips. Selina groaned and moisture flooded her sex. Her arms longed to touch him, but they felt heavy and weighted. All sensation centered on where his lips touched her body.

James's hand slid up her waist and over to her other breast, where his fingers flexed and played with the smooth white skin, reveling in its weight and texture.

Selina gasped at each new sensation, her hips rocking to an ageless rhythm, wanting a nameless fulfillment. She whispered his name over and over as his lips trailed from one breast to the other, exploring both with mouth and hands.

After a long moment, he stood again and the brush of his shirt against her bare skin raised another line of tremors and a moan of pleasure.

Another tug and the shift fell from her hips, leaving her fully nude in front of him. She gasped and emerged from the fresh haze of arousal he had created in her.

Her eyes questioned him and her tongue emerged to lick her lips nervously as she watched him rake over her form for a moment before his mouth plundered hers. She responded with similar enthusiasm, spreading her hands across the expanse of his back before sweeping upward until her fingers found his hair at the nape and spread across the back of his head like the tendrils of a vine.

The feel of him on her skin without corsets, cotton, satin, and silk was intoxicating. Selina's head fell back to allow him better access to her neck. He took advantage of it and turned her so the back of her thighs rested against the woolen blankets that covered the bed.

A thought throbbed through her urgently. This was it. He was going to make love to her and she was going to let him.

"Do you still trust me?" he gasped.

Selina nodded.

"I need you to say the words," he demanded. "Do you still trust me?"

Her mouth opened but no words came out; Selina swallowed and tried again.

"I do," she whispered.

A fourth time, James reached out and plunged the sponge into the wash bowl, then, to her surprise, he sank to his knees. Starting from her lower back and bottom, the sponge brushed along each cheek, then down the back of one thigh and then the other.

Selina spread her legs apart, not knowing why she should do so, only knowing that it was the right thing to do.

James held her securely at her waist, for which she was grateful. Selina's knees seemed unable to hold her weight without shaking.

The sponge laved the tops of her feet and the front of her legs one at a time before being drawn up the inside of one thigh and then the other, just short of the junction of her legs.

The tease was both pleasure and pain at once. The sensation was exquisite, Selina acknowledged, but it wasn't enough. Not nearly enough.

"I think about you like this and all the things I want to do to you, with you and for you..." he whispered hoarsely.

Her feet shifted and her hips swayed, chasing the sponge with small movements as it washed across her belly and then hips before its fluid warmth slid across her thatch of curls. Selina's knees buckled and a cry escaped her lips.

She felt so good, so wanton.

James guided her down until she sat on the edge of the bed, moving in until her legs were spread in front of him.

With a groan that told her that he had reached the limits of control, his hands quickly ran up her thighs and across her belly with his thumbs circling ever closer to the centre of her restless ache.

Half spoken, broken words encouraged him while the first of his fingers slipped between her curls and circled across and beneath her folds, quickly followed by his lips and tongue.

The feeling was ecstasy. Against the rising tide of pleasure emanating from her core, Selina clenched and unclenched her fists in the blankets.

A keening moan stifled by her hand across her mouth and the shudders that moved her body allowed James to feel and hear the exact moment she came.

He leaned down and kissed her, then moved across her cheek to her ear and whispered, "That's what you do to me, Selina. Never doubt how I feel about you."

* * *

Somewhere in the house a grandfather clock chimed the hour. It was one o'clock. Selina lay in a half doze, as she had for a couple of hours, warm beneath the blankets heated by James's naked body beside her.

Her face rested against his bare chest. His arm was around her and his hand brushed and teased her shoulder.

She had whispered that she would like to bring his fulfillment as he had brought hers, and she was aroused again by watching her lover reach his moment at her hand.

Lover.

She and James were lovers.

Although they had not truly consummated—she still remained a virgin—Selina knew that was only a matter of time. The thought filled her with fresh longing and she found her leg restlessly rubbing his. It was stilled by a hand on her thigh as James turned to face her.

"Soon, my darling," he whispered. Selina found that anticipation, too, was arousing.

His features darkened with a thought, and Selina frowned in concern at his expression.

"There's so much more about me that I wish I could tell you Selina, things you may hear that could cause you to doubt me," he began. "I want to earn the same look in your eyes that you gave your brother the night we first met at the ball. I want your love and respect."

Selina opened her mouth to speak, to tell him that he already had both, but he shook his head and stopped her with a finger brushed tenderly across her lips.

"The hardest thing I have ever had to do is leave you tonight, but you have my vow. I love you and we will be together."

She, in turn, silenced him with a kiss.

"Don't promise what you have no control over, James," she whispered. "We love each other, let that be enough for now."

CHAPTER THIRTEEN

Two horses galloped along the wide, sandy shoreline of the River Camel as it stretched to the Atlantic Ocean beyond, their shadows casting long in the early-morning sunlight. Their riders were clearly experienced horsemen.

Reaching the end of the beach, the horses were slowed to a trot, happy to be directed to walk side by side, sheltered in the lee of the low cliffs at Iron Cove.

"You've been preoccupied since yesterday evening and riding like the devil this morning," said Jackson. "Still, I suppose it's understandable with two beautiful women available under the same roof…"

The joke earned a filthy look from James.

Jackson wiped his smile. "I know, not a laughing matter." They rode in silence for several seconds before Jackson spoke again. "You're not the type to get himself caught up in a love triangle, so it's more serious than that. What is it?"

"Abigail attempted to blackmail me last night," answered James.

"She did what?"

"She knows, or suspects, about the siphoned gold. Apparently one of her new lovers told her."

"Do you know who?"

James sighed. "It could be anyone from the Prince of Wales himself through to the Parliamentary secretary. Abigail certainly has the access as lady-in-waiting to the Princess Royal."

"How is she threatening you?"

"Oh, Abigail is too clever to threaten me directly, my friend." James turned in his saddle to face him. "She's set her aim at William Rosewall. Threatens to implicate him in the missing gold if I don't agree to announce our engagement at Pitts's masquerade ball. She has enough clout to see him investigated at least. Depending on who the source of her information is, there might be evidence being manufactured against him as we speak to throw the scent off the real conspirators. And with that much gold at stake, they wouldn't hesitate to let an innocent man hang for it."

Jackson's dismay showed clearly on his face and even more obviously in the brief string of curses, perfected in some of the less upmarket saloons of Pennsylvania, that escaped his lips.

A wry smile lifted the corner of James's mouth. "Well said, brother."

"What about our friends in London?"

James patted his jacket pocket. "I have a dispatch to go to London the moment the post office opens, but it will be at least seven days before I will know whether they can identify and neutralize the threat."

"Nine days is the masquerade ball."

James nodded in acknowledgment.

"Hell, man," said Jackson, "that's cutting it fine. What are you going to do if our friends don't come through?"

"That's why I wanted to speak to you away from prying eyes."

James held his mount's reins in one hand and withdrew from his pocket two envelopes with the other. Glancing at them, he deftly slipped one back in his jacket pocket; the other he handed to Jackson.

The envelope had his name on it and contained more than just a thick sheaf of paper—coins, perhaps—and it was sealed with wax.

"And this is…?" asked Jackson, making note of it as he placed it in his own coat.

"It's what to do if all hell breaks loose."

Jackson nodded. "What do *you* plan to do?"

"I'll be refusing Abigail. But I don't want her to be certain of it until the ball in case our threat lurks closer to home. Much of London has left the city for their country estates, and we don't know who or where they are. If Abigail's threat is real and Rosewall's name is mentioned, I will denounce myself. There will be enough credibility in it to throw off suspicion from him."

Jackson swore bitterly again under his breath.

"My connections and wealth," James continued, trying to assure him, "will afford me protection, but I'm relying on you, my friend, to ensure the entire Rosewall family leaves England immediately and arrives safely in Pittsburgh. There's a letter of credit for three thousand pounds plus ten guineas in gold in that envelope.

"I'll join you in America as soon as the whole mess is sorted."

"And if it isn't?"

"That's my insurance you carry in your pocket. The documents have been signed and witnessed by my lawyers in London. My half of the shipping business will revert to Rosewall. The coal mine and my other business interests will be divided between you and Selina. She'll have all the rights and respect due to her as my widow."

Jackson cocked an eyebrow. "That's a very comprehensive arrangement for a girl you only met two months ago. Does your intended know any of this?"

James shook his head briefly.

"If Abigail suspected she did, she wouldn't hesitate in extending her threat. I won't let that happen."

James was sure Jackson would curse again, but the American swallowed instead and gave a curt nod.

"What of your mother?"

"She'll get Penventen Hall and whatever other hell is due her," James answered bitterly.

"Speaking of hell, what about Abigail?"

"I'm going to have to play up in public to that Jezebel."

"And in private?"

"The thought of dipping my wick in that pool ever again turns my stomach," said James with a curl of his lip. "But she won't care if she thinks she has me in hand.

"Besides, investigating the wreck of the *Pandora* gives us reason enough to be away from the house."

The two men directed their mounts from the beach and over an escarpment where, once again, they let the animals have their head to gallop inland until they reached a country lane about two miles from Padstow.

There, they slowed the grey and chestnut stallions to ensure a steady pace back to the town, where, by then, the post office would be open for James to organize a rider to take his message to London.

* * *

Selina, already seated and partway through her morning coffee, watched Abigail walk into the breakfast room as though she owned it.

In her mind, she already did, Selina supposed.

"Ah!" pronounced Catherine upon spying her friend. "The little sparrow finally awakes! Too late to catch that tasty worm. He's gone a-riding with his manservant."

Selina looked down into her coffee, and Edith emitted a most unladylike snort. Catherine gave them both a sly glance of amusement.

Abigail didn't miss a beat. "One doesn't need to rise early when one's nest has been nicely feathered the night long."

Edith burst out laughing, while Selina's gut twisted. Yes, she knew Abigail's statement was a lie—knew it remarkably well—but it didn't stop the sharp pang of jealousy.

When she looked up from her cup, she noticed Abigail's triumphant expression cast in her direction.

"Well, ladies, since we're all here and the men folk are out doing something or other, what say we decide what we're wearing for the masquerade ball?" said Catherine.

"I wonder what Roger will be wearing? We could match. Wouldn't that be simply sweet?" asked Edith.

The roll of Abigail's eyes revealed what she thought of the idea.

"Edith, darling, your lieutenant is hardly likely to be invited to a ball attended by the most important people in the country," she snipped, as she helped herself to some pastries and a fresh cup of tea. "He's simply the Colonel's errand boy. Really, dear, you must learn to set your sights on something a little better."

In an instant, Edith looked as though she might cry.

"Don't listen to Abigail, Edith. She's obviously tetchy from lack of sleep," responded Catherine. "If the colonel is attending, Roger's likely to be there in uniform."

"Oh, he's so handsome in his uniform!" Edith enthused, brightening again.

"He looks as though he'd be handsome out of his uniform too," Catherine observed. "You'd better offer him some honey to make sure he remains sweet on you, otherwise I might be tempted to take a bite myself."

"Oh, you wouldn't!"

Catherine gave a noncommittal shrug but turned to wink at Selina and Abigail.

"Lady Catherine has a weakness for men in uniform," agreed Abigail. "I could tell you the story of her and a particularly handsome cavalryman—and his friend—in St James Park, just this spring, in which she was nearly caught by—"

"Enough of me, let's not forget that Abigail is also very familiar with any number of uniforms. I believe she is very close to collecting the full set."

"Not quite," countered Abigail, "I believe I might be down a sweet blond-headed lieutenant."

At that, Edith's bottom lip quivered. "You wouldn't..."

Abigail simply arched an eyebrow in reply, and Edith promptly burst into tears and fled from the room.

Catherine and Abigail laughed in her wake. Selina offered a wan smile to their amusement.

Seeing Selina's lukewarm expression, Catherine's smile faded and her expression became serious.

"I promise to apologize to her later, Selina," she offered genuinely, "but you have to admit little Edith is so easy to tease, and she'll need to hold her own if she's to ever move successfully in social circles."

Selina nodded, accepting the truth of her statement.

"She is young and a little credulous, I agree."

Catherine smiled. "No harm done, then?"

"No, I suppose not."

"You're a good egg, Miss Rosewall. More coffee?" she enquired.

"Yes, thank you, I will."

Sensing the focus of attention shifted from her, Abigail interrupted. "We still haven't discussed costumes for the masquerade." Her eyes sparkled with unspoken malice. "I've decided to go as a bride."

Selina stiffened.

"How very clever of you, darling," agreed Catherine, fulsomely. "They say at these things you should go as someone completely different to who you really are. In your case, I can't think of anything so completely opposite than a chaste, biddable virgin."

Selina hid a laugh behind a cough and watched Abigail's face burn with anger.

"You evil cat," she hissed, getting to her feet. "You—with the morals of an alley cat."

"So says the bitch in heat.," Catherine shrugged, sensing her victory. "Meow!"

Abigail gave up and stalked from the room, muttering under her breath. Catherine held herself in check until her friend was gone before bursting into laughter so lusty she held her sides.

"Have you and Lady Abigail been friends for long?" Selina asked innocently once Catherine had settled again.

Catherine gave her a sideways glance and Selina found herself under the woman's scrutiny. She wondered if she measured up and, if so, by what criteria she was judged.

After a moment, Selina decided that she had passed inspection when Catherine answered her.

"Oh yes. Friends. Perhaps not the way you mean," she said, and continued with a naked frankness Selina found surprising. "Abigail and I understand one another. We're friends when it suits our purpose and bitter enemies when our mutual interests collide."

Selina nodded, although she really didn't comprehend at all. Why be friends with someone who would plunge a dagger in your back even as they smiled and kissed your cheek?

Catherine smiled. "I'd imagine our different social stations wouldn't allow us to be friends, but may I offer you a piece of friendly advice?"

"If you wish."

"Standing between Abigail and what she wants is a very dangerous place to be. And you have something she wants…"

Goose bumps rose on the back of Selina's neck.

"I have no control over the affections of Lord Penventen," she answered as evenly as she could.

"Perhaps you do, perhaps you don't. It makes very little difference to me." Catherine shrugged. It seemed to be her favorite way of expressing herself. "But God knows there have been times when Abigail has seduced a favorite of mine right out from under my nose. A little turnabout would be fair play indeed."

Then Catherine paused, her head slightly atilt, as if listening.

Selina heard nothing.

"Come, let's not sit in the house," Catherine announced suddenly, getting to her feet, "let's take a turn about the garden."

Selina followed Catherine through the French doors, across the lawn, and behind the stables to where the hedgerow maze stood. They entered and took several turns in silence before Catherine spoke again.

"Abigail's interest in James borders on obsession. He walked out of an expected marriage with her six years ago."

"Was it any surprise?" asked Selina. "He caught her with another lover."

"I see you've been told the story," responded Catherine. "Very well." She paused briefly, as if selecting her words.

"I've known Abigail since girlhood and she's always been precocious. She has wealth, privilege, beauty, and intelligence too, if you count sheer animal cunning. James was the very first man to leave her. She didn't take too kindly to that. She stormed for weeks. And, when he returned, she was convinced it was out of unrequited longing for her."

Catherine smiled, but it was a cynical raising of the corners of her mouth only. "It also helped that he returned wealthier and more experienced than he left. Oh, of course he doesn't love her. I don't think he even likes her. It was ironic really. When he came back, he treated her with the same offhandedness she treats men with, especially those she's luring into her web.

"Everyone but her could see he'd only taken up with her again under a sufferance of some kind. I mean, even when she started taking new lovers right under his nose, he acted like it meant nothing to him. That only made her more determined to keep him."

Selina was appalled and couldn't help that it showed. Catherine gave her a sympathetic look but continued walking.

"Then you and your brother came on the scene and Abigail was furious, and by that, I mean murderously so. It was the interest James was showing you."

Catherine reached out and drew her fingertips across the leaves of the hedge as she passed and spared Selina a weighted glance.

"Abigail's a very dangerous enemy to have," she warned, "especially with her connections. You do know she's bedded the Prince of Wales, don't you?"

"Oh, dear God."

"No," murmured Catherine, her tone almost self-reflective, as if Selina's reaction was unheard, unconsidered, and unnecessary. "I don't see how you could know."

She pouted a little moue of disdain. "I don't believe James has heard about that one either," she continued.

"That's appalling!"

Catherine let out a tiny snort of laughter. "Yes. Awful isn't it?" she agreed. "No wonder the Frenchie peasants want to murder the aristos in their country."

"I don't understand why you're telling me this," Selina whispered, reeling from the revelations.

"I don't know either," Catherine admitted.

They stopped and Catherine gave Selina a long, considering gaze. "No offence intended, Selina, but we're nothing to one another. We're just mutual houseguests and you're not even in my social class. I don't suppose I'll see you again after this summer. All the same, you seem to be a nice young woman who doesn't deserve to get caught up in the machinations of bored, indolent, and spiteful aristocrats."

"Thank you for your candor, Lady Catherine," Selina replied, stunned by such brutal honesty.

Their walk recommenced and continued in silence until they had found the heart of the maze. In the centre of the square stood a garden of geraniums, their red flowers in full bloom. From the crimson rose a white Greek marble statue of two lovers intertwined.

Selina studied it, recalling the hours she had spent in James's arms. A breeze picked up, carrying with it a hint of salt from the estuary and the ocean beyond. She wrapped her arms around herself, suddenly chilled.

"Well…I'm going to find my own way back to the house, Miss Rosewall," announced Catherine, her voice taking on the slightly imperious tone that was her usual manner of speaking.

"Thank you, again," said Selina.

Catherine dismissed her with a wave of her hand and began to walk back into the maze before stopping.

"Oh, one more thing. If anyone learns I have told you any of this, I will deny it," she said. "I do hope you understand."

CHAPTER FOURTEEN

The day passed pleasantly enough, although Lady Margaret demanded Selina's attention throughout. Selina became secretary, writing memos to the Lady's household and instructions to shopkeepers in Newquay who could be expected to receive her patronage within the week. It wasn't until afternoon tea that the older woman dispensed with her services.

As was her custom, Selina walked down to Padstow to continue her artwork. She posted some letters of her own to Sarah and the children before settling in a favorite spot overlooking the harbor—the one she had discovered a few days earlier, a slight elevation not too far away from the ebb and flow of people whom she delighted in capturing— paying special attention to the array of small ships and boats sheltered there.

The grassy elevation marked the start of an informal path that took the intrepid walker along the length of the peninsula.

For the fourth day running, one man caught Selina's eye. At first, for some reason, she thought he was the harbor master, then that he was one of the other local men who made their living in and around the sea, yet none of the people appeared to speak with him. It was as though they didn't know him.

If asked, Selina would have to confess that she didn't know why he had caught her attention. The man wasn't handsome, in fact his features were rather coarse and his mouth appeared set in a permanent grim line. Perhaps that was the thing she noticed about him—the man's expression never varied.

It might be that he was waiting for a boat to arrive. If so, it must be overdue. While his daily habit of walking along the waterfront appeared unhurried, the hands behind his back, which rolled something though his fingers gently a few days ago, had today increased their actions—a sure sign of agitation.

Selina laid aside her watercolor and started to sketch what features of the man she could glean. Soon pages of her pad were filled with small two-inch drawings, full face, profile, and silhouette.

As the sun announced its intention to end the day with a showy display of pastels splashed across the blue-grey canvas of the afternoon sky, the mysterious man left his vigil around the North Quay Arm and disappeared into one of the side streets.

Deciding the sunlight had dimmed too much to work and that the odd man was not going to make another appearance, Selina finished packing away her kit and looked up to find James approaching from the other end of the path.

"So this is where you spend most of your day," he said. "I couldn't find you at the hall."

"I don't know how many days of fine weather we'll get, so I like to take advantage of it," replied Selina.

James nodded to the sketches of the mysterious man at the quay.

"A friend of yours, a secret beau?" he asked.

Selina smiled.

"He seems to have captured a lot of your attention," James pressed, eyes twinkling.

"I call him Fidget because his hands are never still," she said, then, more thoughtfully, "It might sound odd, but I feel like I know this man, or at least that I ought to. He looks familiar; although I'm sure I've never seen him before."

James shook his head. "Not odd at all. You're a painter who notices things."

Selina shared what she had noticed about the man, pleased that James hadn't dismissed her observations as a flight of feminine fancy.

After the telling, silence stretched on for a few moments between them as they listened to the sounds of the town coming to the end of its working day. The various noises were punctuated by a roar of laughter from the opening door of the tavern on the corner, the Red Lion, where some men had gathered to fit in a pint of ale before walking up the narrow winding streets to their cottages.

Selina accepted James's offer to carry her kit, easel, and folding stool, which he slung effortlessly across one broad shoulder. A traveling box of paints, pencils, and painting boards he held in his left hand, and he held out his right hand for Selina to take.

She hesitated for a moment and James's head tilted in mute enquiry.

"Aren't you concerned about being seen?" she asked.

"Are you?"

"Not for my sake, but what about Abigail?"

"I stopped dancing to her tune a long time ago, and you shouldn't start."

She took his hand, reveling in the feel of its strength and warmth in hers; strong, capable hands that had brought her to the peak of passion last night. She blushed at the memory.

A glance up at him told her that he remembered too. He leaned close, his breath tickling her neck and ear. She closed her eyes in anticipation.

"At midnight, meet me in the hall, I have something special to show you," he whispered.

* * *

James stood at the back of the room, a glass of champagne in his hand, and watched his guests.

All in all, it was a very pleasant dinner. For all of his mother's faults, she was an excellent hostess.

James had had to endure escorting Abigail to dinner and taking his place at the end of the table as master of the house, but it was a small price to pay to see Selina happy. At one stage, he had even seen her enjoying an animated conversation with Alexandre and Catherine, of all people.

His mother had made good on her invitation and Colonel Martin Pickering and Lieutenant Roger Walsh were in attendance as well, much to the delight of young Edith.

And Lady Christina's suggestion that, weather permitting, a day next week be spent exploring the beach and headland with keen amateur geologist the Reverend Ian Kirk, rector of St Petroc's, as guide, was particularly well received—especially by Edgar, who now was playing a game of chess with young Roger.

Unfortunately the young lieutenant was having a difficult time of it.

Edith sat at the piano and played prettily as accompaniment to Lady Catherine's warm contralto singing voice.

In a semicircle of chairs around the piano was an audience comprising Selina; Comte Alexandre; Colonel Pickering; Lady Abigail; Edith's grandmother, Lady Mary; and James's mother, Lady Christina. At the back of the room, close to the low-burning fireplace, was his grandmother, Lady Margaret.

"Are you enjoying your summer, Grandmother?" he asked.

"It's been pleasant enough, although I don't understand why you require me to travel all the way from my home to suffer the presence of your mother."

"I thought you'd like to at least spend some time with your grandson."

"You could have easily paid me a visit instead," she said with a sniff, but the sternness of her words was softened by an affectionate pat on his arm. "I'd like to know the real reason why I'm here, young man. It's not to enjoy the sea air. I could do that as easily in Wales."

James smiled slowly and watched the older woman's face for her reaction as he spoke. "I'm getting married."

The look of surprise on Lady Margaret's face bordered on shock, but the expression didn't last long before it was replaced by a shrewd stare and an exaggerated sweeping glance across the room.

"The young woman must be here, otherwise why bring me all this way?"

James's smile broadened to a grin, and he allowed the old lady to continue.

"It's not little Edith at the piano, she's far too young and too flighty to make a good match," Lady Margaret decided. "Catherine there is a beauty, but there is a stubborn streak in her character that will require her husband to take a firm hand with her. Besides, you've shown no interest in these women before now."

James raised his eyebrows in mock surprise.

"Don't look at me like that," Lady Margaret chastised. "I may live in Cheshire but I still have news of London. Your name is associated with only two women in two months and they are Abigail and Selina."

"Bravo, madam!" He leaned in and kissed her wrinkled cheek.

Lady Margaret harrumphed in pretend annoyance.

"Don't get beyond yourself young man. It has yet to be established whether you have more brains than your father in the choice of a wife."

"Now then," James chided, with a twinkle of mischief in his eyes. "That's hardly the way to speak of your own daughter."

"After what she did to your father, that woman is no daughter of mine. She can go to the devil for all I care. I hope I've been a better influence on you than that hellcat."

"Let's pretend I haven't already made up my mind."

"Well, while we're playing pretend, we'll just make believe that you might heed my advice. Is that the game we're playing?"

"Perhaps."

"Very well...If you marry Abigail, I'll disinherit you as the idiot wastrel progeny of your easily led father and your avaricious, vacuous, social-climbing mother."

Lady Margaret finished her observation and set her mouth in a tight line.

"Now, put an old woman out of her misery and tell me that it's that sensible Rosewall girl."

James nodded.

"Then you do have some brains after all," she said with affection before her expression firmed again. "Now tell me why your fiancée is under the impression she's started a new life as a poor lady's companion instead of the bride-to-be of one of the most sought-after society bachelors."

"That would be because I haven't asked her yet."

Lady Margaret snorted. "Don't you think that might be a good idea? Were you planning on keeping her in the dark until your wedding day? She might go up even further in my estimation and refuse you."

The levity in James's eyes dimmed. "It's complicated."

"Complicated? Tosh! She's pretty and sensible and, for some unaccountable reason, she appears to be in love with you. You have means and seem to be fond of her, so there's no reason why you couldn't be married by the end of summer if you chose."

James shook his head and murmured his dissent low.

"I'm obliged to do a favor for a friend first."

* * *

The last chime of midnight struck as Selina's foot reached the final step. She didn't know why James would want to meet her here, so she changed after dinner into a simple cotton dress in dove grey and a black shawl across her shoulders against the evening chill.

For a moment she thought she was alone until she saw James's silhouette pass a moonlit window as he crossed from the drawing room to meet her.

"Where are we going?" she whispered.

"Sh…" was his only reply as he took her hand and led her to the conservatory and through the French windows to the lawn.

The full moon cast deep shadows over the trees and shrubs, making it difficult to identify the features in the garden.

James didn't stop to inform her of their destination, so Selina allowed herself to trust his sense of direction as they walked farther away from the house and toward the line of trees that marked the northwestern boundary of the grounds.

About twenty yards into the woods, a figure emerged from the gloom to meet them.

Jackson nodded to James and greeted Selina by wishing her a good evening. Then he walked away in the direction in which they had come.

"Only a few yards farther," James said, and continued leading her through to a clearing illuminated by the moon over the Atlantic. The roar of the surf could be heard pounding the rocks somewhere below the cliff.

There were few clouds this night, nothing to obscure the spray of stars that sparkled like diamonds across the inky blackness. The moon itself was bright, big, and full, almost close enough to reach out and touch. Lines of liquid gold shimmered hypnotically on the waves falling toward the shore.

Selina stepped forward, mesmerized by the sight. James's grip on her hand firmed.

"Be careful, the cliff edge is only a couple of yards away," he said softly.

Selina turned to face him and then noticed to her right, two tin lamps on the ground, casting a weak light on a blanket and a wicker basket.

"Oh, this is beautiful!" Selina breathed, squeezing his hand.

James led her to the blanket. In the basket was a bottle of wine, biscuits, cheese, apples, and grapes—a midnight feast prepared by Jackson.

Selina sipped her wine, her back against James's chest, reveling in the smell and the warmth of him.

"I spent a lot of time here as a boy," explained James, his arm around her to protect her from the light breeze. "The view during the day is lovely, but it's at night that I really feel the power of the ocean and the draw of the cliffs. I spent clear nights like this one searching out the constellations and wondering about what life is like on the other side of that ocean. If there was one thing I missed about England, it was this spot. It's home."

"Penventen Hall is beautiful. I understand why it means a lot to you," she said thoughtfully.

"No, I don't mean the hall," he corrected. "That hasn't been a home to me for a very long time. Life here was a pendulum of bitter arguments between my mother and father on one swing and frosty weeks of silence on the other.

"Here though—right here in the wood and this clearing—there was adventure and also solitude when I needed it."

James had not spoken much of his childhood, but Selina knew Lady Margaret disliked James's mother and she suspected that his childhood had not truly been a happy one. She turned in his arms to examine his face in profile, but his attention was fixed out on the horizon.

Then he turned and kissed her sweetly.

"I've never shared this with anyone else," he confessed hoarsely. "I want to give this to you. Do you understand? I want to give you something of myself that no one else has ever had."

Tears welled in her eyes and Selina nodded. She did understand and loved him even more for it.

James's arms wrapped around her tightly and a low thrum of desire infused her.

She wanted him to touch her again, make her feel the explosive surge of pleasure he had given her the night before.

Selina touched his cheek tenderly before following it with kisses she trailed to his slightly parted lips waiting for her. She took her time exploring his mouth while her hands skimmed across his head, his neck, across his shoulders, and down his back. Her hair had become loose from its ties and spread like a halo across the dark grey of the blanket. Her sapphire blue eyes glittered with desire. One arm was flung over her head, and with her other, she beckoned him to join her.

He propped himself on one elbow, using his free hand to explore her face, drifting down her neck across each breast and then seemed content for the moment to just watch her respond to him.

Selina was not content with this; little sighs turned to groans as he teased her.

She rolled to her side and touched him as and where he touched her, delighted to hear his breath catch. Through the linen of his trousers she stroked his hardening length and murmured her approval as his hand found the place between her legs.

"Please," she whispered, not knowing how else to articulate her need.

"Soon," he replied, his hand now bunching up her skirt and drawing it up her leg. "Let me pleasure you like this tonight, but soon, I'll take you completely."

* * *

Selina lay on her back, her head pillowed on James's arm as they watched the night sky together.

"I still remember the first time I went out on my father's ship," she said. "I was five and supposed to be asleep, but I snuck up on deck and listened to one of the sailors play a mouth organ. I watched the stars for what seemed like hours before Papa found me. I thought he'd scold me for being up, but he lay down on the deck beside me and explained how to the find the North Star and told me the legends behind the constellations and how I came to be named Selina for the full moon he saw on the night I was born. I've always treasured that memory."

"Did you know the moon is how sailors find their way at sea?"

"I didn't."

James stroked Selina's arm softly and urged her to continue.

"Papa described the moon as being the hands of a celestial clock. To tell the longitude, the navigator just has to know the position of the moon, the time, and the location of the evening star.

"After Maman passed away"—Selina swallowed at the revived memory—"I would cry whenever he had to leave us. One night he took me outside and pointed to the moon, saying 'as long the moon hangs in the sky, I will always find my way home to you.'

"When he was very sick, not long before he died, we went outside one evening and lay on a blanket and he told me all over again the Greek stories of the constellations. He'll never see the ocean again, but I feel I am experiencing this for him, which means he's alive again. And for the first time since his death, I feel like I'm alive again too."

CHAPTER FIFTEEN

17 July

Selina was glad to have worn one of her shorter walking dresses, a sky-blue one that rose an inch or so above the ankle. Walking along the shore in anything longer would have left her waterlogged. She held a hand to her head to secure her brimmed straw hat from the sea breeze and looked back at the rest of the party.

Edith had been less wise, and the hem of her pretty pale pink walking dress was dark with sand and brine. Its length also made walking a slow-going affair, although Lieutenant Roger didn't seem to mind being a constant companion.

Bringing up the rear were James and Abigail. The woman had latched onto his arm like a limpet the moment they had left the hall.

Comte Alexandre and James's valet, Jackson, kept Selina company. The satchel over Jackson's shoulder was Selina's, which he had offered to carry for her. It contained a few basic drawing materials.

A handful of yards ahead, Catherine and Colonel Pickering were taking an interest in a geological discussion between Edgar and Reverend Kirk. The clergyman was, true to Lady Christina's promise, a wealth of information about the local area.

The Reverend surprised Edith by not wearing his vestments or a dog collar but a simple grey shirt and trousers. When she remarked on it, he told her, "Only when I'm on official business, dear."

Kirk appeared to be in his late forties; his grey hair matched his shirt. While older and a good few inches shorter than Edgar, who was also informally dressed in practical walking attire and sturdy shoes, the Reverend matched the younger man in stride, enthusiasm, and vigor.

He pointed to the outcrop of green- and purple-banded slate that had been quarried for use in Penventen Hall, and to the north-facing recumbent folds in the cliffs that rose from the sand along the mouth of the River Camel.

Selina only half listened to the discussion up ahead, conscious that James and Abigail had slipped farther away from them.

She warred with herself. While Selina was growing to believe that James might actually be in love with her, jealousy and insecurity whispered doubts that pricked at her confidence. She tried to silence the voices by reminding herself that he had gone out of his way each time they had been together to reassure her of his feelings, and she understood the need for a pretence to continue at least a while longer.

So why should the sight of them, Abigail and James, walking along the sand together fill her with such unease?

Perhaps because James had told her that he had informed Abigail their affair was at an end—and Abigail had refused to accept it.

That much Selina could see for herself; there was something in the way Abigail looked at her over dinner two nights in a row—a look of triumph—that made her wonder if she had something over James that might hold him in check.

And if it was large enough that his influence and wealth couldn't dismiss it, then to Selina's mind that left only one thing.

Honor.

Selina knew well enough what women did to capture honorable men.

"Miss Selina?"

Edgar called her forward. "While we're waiting for the others to catch up with us, the Reverend and I would be most indebted if we could impose on you to sketch these formations for us."

Selina was happy to oblige. Even more so because it forced her out of the unpleasant reverie. Jackson held open the satchel, and she quickly extracted her sketch pad and charcoals.

"I've never seen anything like it," said Catherine with none of the cynical archness that so frequently marked her conversation. "How can rock so hard be made to bend like fabric?"

"They are remarkable," agreed the colonel. "What caused those folds?"

"No one is certain," admitted Edgar.

"Certainly a great geological upheaval, perhaps because of or in the aftermath of Noah's Flood," answered Reverend Kirk.

"I find it hard to believe water could be responsible for all of this," said Pickering doubtfully.

"Well, over a great deal of time water can carve very vast swathes. Most river estuaries are formed this way," explained Edgar to the colonel, then nodding to Kirk, "although I do have to say, Reverend, that a flood couldn't be responsible for all of this."

"I do not believe a Noah's flood covered the world," offered the Comte. "It is one of those exaggerated tales. A large flood somewhere in the East perhaps, but there's not enough water in the world to have covered all the land. The flood of Noah is an interesting tale, but one to be discussed as philosophy, not as science."

"I see I'm outnumbered by doubters," responded the Reverend with ease. "However, I don't see belief in the holy word of God as being inconsistent with science. In fact some of the greatest men of science were very devout."

He gestured back toward the folded strata.

"We look at the same feature and you see a gradual wearing away over eons while I see the result of a singular, violent event where rock not yet set was still pliable."

To members of the party glancing back from further along the shore, James and Abigail looked as though they were enjoying a tryst.

"Once Abigail gets her claws into a man, there's no letting go," Catherine observed wryly. "Perhaps her dream of a late summer wedding will come true after all."

"A wedding?" squealed Edith. "How wonderful! James and Abigail make such a handsome couple, don't they?"

"Weddings are a specialty of mine," Reverend Kirk quipped. "We're open all seasons."

Selina started to feel ill and backed away the group.

Oh dear God, she thought, she was going to faint! The panic must have showed on her face because Jackson was immediately at her elbow.

He led her to a shaded rock where she sat.

"Is Miss Selina all right?" asked Colonel Pickering, now alert to Selina's distress.

"I believe so, just a little too much sun," Jackson called over his shoulder.

Jackson looked down at the pale young woman in front of him and dropped down on his haunches to meet her eyes.

"No matter what may happen, please know you have a friend in me."

Selina gave a weak smile and nodded.

"Be strong," he advised.

With a deep breath, Selina stood and was grateful to have Jackson's arm to steady her back to the group that James and Abigail had now joined.

"Reverend?" asked Edith. "Edgar promised you would tell us stories of shipwrecks, smugglers, and pirates—are all those tales true?"

"Well, like the discussion we've just had, there is some conjecture."

The Reverend Kirk smiled, knowing he had a willing audience. Hours spent writing and honing his sermons made him an accomplished speaker, and the opportunity to be a storyteller was irresistible.

"Let's go back along the beach to the other side of the headland where the really tall cliffs start, and I'll tell you the story of Black Heart Pete, the most notorious brigand of Cornwall," he began.

He spun a flagrantly false but utterly engaging tale that kept everyone amused on the two-mile walk across the headland to the rocks and cliffs on the ocean side called Gunver Head.

* * *

Abigail fell into step with Catherine for a while, and James took the opportunity to fall back with Jackson.

"Is Selina all right? I saw her…"

"And she saw you—and heard Catherine announce marriage plans."

James winced and Jackson spoke out to support his friend.

"There's no place we can get a scold's bridle for that one over there? If I have to listen to her petty, spiteful nonsense much longer, I'm going to put her over my knee and…"

James gave a short, bitter laugh.

"You'd enjoy yourself far too much and she'd not learn a lesson."

"Sure, I like them with spirit, but not vain and spoiled."

They soon reached the headland and waiting for them was James's mother, a newly erected marquee, and a small squad of servants getting up tables and chairs.

The Ladies Margaret and Mary sat in the shade while Lady Christina supervised the staff.

The marquee provided respite from the heat of the midday sun while capturing a cool breeze from the ocean.

James had to admit that his mother had outdone herself again. The outdoor luncheon was a stroke of genius, though the memory of what Abigail had said while they were still some distance from the main party bothered him yet.

"Not so fast, lover," she'd begun. "You've been quite skilled in avoiding me over the past two days. I do hope you've been thinking about us."

"Believe me, I've been giving you a great deal of thought," James answered coldly.

"Good. I would hate to think that our arrangement had slipped your mind. Don't think I haven't seen the way you look at the girl. If I didn't know better, I'd say that you had some real feelings for the chit."

"It is no business of yours."

"Oh, I beg to disagree! If the announcement of our engagement isn't to be the cause of too much surprise, you should be seen spending at least a little bit of time in my company."

"And deprive you of time with your other admirers? Not if I can possibly help it," he responded.

Anger turned Abigail's face scarlet. James gripped her hand to his side as she moved to slap his face.

"Never again," he hissed.

"You have one week to effect a change of heart, James," Abigail sneered in response, "because after that I'll see to it there's more than your business at stake."

Despite Abigail's looming threat to him and Selina's family, he felt he could almost relax and enjoy himself right now. Reverend Kirk had just wrapped up his tale of Black Heart Pete, and Edith, Catherine, and Abigail were putting on an impromptu acapella recital.

James sat next to his mother and gave her a kiss on the cheek. She looked at him in surprise.

"James?"

"Thank you," he said. "The lunch was a grand surprise. I don't know when I last enjoyed being home so much."

The older woman beamed.

"You're my son and Lord Penventen. All I have ever wanted is the best for you," she said, taking hold of his hand. "Now if you would do one thing for me to make my summer complete, announce your engagement to Abigail…"

"Now don't go spoiling things," he admonished.

"But nothing would make me happier than if at the masquerade ball next week you would just make an announcement," she wheedled.

He frowned, his good mood beginning to evaporate.

"All right," he agreed. "I promise I'll give you something to talk about at the ball."

Missing the import of his words, James's mother looked triumphant.

* * *

It was midafternoon by the end of the luncheon. With efficiency to make a general proud, Lady Christina announced that the two waiting carts would take the party back to the house and return to collect the marquee and the furniture.

James and Jackson expressed an interest in joining Edgar and the Reverend in exploring some of the cliffs for the remainder of the afternoon.

Selina watched from the second cart as Christina and Abigail behaved as thick as thieves on the ride back to Penventen Hall. They were certainly excited by something, and she had the depressing feeling that she knew what it was about.

Abigail had won.

Whatever hold she had over James was too much to overcome no matter how much he might love another instead.

Selina's eyes flickered down Abigail's maroon walking dress to her belly for any tell-tale sign that she was with child, but there was none. She couldn't be that far along then—perhaps only a couple of months?

She glanced at Catherine. That woman noticed everything and wouldn't think twice about saying something about it, but her attention now appeared completely focused on Colonel Pickering, who was in conversation with Comte Alexandre. Meanwhile, Lieutenant Walsh had Edith seemingly glued to his side.

Well, if the idea of the summer in Cornwall was to establish matrimonial matches, it would appear Lady Christina's party was a complete success.

So, what should she do?

Selina fell back into her familiar habit of problem solving honed by running her father's home.

Let's examine the facts, she told herself.

She was in no worse place than she was a month or two months ago. She could ask Lady Margaret for a recommendation. No doubt the older woman would feel sorry for her, knowing how she felt about her grandson, and would help her find somewhere suitable.

She would have to tell James that she knew. A knife twisted in her gut. She would tell him that she attached no blame to him at all, and the time they had spent together, she would treasure always. She would tell him to be happy, for the sake of his child, who deserved the love of his parents, and he, above all people, should know what life is like in an unhappy home.

There. It was set. A course of action to take, a path to follow. She would make it work.

She *had* to make it work.

* * *

"We can't spend too long down here, there's a change of tide in an hour that will swamp the beach," Reverend Kirk called out over the wind now coming up in squalling gusts.

The four men stood on a tiny strip of shingle surrounded by black rocks and dominated by the tall cliff that they had scrambled down.

James waved to indicate that he had heard the Reverend.

He knew these cliffs. Growing up here, James spent hours exploring every inch of coastline from the river mouth to the craggy cliff of Gunver Head.

The *Pandora* was wrecked here, of that he was certain. But guesswork wasn't going to be enough.

Without evidence, all that remained was speculation that would bring them no closer to discovering the ship's fate.

While the two amateur geologists examined the rock and the strata of the cliffs, James and Jackson climbed up and over the boulders to begin a different kind of exploration. The two men climbed partway up the cliff, finding hand and toe holds to work their way around a jutting promontory.

Before long, they were out of sight of the rest of their party.

"What are we looking for?" Jackson asked, muscles straining to support his weight against the pull of the wind.

"Caves and hollows. These cliffs are…"

The last of James's answer was ripped away by the wind.

Jackson followed as his friend inched his way around. They perched on an outcrop and rested for a moment in the lee of the wind.

James pointed to a hollow in the cliffs about twenty feet away. "That looks promising."

They made their way across slowly. Sea spray dashed by the waves and wind against the rocks made them slick and unstable.

However, what had looked like a cave from a distance turned out only to be a jutting shelf of two feet deep at most. Rendered more visible by the angle of the afternoon sun casting a deep shadow beneath it, the lip was about five feet off the sand at its lowest point, rising to about seven feet as it angled upward over a length of perhaps three yards across the cliff face. At the upper end, it had provided mean purchase for a small shrub to take root in a crack in the rock above the high tide.

Jackson walked in its shadow to the far end of the shelf and stopped suddenly.

"That is interesting," he said. James joined him and looked at the two iron spikes driven across each other into the rock at shoulder height. They were rusty, but not so corroded to suggest that they had been there a great length of time.

James looked up, nudged Jackson, and pointed. A large iron eyebolt with a long shank was screwed into the rock some feet above where the far end of the ledge expired. It appeared to have the same level of exposure to the salt environment as the crossed spikes.

As James observed that the spikes and eyebolt lay in vertical alignment about a foot out from the end of the ledge, Jackson strode back to the low end. With a scramble, he hauled himself onto the ledge and sidled along it. Stretching and leaning out from the upper end, he could easily reach the eyebolt.

Then he spoke. "I've found something."

He reached into the shrub and withdrew a black rectangular object. "Catch!"

James did so. The object that fell into his hands was a book.

By the time Jackson made his way back along the ledge to jump down and rejoin his friend, James had already opened the heavy cover and turned several sodden pages, but the ink of the hand-written entries was too smeared and diffused to read. It appeared to have spent some time exposed to the weather, probably even submerged in seawater for a while.

He peered at it, flipping page after page in hope of a word he could make out. Finally he came across an inscription not in ink, but in pencil.

"It's the log of the *Pandora*."

CHAPTER SIXTEEN

Dinner was an informal affair. Colonel Pickering and Lieutenant Walsh had returned to Newquay Barracks; Edgar excused himself to catalogue his new collection of rocks; Comte Alexandre had letters to write; Lady Margaret, Lady Mary, and Edith retired early.

Just before eight, Selina remained in the drawing room as Abigail and Catherine played a hand of cards and Lady Christina worked with her embroidery loop.

James and Jackson entered the house and came into the drawing room. Both men were grass stained and their boots were covered in sand and silt.

Lady Christina, who would normally have been appalled by such a disheveled appearance and breach of etiquette, ignored her son's filthy clothes and simply informed him that there was plenty to eat—after he had washed.

"Your beloved is practicing for your marriage. He's already rolling around in the dirt," Catherine said to Abigail in a stage whisper loud enough for Selina to hear.

Abigail responded by kicking her viciously under the table.

Selina couldn't stand it. She excused herself, heartsick and miserable, and retreated to her room.

She slept fitfully as she waited for James to come to her as he had done every night since his arrival.

She finally fell asleep at one o'clock with the last grandfather clock chime for the night. Tears stained her cheeks.

* * *

The Reverend Ian Kirk was clearly "on duty" this Sunday morning.

He looked imposing in his black vestments as he delivered the Sunday sermon at St Petroc's, a large fifteenth-century stone church that sat on a rise overlooking Padstow.

With the exception of Alexandre, the guests at Penventen Hall were all in attendance. Selina found herself seated between Lady Margaret and Edith. She knew James sat somewhere behind her, but she couldn't bear looking for him in case she found him next to Abigail.

After the service, she lingered, pretending to admire the stained-glass window above the altar when in fact she was hoping to avoid James.

She knew her resolve would waiver if she looked at him and he couldn't be strong enough to do the right thing for his child; then she would have to be strong enough for the both of them and walk away.

She joined the end of the queue to leave the church and could hear James ahead of her asking Reverend Kirk for an appointment to meet him in private this afternoon.

The Reverend readily agreed, suggesting that James and his friend arrive in time to join him and his wife for afternoon tea.

Selina steeled her courage again as she shook the rector's hand and thanked him, not quite able to meet his eyes.

Outside, the congregation had started to disperse, with groups of family and friends clustered together on the path between the steps and the low stone wall that surrounded the church and grounds.

Catherine, Abigail, and Lady Christina had already started on the walk back to the house—a distance of a quarter mile was certainly no hardship on a day as sunny as this one.

Selina noticed there was no sign of James or Edgar or Jackson, who seemed much more James's friend than manservant. They must have gone on ahead too.

She picked her moment carefully.

From a corner of the church, she watched Edith and her grandmother pass the seat by the church gates to make their way up to the house, leaving Lady Margaret talking with a villager, whom Selina recognized as a local dressmaker.

She waited a few minutes more to be sure that no one else would disturb them before walking toward her with purpose and determination.

"I'm sorry to disturb you, Lady Margaret, but may I have a word?" There, Selina told herself, her voice hardly shook at all.

The villager smiled and took her leave of the two women.

"Be seated."

Selina sank to the seat beside her.

"I hope to ask…that is, I was…I…" Selina stammered.

"Spit it out!" Lady Margaret demanded with a small degree of irritation.

Selina drew a deep breath.

"Have I been satisfactory as a lady's companion?" she asked.

Lady Margaret saved the page of her prayer book with her marker ribbon and closed it with slow deliberation before looking at Selina with intense scrutiny.

"Why?"

"I have been considering my future after this summer, and I thought if you had found my services satisfactory, that I could impose upon you to…"

"No."

"I beg your pardon?"

"I said no," Lady Margaret snapped. "I will not write you a reference, I will not recommend you, and I will not put your name forward as lady's companion or governess or for any other type of service!"

She emphasized the rejection each time with an angry tap of her cane.

The heat of mortification rose through Selina's cheeks. She blinked rapidly to clear her eyes and disguised a small choke as a cough.

A whispered, "May I ask why?" was all she could muster.

"Because you're supposed to be marrying my grandson, that's why," Lady Margaret answered firmly.

"Excuse me?" Selina squeaked.

"Are you deaf? You are supposed to be marrying my grandson, so what is this nonsense about you going into employment?"

"I'm afraid you've been misinformed…"

"You still love the boy, don't you?"

"Yes, I do but…"

"There's no 'buts' about it, unless there is something I don't know about."

Lady Margaret looked at her directly.

"Lady Abigail—"

"That trollop!"

Selina jumped.

"What has that little slattern done?" Lady Margaret fumed.

Selina wondered whether the older woman should be using such language in front of a church, but with a lick of her lips, she plunged in with her explanation.

"I believe she might be expecting a child. James's child."

The older woman pounced on the uncertainty.

"Believe? How did you come by this information? Begin at the beginning and leave nothing out."

Selina left plenty out—James bringing her to the peak of desire, touching her intimately, her learning the hard-muscled warmth of his body—not the topics of conversation suitable for her lover's grandmother.

So she explained simply what James had told her of his complex relationship with Abigail, his intention to break off with her, learning that Abigail had refused to acknowledge the break, the scene she had witnessed on the beach, and his wish to meet with the Reverend Kirk privately this afternoon.

Lady Margaret paused and Selina waited. The older woman bent her head as though in deep contemplation before raising her head. Instead of sympathy or pity, there was anger in those sharp eyes.

"You disappoint me," she announced. "I thought you had more spirit in you than that."

Selina was stunned mute. She had hoped for help from this woman, not a tongue lashing.

"Instead you are a craven coward," Lady Margaret continued. "All it took was one advance on the battlefield by your opponent and you retreat under a white flag even before you know the strength of her position."

Selina found her voice and was livid.

"You make James sound like a piece of ground to war over. He's worth more than that."

"Indeed he is, so how dare you think of abandoning my grandson to that creature on the basis of speculation, suspicion, and assumption?"

Lady Margaret stood and dusted off her skirt.

"You've panicked under fire but I'll forgive you this once. However, this is the last time I will hear you planning to go into employment." She turned abruptly. "Good day."

Unable to move from the bench, Selina watched Lady Margaret walk up the street to the house. She shook with fury.

How dare the old woman speak to her like that? Then, as the seconds passed, Selina realized to her shame that Lady Margaret was right and her head fell.

She recalled the night James first came to her room…

"There's so much more about me that I wish I could tell you…things that you might hear that might cause you to doubt us…I want to earn the same

look in your eyes that you gave your brother the night we first met at the ball. I want your love and respect. You have my vow. I love you and we will be together."

How could she claim to love James and then run away at the very first difficulty? Were her feelings for him as mercurial as all that?

Selina lifted her gaze to follow Lady Margaret's progress up the street.

God bless her. The figurative slap across the face was exactly what she needed.

She hurried after her, then slowed to match her pace. Lady Margaret ignored her.

"Thank you," Selina said without further explanation.

The older woman harrumphed and carried on, but Selina could see the edge of her mouth crease into a smile.

* * *

The day dragged on as it seemed that James had disappeared altogether. Selina swallowed her disappointment at his absence and masked her features to hide it. She learned from Bridget, the upstairs maid, that he had ordered lunch be brought into his study, and that's where he and Jackson had locked themselves—literally—since returning from church.

She considered Jackson's urgently whispered words to her on the beach, and the more she thought about it, the more she became certain that Jackson knew the full story of James's past.

She decided that if James would not come to her this evening, she would go to him.

Keen to spend the hours productively, Selina spent the afternoon in the conservatory. With its series of large windows running the full length of the room to capture the afternoon sun, it was the ideal place to paint.

This time her canvas was a piece of fine ecru silk, held taut in a simple pine frame she'd asked one of the gardeners to make for her.

After having penciled in her design, Selina used a fine soft brush to paint the outline with a liquid wax before watering down her watercolor pastels far more than she would if she was painting on board or paper.

After about an hour, Selina heard someone enter the room. She chose to say nothing, hoping they wouldn't notice her in the corner.

"Another painting, Selina? Oh, what are you painting on? I can see right through it!"

It was Edith. Selina continued painting without looking up.

"It's silk and part of my costume for Saturday," she replied.

"Going as one of your own paintings, now that *is* imaginative…" That was Lady Catherine, who had entered the room with Edith. "…Although a gilt frame around your neck would make dancing difficult."

Selina looked up and offered a half smile.

"And you still won't tell me who you're going as," Edith pouted.

"I thought the whole purpose of a masquerade was to conceal your identity?" Selina replied.

"It is," assured Catherine. "It's just that little miss here has not the patience, nor the attention span, of a gnat."

Edith pulled an unladylike face before skipping around the room, singing, "Catherine is more tetchy than usual because she's in love with the colonel and is so sad that she won't see him again for three *whole* days."

Selina watched as Catherine's face darkened with thunderous rage.

"You little minx! I told you that in confidence!"

Catherine darted toward her. Edith squealed and ran from the room, dodging around Abigail sailing in through the door.

Selina decided to ignore her and continue painting her silk, but Abigail would not let her.

"Are you feeling well, Selina?" Abigail asked in an exaggeratedly conciliatory tone. "You were looking awfully pale this morning, and after the fainting spell yesterday, James and I are most concerned for you."

So that *hadn't* gone unnoticed, Selina thought with chagrin.

"*Your* concern for my welfare comes as an unexpected surprise," she responded. "James, on the other hand, makes his interest abundantly clear."

Abigail's eyes flashed with anger momentarily, then were cool and calculating again.

"I'd like to give you the opportunity to be the first to congratulate me," she began. "There's going to be an announcement at the masquerade ball. James and I will be announcing our engagement then. I did warn you."

"Does James know about your supposed engagement?" Selina enquired sweetly.

"Why do you think he's having tea with the vicar?"

"To repent?"

Catherine, listening some yards away while pretending to read, snorted, then feigned interest in the *West Country Farmer's Almanac*.

"James knows what his obligations are and as an honorable man he knows what he must do," Abigail pronounced.

"At least we can be agreed on something." Selina nodded. "James *is* an honorable man, but I fear where we differ is whether you and I have the same definition of honor. Now," she continued, shifting on her stool and picking up a paintbrush, "if you'll excuse me, I'd like to finish some more painting before the light goes."

From the corner of her eye, Selina watched Abigail consider her and then Catherine, who had withdrawn to a farther distance, determined to keep out of the discussion.

"By all means, dear," said Abigail as she seated herself on a wicker-back sofa. "It's nice to have a little talent, so important to keep the wolf from the door. You keep up the good work; you'll need to earn your living one day."

Catherine was unable to resist. "Abigail's little talents earn her an income too," she chimed in, "but there's a lot of competition on the streets around Covent Garden."

Abigail gave her friend a hateful stare, then Selina too, who was doing her best not to laugh.

CHAPTER SEVENTEEN

James sent his apologies and didn't join his guests for dinner. The study door remained not only closed but also locked, leaving his mother slightly anxious about how she was to entertain his guests, despite the fact that everyone assured her they could very ably amuse themselves.

Thinking ahead, Selina arranged for a supper tray to be taken to the study at ten o'clock and, at the appointed hour, was there by the door when Alice, one of the kitchen maids, promptly arrived.

If Alice thought it odd that one of Sir James's guests offered to take the tray from her, she didn't mention it, nor comment on Selina's asking her to knock on the door. To the query from inside of *"Who is it?"* she replied, "It's Alice from the kitchen, sir. Miss Selina thought you might like some supper."

At the sound of the internal latch being opened, Selina quietly dismissed the maid. Alice smiled and curtsied then headed back to the kitchen.

Jackson opened the door and showed momentary surprise, then put a finger to his lips in warning to be quiet. Selina stepped through the doorway and breathed in the distinct masculine scent of a room that had been shut up for too many hours.

James didn't look up. He was transcribing notes from the curled and stained pages of a large book onto crisp new sheets.

"Just put the tray on the side table, Alice," James instructed, absorbed in his work.

Selina did so and was about to correct him about the name when Jackson shook his head violently, instead clearing his throat in an exaggerated fashion.

James raised his head with a frown, then, as his eyes focused on Selina, the puckered brow cleared and his expression was replaced with a smile; a tired-from-work one, but a smile at seeing her nonetheless.

"You both have not left this room for hours. I thought you might be hungry," she explained softly.

Jackson had already removed the tray's linen cover and hastily devoured two quarters of one of the cut sandwiches, but instead of pouring tea, he had crossed to a glass cabinet and removed two tumblers and a decanter of whiskey. He was now in the act of pouring a healthy measure. In both actions, he behaved as though he owned the room.

Clearly, Selina decided, Jackson was someone whom James considered not a servant but an equal.

One glass Jackson placed beside his friend, then loaded a plate of sandwiches for his own consumption before helping himself to a cigar from the oak box on the desk.

He stood briefly with glass in one hand and plate in the other, then announced around the unlit cigar between his lips, "I'm heading out for some fresh air." He slipped through the French door to the private courtyard outside.

Selina turned her attention back to James, who rose from his desk and stepped over to her. He enfolded her in his arms.

"You're a sight for sore eyes," he whispered in her ear. "I've missed you."

"You saw me only this morning," she teased.

"Too long," he replied, running kisses along her ear. Selina shivered and clung to him, savoring the feel of his body against hers, but only for a moment.

"Stop. You must eat."

"I am."

"I didn't mean me!" Selina giggled. "Come, have some sandwiches and get some tea before it gets cold."

James began with the whiskey, slugging it back. Then he ate greedily, finishing the platter and two cups of tea poured by Selina.

"Everyone is wondering what's so fascinating in here that has kept you locked away for almost a full day," said Selina. "It's been just as well that Abigail has kept me in sight for most of that time, otherwise she would have beaten down the door hours ago. I'm fairly sure that she doesn't believe you're having an assignation with Jackson."

That earned her a grin, but no other explanation.

"You can't tell me, can you?"

James shook his head regretfully. "There are people who know part of it and shouldn't. As a result they have complicated this affair even more."

"Abigail, you mean?"

James's answer was a huff and a frustrated nod.

Selina stepped forward, back into his arms. "I trust you, James," she said. "That is explanation enough for me."

James groaned and turned the embrace into a bear hug before pulling his head back to look at her.

"You don't know what it means to hear you say that." He smiled before adding a soft kiss to her lips.

"But it has something to do with that ship's log," she persisted, nodded toward the desk.

"You can tell?"

"You did know that I'm a sailor's daughter, didn't you?" she said playfully. "Of course I know a ship's log when I see one."

"Can you read one?"

"Of course!"

Selina found herself the subject of James's intense regard. She could see behind his rich brown eyes that he was warring with himself. Quickly, as though he'd come to a decision about something, he steered her to his desk.

"This is the log of the *Pandora*. Jackson and I found it yesterday afternoon when we went out with Edgar and Reverend Kirk."

The *Pandora*… Selina recalled that James and William spoke briefly of the ill-fated ship and its captain on the first night they met. Her eyes scanned the columns—hours, knots, fathoms, courses, winds, and remarks—all there, all painstakingly transcribed from the water-damaged and faded originals that had been entered in the hand of Captain Francis Armsden or his first mate.

Selina turned to the final page. Pencil lines marked out columns that were only half-filled. The last entry read "9."

"It was the beginning of a tremendous storm. You can see there was a change in the barometer reading over the preceding three entries," Selina explained. "All the same, the *Pandora* appears to have been making very good time…"

She paused. "There's something not right here…"

Selina worked her way back up the rows until she reached the entry that noted when the ship had left Bristol.

"Do you have a map of Cornwall and a drafting compass?" she asked James hurriedly.

Without asking why, he pulled out a map and spread it on the desk beside the *Pandora*'s logs and his transcription.

Selina adjusted the caliper and traced the route of the *Pandora* down the map, following the journey as told through the log.

"In the last entry, Captain Armsden wrote that he'd passed the headland beacon at Trevose," she began, "but that's wrong. The *Pandora* couldn't have been there. At the speed she was traveling, they would not have been that far south by nine p.m."

Selina had James's full attention.

"An experienced captain would not have made a mistake like that," she asserted.

"Even on a violently stormy night like the *Pandora* was going through?" asked Jackson, who had begun to listen in. He leaned against the doorframe, half in and half out of the room, his half-finished cigar trailing smoke outside.

Selina turned. "Perhaps, but it should have been picked up by one of the other officers. It likely would have been the next day."

"But there was no 'next day' for the *Pandora* or her crew," said Jackson. "She ran aground that night."

"Or was deliberately run aground."

All eyes turned to James.

"Let's assume the log is correct and the captain or his first officer made the entry accurately," he said. "The light they see is not at Trevose but further north. The captain adjusts course…"

"…and runs aground on the rocks here," finished Selina, pointing to the spot at which the ship and its crew met their doom.

"The only way that could be is if someone had foreknowledge of the *Pandora*'s planned course and deliberately lit a beacon to deceive," said James grimly.

Selina frowned deeply. "For such a thing to happen would require the conspiracy of a dozen or more men," she murmured. "Surely the insurers already know about this."

"Or, in the absence of the *Pandora*'s log, they must at least suspect," suggested James. "The more important issue is whether the full cargo can be accounted for."

"If smugglers deliberately ran the ship aground, just about everything of value will have been taken or destroyed in the attempt, no doubt?" asked Selina. "It should be a simple matter of checking what has been recovered against that which is still missing."

"We don't believe that everything on the ship was on the cargo manifest," said Jackson, closing the French doors behind him.

He paused and looked at James. His expression queried *how much do you want to tell her?*

James gave his friend a slight nod before turning to Selina. Her face still betrayed her surprise at the idea that the *Pandora* had been carrying unregistered cargo. James placed his hands on her shoulders.

"You've just got a taste of what I've been up against since I returned to England," he told her urgently. "There's more I want to tell you but I can't right now—for your sake and that of your brother."

"William?" Selina sat upright in her chair. "What does he have to do with this?"

"I needed someone I could trust. Someone who could ask the right questions of the right people and not arouse suspicion."

Selina was appalled. "So the business venture with my brother is some kind of ruse?"

"No. Our partnership is real—real enough to pass the forensic examination of Earl Canalissy," responded James bitterly.

Viscount Canalissy's father? "I don't understand," said Selina. "Why should this be any business of the Earl's?"

"I have as many questions as you do, Selina—perhaps more—and no real answers for them, but I'm hoping to find them before the masquerade ball."

* * *

The Wednesday before Saturday's ball saw the majority of the Penventen Hall party travel ten miles south of Padstow to Newquay for a stroll along the wide sandy shoreline, lunch, and a matinee concert. Only Edgar and the Comte Alexandre had declined the invitation.

The ladies traveled by carriage, with the exception of Abigail. She rode behind the carriage on a bay gelding selected from the Penventen stable. Seated on an elaborately decorated black leather and silver saddle, she wore an impeccably tailored riding habit in garnet red that showed off her figure to its best advantage.

Selina had to admit that Abigail looked impressive on horseback. However, Abigail did not appear to be enjoying herself as they progressed along the road on the hour-and-a-half-long journey.

James and Jackson were also on horseback but they rode some yards ahead of the carriage, James having led them away from Abigail almost immediately on setting out. Her opinion of the rebuff was evident in the set expression on her face.

Eventually, the group passed the curve of the headland to Newquay Harbor, a natural protection from bad weather around which a small fishing village had thrived for centuries.

The "new quay" after which the town was named had been built in the fifteenth century. It had transformed what had been a village into a decent-sized port town from which copper and tin were shipped from the famous Cornish mines.

Through glimpses from the carriage windows, Selina looked out for her brother's ship, but the confusion of masts and rigging of other boats and ships sheltering there obscured the familiar lines of the *Diamond*.

Selina was separated from most of the party within moments of arriving. James had disappeared, while the ladies, having freshened up, took a stroll along the promenade. Jackson kept Selina company as they walked to the harbor master's office to confirm the arrival of the collier.

As they waited for the clerk, Selina watched the sailors and fishermen hard at work.

One boat was dry docked and a dozen men wearing leather gauntlets and wielding hammers and broad-bladed chisels scraped the hull free of barnacles. Another group sat cross legged on the deck of a larger boat using long, straight needles to effect a repair on a sail, while nimble young men scampered up rigging to varnish masts.

A figure caught her eye as it made its way down one of the jetties and back onto the harbor side. She tracked the man's movements for a moment as she tried to place him. It was Fidget, the man she had sketched at Padstow.

As he passed the entrance of the harbor master's office, Selina noticed the man's hands were behind his back and he still rolled the familiar dice between his fingers, but the movement was less frenetic than when she saw him last. Maintaining her assumption that he had been anxiously awaiting someone, Selina took it that the man's party had arrived safely.

"The *Diamond* docked yesterday afternoon," Jackson told her. "Your brother is waiting at the King Charles hotel."

They walked to the nearby hotel to learn that William had left word he would return in a couple of hours time, so they ordered refreshments and sat at a round white-washed table by a window that offered a magnificent view of the sun-dappled ocean.

Selina saw no point in beating around the bush. "You and James are equals," she observed, "indeed more than that, you're friends. Why do you play the role of valet?"

There was a long pause.

"It was my idea," he confessed. "You'd be surprised how much you can find out if people think you're merely the hired help."

He then told of how he and James met, of life in America and some of the misadventures they'd had in the four years they had known one another.

Listening to the stories over tea and cake, Selina suspected some of the tales had been embellished to entertain her—or sanitized so as not to shock her.

Nevertheless she was touched by the depth of the friendship.

"James is very fortunate to have a true friend in you."

"It goes both ways," Jackson responded. "And it extends to you too, Selina. I meant what I said at the beach," he added earnestly. "If there is ever a time you need help or need a friend, I'll be there for you as I am for James."

Not trusting herself to speak, she merely whispered "Thank you," and reached across the table to squeeze his arm.

In the next moment, a familiar voice called out, "Dearest Selina! My summer is now immeasurably better for seeing you."

Selina stiffened at the sound of Viscount Canalissy's greeting.

Selina and Jackson stood, offering the respect due the title if not the man.

Geoffrey wasn't alone. Abigail had her arm through his as though lifelong friends had been recently reunited.

"Jackson, I'm glad I've found you," said Abigail. "I have work for you; come with me, there's a good man."

Selina bit her lip, struggling not to smile at the look of distaste that washed briefly across Jackson's features. His eyes held hers for the moment as if torn over the right course of action.

Selina's nodded almost imperceptibly to him and he sighed and turned to Abigail. "How might I be of service, milady?"

She beckoned him to follow her, leaving Selina alone with the viscount. He took her hand and planted a full kiss on her wrist. He then urged her to take her seat at the table before he himself sat opposite.

"It's an honor to see you again, my Lord," said Selina formally in response.

It was plain her cool greeting displeased him, and inwardly Selina shuddered as an expression of malice briefly crossed his face.

"I see your act of charitable forgiveness extends only so far," he stated.

"I mean no disrespect," answered Selina.

The viscount was livid.

"And yet you've shown nothing but disrespect for months— disrespect for me, disrespect for your hostess, disrespect for Lady Abigail, who informs me that you've been shamelessly throwing yourself at Penventen for the past week," he hissed angrily.

Selina's own temper flared, but mindful of being in a room now beginning to fill with lunchtime diners, she swallowed her ire.

"If you'll excuse me."

She began to rise to her feet, only to find her arm clamped to the table by Canalissy's much stronger grip. Fortunately his overt temper had abated somewhat, leaving only the mildest expression on his features.

"You'll not walk away from me again, Selina."

"Are you planning to hold me against my will?"

The viscount paused, reconsidering his approach. His hand released her arm and his eyes softened indulgently.

"I do this because you fill my thoughts. I can hardly contain myself around you because you drive me to such wild passions…"

Selina involuntarily licked her dry lips. Canalissy's expression turned hungry.

"I can't return your feelings, my Lord, I'm sorry," she responded softly.

"You can't…" he echoed softly in disbelief, then added in a rush of words, "That's because you've been bewitched by Penventen, and I don't blame you. You're such a lovely, trusting, innocent girl, you have no idea of what that man is really like or what he's capable of."

"I believe I know him well enough."

"Oh, you have no idea, you poor darling." His voice gained strength. "James Mitchell is a traitor to the Crown and is responsible for the deaths of twenty sailors, including Captain Armsden of the *Pandora*…"

Selina stared at him in shock.

"I don't believe you."

"…now he's trying to involve your brother…"

"You're lying."

Geoffrey reacted as though he'd been slapped.

"I have proof."

"What kind of proof?"

"Documents, transcripts, notes…some of which appear to implicate your brother in the loss of the *Pandora* after the fact," Geoffrey responded. "There's enough evidence there to see both men hanged."

Selina felt sick to her stomach.

Canalissy's mouth split in a wide grin.

"Would you like to see the evidence?"

"Yes," she answered weakly.

"At Saturday's masquerade—I'll have them with me and you can see for yourself."

He stood and, taking hold of Selina's arm, forced her to stand as well, leaning in as though to kiss her on the cheek.

Instead he whispered, "Breathe a word of this to anyone and I'll go straight to a magistrate to have both Penventen and your brother arrested."

He straightened and drew his hand down Selina's arm until once again he gripped her hand. He raised it to his lips for another kiss.

"Until then, my dearest."

Chapter Eighteen

Selina debated whether to speak to James and William about the encounter with Viscount Canalissy. However, the look of delight on her beloved brother's face at seeing her made Selina decide to say nothing about the man's appearance and threat.

She determined to find out what "evidence" he had and then she would tell them, although she strongly suspected it was nothing James was not already aware of. She was now convinced it was the same threat that Abigail held over James.

Pleased to see her brother again, Selina pushed the unpleasantness out of her thoughts. Saturday would come soon enough.

It was a light supper that evening back at Penventen Hall. Colonel Pickering and Lieutenant Walsh had accepted an invitation to attend while Lady Abigail begged off, apparently tired from her lengthy ride. It had been suggested she squeeze in with the others in the carriage for the return journey, but her pride would not allow it.

After supper, the younger members of the party retired to the drawing room.

Some conversed, others read. Selina was delighted when James suggested they play chess. It placed them quietly together apart from the others.

After a few minutes, James, surveying the pieces on the board, murmured casually, "What did Canalissy want?"

"How did you know...oh..."

Jackson. Of course. How could she have expected him not to tell James?

"It was nothing," Selina said quietly. "He was being a nuisance, that's all."

"Are you sure?"

"Yes. Just making mischief."

She felt James's eyes on her and sensed his doubt, if not of her then of Canalissy's motives, as she moved one of her chess pieces.

"If you're sure, then," replied James, and he reached in and took the rook she had just moved with one of his knights.

Selina looked up at him with a scowl at the loss. James grinned back at her.

Some time later when the lieutenant took his leave to organize the evening patrol, Lady Edith decided on an early night for herself.

Inevitably, being the fashion of the salon, the conversation among those who remained turned to politics, the intent among the men especially to engage and savor in the cut and thrust of debate.

"Personally, I believe the likes of Wilberforce need to be held accountable to the nation for trying to ruin the lives of hardworking Englishmen," announced Edgar over his brandy.

"Without the African, our plantations would grow back to jungles and further costly tariffs would be needed to protect our sugar trade from the French. Not to mention that copper and guns manufactured in Birmingham are greatly sought after in Africa, where some of the most despotic and cruel slave drivers are the Africans themselves."

"The fact that some of the Africans themselves behave poorly toward their fellow men is hardly a ringing endorsement of slavery," observed the colonel coolly as he swirled the amber liquid in his own snifter.

"Well, perhaps," said Edgar. "I concede that slavery is not a perfect means of labor organization by any means, but it is certainly one of the most enduring. No great political or military power has ever emerged except through the economic benefits of slavery.

"It could easily be argued that slavery is the very best thing for the Negro. In the hands of a responsible slave owner, he's fed, clothed, housed and given productive work to do. If Wilberforce cares so much about their spiritual well-being, he should drop his damnable abolition bills and embrace slavery as an opportunity to promote Christianity."

"That's a ludicrous argument," scoffed the colonel. "Enslavement of a people in the hope some benevolent master will teach them the fundamentals of religion?"

"Would that be so bad, Martin? Surely it would be better to have food and shelter in exchange for labor," Lady Catherine ventured beside him on the divan. "Surely that's not so different from having servants."

The colonel turned to her.

"The difference is free will, my dear. A servant here is free to take his labor anywhere he chooses. A slave cannot unless he buys his freedom," he reasoned. "And the law has already determined that an African who arrives on our shores is a free man—free to make his own decision and his own choices."

"And that's exactly the point that I'm trying to make to the colonel here, Lady Catherine," said Edgar. "Without the slave and master relationship, the lot of the Negro would be far poorer. It has been observed in plantations in Virginia where slaves have been freed, that they are lazy, indolent, and live like paupers."

Colonel Pickering frowned mildly. Edgar had earlier spoken enthusiastically in support of Thomas Paine and of France's Declaration of *The Rights Of Man And Of The Citizen*.

"How do you reconcile the French Declaration of Rights which says 'men are born and remain free and equal in rights' with not supporting those rights for all men?" he enquired.

Edgar shrugged. "You've lived in America, Colonel. The Declaration of Independence says all men are self-evidently created equal and yet the Americans show no signs of freeing their slaves. Compromise abounds even in the pursuit of the ideal, does it not?"

Comte Alexandre cleared his throat politely from across the room where he was seated at a small table, writing a letter. As he spoke he folded and slipped the letter into his coat pocket.

"Lady Catherine, may I be permitted to observe that the Africans are not like us at all? It is quite unlikely that we share any of the same blood with them."

"I thought we were all the descendants of Adam and Eve," Selina observed, looking up from her chess game with James, unable to resist entering the conversation.

Lady Catherine nodded. "I agree with Miss Selina, we're all children of God aren't we? Surely if some people have the right to be fully free human beings, then shouldn't we all?"

The Comte and Edgar laughed.

"Adam, Eve, and the Garden are at best allegories—stories for children," said Edgar. "The greatest scientific minds of our age are quite sure that Negroes and Europeans come from separate species altogether."

He was supported by the Comte. "As we eschew superstition in pursuit of enlightenment through reason and science, we will see man less reliant on stories from ancient tales," he pronounced.

"There is no question that the Negro is hardly a man like the European. To quote from one of France's greatest philosophers, Voltaire, 'the race of the Negroes is a species of men different from ours...we can say that if their intelligence is not from another species of our understanding, she is much lower...'"

The Comte paused briefly, searching for the words in English, and continued, "Ah, yes—

'They are not able of a great attention, they combine little—'"

The sound of a crystal tumbler smashing with force against the fire grate caused most everyone in the room to jump and brought the Comte to stunned silence.

Selina had forgotten that her brother was in the room.

He'd been uncharacteristically quiet during the conversation. Now he stood before the fireplace florid with anger.

Selina started to rise, intending to calm him, but felt James's hand cover hers to still her. She looked at him across the chess board, eyebrows raised. James answered with a shake of his head. Her facial expression asked a new question silently.

"Let him speak," he whispered to her.

All eyes in the room were on Captain Rosewall. He pinned both Edgar and Comte Alexandre with a hard stare, the kind he usually reserved for subordinates who were about to receive a tongue lashing.

When William started to speak it was through clenched teeth.

"Have you ever seen a slave ship, gentlemen?"

Edgar and Alexandre shook their heads in silence.

"I have. As you approach it, the first thing that assaults you is the stench of humanity. It stays with you, no matter how many times you wash. It sets up residence in your nostrils and not even the heaviest smell of ocean brine will clear it.

"Hundreds of men, women, and children are chained in a hold with less space than we afford penned cattle. Believe me, you never forget their cries and groans.

"I was seventeen, just an able seaman on my first position outside of my father's fleet. We made the voyage from Bristol down to Guinea in West Africa, and while we unloaded our cargo of guns and ammunition, slaves were waiting at the docks.

"The men had their necks trapped between planks six feet in length to keep them separated. They were also chained around the wrists. Women, even those with child, and children were forced to follow behind by the chains attached to their necks.

"You could smell the fear on them. On some you could also still smell their burned flesh from being newly branded.

"I was on the middle watch for the first few weeks of the voyage. It's a quiet time and if the weather is fair, there's nothing finer than watching the passage of stars across the night sky. On one of those nights I met Jacob.

"In the darkness I heard a voice singing a lullaby Maman used to sing, one she sang to Selina often."

William half sang, half spoke:

La poulette grise

Qui pond dans l'eglise

Elle va pondre un petit coco

Pour son petit

Qui va faire dodiche

Dodiche dodo.

"I put my ear to the grate above the hold because I thought I was imagining things, but no, the same voice kept singing, 'The little grey chicken who lays eggs in the church.'

"I asked '*Qui est-ce qui chante?*'—Who is it who sings? And the voice laughed. '*Qui est en Anglais qui parle Francais?*'—who is the Englishman who speaks French?

"Jacob spoke and read fluent French and spoke at least two African languages. He could also speak some English and read it a little. He was more educated than most of our crew.

"He was an orphan raised by French missionaries in Cote d'Ivoire and he was joining them on a mission trip to the highlands when he was captured by a slave gang. Over two weeks we spoke every night through the grate on deck.

"He told me of his home and the stories of the men chained beside him. He wanted to know what England was like. I told him of my home with my mother, sister, and father.

"Most of the other crew treated the Africans like cattle and I mightn't have thought much about them either if not for Jacob."

William procured a replacement glass from a tray and poured himself another whiskey. He sat heavily in a chair and took a mouthful of the alcohol, hesitating before he continued.

"Because of the heat and the first leg of the voyage out of Guinea, conditions onboard ship were nearly putrid to begin with. And you know that if the weather is against you, the Atlantic crossing may be two and a half months of hell.

"Well, after just three weeks at sea, the forces of hell were unleashed. We hit a run of violent storms that followed us for two weeks, and we lost three crewmen overboard. It was a mess.

"But if things were bad for the crew, they were worse for those belowdecks.

"Vomit, blood, feces…the smell below got so bad the crew slept on deck for the fresh air rather than spend too long in their quarters below.

"It was another week before I could speak to Jacob again. He told me that there were dead bodies below that had been there since the storms began, and now more people were becoming sick. I told the captain but he was indifferent. He was more concerned about repairing the damage to the ship in order to make up lost time to Jamaica. He wouldn't listen until some of the crew started falling ill."

"Dysentery?" queried the colonel.

"Yes," answered William. "We were ordered to pull the slaves up in chained groups. In each line of seventy between seven and ten were dead or dying. The dying we lay on the deck to either recover or die. The dead we simply threw overboard.

"I didn't know where Jacob was. In fact I had no idea what he looked like—I'd never seen him in the light of day—so I started whistling the lullaby, hoping he was one of the living. His chain was one of the last to be pulled out. He was weak but he looked at me as I whistled, and he smiled. The men on either side of him were dead, by the looks of the corpses, for at least three days.

"I unchained Jacob myself and carried him to where the sick lay dying. He was shorter than me but still weighed far too little for a man. Cramps seized his body. I could do nothing. I laid him down on the deck and, as I did so, he whispered to me, 'See you in Heaven, my brother.' Then another seizure took him and he died."

William shifted restlessly in his chair for a moment, then threw back his glass of whiskey in a single gulp. He suddenly realized Lady Catherine was weeping silently, tears flowing down her cheeks.

"I'm sorry," he said, "but some things need be told."

"You are forgiven, Captain Rosewall," she replied in a breaking voice. "I believe you are right."

Pickering slipped his arm around her. "Yes," said the colonel, "go on if you wish, Captain. It does bear telling."

William looked about the room, then stood and placed his empty glass on the mantelpiece. Looking down into the fire, he directed his comments to no one in particular.

"I don't pretend that I've studied the works of Voltaire or discussed Enlightenment philosophy in fashionable salons or know that much about theology," he said.

"But I do hope there's a heaven for Jacob's sake, because if anyone deserves a place there he does, and I do so want there to be a hell for those who profit from this day after day.

"We talk about the high-minded ideals of egalitarian common humanity or because they are our brothers in the eyes of God, and yet the world persists in continuing this cursed trade because it makes money."

With that William muttered an "excuse me" and left the room.

Lady Catherine allowed her silent tears to become an audible sob as Colonel Pickering held her.

Edgar kept his eyes to the carpet while Comte Alexandre poured himself a large measure of brandy.

Selina turned wide blue eyes to James, tears just starting to drip over lashes.

"I had no idea," she whispered. "He's never spoken of this before." Then more strongly, "I'm going to go after him."

"Don't Selina," advised James, stroking her hand when it lay on the little table. "Give him some time. He's raised ghosts from his past tonight. He needs time to lay them to rest."

* * *

Some time toward midnight, James walked into the conservatory. By lamplight it looked deserted, but he caught a movement in the shadows.

James elevated the chimney of a hurricane lamp and drew on a cigar until the end caught light and glowed. He inhaled strongly and expelled the smoke in a long, controlled breath. After a moment, he changed his mind and spoke.

"I have another one of these if you're interested."

There was silence for a long moment.

"Yes, I think I will."

William emerged from the shadows to accept the cigar. He lit it on the lantern as James had done.

"How is Selina?"

"She's concerned about you," replied James.

"I'll make sure I see her before returning to Newquay in the morning. Does she know what's going on?"

"Some…certainly not all of it."

William sighed. "She deserves to know the truth. I like you Penventen, but just…just do the right thing, will you?"

"I promise. Upon my life," James vowed. "This nightmare should be over after the ball, and I will tell her everything, even if she should hate me, she will have nothing but my honesty."

Selina had not meant to eavesdrop; she was simply walking by the conservatory to fetch a shawl when she heard her name. There she had stopped and lingered in the shadows outside, listening to the two men who meant the most to her in the world.

Now Selina briskly continued her original errand, but apprehension settled in her chest.

After the ball might be too late if—false or not—Viscount Canalissy did have evidence against James that also implicated William. She was under no illusion that Canalissy would not want to exact a price for his silence, and she wondered whether she had it in her to enter such a bargain.

CHAPTER NINETEEN

24 July 1790

Free from the stench and fetid air of London in the summer, the green open spaces and bracing sea air of Cornwall attracted the well-to-do every year. Aristocrats and successful merchant families rubbed shoulders without class distinction.

One of the grandest families of England's southwest peninsula was that of Thomas Pitt.

Successful trade with India—including the discovery of the 410 carat Pitt Diamond—had made him very rich indeed, and much of the family wealth was invested in the family seat of Boconnoc House at Lostwithel, a magnificent estate first noted in William the Conqueror's Domesday Book.

Each summer the Pitt family staged a grand occasion at Boconnoc, and their decision to hold a masquerade this year had created one of the most anticipated events on the calendar.

As the guests from Penventen Hall arrived on the Friday afternoon, staff swarmed the lawns, hard at work erecting four large white marquees and setting up trestle tables, as well as staging for the orchestra. By Saturday evening, the gardens would be transformed into a wonderland of lantern-festooned trees, with still more lamps clustered together to offer pools of light at strategic points. At nightfall, lines of torches would be lit to illuminate a path from the ballroom to the marquees.

Like many of the other guests, those from Penventen Hall would spend the entire weekend.

Selina found herself sharing a room with Edith, and, although they had been together only for an hour, Selina was exhausted. The girl was like a flea in a bottle, and most of her jumping about was related to Lieutenant Roger.

"Do you think he's here yet? I wonder where he's staying?" Edith pondered uselessly. "Don't you think he'll be magnificent in his dress uniform? Do you think he'll recognize me in my costume?"

After the first twenty minutes, Selina realized an occasional *uh-hmm* was the only answer Edith actually required, and after an hour, a summons by Lady Margaret was a welcome distraction.

Selina lightly tapped on her door. "You called for me?"

The older woman turned from her writing desk and waved her hand, beckoning Selina in.

"Good, I'm glad you're here," she replied crisply. "I want to talk to you about your costume for the masquerade."

Selina was surprised. She'd been keeping her Greek costume a surprise for days. Only Bridget had seen it because she'd helped with the sewing.

"Don't look at me like that young lady. I know what's been going on. I want to see what you're going to wear."

She nodded toward the anteroom.

"You can get changed in there."

Selina was stunned.

"Don't dawdle, girl! I'm not getting any younger!"

* * *

James closed the door to his room as soon as Jackson came in with a parcel from London that awaited his arrival at Boconnoc House. That was a surprise. He had expected a note, a letter perhaps, but not a parcel.

He cut the string with a knife and ripped open the brown paper wrapping, uncovering dark green fabric. A small note folded in half sat on top:

I heard you couldn't make your mind up, so I've taken the liberty of deciding for you. Wear this to the masquerade and watch out for the sheriff and his men.

-Percy

"What the hell? Is this some kind of joke?" spat James.

Jackson picked up each piece of fabric in turn. It was a short waistcoat in twill and, in felt, a close-fitting hat with a forward-pointing brim with a large brown quill.

"I think Percy intends you to go to this shindig as Robin Hood."

* * *

Selina looked at herself in the full-length mirror. What on earth had she been thinking? She was half-naked.

The crisp white cotton tunic featured a low scoop neck held at the shoulders with two gold-colored buttons about an inch in diameter that looked like coins. Gold cord threaded through a pocket beneath her breasts to emerge behind, where it wrapped around her back, before crisscrossing at the front to emphasize her slim waist. The cord, weighted with gold-colored glass beads, adorned the ends and fell from her side.

Her feet were shod in simple sandals to which she had added thin gold cord to act as thongs that crisscrossed from ankle to knee.

However, her skirt was obscenely short; it only just covered her knees.

At the time, Selina had figured a moon goddess like Diana the Huntress would not hunt in ankle-skimming skirts, but probably wouldn't do it in garters and sheer silk stockings either. However, she now realized that to go bare-legged would also be far too scandalous.

Entering a major gathering with bare arms was daring enough.

As she looked at herself now, she wondered in horror what Lady Margaret would say.

She closed her eyes. Well, it was too late now. She had several inches of fabric that might make the costume more acceptable, but they were lying in a sewing box in her room back at Penventen Hall.

Selina gave a long, loving look at her cape, an evening seascape of deep blues, greens, and purples highlighted with a rising golden full moon on silk. It had taken her the better part of the week to paint it. If she was to have only one reminder of James's love for her, then let it be this and let the whole world see.

She fastened her cape to the buttons at the shoulders and let it fall to her hips.

"I'm waiting!" Lady Margaret called from the other room.

Selina sucked in a deep breath and opened the door.

The older woman's eyes widened in surprise. She crooked her finger three times, beckoning the young woman. Selina walked forward three paces and stopped.

Lady Margaret rotated her index finger once, slowly. Selina moved to comply, afraid of the expression she might see when she finished the turn.

Grinning from ear to ear was not in the catalogue of expressions Selina expected.

"Well done, my girl!" she enthused. "If I were fifty years younger, I'd be jealous.

"I'm glad you've put that nonsense of going into service behind you. If that idiot grandson of mine can still wed Abigail after seeing you tonight, then we'll know that horrendous monster has already sliced off his manhood. As for you, you'll have your pick of suitors throwing themselves at your feet, dowry or not."

Selina choked.

"There, there, sit down and take a glass of water," Lady Margaret directed. "No, better still, a glass of brandy. I'll join you."

Selina sank onto one of the delicate bedroom chairs, not trusting herself to speak. Lady Margaret unlocked the traveling tantalus on her dressing table and meted out two small glasses of brandy. She passed one to Selina and sipped delicately at her own, surveying the costume once more.

"It's incomplete," Lady Margaret announced. She turned her back on Selina and opened her jewelry box. Selina allowed herself a sip of brandy, which burned her throat.

"You need these." Lady Margaret placed in Selina's hands earrings of cascading moonstones set in silver. "They're a gift from me to you. You may keep them."

Selina was nearly speechless. "They're beautiful," she breathed, "thank you."

The afternoon sunlight falling through the window caused the stones to glow and seemed to throw moonbeams across each stone in turn.

"The second piece is only a loan," said Lady Margaret softly, and she revealed a crescent moon hair ornament about three inches in height made from a single piece of mother of pearl.

"I wore it when I was about your age and I had intended to pass it down to my daughter, but now I intend to pass it on to my grandson's wife."

She gently twisted Selina's loose hair and firmly brought the pin down to hold the ornament in place. Mahogany curls framed her face.

"There," she said, examining her work with satisfaction.

Her expression softened as she saw small tracks of tears make their way down Selina's face.

"Sh, sh! There's no place for tears," she soothed, patting Selina affectionately on the shoulder. "You love my grandson, do you not?"

"I do."

"Then have faith that this disorder will sort itself out. Don't give up on him, and don't give up on yourself."

* * *

The reception hall was a zoo—literally. A pride of guests were dressed as lions and tigers, at least two wore large headdresses that turned them into giraffes, another four wore smaller versions and appeared as horses and zebras.

Selina descended the staircase as the Goddess Diana and immediately found herself the subject of whispers by some women and admiring glances by many more men.

In elaborate costumes that covered their faces or in masks, everyone was unrecognizable. Selina would have been hard pressed to have known Edith if she had not helped her into her fetching shepherdess costume. At least the tall shepherd's crook made her easy to spot in a crowd.

As she made her way through the ballroom to the marquees outside, Selina brushed shoulders with kings and queens, pirates and Vikings, fairies and hobgoblins.

A glass of champagne was pressed into her hand as she emerged through the French doors to the lawn.

Edith had disappeared from view, leaving Selina to be carried along by the crowd to the marquees.

The orchestra had already started playing lively country tunes—no minuets would be danced tonight. Despite the wealth, renown, and nobility of the guests, the ball would be informal, perhaps even bordering on bacchanal.

Selina's arm was grasped by a complete stranger, and she found herself amidst the dozens of dancers. It was five dances with three unknown men before she begged off and backed away from the throng.

She skirted the edges of the marquee, hoping to identify a familiar face, when she bumped into a masked Robin Hood.

"Excuse me," they said reflexively, then the light of recognition dawned on them both.

Although dressed nowhere near as elaborately as some of the other guests, James looked magnificent in his tan breeches with a lightweight epee hung at his waist. A white long-sleeved peasant shirt was tied loosely at the neck, and his costume finished off with a Lincoln green waistcoat and feathered cap.

His eyes beneath the mask glittered darkly as they raked down Selina's form. He looked dangerous, and Selina's heart beat faster.

The look of desire thrilled her, and something mischievous rose in her. She turned in a circle, the silk of her cape fluttering and giving movement to the sea it depicted.

"Do you like it?" she asked innocently.

James had recognized the seascape and the full moon instantly, and desire coursed through him.

He snagged an arm around her waist and pulled her to his chest and held her there. "I'm not letting you out of my sight dressed like that," he told her.

"James! Someone will see us," she protested.

"Do you care?"

"What about your mother and Abigail?"

"Damn the both of them," he bit out harshly, causing a couple of people to look in their direction. He glared back and pulled Selina from the shelter of the marquee toward the gardens and into the night. James said nothing until they were far enough away from the crowds.

A pool of light cast by a collection of two-inch-high oil lamps highlighted a garden seat hidden from view of the party by a stand of flowering red azalea shrubs, but they did not sit.

Once safely hidden from sight, James tore off his mask and gave her a crushing kiss. Selina clung to him tightly.

His lips blazed a trail across her face to her ears and her neck before claiming her mouth again.

Selina responded with equal passion. Her nipples hardened under the light fabric and she pressed herself against him restlessly. He stilled her movement with his hands on her buttocks, pressing her core against his growing erection.

"Have I told you that you are beautiful tonight?" he asked, breath still ragged from their kiss.

"Not in so many words, but I had an impression you were pleased." She smiled.

"Hmmm, more than pleased," he agreed, placing small butterfly kisses on her neck, which kept her giggling.

"Your cape, that's the moon we watched together, the one you're named after," he observed, and then fingered the mother-of-pearl moon nestled in her hair.

"I recognize this too. My grandmother wore it for her wedding portrait. It was a gift from my grandfather."

"She loaned it to me," added Selina. "She says it's to be a gift to your wife."

James closed his eyes. His grandmother's message to him was as unsubtle as it could possibly be. But how could he expect Selina to become his wife when the threat of a charge of treason hung over his head? Especially when the same threat attached to her brother?

He wanted to give her everything he had and more—the sun, the moon, his very life—but until Pitt's intrigue was through, his life wasn't his own to give her.

He had mingled with the ball-goers for a couple of hours, feeling like a fool in this damn costume and fearing that Sir Percy had played some kind of perverse trick. It wouldn't be below him.

James had been promised answers and until he had them, he ought to stay at arm's length from Selina.

But as he held the woman he loved in his arms, he appreciated the absurdity of it all. And he started to laugh manically between desperate kisses and caresses he bestowed on her hair, cheeks, ears, and lips.

He meant what he told Selina. Damn the whole lot of them. Abigail no longer owned him, and from tonight, no longer did the Parliament of England.

For better or for worse Selina would be his wife. "Till death did they part"—that was the part he was desperate to forestall.

Although confused by James's mercurial expression, Selina allowed herself to be carried along by her passion, thrilled to feel his hands and lips over her, yet she sensed that his lovemaking was desperate, as though this moment would be the last they'd have.

"We're getting married…next weekend," he groaned.

Selina stilled, sick to her stomach. Whatever power or threat Abigail held over James had been too much to overcome. But she had to hear it fully from his lips so that there would be no more misunderstandings or assumptions.

"Who?"

James stopped his assault on her neck and blinked at her.

"Who?" she repeated, and urgently grabbed his hands. "Who is getting married next weekend?"

He looked at her askance. The longer he failed to respond, the worse she feared the answer was going to be.

To Selina's alarm, James dropped to one knee.

"I'm hoping that we are, my love. Well, obviously not next weekend, but as soon as the banns have been read."

Selina's mouth fell open and tears filled her eyes. She was speechless.

"That's not the response I was hoping for," he responded uncertainly.

Finally Selina found her voice. "Are you sure? I mean, can we?" she whispered.

"Should I take that as a yes?"

Selina nodded vigorously, tugging at James's hands, and he stood, enveloping her in a relieved embrace.

"Good, we'll announce our engagement tonight."

"But what about Abigail and your investigation into the *Pandora*? I know of the threat to you and my brother."

James groaned. "How?"

Selina was about to tell him about Viscount Canalissy, when James shook his head.

"Never mind, I can guess who."

Her resolve to face Canalissy alone now wavered. She realized she should tell James everything, but how would he react?

Unfortunately, she had a pretty good idea. James would ignore the threat to his own safety and confront Canalissy over the threat to her and her brother.

No, she decided. Better that she try to reason with the man on her own.

"We'd better get back before we're missed," she suggested.

Hand-in-hand they started back to the pavilion, when four men emerged from the shadows.

"Ho, Robin Hood," said the one in the centre, wearing a lavishly ornate medieval costume comprising red breeches and matching coat with puffed sleeves slashed with green satin. The man's features were covered with an elaborate mask.

James went instantly on alert. Despite their costumes, these men weren't revelers; they were all business.

He let go of Selina's hand to reach for the hilt of his sword. She noticed it was only a fencing epee designed for sport.

"We thought we might find you hereabouts with the delectable Maid Marian," the man continued.

Selina felt James relax. He obviously recognized the speaker. She, however, was less inclined to give him the benefit of the doubt.

"Who are you?" Selina demanded.

"Now then, no need for concern, my dear. The Sheriff of Nottingham at your service," the man said with a flourish, then to James, "She is a fine one isn't she, James, no wonder you prefer her. I like them spirited."

"If I recall the legends, meetings between Robin of Loxley and the Sheriff of Nottingham never went well," James replied.

"Alas this is true, which is why I have to inform you of my intention to take you into custody."

CHAPTER TWENTY

To Selina's astonishment, James laughed. All the men laughed, apparently all in on some kind of joke. "Before my fiancée runs you through herself, you'd better introduce yourselves," he advised after catching Selina's perplexity.

The sheriff stepped forward, bowed, and took Selina's hand.

"Fiancée! Congratulations to you, Miss Rosewall, and to you, James," he exclaimed. "If I might introduce myself, I'm Sir Percy Blakeney, personal secretary to our Prime Minister and host tonight, Mr. Pitt."

Selina looked at Blakeney askance for a moment, then burst into laughter and curtsied to him.

Blakeney smiled broadly in response before a theatrical frown swept across his features. "Unfortunately we do have to monopolize a little of Lord Penventen's time, but I do hope to return him to you soon in not too worse a state than that in which you found him," he explained.

The group walked to the marquee, where Selina spied Jackson dressed as an American Native in buckskin breeches, a shirt, and two long false braids that fell down his back and were held in place by an elaborately and colorfully beaded headband. A feathered tomahawk was tucked in a belt around his waist.

He was conversing with Lady Margaret and Lady Mary among a group of older women, all seated on chairs that had been brought from the house. The ladies were elaborately dressed but not costumed. Jackson was costumed but not masked.

On seeing the group approaching, Jackson excused himself and crossed to them. He broke out in a grin.

"Hau!" he grunted with hand raised.

"Priceless!" quipped the Sheriff.

James turned to Selina.

"I won't be too long," he said, and kissed her, ending his caress with a gentle touch to her cheek.

Jackson's grin broadened further.

James and the four men took their leave and made their way to the house. Jackson walked Selina toward the circle of ladies.

"Can I assume congratulations are in order?" Jackson asked.

"For what?" said Selina, pretending not to understand the question. Her beaming smile belied the ruse.

"Come on, don't tease," he said. "Until I go home to Pennsylvania, my love life's experienced vicariously, so please tell me that James proposed and you've accepted?"

"Yes."

Jackson let out his attempt at a native battle whoop, enfolded her in a bear hug, and swept her in a circle, her feet flying off the ground.

Lady Mary, observing the actions of Lord Penventen's decidedly unusual valet, turned to Lady Margaret.

"Do you know what on Earth is going on?"

Lady Margaret smiled.

"I think my grandson has made the wisest decision he's ever made."

* * *

In public, Sir Percy Blakeney was assumed to be a vapid fop or a carefree bon vivant, depending on whether one liked him or not. Either assumption suited his purposes.

Tonight, he led a group of men through Boconnoc House and his expression was not foolish; it was deadly serious. The three men of the escort were accustomed to Sir Percy's ability to switch personae, and they trusted his judgment implicitly. In a corner of the house far away from the festivities, they entered a large library. At the far end of the room was a desk behind which sat King John.

He remained still and silent until the last man had entered the room and the door was shut and locked, then raised his mask and surveyed the group before him.

"I have to give you your due, Percy," said Pitt, casting his eye at Robin Hood, the Sheriff of Nottingham, Will Scarlett, Little John, and Friar Tuck. "You do have a sense of the theatrical."

"It does make it easier to find people in a crowd," Sir Percy shrugged.

"Well, next time make me Richard the Lionheart, if you don't mind. Now James, let's address this issue of Lady Abigail Houghall's blackmail.

"The envelopes on my desk contain letters of commission giving you and William Rosewall diplomatic status as agents of the King. Anything you have done or will do in connection with this mission has the full sanction of the Parliament of England, so put your mind at ease on that account."

"That's welcome news indeed. Thank you, William," James responded.

"Well, we can't have the groom face the gallows before the wedding, can we?" Pitt suggested wryly.

James raised an eyebrow and glanced at Sir Percy. "News travels fast. I only proposed to Selina tonight."

Percy examined his manicure and hid a small smile.

"On receipt of your letter, we've had men investigate Lady Abigail and learned she is heavily in debt and has been for the past two years," continued Pitt.

"While the findings are still preliminary, we are aware her financial position became more perilous six months ago when the Prince of Wales's common-law wife found out about young George taking Abigail as his mistress."

"And we know what a fierce temper Maria Fitzherbert has," added Percy.

Everyone in the room nodded.

"Indeed," said Pitt. "Lady Abigail's standing in court has been diminished since Mrs. Fitzherbert insisted the Prince break off with her. She's been forced to find another patron."

James wrinkled his nose in distaste. "Well it hasn't been me," he said sullenly.

"Yes, we know that dear chap, and that is what's caused us a deal of confusion," Pitt continued. "Your return to England happened to be a fortunate bit of timing for her.

"Your squiring her around this season as the handsome reunited Lord is just the tale ready-made for the society pages. Our focus was so much on Radicals in our midst that we didn't see the threat already under our noses. Lady Abigail has been a most accomplished spy."

"For whom?" asked James, coldly.

"We can't say for certain but there may be a clue in who is paying her bills—Randall Dobell, the Earl of Canalissy."

James looked thoughtful. "That makes perfect sense," he said. "There is a family connection there, cousins or some such. The Earl has made enquiries into my business arrangement with William Rosewall, but I thought that might have been on behest of his son Geoffrey, who developed an interest in Selina."

"There's something we need to tell you about Randall," said Pitt. "He's not the man you think he is, but don't underestimate the son. He is just as cunning and ambitious as his father, but he has a short temper and that makes him far more dangerous."

* * *

Selina accepted a handful of dances in between listening to Jackson being quizzed by the ladies and entertaining them with tales from the wilds of America that even to Selina's ears sounded completely fictitious. The men with whom she danced were, it seemed, entertained by her costume. Strange, thought Selina, that such a relatively short time ago she was concerned about too low a cut.

She declined her dance partners' further invitations.

Through the course of the evening, she identified Edith taking a walk in the moonlight with her lieutenant.

Then she spotted Catherine, wearing an exquisite ruby-and-emerald-colored sari made even more remarkable with its elaborate embroidery in gold. The young woman was almost unrecognizable; not due to her mask, but because of the way she wore her hair loose to her waist and decorated with a filigree gold band along the centre part.

Much to Selina's surprise—and the reason she was able to know her as Lady Catherine—was that she was accompanied by the uncostumed but uniformed Colonel Pickering and, further, seemed content to sit out the dancing and spend the evening in apparently pleasant conversation with him.

The reel ended and Selina curtsied and thanked her partner. Walking away from the dancers, she felt her bare arm snagged by a firm grip.

"I seem to recall asking for a dance two months ago," said Viscount Canalissy, close to her ear. "I'm planning to claim what's mine."

He was dressed head to toe in black, its starkness relieved only by silver buckles on his belt and shoes and by silver button cufflinks. His black satin domino mask was edged in silver thread too.

With no more preamble, the viscount dragged Selina back to the dance floor just as the opening strains of a waltz were played by the orchestra.

As they turned and moved in the crowd, Selina kept peering over his shoulder to see if Jackson had noticed where she was. It was impossible for her to see. Canalissy, on the other hand, kept his eyes focused on her face with a close stare that was unnerving.

By the end of the dance, Geoffrey had steered her to a far corner of the pavilion. She took two paces back to put some physical distance between them.

"Consider my debt to you paid, sir," said Selina. He responded with a mocking look.

She felt his eyes roam over her, and she reminded herself that she was not here by choice. Selina decided to remind him of that too.

"You claim to have evidence of wrongdoing by James and my brother. Where is it?" she demanded.

"My dearest Selina, you don't expect that I would have it on me, do you?" he asked, raising his arms in emphasis. "You are welcome to search me if you like," he added with a leer.

Selina could not prevent herself from expressing her distaste for him. "You're disgusting."

She turned to leave.

Canalissy gripped her arm, blanching it beneath his grasp.

"Forthright, aren't we? Not an attractive quality in a woman. Neither is impatience."

"Blackmail is hardly amongst the list of virtues either," she spat back, shaking her arm free, "so before we start comparing sins, show me what you believe you have against James and William."

"Blackmail? Who said anything about blackmail? Have I made threats? Have I coerced you into doing anything against your wishes?"

No, thought Selina, he was too devious for that. Anything Geoffrey had done so far that she might call amiss could easily be explained away to a third party.

"Right now, for instance," he continued, "I won't make you accompany me to the stables. You will do so of your own volition. You will join me because you're anxious to see the evidence I have that implicates Penventen and your brother in seditious acts against the Crown.

"As a loyal subject to our King, it is my duty to present this evidence to the appropriate authorities at the earliest opportunity—which might be as soon as tonight.

"You may even wish to strike a bargain with respect to it. But don't call it blackmail, my dear, because I have asked you to do nothing."

Selina realized that she was being out-maneuvered and warred with herself. *This was a mistake, don't listen to him, walk away now!* one part screamed, while another told her that if there was the least bit of truth in Canalissy's claims, she owed it to both the men she loved to find out what it was.

"If it's your duty to present this evidence to the King, why tell me any of this at all?" asked Selina.

"Have you forgotten my offer of friendship? My vows of devotion? I'm doing this for you."

Selina viewed him askance. "Doing what for me?"

"I'm not without influence," he offered. "I can certainly provide evidence that would offer mitigation for your brother."

"And for James?"

Canalissy let out a small laugh. "Alas, I cannot save him, from himself least of all. However, Lady Abigail might have more sway with those in power. Why do you think she's so devoted to him despite the fact that he has strayed with you? His only protection is to marry her."

"James has proposed marriage to me," Selina said firmly, noting with satisfaction the surprise, or perhaps anger, that momentarily flared in his eyes. Then he sniffed contemptuously.

"My poor, sweet, innocent darling, don't you know a man will promise anything to get a woman into his bed? Haven't you ever wondered about the secrets he keeps from you? And why, for all his supposed antipathy for her, he still keeps Abigail at close quarters?"

"I trust him. There must be a good explanation," she answered.

"I can tell you what that is and what Penventen will be forced to do if he wishes to stay alive," Canalissy replied. He began to move away from her. "I'll be in the stable, checking on my horses. It's your choice to join me there or not."

* * *

Pitt pressed a glass of whiskey into James's hand, watching the young man's ashen face with concern.

"I only learned of the rumor on news of your father's death," he explained. "I'm sorry to have to rake through family scandal but it may go to Lord Randall's motivation and that of his son, come to think of it."

"Do we know this as a certainty?" interjected Sir Percy.

Pitt shook his head. "I doubt Lady Christina would cooperate. There's no advantage to her if the scandal becomes public knowledge."

James looked up, the shock of the revelation ringing in his mind. He swallowed a stiff measure of the drink, using its impact to waken himself and sharpen his thinking on the matter just revealed to him.

Earl Canalissy might be his father.

"Randall has an heir, so why pay attention to me?" James asked, the question somewhat rhetorical.

One of the other men, the one dressed as Friar Tuck, offered a response. "He could be planning to acknowledge you in Geoffrey's place as his true firstborn. It's no secret that Randall has been increasingly disdainful of his son. There's an elegant logic about it, you have to admit."

James nodded. It was logical indeed. And memories from his childhood came flooding back and made more sense through the prism of this revelation.

Ah Selina, James thought to himself, he had warned her there were secrets about him, but he had no idea there were secrets being kept *from* as well!

He thought about his grandmother and wondered if she knew of her daughter's secret. Was that her reason for the animosity toward his mother? He groaned inwardly as he realized Abigail might be aware of this too.

It was hardly fashionable to wed a bastard son, but if he was rich and in line for an Earldom…

James drained the rest of the whiskey. One thing at a time, he decided.

"Let's put my questionable lineage to one side for now," he said, "and concentrate instead on another questionable character. His name caught my eye on the list of suspects you gave me, Prime Minister.

"I had only heard of him by chance a little earlier, and I don't believe in coincidence. He was Francis Armsden, captain of the *Pandora*."

Pitt looked grave as James revealed the outcome of William's investigation and his and Jackson's own enquiries.

It appeared that Captain Armsden had, some weeks before his death, made enquiries about purchasing a holding in Virginia. According to his widow, that fateful trip was to have been Armsden's last before an early retirement. She had expressed regret not only at that coincidence but also that her husband had spoken of a bequest of a thousand pounds that was to support their migration and transformation to the landed class of the New World, but of which there was now no record.

It was generally agreed unlikely that as experienced a captain as Armsden had allowed his ship to get so far off course by accident. So too was the idea that the crew struggling to shore had fallen foul of opportunistic killers and thieves who had simply observed a foundering vessel. It was nearly certain they had created the craven opportunity themselves and lured the *Pandora* off-course and onto the rocks.

Yet deliberate wrecking was not a simple affair. It involved many participants. Nor was it to be entered into lightly, since involvement might easily lead to a short affair with the gibbet. So ships that were lured to their doom were only infrequently selected at random. Rather they would be targeted for the best pickings from the risky business.

"The *Pandora*'s manifest was nothing special, just pots and pans, fabric, and the like. Not worth twenty men risking their necks for," said James. "It suggested someone was aware of an illicit cargo that was compact enough to bring aboard without arousing suspicion, perhaps among Armsden's personal effects. Could it have been the mysterious bequest?"

"Armsden was in London the week before he sailed. He collected a small trunk from a dealer in Bond Street," said Will Scarlett, providing a scale of the trunk with his hands—about twelve inches wide and twenty-four inches long.

"We've had that business under watch for several weeks. We think it's a Foxite drop-off point, but we've not be able to prove it. But a trunk that size would hold a thousand pounds worth of gold very handily."

"So, Armsden was in the Foxites' pay and in possession of a thousand pounds worth of gold as some sort of final payoff. Is that what you're saying?" asked Pitt, his brow now even more deeply furrowed.

James and Scarlett looked at each other for mutual assent.

"It appears so," said James.

Pitt sighed. "Forgive me, gentlemen, but is this connected to anything or is it simply cut-throats stealing from traitors? And would such booty have been enough to tempt a group of men to embark on such an elaborate and vicious undertaking?"

"I've pondered the same questions," said James. "It does seem a lot of danger for little gain. If it wasn't the gold, what other motive might there have been?"

"How about seeing off Armsden?" offered Scarlett. "If he was getting out of the game, maybe they thought it safer if he was silenced. And they could take back their gold at the same time."

"By wrecking the *Pandora* and killing his entire crew along with him? Simpler to slip a knife between his ribs dockside and make off with the chest," said Sir Percy. "We're missing something."

For a moment, the room of costumed men looked blankly at each other, then James spoke.

"What if seeing off Armsden and recovering the gold were part of it, a convenience so to speak, but there was something more?"

"Three birds with one stone? A pretty shot," said Pitt. "Do you have anything in mind?"

"I don't know. It's nothing solid. But ever since I saw Armsden's name on that list, I've been convinced there was more to the destruction of his ship than met the eye."

"And?"

"Something like this doesn't come together by chance," James began.

Garnering their full attention, he understood momentarily why Percy enjoyed playing to an audience.

"You get closer to the bull's-eye the more arrows you shoot. Now how do you get better at wrecking ships while making it look like an accident?"

"Gad..." muttered Percy. All eyes turned to him as revelation dawned on his face.

"You're saying the wreck of the *Pandora* was a practice run?"

Percy warmed to the thought. "Of course! A practice run.

"The *Zeus* is to set sail from Bristol with a shipment of gold for Louis from His Majesty on the fifth of the new month. It's an amount that will be, shall we say, somewhat more substantial than would fit in a small trunk from Bond Street.

"It's not inconceivable that the perpetrators who preyed upon the *Pandora* would use the methodology that proved so successful for them on the *Zeus*."

Pitt straightened. "Then it's settled, we'll need men from Tintagel to St Ives."

"That's a coastline of almost sixty miles!" Friar Tuck exclaimed.

"We will be stretched," Pitt admitted, reaching across the desk for a map. "But there are barracks at St Ives and Newquay with men we can call on."

* * *

Selina cursed herself for her foolishness with every step she took. The stable loomed before her. Distant sounds of merrymaking and music told of how far she was away from the party.

In his dark costume, Geoffrey had all but disappeared into the inky blackness.

Yellow light from smoky lamps dotted the entrance of the stable. Selina entered and paused, allowing time to get accustomed to the gloom. The whicker of a horse in one of the dozen stalls drew her attention, but otherwise the stable remained quiet except for the occasional sound of hooves shuffling in the hay.

To her left, both halves of a split door were open. She sensed a slight movement within the stall and moved toward it. It appeared to be empty.

She stepped inside and took several paces until she could perceive the back wall.

Geoffrey's voice emerged soft and low from the semidarkness behind her.

"I knew you would join me."

Selina jumped and spun on her heel. Her leg bumped into a large open sack filled with grain.

Geoffrey remained hidden in the shadows.

"You see, I know you better than you know yourself."

"You promised to show me evidence."

"I have lots of things to show you. What would you like to see first?"

His tone of voice, rich with double meaning, put Selina on guard. If she knew where he was, she could plan her next move to get out of the mess she had created for herself.

"Show yourself instead of hiding in the shadows like a mouse," she said with more bravery than she felt.

Geoffrey obliged, stepping forward from the shadow of a brick pier. He blocked her direct path out of the stall and took another step forward. Even behind his mask she could detect his malevolent intent.

"A roll in the hay is an appropriate-enough initiation for someone of your standing. You might learn to enjoy a little rough and tumble."

Selina scanned about for a weapon to defend herself. She found none. Then the roughness of the hessian sack at her leg provided a reminder, and she scooped a handful of corn, oats, and barley.

As Geoffrey lunged, Selina threw the grain, momentarily blinding him. She ducked beneath his sweeping arms and darted past, feeling the glancing touch of his fingertips as he wheeled and reached to grab her, but she was a fraction too quick.

As she ran past the threshold of the stall, Selina grabbed and swung back the top half of the split door. An instant later, she heard a thud and a howl of pain as the heavy wood connected with Geoffrey's nose.

Selina heard him scramble to his feet. He would be on her in seconds.

She ran.

CHAPTER TWENTY-ONE

James took a deep breath of night air as he walked away from the house, down the sloping lawn to the masquerade marquee. On the one hand he was thankful that a significant weight was off his shoulders. On the other he was considering the burden of a new load.

No wonder his father became such a disillusioned and bitter man.

He undoubtedly knew. He must have, or suspected at least, when year after year no further children were added to the Mitchell name.

He wondered about Edward Mitchell's family; were there any still alive? If so, they could rightly challenge on the basis that he was not his father's son and rightful heir to Penventen, and although he was successful in his own right, James also relied on the funds and connections his family name gave him.

And what of Selina? He couldn't offer her a title or even the security of his name. He would need to talk to her before the evening was out. If she wished to break off their engagement he would not dissuade her.

He lit a cigar on one of the torches and looked up at the night sky.

Dear merciful God in Heaven, he pleaded silently, *help me.*

The voice that spoke beside him was not that of God.

"It's a lovely night to announce an engagement."

James turned sharply to find Abigail standing next to him.

She was dressed as Cleopatra and astonishingly beautiful. Her curly white-blonde hair was hidden under a straight black wig that fell to her shoulders. Her full-length gown was in white, decorated at the bust, hem, and sleeve by broad ribbons embroidered in gold, turquoise, black, and green Egyptian motifs.

Noting James's observation of her, she turned slowly for his perusal.

"Do you like it?" she asked.

James recalled Selina asking him the same thing about her costume. Astonishingly beautiful or not, he realized that, to his mind, a comparison between the two women would leave Abigail wanting.

In answer to her question, he shrugged and looked back to the marquee, hoping that from a distance he could see Selina.

The sharp dig of fingernails at his chin forced James's attention back to Abigail, who was furious at the snub. James found he could care less.

"We have a bargain," she hissed.

James nodded. "An engagement, announced tonight," he answered absently, taking a step away from her.

"There's something you ought to know," he intoned hollowly. "I'm already engaged."

Abigail's temper exploded. "You *dog*!"

"Don't you mean 'you *bastard* dog'?" he asked mildly with another step's distance between them.

He watched as the meaning of his words came home to her.

"You weren't supposed to know. Not until…"

"Not interested."

"What do you mean, 'not interested'? The chance to one day be an Earl means nothing to you?"

James gave a regretful shake of his head.

"I no longer have my own name, Abigail. What good does a title do me?"

Abigail's expression was utter bewilderment. James allowed himself a half smile. Of course she wouldn't understand.

"Oh, and don't think about spreading rumors about William Rosewall or myself," he added, thinking of the diplomatic commissions in his coat pocket. "You're not likely to get a sympathetic hearing—that is, unless you fancy transportation to New South Wales for blackmail."

James glanced up the hill past Abigail. Friar Tuck and Will Scarlett had emerged from the house and were walking down the lawn in their direction.

With a nod, he drew Abigail's attention to the men. She looked back at James with wide eyes.

"James?"

"I think these gentlemen want to have a word with you," he suggested.

"But..."

He regarded her with sudden compassion.

"I hope you find what you're looking for, Abigail."

* * *

Selina ran toward the light of the marquees, not knowing if Viscount Canalissy was in pursuit.

Her light, flat shoes provided no protection from the stones in the gravel, so moving across to the grass, while kinder to her feet, made every step a half-slip due to the late-evening dew.

Becoming breathless, she turned the corner of a small outbuilding, running behind it and trying stealthily to double back, hoping that if Geoffrey was in pursuit, he would head in the direction of the pavilions.

Sure enough, long booted steps crunched along the path but then slowed to a stop not far from where Selina had turned behind the building. At the far back corner, she forced her breathing to steady and concentrated on identifying the location of her pursuer.

"Selina?" Geoffrey sounded deceptively calm but somewhat nasal. "Why are you running away from me?"

He took a few steps on the gravel and paused again. Selina, now all the way around the building, peered around the corner. As Geoffrey was dressed all in black, it took her a moment to find his silhouette in the darkness. He stood on the grass off the gravel with his back to her.

Selina looked across the drive to a tall, spreading oak whose wide trunk would provide cover in the shadows, and had the added advantage of placing her just a few dozen yards from the door of what appeared to be a cookhouse off the side of the main building. Inside, she might find assistance. Indeed, as she watched, she saw a staff member inside move past the window.

She determined to risk a careful crossing of the gravel then over to the door, and she looked back along the path to gauge Geoffrey's distance.

He had disappeared!

Selina cursed beneath her breath. She hadn't seen or heard him move off.

"You've bloodied my nose, darling! I had no idea that you liked to play rough…"

Selina jumped and covered her mouth to stop an involuntary scream. Geoffrey was behind the outbuilding, having circled around after her. Now he was only a few feet away from turning the back corner and seeing her.

"You know, you really shouldn't run on wet grass."

Closer…

"It leaves tracks."

Closer…

"But I think you really want me to find you, don't you, my pet?"

Selina turned and ran across the drive as fast as she could, four or five paces crunching in the gravel, and threw herself in the shelter of the oak in the second before Geoffrey appeared as an absence of light around the back corner of the outbuilding.

From the shadows, Selina saw him run to the edge of the path. He looked left and right along its length, then across at the oak.

Selina took off again, this time running for the door while trying to keep the bulk of the tree between her and Geoffrey in the hope it would provide cover and valuable seconds before he spotted her. And it did render the protection she coveted, but the door was locked.

"Selina!"

She heard Geoffrey call her name, heard his rapid footsteps on the path, and she ran again, along the side of the main house toward the front of the building.

The sounds of the party grew as Selina cleared the eastern corner of the building at full tilt, turning, almost falling. She pitched again momentarily along the front of Boconnoc House, then pulled up so quickly she almost overbalanced.

A dark-haired woman dressed majestically in white stood motionless at the front door, looking down the lawn to where the masquerade continued in full swing. She turned and regarded Selina with surprise.

"Miss Rosewall," she offered, "you seem to be in somewhat of a hurry."

Selina, breathless and confused, stared at the woman, trying to place her.

"Is aught amiss?" the woman asked with a small degree of concern.

Selina was suddenly aware that Geoffrey had burst around the corner also and likewise had skidded to a halt just behind her.

The woman looked past Selina to her pursuer. "Cousin."

"My lady," said the breathless Geoffrey, panting.

Selina suddenly realized the woman now walking toward her was Abigail, costumed as Cleopatra in a dark wig. She was trapped between her enemies.

But when Abigail frowned, it was at Geoffrey.

"Your nose. It's bleeding."

"Um…yes."

Abigail scowled at him.

"Perhaps you should go and address your wounds, my lord."

Geoffrey drew breath to reply, then thought better. He turned and walked away in the direction he'd come.

Selina looked at Abigail; Abigail fixed Selina with a weary grimace.

"You'll find James somewhere down there," she said, nodding in the direction of the marquees, then turned and walked back toward the portico door.

She tossed her words acerbically over her shoulder, not looking back.

"Tell him to take better care of you in future."

Abigail disappeared into the house.

Selina blinked, unsure of what had just happened.

She walked down the lawn and reentered the party in search of James.

* * *

James was distracted and sullen, not the man who had just had his proposal of marriage accepted by the love of his life.

James and Jackson steered clear of the cadre of familiar faces with whom James would be expected to make polite chitchat. Instead, like a caged tiger, James stalked the grounds between the marquee and the hedgerows that had become popular trysting sites during the evening.

After ten minutes of aimless walking, James stopped as if he suddenly remembered something.

"Where's Selina?"

"I don't know, I lost sight of her well over an hour ago amongst the dancers," said Jackson. "She looked as though she was enjoying herself."

James threw a newly lit cigar to the ground and stomped on it ruthlessly.

"What the hell do you mean, you don't know?" he fumed. "You were supposed to be looking after her!"

James was off, breaking through crowds of people to follow any glimpses of a white costume and mahogany hair in the crush of people, animals, and otherworldly creatures, carousing and singing drunken ribald ditties.

On the edge of the dance floor several minutes later, James's head spun from his anger, the loud music and voices, too much alcohol, smoky air and sweaty bodies, and the dizzying twirl of dancers.

Mercifully, Jackson appeared and rescued him from his fugue state by shoving him out the other side of the marquee into the fresh air.

James back threw his head and filled his lungs in an attempt to stop the pounding in his head. It helped somewhat.

He looked at Jackson, who offered no reproach, but wariness was evident in his expression.

"I'm better," James offered with a half smile of an apology. "Thank you."

His friend nodded his acceptance but his expression didn't lighten. James had never spoken to him the way he just had ever before.

"I asked Lady Edith. She saw Selina with Geoffrey. Selina didn't look happy about it. I've had a discreet word with Pickering and Walsh; they're keeping their eyes open."

Jackson spoke softly, as if trying to gentle a skittish horse, which James had to admit he was doing a very good impression of.

"Let's head back around the other side. She might have returned to the house for some reason."

James took another deep breath and nodded, but it was Selina who spotted them first from her elevated vantage near the house. She ran and threw her arms around James, holding him tight.

"Geoffrey says he has something against you and William," she said breathlessly. "He is threatening to implicate you both in the loss of the *Pandora* and have you arrested."

Jackson groaned as James stood back from Selina, ramrod straight.

"And how do you know this?"

"He told me. At Newquay. And tonight he said he would show me evidence at the stables…"

Unalloyed fury flashed across James's face.

"I don't believe it! I ask you not to trust that man or trust anything he does and here you go swanning off into the night with him!" he roared. "How could you be so naïve? What the hell did you think you were doing?"

"James! Calm down, man!"

Jackson's rebuke brought him back to himself. He looked at his friend, who regarded him as one might a madman. Well, perhaps he was.

James turned back to Selina. Her face was pale and her eyes were wide with shock. James swept her hands up with his and rained kissed on her knuckles as he murmured profuse apologies.

Jackson shepherded the couple to a quieter part of the garden and withdrew to a discreet few yards away. Standing rigidly with his back to them, arms folded, he looked every bit his party character.

"First things first, Selina. Did Geoffrey harm you in any way?" James asked.

"No. No, he didn't," Selina assured him. "He said he was planning to have you arrested tonight."

Jackson was unable to resist a snort of derision. Selina looked over at him. "I didn't know what to believe," she said to his back, then looked up at James.

"The evidence was only a ruse to get me alone. I'm very sorry James, you were right; I should never have trusted him."

James's expression was grim.

"I'll call him out tonight."

"I'll stand as your second," said Jackson, returning to the conversation.

Selina was aghast at the thought of a duel.

"No, please don't. What if he does have something against you? What about William?"

"You can rest assured on that count; any 'evidence' is fake," James promised. "Tonight Pitt has given me warrants that name Jackson, myself, and William as diplomatic agents of the Crown. We have full immunity."

Twin expressions of relief came over Selina and Jackson. James couldn't help but smile, feeling the same way himself.

"But Canalissy can't be allowed to harass you any more, sweetheart," he explained.

"I don't believe he will…I fear I may have broken his nose," said Selina, wincing at the sound she recalled when she slammed back the door into Geoffrey's face. She briefly explained the circumstances, taking special care to downplay the fear she felt at the time.

James was astounded; Jackson whooped with laughter.

"Oh man, I'm going to see if I can find him. This is too good not to see for myself," chortled the American. He bade them farewell temporarily and strode up toward the house in search of his amusement.

As Jackson disappeared from view, James's mood ebbed.

"I also discovered something else tonight that should cause us to reconsider our engagement," he started.

Pained, Selina shook her head desperately. "No…not now!"

Taking her by the hand, he sat on the stone coping of a raised garden bed and urged her to sit next to him.

"There's the strong possibility that I may not be Lord of Penventen; in fact, I may not even be a Mitchell at all," he said.

"I don't understand. How?"

"I learned tonight that my mother entered marriage carrying another man's child."

"Oh James! I'm so sorry. I understand why you are shocked." She squeezed his hands. "Do you know who?"

"Earl Canalissy, Geoffrey's father."

Selina's expression was pure astonishment.

"I can't marry you. I have no name to call my own and no title to offer you," he continued bleakly.

"Should any of my father's, rather, Edward Mitchell's family learn of this, then by rights I lose the title, Penventen Hall, everything…It's not what I want for you and not what you deserve."

Selina took James's hand and kissed it.

"Do you love me?" she asked.

"With everything I am, I love you. But…"

Selina interrupted him with a finger to his lips, then leaned in and softly pressed hers to his. She looked at him gently.

"I don't want to marry title or lands," she whispered. "I want to marry you. You're a good, kind, honorable man, James. I love you."

She kissed his cheek.

"…for better or for worse…"

Selina moved another kiss closer to his mouth.

"…'til death do us part."

Selina's mouth coaxed his open and they kissed long and deeply before James broke off.

He regarded her carefully.

"It won't be an easy life if we have to leave England permanently. America is barely civilized."

"It doesn't matter as long as we're together."

James stood, bringing her to stand up with him.

"Then, tell me again, Selina. Will you marry me?"

"Absolutely yes." She smiled.

He swooped down to claim her lips, devouring them thoroughly. Selina matched his intensity, bringing her arms up under his to press herself against him more completely, restlessly yearning for more of him, more of the heady, sensuous feeling he released in her.

"Three weeks from tomorrow, Selina," he whispered between kisses. "Then nothing will keep us apart."

CHAPTER TWENTY-TWO

2 August 1790

The week following the masquerade flew by, a parallel to the arrival of the late-summer winds that roared up the coast, stealing hats and parasols on fashionable seafronts and making the way of ships in and out of Bristol even more hazardous.

James saw Selina less in this week than in the three weeks prior.

Selina was out of the house from early morning until well after dinner some evenings, her life a whirl of dress fittings, social calls, and introductions facilitated by Lady Margaret, who was taking her motherly role very seriously indeed.

James counted down the days to his wedding. When they did dine together, he saw the longing looks Selina gave him over the dinner table and, propriety be damned, all he wanted to do was sweep her into his arms and make love to her until dawn.

Perhaps that was his grandmother's intent—to keep her so occupied that she was out of temptation's reach. He began to regret his decision to place Selina in a bedroom more fitting her new position as his fiancée, since the room was next to his grandmother's and she, when it was convenient to be so, turned out to be a very light sleeper.

This was madness! He was even beginning to resent Jackson, who appointed himself Selina's protective shadow. James grumbled to his friend that he, Jackson, had seen more of his wife-to-be than the groom had.

It had now been mutually agreed by all three that little would be served telling William about Selina's confrontation with Canalissy.

Jackson had been unable to locate the viscount that evening, and the following day the Canalissy party had made an early departure from Boconnoc Hall.

Selina was confident that would be the end of the matter. Jackson and James were less certain, and that was when Jackson volunteered to be at her service if James himself couldn't be present.

Abigail had surprised Penventen guests by announcing her intent to stay with friends in the fashionable Cornish city of Truro, her departure to be so immediate that Lady Catherine was charged with the responsibility of forwarding on Abigail's possessions to an address to be supplied by Sir Percy.

The morning after the ball, James had asked Sir Percy what plans he had for Abigail and was kindly but firmly told it was no longer his business.

So it was a surprise when, as other guests attended the informal buffet breakfast—the civilized way to cater to the gentleman or lady who suffered to a lesser or greater extent from the excesses of the night before—Abigail asked to walk with him in the gardens…

Her pale skin and dark-circled eyes didn't look out of place among some of the other hung-over guests, although James knew the cause was different.

"You will forgive me for not returning with you. It seems I am to assist Sir Percy in some matter and I'd rather not talk to his men at Penventen. Anyway, I'm not sure I feel up to attending your wedding. I think a clean break would be best."

James accepted her decision without comment as the steady crunch of gravel under their feet marked their progress along the path.

"I did love you, you know," she offered after a long minute of silence.

A bitter retort hovered at his lips, but he swallowed it. He shrugged and tried to find the better angel of his nature he had once been assured existed somewhere.

Another minute passed before he felt he might have found it.

"I meant what I said last night," he said quietly. "I truly hope you find what you're looking for. I never could understand why you had to cheat and connive to get ahead. You're a beautiful woman with all of the advantages of wealth and status. You're accomplished, intelligent, and witty. Men fall over themselves to be beside you."

"Not you," she replied.

"I did once," he responded. "I ought to thank you for helping me see clearly all those years ago. Our marriage would have been as miserable as the one I grew up witnessing.

"I know I probably haven't treated you fairly over the past year but you are someone I once cared for. I hope you find the right man to love, the one who understands you and treats you well."

Abigail smiled mockingly.

"I thought I had found him."

"It could never be"—James shook his head—"and you know it too, especially from the first night I met Selina."

"I think I did know even then. I hated her on sight, you know."

James nodded. He had known, right from the start.

"But now I don't hate her at all. I haven't the energy. I hope she will love you in the way you deserve to be loved and in a way that I simply don't know how. Perhaps you'll both give everyone hope that marriage is still an honorable institution," she conceded with an attenuated degree of flippancy that made James consider her words were less cynical than they sounded.

James stopped and turned, looking back at the house.

"I'm glad we've cleared the air," he said. "But let's not make any false promises of future friendship. If nothing else, you're not a hypocrite. And I don't bear you any ill will or malice, but I want to be perfectly clear…I don't want to see you again."

With that, James walked back to the house and did not glance back.

Now, at the start of August, James found himself alone at Penventen Hall with other unpleasant arrangements to make.

He called for a servant to send for his mother.

* * *

The stop at the teahouse overlooking Padstow harbor was welcome following the seemingly endless engagements with bakers, cooks and confectioners—both in the village and in Newquay—regarding the wedding breakfast and the obligatory village celebration.

A letter had waited for Selina at the post office, a fulsome communication from Sarah, delighted by her sister-in-law's news. She and William would be back in Padstow within the week, along with the children. The boys had been delighted to learn they would be pages at the wedding, and were looking forward to welcoming Uncle James into the family.

Reading the letter, Selina realized how dearly she missed Sarah and the children.

The bride-to-be was relieved to sip tea and take the weight off her feet, and she spared a glance at the new weight she wore on the third finger of her left hand, an engagement ring—a sizable ruby set in gold and surrounded by smaller rubies.

She sat alone. Even now, James's grandmother had appropriated Jackson for another errand involving the florist. Selina had no idea where Lady Margaret found the energy.

Jackson would be pleased, she giggled to herself. Selina decided to have a box of cigars sent directly to his quarters as an apology.

While watching the passing parade of fishermen, housewives, and vendors on the Strand, Selina's eye found Fidget, dressed as she had always seen him in dark blue trousers, a grey shirt, and a matching grey cloak, walking quickly along the street.

Things must be well with him, she decided; he was doing far less fidgeting with the dice in his hands.

Then he stopped and greeted a man. It seemed obvious they had an appointment.

At first Selina couldn't see clearly whom he was meeting with, but as a knot of sailors passed the window, the man turned in profile and Selina was surprised to recognize him.

It was Comte Alexandre, now in an animated conversation with Fidget.

Odd. How did they come to know one another?

At that moment, Edith bounced through the door of the teahouse like a beribboned rubber ball.

"Selina! You'll be the first to know," she announced breathlessly, talking even before the doorbell had finished clanging and she had arrived at the table. "Roger and I are to be married at Christmas!"

Other customers glanced over at them, smiling indulgently.

Selina rose to her feet and hugged the girl warmly.

"Edith, I'm thrilled for you both. That's wonderful news!"

They sat and a waitress brought another pot of tea and crockery.

"Roger is accompanying me to Cheshire after your wedding to meet Mama and Papa."

"Shouldn't Roger have settled matters with your father before he proposed?" Selina teased.

"Oh!" giggled Edith. "He did! But the sneaky man kept it from me. Roger had grandmother's approval, so that was enough for father."

Selina found herself only half listening as Edith chattered. Beyond the window, Fidget and Alexandre had concluded their conversation. The men parted, with Fidget handing a sealed envelope to the Frenchman.

* * *

Christina glided into the study in Penventen Hall with all the poise of the lady of the house, although she had not been seen for days. The announcement of her son's pending marriage to Selina and not to Abigail had resulted in the woman's locking herself in her bedroom, claiming she was too ill to give the bride-to-be her blessing.

Now, with her mother and imminent daughter-in-law out of the house, Lady Christina emerged like a butterfly from a chrysalis. She looked regal in her blue-and-cream striped morning dress, though her eyes were wary.

James had to give his mother credit; she looked as though butter wouldn't melt in her mouth. He could suddenly see her as the debutant. All she would have needed to do was bat her calf-brown eyes and no man would deny her a thing.

His grandmother was right, he realized; men were fools all too easily manipulated with the promise of sex and admiration.

James had grown up watching his mother flirt coquettishly with men. In his youth, he had found it amusing to observe her at parties, trading a few kind words for a rush to fetch her refreshments or a smile to garner a more favorable seat. There was no doubt she had used her same charms on his father—or should that be "fathers"?

James wondered what feminine wiles she'd try to use on him today.

"I have never been more embarrassed in all my days! Such a debacle at the masquerade…How could you let this happen, James?"

Attack instead of defense, he noted. Excellent, much better than crocodile tears and fainting spells.

"The Rosewall girl has you utterly bewitched," she continued. "Running around like a half-naked savage in that revealing outfit! She was the subject of talk all evening, and now you announce to the world that you're marrying the chit?"

"Be careful how you speak of my fiancée, mother," he warned.

She huffed dismissively.

"You're supposed to be marrying a woman of quality like Lady Abigail Houghall."

"Quality? And what qualities would they be?" James scoffed. "Avarice, lust, envy, and pride are hardly qualities to boast about. But be sure, this is the final time we'll be discussing Abigail. In the meantime, I've had Selina moved to the suite next to Grandmother until the wedding, and I expect you to treat her with the all the courtesy and respect due her as my bride."

Christina's eyes flared. "I will not let that woman become mistress of Penventen Hall!" she vowed, stamping her foot for emphasis.

"That hardly matters since I'm not truly the master here either, am I?" James responded harshly. "You've seen to that too."

His response was plainly unexpected. Open-mouthed for a second, she seemed to be grasping for a reply. James waited.

"Who have you been speaking to?" she asked darkly.

"It hardly matters. The rumor seemed well enough known at the time of your wedding," he parried. "My main question is why it should make a strategic appearance after the death of my father? Just how close are you and Lord Randall? I seem to recall now that he spent a lot of time visiting when father was away.

"Bringing Geoffrey with him was a convenient excuse, wasn't it? While two little boys played in the garden, you played the whore in the bedroom."

An angry slap across James's cheek brought the exchange to a halt. Mother and son stared at each other angrily for a moment.

"At least you're not further insulting me by denying it," James muttered.

Lady Christina seemed then to sag. She crossed listlessly to the settee and didn't so much sit as fall into the cushions.

"I suppose you want to hear the truth?" she asked tiredly.

"It would make a pleasant change."

James sat on the corner of his desk and crossed his arms, steeling himself for the revelation.

His mother looked away, suddenly appearing to find fascinating a painting on the wall to her left—a small, inconsequential hunting scene. She began to speak in a brittle voice.

"Randall and I were lovers long before I married your father. We were discreet for the protection of my reputation and, in order to keep our secret, I cultivated a suite of suitors, all the better to hide the truth.

"Randall was formally unattached when we began, but he was obliged to go through with his arranged marriage to Baroness Sophia. I would have been content to remain his mistress except I discovered

I was..." Her eyes flickered involuntarily toward James for a split second. "With child."

She looked down momentarily, as if gathering her thoughts. When she raised her face again, though still unable to look at James, her expression had hardened.

"Edward Mitchell was an *honorable* man as well as one with means."

She betrayed a moue of distaste at that word.

"So I seduced him and told him three weeks later that I was pregnant. We married immediately. "Oh, there was talk as there always is with hasty weddings and sudden confinements. He was aware of the rumors, but he maintained that you were his son. But I...I resented the useless cuckold and his damnable honor. All the more when it became evident that he couldn't father his own children.

"In the meantime, Sophia bore Geoffrey six months after you were born and she died just three years later, giving birth to child number four. One night soon after, I had enough of Edward trying to mount me and I told him the truth. I begged him to set me aside."

Lady Christina offered a bitter laugh.

"Do you know what that fool said to me?"

James's lips were drawn tight and he gave a curt shake of his head.

Lady Christina's gaze fell on the portrait of Edward Mitchell that hung over the fireplace behind her son.

"He said he didn't care. He was in love with me and was proud to claim you as his.

"I hated him until the day he died."

James pushed away from the desk and turned his back to her, looking up at the portrait, staring into the face of the man he had called Father. He could not speak.

His mother broke the silence.

"Edward might have been a fool in love, but he was no fool as a lawyer. Your inheritance is safe. You are secured as Lord Penventen. There will be no other claimants. And, yes, Randall is considering acknowledging you as his eldest son and heir. It would appear Geoffrey is a disappointment to him."

James felt sick to his stomach. Without saying a word, he sat down at his desk, found a pencil and paper, and started making notes.

After a few moments, he raised his eyes to his mother, who remained on the settee.

"Madam, you should know that I will deny the Earl's acknowledgment and any offer of inheritance," he said gravely. "As far as I and anyone else are concerned, I am James Mitchell, son of Edward Mitchell."

Lady Christina straightened.

"My father wouldn't set you aside, but I will. From next month you will no longer be able to draw on my credit. Instead, you will have a pension that, if you're frugal, will allow you to live modestly well for the rest of your days. You will have a townhouse in Mayfair and a small house in Truro.

"You will leave Penventen while Selina and I are on our honeymoon, and any future communication between us will be through my lawyer."

James was prepared for her to bluster or go into hysterics, but she surprised him by calmly nodding.

"Thank you. You're most generous, son."

CHAPTER TWENTY-THREE

5 August 1790

Selina drew her tongue nervously over her lips as she watched the groomsman saddle the bay mare. For the third time that morning, she looked over at her rose riding habit with a view to actually wearing the outfit for its intended purpose.

"I have to confess, James. I've never learned to ride."

He laughed.

"Please. Could we not walk instead?"

James refused with a grin.

"It will be another of your accomplishments as wife of a baronet," he said, supervising the addition of wicker panniers onto his horse, a large chestnut stallion.

James looked, in Selina's estimation, particularly handsome in his tan riding breeches, linen shirt, and navy blue riding jacket. She admired the way the jacket's crop to the waist accented his figure.

"Besides," he continued, "I intend to have you all to myself today, so I want to be as far away from the house as possible."

Now Selina smiled too. She had missed their late-evening rendezvous, and if it took learning to ride a beast to be alone with him, then it would be a small price to pay.

After a twenty-minute instruction on basic horsemanship, Selina was confidently controlling the gentle mare around the stable grounds.

Then James set a walking pace up the hill away from Padstow across open fields toward the cemetery about a mile away from Penventen Hall.

There they dismounted—Selina somewhat stiffly—and James tied their horses at the post by the gate.

Walking in, Selina observed how many of the headstones were weathered by the ferocious wind and rain that lashed that part of Cornwall. Other, more recent markers glistened freshly in the sunlight.

The elderly sexton, who lived at the edge of the village, supervised a couple of the village youngsters slashing the tall grass with scythes at the far wall of the graveyard. He doffed his hat in greeting from the distance, and James acknowledged him with a raise of his hand.

Selina didn't need to be told which was Edward Mitchell's grave.

Whatever Lady Christina's ambivalence about her husband in life, she made sure that he was suitably commemorated in death with an impressive monument made from locally quarried greenstone.

As Selina approached the marker, the Mitchell name, chiseled in sharp relief on the plinth, caught the morning sun, which caused it to stand out even more strongly.

This was to become her name in a little more than two weeks' time.

Glancing back at James by her shoulder, she saw his lips set in a thin, straight line. This was his first visit to the grave since the confrontation with his mother. He was holding his emotions on a tight rein.

Selina's heart filled with compassion and love for him. She couldn't begin to fathom the turmoil of emotions he had experienced on learning of his true origins. He had done his best to ensure it didn't cast a shadow over their wedding, but a long day preparing a brief for his solicitor, who was expected to arrive from London shortly, had taken a toll.

She took James's hand and read the inscription.

Here lies
Sir Edward Mitchell
Lord Penventen
5th Baronet
1732–1789
Aged 57 years

"I wish I had taken the time to understand him better when he was alive—the way I believe I know him now," said James after a while.

"I knew what my mother was, and like everyone else I thought he was weak. I can't begin to tell you of the surprise I had when he encouraged me to leave after the affair with Abigail. At first I thought he was glad to simply have the scandal quickly disappear, but I see now that he was telling me to escape, to do the thing he was incapable of doing."

"There's something else," Selina added softly.

James turned to her with a question in the tilt of his head.

"What would have happened to that little boy had your father left? What would have happened to you? I think your father knew that and he stayed to give you everything he was capable of giving, including permission to find your own way. I think he would be proud of the man you are today."

James enfolded her in his arms under the dappled shade of a nearby tree, drawing comfort from her and whispering words of thankfulness and love.

The elderly sexton glanced over, saw the couple embracing, and smiled.

James and Selina's ride continued with a lesson in brisk trotting. From the graveyard, they moved along the headland, then down onto the beach at Iron Cove where James encouraged Selina to bring the mare to a gallop along the hard-packed sand.

She began to understand that despite the mare's size, controlling her was not so difficult after all. Once you understood the animal and had mastery of the reins, subtle shifts of movement effortlessly communicated between rider and horse.

The sun had traveled well past its zenith, its afternoon trajectory heading toward banking clouds that had emerged along the western horizon, by the time James and Selina stopped for lunch. They sat in the lee of a grove of trees that hid the cliff edge, but not the pounding of the surf below, or the salt air tang the wind brought with it.

After dining, they lay side by side on the blanket Selina recognized from their moonlight picnic weeks earlier. Together they watched the sky begin to fill with clouds; tiny, innocent, and white at first but growing steadily larger and becoming darker shades of grey.

"We're in for bad weather tonight," Selina observed.

James nodded in agreement. He rolled onto his side and observed his bride-to-be.

His gaze followed the shape of her forehead, her delicate nose, her cheeks and sensuous lips, and down over the perfect outline of her breasts to her waist, taking in the flare of her hips and eyeing her legs and neat black booted feet.

He allowed his fingers to trace a portion of the journey his eyes had undertaken a moment before, his hand coming to rest on her hip.

Selina sighed languorously and, as James lowered himself to capture her lips—which opened to receive him eagerly—she pressed herself to him.

They kissed and touched each other for long minutes before James pulled away from her lips and concentrated his efforts at her earlobe.

"Let's elope," he breathed. "Let's leave everyone here with their grand wedding plans and tiered wedding cakes and boring guest lists. We can be in Gretna Green within a week."

"It's tempting," Selina said with a sigh. "But it's only two weeks more."

"Two weeks and three days," James grumbled, rolling away from her. Selina giggled and sat up.

"Let me come to you this evening," she asked, stroking his back with trailing fingers. "My bed is too large, cold, and lonely for one, and yours must be even more so."

"Why, Miss Rosewall! Are you trying to seduce me?" James teased.

"If you have to ask, then I fear I must be doing it wrong," Selina responded in kind.

"Have you no care? Won't you think of my reputation?"

"And what reputation would that be?"

His answer was heavy with irony: "A reputation for being the luckiest bastard in England."

James swooped back in for a kiss.

"Have I told you how much I love you, Selina?" he asked.

"You have and it seems that I don't get tired of hearing it," she answered. "Nor do I tire of telling you how much I love you in return."

Their embrace was interrupted by a gust of wind and a dark cloud scudding across the sun, turning off the light in their picnic place almost as surely as an extinguished candle. The weather had turned.

As James repacked the saddle panniers, Selina kept watch on the sky. This had the potential to be a bad storm.

After a few minutes of riding, Selina edged her horse closer to James's. The wind had increased in strength and was now howling through the trees. She was certain that they had changed course subtly in the last minute and were moving farther away from the direction of the hall and closer to Gunver Head.

"Why are we moving away from the hall?" she called.

James put a hand up and brought his mount to a halt.

"Wait here," he ordered.

James dismounted and disappeared into the thicket ahead.

A low rumble of thunder announced itself in the distance, and Selina bent low to give her horse a reassuring pat on the neck.

* * *

James had heard snatches of sound carried on the gusts of wind, the noise of hammers and of voices yelling instructions. He stayed as close to the hawthorn bushes as he could without snagging himself until he reached the edge of a clearing. He remained hidden and looked upon the activity in front of him.

Six men were erecting what appeared to be a temporary scaffold of timber, pegs, and ropes. He watched four of the men mate two thick timber beams at a single point and lift it to form a jib. From its apex, a sturdy iron pulley swung in the wind.

A temporary crane, James realized. That was how the wreckers were able to quickly take cargo up from the wreck of the *Pandora*.

The purpose of the metal eyebolt and spars he and Jackson had seen driven into the cliff face now made sense as guides and tie-points for the ropes.

As James watched, the lowering clouds overhead deepened from charcoal to black as the storm started its approach to shore. Suddenly, lightning split the sky and with it came the first drops of rain.

Behind the following boom of thunder, James heard a scream and realized it came not from the seabirds retreating to shore for shelter, but from Selina. He turned and made his way as fast as he could back toward her. Rain spattered the ground with increasing impatience as James burst from the thicket.

He saw a man silhouetted against the sullen sky grabbing the bridle of Selina's mount. The horse tugged back, trying to free itself from him. Unable to do so, the animal started to buck.

"Selina!"

James ran toward the scene as Selina tried to control the horse.

He watched her kick out at the man with one foot, but it was not enough to dislodge his hand.

Yard upon yard James closed on them, calling Selina's name once more.

The man looked at him and in one swift movement released Selina's ankle and snatched a pistol from his pocket.

Even at the sight of the pistol coming up to point at him, James ran headlong at the man.

Selina kicked her assailant again, landing a glancing blow to his shoulder just as he fired.

James saw the flash at the muzzle and felt the ball hurtle past his head.

The sound of the report merged with a clap of thunder. Selina's horse reared and she was thrown to the ground.

The man sidestepped as James came on and fled. Seeing his retreat, James yelled after him in impotent fury and threw himself to his knees beside Selina.

He called her name and tapped her face gently to rouse her, and after a moment she opened her eyes and tried to speak, but no words came out. James found his panic ebbing as Selina squeezed his hand strongly to reassure him.

"Where are you hurt?" he asked.

Selina blinked the rain from her eyes and sought to answer the question.

"Everywhere," she said.

"But no place worse than any other?"

Selina shook her head, and James assisted her to her feet. She leaned against him heavily. Bruised and winded, he guessed.

A glance around told him her mare had fled into the gloom and roiling rain and wind, along with her assailant. Without pause, James pushed her toward his horse and mounted before reaching down to pull Selina onto his lap. She collapsed gracelessly against his chest.

She was going into shock.

"Stay with me, sweetheart, I need you to hold on tight," he instructed as he wheeled his horse around and encouraged it at a gallop toward Penventen Hall.

James pushed his horse as fast as he dared. Time was of the essence—not only to get Selina home safely, but also to give warning about the wreckers on the cliffs.

As the lights from the Hall emerged out of the lashing rain, he chanced a glance down at Selina. Her head was tucked into his shoulder, protecting her face from the downpour; her breath warmed his sodden shirt.

In one easy movement, he dismounted with Selina in his arms and burst through the front door.

He ignored the cries of surprise from Mrs. White, but her startled reaction brought William and Edgar to the door of the drawing room, where Comte Alexandre, Edith, Catherine, and a heavily pregnant Sarah were beginning to rise from their seats.

He could hear Mrs. White trail behind him, calling to one of the upstairs maids to fetch warm, dry clothes for the master and Miss Selina.

Lady Margaret and Lady Christina, hearing the commotion, emerged from the suites on the second floor and joined the procession through James's private reception room and into the bedroom itself.

Sarah moved past him as he gently placed Selina on a footstool. The four women, along with two maids, set to work divesting her of her now-saturated clothes. James gave her one last glance before closing the bedroom door.

In his reception room, he accepted a towel from Jackson and began stripping off his own wet clothes.

He found himself faced by a furious William Rosewall.

"What the hell is going on, Penventen? What's wrong with Selina?" he demanded.

"She fell from her horse but she's unharmed," James assured him. "She's winded and wet from the rain."

William let out a pent-up huff of breath and laid aside his anger.

James turned to Jackson, toweling himself as he spoke.

"There are wreckers on the cliff at Gunver Head. They're after the *Zeus.*"

William straightened. He knew that ship.

James didn't let him ask the inevitable question before he answered it.

"She's carrying a king's ransom in gold. We must raise a posse to go to them."

Jackson had gathered dry clothing for James. He tossed it across a chair and disappeared down the hall to recruit men among the staff to help give pursuit to the gang on the cliff.

"I have men in Padstow," William offered.

"Then get them to the cove beneath the cliffs. Jackson and I will lead a party to the top of the cliffs and send a rider to the barracks. Pray that Colonel Pickering and his men are able to stop the gang setting up a false beacon at Polzeath."

CHAPTER TWENTY-FOUR

6 August 1790

The setting sun painted the late afternoon clouds with streaks of bloody red. The old saying "red sky at night, sailor's delight" came reflexively to James as he scrubbed his tired face and looked from the window of Custom House where a man of interest was being held.

The *Zeus* had sailed safely along the Cornish coast and was now well into its journey toward Europe.

James's posse and William's crew had captured eight men the previous night, five on the shore and three on the cliffs above. Another five men on the cliff escaped in the melee just as Lieutenant Walsh arrived with reinforcements and news from Colonel Pickering that his force had stopped a false light beacon on the headland of Polzeath. Three men were in custody there; three escaped.

The clash with the wreckers at Gunver Head was not without casualty among the forces of order. Two of William Rosewall's sailors were moderately injured in the fight on the beach, while on the cliffs overhead, Jackson had received a gash to his arm.

After seeing to the welfare of the men under his charge and the secure incarceration of their prisoners, James sent for word of Selina. When the message came back that she was still sleeping, he fixed on an interrogation that went through the rest of the night and into the next day.

A small number of the men were ruffians—career criminals for hire; others were locals who considered the extracurricular activity of smuggling an acceptable way to supplement their income.

However, none knew who was the mastermind of their venture, only that they would be paid well for their work.

Now they faced an audience with the magistrate, a trial after that, and, should they be fortunate enough to avoid a hanging, they would be unfortunate enough to face transportation.

One of the captured men was, time and again, identified by his cohorts, as the organizer and paymaster. It was he who James now waited to question for a second time.

In an initial interview, the man had disavowed his role of organizer, claiming that he had simply relayed instructions and resources that had come from a Mr. Reynold.

The name Reynold was the reason why James remained in the small office. It was the name that had been invoked when he and Selina had been followed through the streets of London.

Reynold's man had tried to warn him off and made the oblique threat to Selina.

James was going to see this through to the end.

The office door opened. Colonel Pickering entered looking less polished but more dangerous than James could ever remember seeing him. His overnight stubble matched the grey of his temples, and the darkness under his eyes gave him a vaguely threatening air.

Nonetheless, his voice was brisk. "You should be at home, Lord Penventen."

"Not until I find out who this Reynold character is," replied James.

Pickering folded his arms. "Well you're not going to learn anything further for at least another twelve hours."

"This man threatened my wife-to-be and me."

Pickering would brook no argument.

"My men are going off-duty to rest," he told James firmly. "Our prisoners are in custody and are going nowhere. I have a unit from Newquay that will be patrolling the roads out of Padstow and Newquay. Go home."

James shook his head as much to clear the fatigue as to refute the colonel's argument. Through heavy lids he looked at the older man.

"You'll send someone to the hall when you're ready to interrogate Morgan?" he asked, reluctantly taking up his crumpled jacket as he stood.

"The man's name is Morcombe, and, yes, I'll personally let you know."

Pickering slapped him on the back in camaraderie.

"Lady Catherine saw to your wet kit being returned to Penventen Hall," he told James. "She says the doctor has seen Miss Selina again, and she will be well when she has recovered from bruises and a chill. Oh, and he's put a few stitches in the arm of your man Jackson."

"The other wounded men?"

"I'm told they're no more worse than they would have been on a Friday night brawling at the tavern."

James offered a tired smile in acknowledgment and paused in the doorway.

"I'm convinced Reynold is the key to this," he explained. "If we find him and the puppet master who pulls his strings, then we have the potential to end the means to fund revolution on English soil."

With a firm hand on James's shoulder Pickering steered the younger man down the stairs and through the passageways to the front door.

A young soldier on guard stood to attention at the colonel's appearance.

"Bring Lord Penventen's horse, private."

The man saluted and went to carry out the order.

"I know my duty, my Lord, and I don't underestimate its importance," Pickering said kindly.

"Lady Catherine and I are looking forward to attending a wedding in two weeks, and it wouldn't do for the bride and groom to be indisposed. Go home and get some sleep, sir."

* * *

Selina woke to whispering voices. Her head pounded furiously, so at first she refused to open her eyes in order to keep the pain to marginally tolerable levels.

Then curiosity got the better of her, and she ventured opening one eye and then the other, surprised that the very act hadn't exhausted her completely.

The curtains on the bed, gauzy white inners and heavy red outer drapes, were closed between the four barley-twist posts.

"I'm awake," she croaked hoarsely.

The bed curtains opened swiftly and the sudden infusion of light was as startling as it was agonizing. She clenched her eyes shut.

Selina counted to ten in her head before she attempted to open them again. The face that came swimming into view was Sarah's.

"Selina, darling," she exclaimed softly. "We've been so worried about you! Here, take a small sip of water."

Despite the growing weight of her pregnancy, Sarah moved with the brisk assurance of a mother well used to soothing and tending invalids.

Selina accepted the water gratefully, letting the cool liquid trickle down her raw throat.

Sarah smiled at Selina's expression and leaned in.

"Although it's highly improper, I have someone here to see you." She grinned.

Sarah now had Selina's full attention, and, over her shoulder, James appeared, looking haggard and concerned.

Sarah withdrew, telling them that she would be back after consulting with Lady Margaret and Lady Christina. It appeared that Sarah Rosewall was the only woman in England who could effectively marshal both mother and daughter.

James smiled tiredly, sat on the edge of the bed, and took her hand. He kissed Selina on the forehead.

"You're running a temperature," he noted.

"A small one," she assured him with a squeeze of her hand. Her eyes wandered over his form looking for injuries but found none.

"You look tired," she observed.

"Nothing a day's sleep won't cure."

"Not the most romantic way of getting me into your bed." Selina smiled.

James allowed himself a chuckle. Selina tried to join in but it ended in a hacking cough. Another sip of water eased the spasms.

She spoke briefly, the pain in her throat acute. "What happened?"

James held a finger to her lips.

"I'll speak, you rest, agreed?"

Selina nodded and listened intently as he outlined the events of the past twenty-four hours.

"The *Zeus* is safely on her way to Gibraltar but, more importantly, you are safe and my duty to William Pitt and the Crown is complete," he finished. "No more intrigue, no more scandals, just you."

He punctuated the words with a kiss to her cheek.

"And me," he said, ending the sentence with a soft kiss to her lips.

"Your sister will be back soon. Will you promise me you will get some rest? You have a wedding to plan."

Selina smiled and James stood.

As though on cue, the door opened and Sarah peered in. William hovered over her shoulder.

"Get some sleep?" she asked James hopefully.

"I will. They won't interrogate Morcombe again until tomorrow morning."

James leaned down and gave her another sweet kiss. He was about to leave, when Selina firmly grasped his hand.

He looked at her, surprised by the alarmed expression that had appeared on her face.

"Selina? Are you ill?"

She shook her head.

"No. It's the man." She coughed. "The man who tried to unhorse me…it was Fidget."

"Who's fidgeting?" William approached the bed.

He too looked tired, and there was a sizeable bruise on his cheek.

Selina shook her head again in frustration, aware that her voice wouldn't hold out much longer. She squeezed James's hand harder, trying to make him appreciate the importance of her news.

"Fidget…the harbor…my sketches."

"Sketches?" asked Sarah. "Shall I fetch them for you?"

Selina nodded. "Secret drawer…writing box."

Her eyes implored James.

"Where's the key, Selina?" he asked.

Selina struggled to sit up in bed. Every muscle ached. Whether it was from the fall or the subsequent chill, she couldn't tell. She reached for a fine gold chain around her neck. Beneath a locket that had been her mother's was the key.

Sarah left the room and both men hovered by the bed.

"Are you telling me that you know the man who attacked you yesterday?" James asked.

"Attacked? What's this?" demanded William. "When were you going to tell me this?"

Without the energy to deal with her brother, Selina concentrated on James and the vital message she had to tell him.

"I call the man Fidget. From the Harbor."

Sarah came back into the room with a small sketchbook bound in leather, and Selina reached for it immediately. After flicking through a few pages, she found what she was looking for and presented the book for the two men to see. Many faces, but all of one man.

"Fidget," she announced.

"You're sure that's the man?" William asked.

Selina gave an emphatic nod of her head.

"He's not amongst the men arrested," he observed.

"That might be something in our favor," reasoned James. "Let's see if Morcombe knows. If we can identify this man, we might be a step closer to finding Reynold and ending this conspiracy for good."

* * *

7 August 1790

Weak, diffuse light from a high, narrow window, its thick panes salt-encrusted from years of Cornish coastal weather, was all that lit the holding cell. A wooden slatted seat stood in the pallid beam of light as though it were the only piece of furniture in the room.

A soldier nudged Morcombe forward into the room and pushed him onto the seat, then took up station on the wall behind him.

The room was little warmer than the cell in which he had spent the night. His shackled hands were still on his lap, but his eyes darted furtively around the room.

Colonel Pickering entered the room carrying a leather-covered notebook in one hand and a lit candle in a tin holder in the other. He placed both objects on the table and sat down. He said nothing to the man in front of him, instead opening the notebook and spending some time studying several pages.

Although just a couple of years separated the two men in age, the difference in their physical bearing couldn't have been starker.

Where the colonel stood tall, Morcombe stooped, a legacy from the back-breaking labor of mining. Pickering was graying at the temples, but healthy and stalwart in appearance; Morcombe was grey in complexion and missing three top teeth and two below, causing his mouth to appear misshapen.

Pickering closed the book and met Morcombe's sideways look of curiosity.

Morcombe returned his gaze, more from defiance than confidence.

The colonel smiled. He withdrew from his jacket pocket his pipe and a chamois tobacco pouch, pulled out a wad of freshly cut tobacco, and tamped it down into the bowl of the pipe. The pipe stem between his teeth, Pickering felt inside the pouch once more, found a taper, and lit it on the candle, then transferred the flame to the bowl of the pipe, causing the tobacco to glow and sputter.

The colonel blew out the taper with a mouthful of smoke, pinched its end between thumb and forefinger to ensure its complete extinguishment, and looked across at Morcombe while drawing thoughtfully on the pipe. The prisoner inhaled audibly as the plume of smoke drifted lazily across the two yards separating the men.

Pickering smiled again. "Not much longer to go, Morcombe, then you can have some tobacco yourself."

"I dunno what more you want to know," Morcombe replied gruffly. "If you ain't onto Reynold by now, then I can't help ye."

"I think you know more than you're telling us," said a voice from the shadows.

Morcombe jumped. He stared in the direction of the voice, a darkened corner beneath the high window.

"Do you, Morcombe? Do you know more than you've told us?" the colonel asked mildly.

"I swear I told you everythin' I know!"

"Everything except where Reynold is, who Reynold is, and why he'd hire a group of ne'er-do-wells and misfits like you." James emerged from the darkness.

Morcombe looked at the young Lord with a bitter sneer.

"I never met the man a'fore this year. He seemed to know about me though. Tol' me all about m'past an' asked if I wanted to make five quid."

"Doing what?"

"I've already said."

"So say it again."

Morcombe's nostrils flared and he pouted as he answered.

"He said I had to get twelve men what I trusted who wanted to earn a pound each for their troubles."

"When was this?" James prompted.

"In January. In Newquay. In a pub," Morcombe answered impatiently. His face hardened with surliness. "Look, I've already told about all of this. It's a waste of your precious time, milord…"

"Tell me about the *Pandora*," James interrupted.

"The what?"

"The ship wrecked in February."

Morcombe's eyes narrowed.

"That were Reynold's doing," he started cautiously, "I did nothin' but take barrels of brandy. That were after the ship were already wrecked. I know nothin' 'bout the men that was killed."

"How many times did you meet Reynold?" asked Pickering.

"Not more than a dozen times."

"How did you know how to find him?"

"I never did. 'E found me." The prisoner offered a sharp laugh on fetid breath. "Not that I was hard to find—at the pub 'til closing time every day 'cept Sunday, when I've an 'angover."

He smirked at James.

"Does Reynold have a Christian name?" James asked.

Morcombe turned his face up to his questioner with contempt clear in his face.

"I'm sure 'is mother knows."

James cuffed the man hard across the side of his head, the slap loud in the confines of the cell. Morcombe started to rise from the chair with a bark of rage, only to be firmly pushed back down by the soldier who stepped up behind him.

"Try again," James growled.

"I heard 'im speak to someone in Newquay a couple of times, a foreigner or maybe a toff. I can't tell the difference. 'E might have called him 'Enry."

"Why do you say he was foreign?"

"Or a toff. He dressed like a gent. Maybe 'e's one o' your friends."

James glared but made no move toward the prisoner.

Pickering spoke mildly, almost with disinterest, forcing Morcombe to switch his attention between his interrogators again.

"We won't keep you for very much longer."

Pickering rose from behind the table, bringing the leather-covered book with him.

"We simply want you to look at this and tell us if you recognize anything."

Morcombe glanced at James, who had stepped back out of the shaft of dirty light falling from the window and slipped into the shadows. Then he looked to Pickering, who was now standing in front of him, holding open Selina's sketchbook.

Morcombe glanced down and, page by page, the colonel turned the leaves for the man to look.

Quick studies of trees, boats, and fishermen filled the early pages and, from his position, James could see Morcombe physically relax. There was nothing to concern him in any of these pictures.

Then the middle of the book was spread before him and across two pages were finely detailed mini portraits, twelve in all, and all showing the same figure, some full face, some in profile, some full length, another just a sketch of eyes and a brow.

James saw Morcombe stiffen and stare.

"Do you recognize the man?" asked Pickering evenly.

"This is a trick. You ask me about Reynold and you know who 'e is all along!"

Pickering glanced at James, who looked as shocked as Morcombe himself.

He held the sketchbook closer to Morcombe.

"You know the man illustrated here?"

"Aye, we've only just been talkin' about 'im!"

"Name him," Pickering commanded, "but remember that you will be obliged to swear it under oath before a magistrate."

Morcombe nodded at the dozen portraits drawn by Selina.

"That there is Henry Reynold."

Pickering closed the book and returned it to the table. As he did so, without looking back at Morcombe, he addressed the guard.

"Take him back to his cell."

As the door closed behind the prisoner and escort, James dropped into the seat vacated by Morcombe.

"Have you found your answer, Sir James?" asked Pickering, turning to regard him.

James shook his head.

"I have even more questions now."

CHAPTER TWENTY-FIVE

22 August 1790

By daybreak, Selina was up and dressed in one of her old grey gowns. She slipped away from the house, retreating to the relative seclusion of the hedge maze, where the noise of the household at work faded into the background.

She had recovered well from her fall and the chill, and after three days of confinement she had started to chafe under the well-meaning hovering of so many people. The application of a pungent salve saw her bruises fade, and she insisted that she be allowed fresh air and a stroll in the gardens twice a day, which she was convinced assisted her recovery.

Even Lady Catherine had been genuine in her solicitude. Without Abigail to needle, and with the burgeoning romance between her and Colonel Pickering, Catherine appeared to have changed for the better.

It was nothing short of miraculous, in Selina's opinion. Every now and again, the edge of Lady Catherine's acerbic manner would slice through—particularly in frustration with Edith's flightiness—but it was now more often than not tempered by greater self-control.

In the hedge maze, Selina basked in the gentle morning warmth as early light clouds retreated. She traced the lines of the sundial with her finger; its bronze gnomon glinted in the sun, casting a shadow to reveal the time.

In just five hours' time, she would be Lady Selina Ann Mitchell, wife of Sir James Mitchell, sixth baronet and Lord Penventen.

In so many ways she felt that she was already James's wife in everything but name. Yet knowing he was to become hers for life, this sought-after society favorite who had swept her off her feet at a royal ball in far-off London, still seemed unreal.

Thanks to the determinedly diligent assistance of Lady Margaret and her beloved sister-in-law, Sarah, all preparations for the wedding were complete. The house was, as her father would have said, "ship-shape in Bristol fashion."

She smiled as she thought of her father. She intended to wear a miniature of him and her mother tied to her wrist with a blue ribbon for remembrance. William, of course, would have her other arm to give her away.

James had spent the night in Newquay with Jackson and some of his friends from London and would meet her at St Petroc's church at eleven o'clock. Their wedding breakfast would take place in Penventen's Great Hall, while a festival for the people of Padstow would be held in the grounds of the hall.

Lady Christina, who was at least speaking to her directly now she was to become James's wife, had been determined to play a role in preparing her son's wedding. But with Lady Margaret firmly establishing herself as a surrogate mother of the bride and flaunting the fact to her daughter, Selina was thankful that Sarah was masterful in her role as peacemaker. In the end, Lady Christina was to arrange the reception, and the compromise was deemed acceptable by both sides.

By now Selina found, as much as she loved Lady Margaret, the tension between her and her daughter was draining. However, James had told her that would cease to be an issue after today.

Lady Christina would be in Truro by the time they returned from their honeymoon, and Lady Margaret would have returned home to Cheshire.

The sound of workmen erecting tents and marquees competed with the calls of peacocks annoyed at the disturbance and awoke Selina from her thoughts.

The sun caught the ring she wore on her left hand. She studied the beautiful ruby posy James had given her the afternoon they arrived back from the masquerade ball.

In the light and warmth of their wedding morning, Selina returned to a treasured memory of how they had managed to slip away from the rest of the household. James had brought her to the centre of the hedge maze, where he kissed her deeply. She felt the taste and texture of his lips and his tongue imprinted on hers.

Selina hugged him tightly, rubbing her cheek against the linen of his shirt. She reveled in the strength of his arms around her and the steady beat of his heart.

"Not too many people know yet. It's not too late to change your mind," he whispered.

She looked up at him.

"I won't if you won't," she replied, eliciting a laugh for her husband-to-be.

He continued soberly. "I never thought I would be so glad to be married. I never realized how empty my life had been until I met you, and with each day I appreciate how impossible it is to live without you."

James dipped into his waistcoat pocket and placed the ring on her finger.

"'Who can find a virtuous woman? For her price is far above rubies,'" he recited. "'The heart of her husband doth safely trust in her, so that he shall have no need of spoil. She will do him good and not evil all the days of her life.'

"I think I begin to understand what the Bible means when it talks about 'two become one flesh.' You are as much a part of me as I am of myself. The one thing I know for certain is that I'm the one getting the better end of the bargain."

Selina drew in breath to hold back tears. She kissed the hands that still held hers.

"I know you, James. You're a man of honor and passion and I have to confess that I may have fallen in love with you on the first night we met," she declared. "And I love you more now and I will love you even more with every year we're man and wife."

Selina was still smiling at the recollection when she was startled back to reality by the voice of Lady Catherine.

"Selina! What are you doing hiding here? People are looking for you. You'll bring on Sarah's labor early; Lady Christina will have a stroke, which will cause Lady Margaret to die of happiness; and Edith will become hysterical."

"I certainly wouldn't want to be responsible for all of that," Selina answered gravely but with a twinkle of merriment in her eyes.

Catherine drew the cord of her emerald bed robe more securely around her waist and scolded with an equal spark.

"Then get back inside to be plucked, primped, and preened within an inch of your life and made completely unrecognizable to the groom."

* * *

To her dismay, Selina discovered that Catherine was only half joking.

She had already determined how she would wear her hair and was forced to resist when she saw the curling tongs being heated over the fire. Her chestnut locks were held in place with a double gold hair band and dressed in only light curls.

Another battle loomed over makeup. Here Selina compromised, refusing to have her face powdered but consenting to her cheeks being lightly rouged and her lips being touched with color.

Fortunately, it was too late for others to make changes to her gown. It was one of her own choosing, in peach satin with a wide scoop neck, embroidered with blossoms in pink silk thread. Two pink bows were stitched just below the shoulders.

The gown fitted her slender waist and flared out to reveal a split skirt embroidered with larger flowers in pink silk along its edges. The under skirt was in pale rose satin, a shade lighter than the pink embroidery on the skirt above.

Her traditional bouquet was pale pink roses interspersed with orange blossom. Her only jewelry was her posy ring, the miniatures of her parents at her wrist, and pearl studs at her ears, a gift from her brother.

Now, as the hour approached, William arrived at her bedroom door and watched his sister examine her ensemble in the cheval mirror.

"You are the second most beautiful woman I have ever seen," he told her.

"You can save your flattery, Sarah's already left for the church," she told her brother's reflection with good humor.

"Both Father and Maman would be proud of you," William affirmed, taking her arm to lead her to the carriage that waited at the front of Penventen Hall.

"And I couldn't be happier that you're not only marrying for love, but also marrying a man that I'm proud to welcome into my home. Sarah tells me that she knew he was the one for you the moment she laid eyes on him."

"Your wife is an incurable romantic," Selina retorted.

"I know. Why do you think I have four children and another on the way?"

* * *

James cast an eye down the aisle of St Petroc's Church, nodding and smiling at people in the pews as he recognized them, nervously twisting the ring Selina had presented him two weeks ago. It was gold, with a square-cut ruby set flush in the band. He'd not given much thought of wearing a ring himself, but Selina insisted that she provide him with a token for the wedding.

St Petroc's was filled to capacity with a mix of the "right" people and genuine friends from both London and the local community.

"So, any last words of advice before Selina arrives?" James whispered to Jackson, who stood beside him as his best man.

Both men were dressed alike in navy blue. Their breeches were tucked into highly polished black boots. The jackets were fitted to the waist, and their cream shirts were complemented by cream satin cravats.

In fact, they looked so similar it was only Jackson's fair hair that distinguished the men from a distance.

"Don't forget to breathe," Jackson answered sagely.

James gave him a quizzical look.

Jackson nodded in confirmation. "Back home I saw a man so nervous on his wedding day that when the preacher asked if he did, his eyes rolled in the back of his head and he dropped to a dead faint on the floor of the chapel."

"What happened?"

"They didn't get married that day. His bride burst into tears and wouldn't talk to him for a month, and her parents stuck him with the bill for the nuptials."

"You know how to make a man feel better," James grumbled.

"So, that's why my advice to you is 'don't forget to breathe.'"

"Do you think I'll get to return this pearl of wisdom?"

"Ask me in six months' time."

Jackson nudged his friend as Reverend Kirk, resplendent in a crisp white surplice over his black clerical robes, approached briskly.

The Reverend nodded to his wife, who was also church organist, and took his place at the altar.

The church stood at the opening strains of the first hymn.

James's breath caught in his throat at the first sight of his bride. She was beautiful. Selina caught his eye and gave him a shy smile. The groom found himself grinning back. Jackson's estimation of his expression was "like an idiot," he was informed later.

James remembered the first time he saw Selina all those months ago at the Chesterfield House royal ball. He recalled their banter as they were introduced, the feel of her in his arms as they danced, the passionate nature that exhibited itself at almost every opportunity they had to be alone.

And now she was to be his for life. Each morning he would awake with her beside him. Each night they would go to bed together. He would touch, taste, and make her a true part of him, and himself, a true part of her.

Now, as Selina moved closer to him, it seemed the other guests in the church had disappeared. All he could see was his wife-to-be approaching, and, within half an hour, they would have made their vows to each other before God and the congregation.

Selina was halfway down the aisle when Jackson nudged James discreetly.

"You've forgotten to breathe."

* * *

The day that had begun with light cloud fulfilled its promise of a perfect late August day. The sky cleared and sea breezes tempered the warmth of the late summer sun.

At Penventen Hall, guests from all strata of society strolled the gardens to the sounds of a string quartet while blue uniformed and bewigged footmen circled the crowd with trays of refreshments.

Not long after she and James returned to the hall, a dispatch rider arrived to hand James a packet. Letters from more well-wishers, she presumed.

James disappeared inside the house with the letters.

Selina's cheeks were starting to hurt from smiling, and her throat was parched from welcoming guests and accepting best wishes from Padstow villagers by herself. She sent one of William and Sarah's boys on an errand to get her some punch, but it was James who returned with it.

"Ah, I thought I was being abandoned on my own wedding day," she teased. She took a grateful sip of the chilled beverage. "There are so many people here. I had no idea you were so well regarded."

"Me? I thought these were all your friends."

Selina smiled.

"I saw the post rider; if he delivers any more letters I can see the first month of being your wife doing nothing but writing letters of thanks," she said.

"Well, perhaps during the day." There was a twinkle of mischief in James's eyes. "I have very definite plans for the evening."

His words, heavy with promise, thrilled her and colored her cheeks unbidden, but not unnoticed.

"Oh yes, very definite plans," he said, and planted a soft, lingering kiss on her lips. The villagers roared their approval.

Selina blushed deeper.

"How soon before we can be alone?" she whispered as they strolled farther along the grounds.

"Right now if you like."

Selina raised a skeptical eyebrow.

"You shouldn't tease with false promises. We're the centre of attention. We'd be missed even before we reach the house. Besides, we have the Prime Minister of England and the Duke of York as guests."

"And my mother complained it was a small wedding," said James.

He cast his eye across the grounds. White marquees were decorated with garlands of pink silk roses. Studding the lawn in groups, white wicker chairs and lounges had been made more comfortable with peach cushions and rose pink bolsters monogrammed with either the Penventen coat of arms or the letters J and S intertwined.

"She will insist we sit through every moment of her reception," he observed with a twinge of bitterness in his voice.

He drew Selina behind a gardenia shrub, placing them slightly out of sight of the main festivities, and wrapped his arms around his wife.

"By my calculation," he told her, "we should be able to take our leave in about eight and a half hours' time, so I believe we both need something to sustain us until then."

She met his kiss without shyness or hesitation. She savored the touch of his lips and opened her own to encourage his tongue to plunder her mouth.

CHAPTER TWENTY-SIX

With a fanfare, the doors of the Great Hall at Penventen were opened for the first time in thirty years. The last major event held in the hall was the ball in honor of King George III's ascension to the British throne. Although mostly unused, the Great Hall hadn't suffered the neglect of other areas of the house, however. It had been generally maintained over the years and a conscientious cleaning had revived the elaborate if somewhat old-fashioned grandeur of the double-story room.

The Great Hall, an addition built during the reign of King Charles the First, was three times as long as it was wide and its opulence belonged to its age. Damask silk wall coverings, the color of fine Bordeaux, provided the backdrop to large stylized burnished gold Arabesque flowers that rose to the ceiling over oak-paneled chair rails.

Mirrors six feet high were encased in elaborately carved gilt frames and angled in such a way to catch the afternoon light from the floor-to-ceiling windows on the opposite wall and then later to disperse light from elaborate silver candelabra that stood on solid oak console tables in front of them.

Ordinarily, chairs would have lined these walls. Tonight, they were placed the length of dining tables set with starched white cloth and covered with candelabra. Epergnes filled with fragrant damask roses and an impressive range of crockery were set in their place to indicate the start of an elaborate, multiple-course feast.

The booming voice of the Master of Ceremonies announced the arrival of the bride and groom.

Side by side, James and Selina were introduced to Prince Frederick, the Duke of York, King George's second son, and Prime Minister William Pitt before taking their place at the end of the reception line. In all 120 guests filled the room, greeting first royalty, the head of government, and then the bride and groom.

As soon as James sat down with Selina at the raised reception table, he pointed out the intricate mural that ran the length of the ceiling.

The hanging chandeliers were already lit, partly obscuring the exquisitely painted mythical Greek scene, but Selina could still see the frolicking nymphs and dryads playing by the waters' edge while human dancers with festoons of grapes between them entertained another crowd as they stamped out a new vintage.

In another corner of the room, Pegasus grazed in a peaceful lea away from the gathering.

"See just over there?" James asked, pointing to a third of the way along the hall.

He indicated a shirtless bearded man in a cloak that covered his hair and swirled to shield his lower body from view. He played a reed flute for an enraptured young woman who reclined on a white fleece. She wore only a crescent moon crown, but most of her nudity was obscured by well-positioned foliage.

"Is that Pan?" Selina asked.

"Do you know the story of the seduction of Selene?"

Selina shook her head.

"Pan, as you probably know, was a great seducer of women," he began.

"I'm beginning to see similarities already," she mused.

"Ah," James held up a finger to silence her. "But Selene was in love with a humble shepherd by the name of Endymion."

"Oh dear, that's very inconvenient," Selina responded giving James her full, if somewhat amused, attention.

"So, disguising himself as Endymion, Pan tempted Selene from the sky with a fleece—soft, white, and silky—beautiful to lie on. Remind me to show you one day how soft a sheepskin can be…"

Selina smiled sweetly. "You were saying?"

"Still believing that he is Endymion, Selene allowed herself to be seduced only to discover too late that her lover was the notorious Pan."

"What happened to Selene and Endymion?"

"Oh they still remained lovers," James added dismissively. "But when Zeus offered Endymion the choice of either living a mortal life or being forever young, he made the wrong choice and decided to remain forever young."

"Why was that a mistake?"

"Well," James smiled, clearly warming to his story, "because, to remain forever young he had to go into that eternal sleep—death. Selene was heartbroken."

"These Greek legends never end well do they?"

They laughed and returned their attention to the evening's activities.

* * *

Finally, accompanied by a retinue of servants, the couple were able to take their leave to the applause of all and a dash of ribald commentary from some especially ebullient guests.

James reached for Selina's hand as the sounds of the merrymaking faded and they entered the living quarters of Penventen Hall, and finally the bedroom. Although Selina had spent three nights sleeping and recuperating in this room only two weeks before, she now saw it anew.

It was typical of predominantly male quarters. The walls were cream in color, but on them hung original paintings of pastoral scenes. The room was simply but expensively furnished. The furniture was in dark oak without the inlay popular in more fashionable French-inspired pieces, but was still, nonetheless, superbly carved.

But this was no longer only James's suite. It was hers also.

Selina glanced at her new husband; she couldn't see his face as he sat and leaned over to remove his boots.

As for herself, she was uncharacteristically impatient and growing annoyed by what appeared to be the inordinate length of time it took for the house maids to fuss over the evening preparations.

Slipping off her peach-colored shoes and undoing the garter at her knee, Selina absently noted a maid taking slippers through an adjoining door. Apparently her wardrobe had been moved into the Lady's bedroom. Apart from dressing, she couldn't imagine that room getting much use. Perhaps she could suggest to James that they turn it into a nursery.

She blushed as she imagined the result of their lovemaking. From the corner of her eye, she saw the play of muscles beneath James's shirt as he removed his jacket and waistcoat and could understand why lust was considered a sin for the unmarried.

James was an incredibly handsome man, but also so kind, witty, intelligent. She thought it a wonder the whole world wasn't in love with him.

Selina kissed him eagerly the moment the door was closed behind the last servant, but he stopped her with his hands on her shoulders. She looked at him, puzzled.

"We have all the time in the world now, and I want to take it slow," he said.

His eyes were dark and his expression revealed the depth of his desire for her.

Selina met his gaze and spoke the words he had asked to hear from her that first night. "I trust you."

He groaned and fell on her lips, lavishing them with kisses before turning her around so her back was to him.

A small fire burned in the grate and its heat warmed her front while the heat of James's body heated her back.

One by one, he released the small silk-covered buttons on her dress as he pressed warm, tender kisses along her neck.

With the last of the buttons undone, James pushed her dress slowly and deliberately from her shoulders, down over her arms, where the fabric hung formless over her waist. His hands swept up her arms, across her shoulders, up her nape, where he removed the dozen or so pins that held her coiffeur in place.

Selina's hair tumbled free, and, as it did, James's hands began to loosen the stays of her corset. With her assistance, he pulled the garment over her head and tossed it on the floor where it would soon be joined by her other clothing.

The rose pink underskirt was fastened with a set of four buttons at the back; they too were released, and the weight of the skirt without the support of the female form fell from her hips in the form of rustling satin and silk, whispering its seductive encouragement.

James turned his attention to Selina's ears; his breath eddied in its shells and Selina shivered with pleasure, restlessly rubbing herself against him as one hand explored her breasts while the other drifted lower, teasing her hips with light, gentle caresses and moving again below her belly, where, through the fabric of her chemise, he softly stroked her with teasing touches of his fingertips, enough to arouse but not yet satisfy.

Selina moaned softly, enjoying the feel of him so close, but she wanted more. She stilled his hands with her own and turned to him.

James swept her into his arms and laid her gently on the large expanse of his bed.

Although fully clothed, he joined her on the bed, claiming her lips again with his. Selina wrapped her arms around his neck and kissed him hungrily for a time.

"You're still dressed," she complained.

With a hand pressed firmly to his chest, she pushed him up and off the bed, arose herself, and beckoned him near to the fire where her dress lay.

Obeying her unspoken instruction to stand at ease, James obviously reveled in the pleasure of his wife undressing him.

Although she had seen him fully unclothed only the once, Selina paused to study the man now standing nude before her, evidence of his desire for her unashamedly present.

She tore her eyes away from his manhood only after considering whether her lips on his sex would bring him same the ecstasy that his lips on hers had done. Selina looked forward to finding out—perhaps tonight, perhaps some other night. James was right. They had a lifetime to learn one another.

So for tonight she set about learning his neck and his chest with her lips, noting in delight that his smaller nut-brown nipples puckered and gave him pleasure. While her nails lightly grazed his back, raising goose bumps, his hands were on the ribbons on the stays around her shoulders and under her breasts.

Then they were loose and bunched at her chest.

With deliberate, slow provocation, James snaked one arm around her back and with the other touched one creamy white breast, then the other, before decisively yanking the fabric down, letting it float to the floor.

Now his bride was as naked as he was, and the feel of her standing completely flesh-to-flesh was more intoxicating than any of the champagne he sipped at the reception.

Once more without speaking, he scooped her into his arms and returned to the bed.

Against the crisp linen sheets, his eyes drank in her form. Although he wasn't touching her, Selina's eyes were dark with passion, her lips full, red, and slightly parted. Her rosy pink nipples on firm, high breasts were already standing erect for him.

He lowered his head for a taste, rolling first one and then the other between his tongue and his lips.

Selina encouraged his attentions, both with her lips and her body. He stretched up to kiss her gently on the lips.

"I love you, my darling," he whispered.

"And I you."

His hands moved lower and grazed the soft curls between her legs, which parted to inspire him further. His fingers explored her and would find her moist and ready for him.

He watched her closely as he seduced her with his mouth and fingers. She called his name at the peak of her pleasure.

James moved himself over her and brushed her face lovingly to bring her back to herself.

"Sweetheart, look at me," he said.

She looked up and he was in awe again at the longing in her eyes. James was sure it mirrored his.

"I've been waiting for this moment," she told him huskily. "I want you."

As he kissed her face passionately, his manhood nudged her entrance. Instinctively, Selina's legs wrapped around his hips, encouraging him on.

Leaning heavily on one arm, he stroked her with his fingers, coaxing a new responsiveness as he entered slowly and then deeper with every stroke. He broke through the delicate barrier before she reached the zenith.

Selina cried out in surprise, but the slight pain evaporated quickly as her body accommodated James, whose firm, even strokes were stoking a new fire.

She gave in to the pleasure that began at her centre and radiated out, sparking awareness in every nerve of her body.

As her orgasm receded, she squeezed to prolong her pleasure and with delight watched her husband moving over her and in her, cataloguing his changing expression as he came to his own fulfillment with a guttural cry.

She kissed him back into awareness of her, which he then returned with a rain of kisses on her lips, throat, and breasts.

He rolled her with him so they both lay on their sides facing one another. James watched her closely as pinpricks of tears edged at the corners of her eyes.

"Oh, I've hurt you, sweetheart, I'm sorry," he soothed, stroking her hair gently.

Selina vigorously shook her head.

"No! Not at all, my love, it's just that was…" She paused, struggling for the words to describe the intensity of her experience. Instead she looked directly into his eyes, understanding that he needed reassurance. "The most incredible feeling."

Furrows in his brow smoothed and a grin appeared like the sun on a new morning.

"Really?" he asked.

"Mind you, I have little experience to compare," she told him with mock seriousness.

James laughed.

"I think it is incumbent upon me to help you with some field research, Mrs. Mitchell." He kissed her thoroughly and ran his hands along her body until he found a fist full of bedding that he pulled up to shield them both from the evening coolness.

"Field research?" she asked, snuggling herself back up against his chest.

"Mmmm, field research," he whispered in her ear as he stroked her again, "in front of the fire research, in the garden research, in the bath research, in the carriage research…"

Low-grade arousal was tempered with fatigue from a long day and the warm cocoon of their bed.

"That sounds like a lot of research," she replied.

"A lifetime's worth," he assured her.

CHAPTER TWENTY-SEVEN

October 1790

The month after the wedding, chill winds from the North Atlantic heralded the beginning of autumn. The rich mantle of green that had shrouded the mature trees around Penventen Hall compensated for the falling temperatures by mimicking the sun—turning gold and ruby in color. As their leaves were shed and the canopy receded, shimmering glimpses of the sea beyond lit up afternoon walks and rides along the peninsula above Padstow.

One by one, the summertime guests took their leave.

Lady Christina was gone the morning after the wedding and bade farewell in a letter delivered by a local solicitor one week later. James hadn't revealed the contents of it to Selina, but, judging by his sour expression upon reading it, Selina suspected that the missive was not a happy one.

He chose not to speak of it, and Selina decided not to press. She knew he would tell her in his own time.

Next to depart was Edgar, whose geological dispatches had resulted in a commission to write a book on the Cornish coastline for Cambridge University. They also offered apartments and a teaching position for the new academic year.

Selina savored the three weeks of late summer in the company of her husband and her family, knowing that it would be at least six months before she would see William, Sarah, and the children again.

By the time Selina and James ended their honeymoon in Pennsylvania, she would be an aunt over again.

While Sarah and the children would winter in Bristol, William and Jackson would travel with the *Diamond* to establish its new role as a coal transporter along the Allegheny River, supplying the newly opened areas in the United States.

William promised, all being well, that his family would soon join them in America to try life for a couple of years in the New World.

On their departure, James clasped Jackson's shoulder, wished him Godspeed for the voyage, and thanked him once again. Selina hugged him as she had done William, telling him that as far as she was concerned, she now had two brothers.

Edith, her grandmother, and Lady Margaret were to return to Cheshire escorted by Lieutenant Walsh, who had obtained a leave of absence. Selina was surprised when James's grandmother hugged her fiercely as the coach was being loaded with luggage.

"You've made me happier than I have been in decades, Selina, thank you," she told the younger woman. "My grandson has married a woman worthy of him in every way. Make sure you remind him of that often."

Selina laughed and returned the embrace before kissing the woman on the cheek.

"Thank you for believing in me when I didn't believe in myself or James," Selina told her sincerely.

* * *

It was midmorning on the road to London. The sun struggled valiantly to make its warmth felt through a blanket of cloud that had brought with it a brief but heavy fall of rain.

The party from Padstow was on the fifth day of the seven-day journey to the capital. Selina edged a travel blanket over her skirt and raised her eyes from her book to watch the passing scenery.

She glanced at James beside her. His interest at that moment was immersed in a thick packet of letters. Judging by the frequent appearance of the Prime Minister's crest, much of it appeared to be from Mr. Pitt himself.

Lady Catherine and Colonel Pickering sat opposite. They had announced their intention to hold a small wedding in the city ahead of his accepting a commission to India.

Comte Alexandre was the fifth member of their group, and on this stage of the journey, he joined the two coachmen on the roof seat, as much for the fresh air as the change in company, Selina suspected.

Alexandre had been somewhat introspective since the receipt of letters from his homeland and had spent the previous two weeks writing a series of missives, often going to the post office twice a day.

His avid correspondence had not gone unnoticed by his hosts, and one night over supper James had asked if something was amiss.

"My cousin has written to inform me that the revolutionary government finally nationalized the churches last month," Alexandre told them.

"Why should they do that?" asked Selina.

"Ah, for two very good reasons, madame. The first, which will be no surprise to you, is that France is bankrupt. The second is that the church, this foreign power in her midst, owns nearly a quarter of her land and takes a tenth of all in tithe.

"If the people of France own the land and the properties instead of the Pope, then there will be a few sous in the coffers at least."

"Doesn't the church use the tithe to operate the hospitals, orphanages, and schools?" Selina enquired.

"Some do, but the rest goes to useless second sons who live off the income without any pretence of being interested in matters of the church or the welfare of the people."

"And what of those who do the right thing?"

"The government will let them keep doing it," the comte had replied.

Now on the post road heading for Swindon, the comte remained aloof from the party, while the colonel took the opportunity to produce his travel chess set and made effort to improve Catherine's skills.

Selina was content to watch for a while as the first two games went the colonel's way decisively, but Catherine fought back to at least an honorable loss in the third, when just three pieces remained in play.

Catherine, encouraged, began resetting the board for a fourth game, pegging the small wooden pieces into the holes in the centers of their respective squares.

Selina turned to James, who had also looked up at the break in play.

"Was that the correspondence that arrived on the day of our wedding?"

"It is. It's a report from Pitt's office about the man we arrested. It's always bothered me that we never identified the man Morcombe said met with Henry Reynold."

"These things aren't always neatly tied in a bow," said Pickering. "We might never know his identity, or if we do, it may be more a matter of coincidence or sheer good luck."

"Did your prisoner describe the man?" Selina enquired.

The colonel shook his head regretfully. "No, he did not. At least not in any useful detail."

"I certainly saw enough of Fidget, I mean Reynold, for him to make an impression on me, not only in Padstow, but also in Newquay," said Selina

"When was that?" asked Pickering.

"When William arrived," she recalled. "Jackson was enquiring after the *Diamond* and I saw Reynold from the window of the Harbor Master's office. In Padstow, I always had the sense that he was waiting for someone because of the way he'd fidget with his fingers. A few days before I saw him in Newquay, he was very agitated indeed. But at Newquay I had the impression that whoever he was waiting for had arrived."

"Perhaps not 'who' arrived, but 'what,'" mused Pickering.

"No, no, I think Selina's right," considered James, "because Morcombe did tell us that he saw Reynold meet with a man who might have been a man of means and not necessarily an Englishman."

"Why do you say that?" asked Catherine, who had been listening to the conversation while resetting the chess board.

"Because Morcombe said the man was dressed like he was either a 'toff' or a foreigner," Pickering answered.

"Oh, dear Lord!" Selina gasped, holding her hand to her lips as realization dawned.

Everyone reacted at the alarm and waited for her to speak.

"Selina?" prompted James.

"Oh James, I'm so sorry, with the wedding and the journey, I forgot all about it. But that's silly. It could be nothing at all."

"Sweetheart? You're not making any sense."

Selina took a deep breath and lowered her voice so as not to be heard outside the carriage.

"After we returned from Boconnoc House, I saw Comte Alexandre talking to Fidget…to Reynold."

"Where?"

"On the Strand at Padstow."

"Could it have been a casual acquaintance?" Pickering inquired.

"No, I don't think so; they looked very deep in conversation. And Reynold gave him an envelope."

"James, do you know how the comte would know anyone in Padstow?"

James shrugged. "Unfortunately I know very little about him at all. He was someone my mother found witty and amusing while in London. I hadn't heard anything against him so I didn't object when she said she wanted to invite him."

Pickering glanced at the carriage clock secured in its niche in the wall.

"We'll be stopping for lunch in an hour, why don't we ask him then?"

* * *

Alexandre didn't seem offended when the two ladies elected to leave lunch early to take a constitutional before the afternoon's travels.

He ordered brandy and three cigars for the gentlemen at the table with him.

"Salut, gentlemen," he gestured, and drank.

Placing his glass on the table, he regarded James and Pickering with a smile.

"Since you are monopolizing the attention of two beautiful women as traveling companions, I cannot believe that I am your first choice for company while dining," he offered.

James considered the first card played well but wondered what game the Comte was playing.

"You're quite correct, Comte," answered Pickering smoothly. "Both Lord Penventen and I have a puzzle to solve. We wondered if you might be able to assist us."

Alexandre shrugged and settled back into his seat. "But of course," he answered mildly.

James, less willing than the colonel to play games, decided to show his hand directly.

"Henry Reynolds. Who is he?"

Pickering gave James a brief sideways glance of disapproval.

However, Alexandre's green eyes met James's without reservation. He did not appear surprised, but he paused, as if considering several answers, before responding.

"You may have more success if you enquire after him under his actual name. It is Henri Renauld," said Alexandre at last, giving the man's name its proper pronunciation.

"You don't deny you know him?" asked Pickering.

"My dear colonel. Why should I?"

"He is accused of organizing the wreck of the *Pandora*, with the loss, or, rather, murder of all hands; also the attempted wreck of the *Zeus*, the assault on Lady Mitchell, and the attempted murder of Lord Penventen," responded Pickering, elucidating the charges against Renauld in an even tone that belied their gravity. "I'd be most distressed if a man of your caliber was keeping such company, Comte."

"I have to confess to not knowing the man well, and, to the extent of his nefarious activities, I would have to say not at all," said Alexandre, gesturing with his unlit cigar.

"I merely heard him talk and recognized him as a fellow Frenchman. It was a superficial acquaintance, enough to learn his name and for him to tell me his profession."

"Which was?"

"He said he was a merchant and had interests in London, Calais, and Paris."

"Did he reveal what he was a merchant in?"

"Alas, no, and it never occurred to me to ask."

Alexandre shook his head sadly and lit his cigar from the candle that had been left at their table for that purpose.

"Now, if you will excuse me, please, I have letters I'd like to post before we move on."

The Frenchman departed.

"What do you think?" asked James as soon as the man was out of earshot.

"I believe the comte is telling us the truth as far as it goes, but not the complete truth, obviously," said Pickering. "For instance, why would a man he barely knows give him an envelope?"

Pickering smiled and added, "I'm glad you chose not to play that card after showing the rest of our hand at the very start, my Lord."

James shrugged off the colonel's gentle dig. "It worked, didn't it?"

"Indeed it did, you read him well," said Pickering, "but whether we ever get the full story out of him is another matter altogether."

"That was the impression I had too. We'll need to get an urgent message to Pitt's office. If anyone can find him, it will be Sir Percy."

* * *

London
10 October

If James was preoccupied at all with thoughts of wreckers and conspiracies, he did a good job of hiding it. Almost immediately on arrival in London, he insisted on lavishing on Selina what she considered an obscene amount of money on dresses and jewelry as part of her honeymoon trousseau.

Her first instinct was to refuse, as she had done her brother.

She could hardly believe one person might need or wear so many clothes, but Selina soon realized she was something of a subject of interest. The young woman who had captured the bachelor of the season attracted invitations for morning and afternoon events.

All were addressed to Selina, Lady Mitchell, a reminder that she was to honor her husband's name as it was now her own, and James encouraged her to attend.

She acquiesced to his generosity, but also satisfied herself that the expenditure was in budget.

The latest event was, however, an evening affair to which they were both invited—the post-wedding party of Colonel Pickering and Lady Catherine. The wedding, owing to Pickering's rank as colonel, was held at Royal Military Academy Chapel at Sandhurst.

It had been as intimate as promised, only forty guests, including James and Selina, attended, though there were double that number now at the party held at the Officers' Dining and Reception rooms.

Instead of liveried footmen, young cadets in uniform waited on the guests.

Selina complimented Catherine on her dress, a silver gown with delightful aqua embroidery.

"Don't you think it goes rather nicely with this?" inquired Catherine, flashing her diamond engagement ring, making it sparkle in the light of the chandelier.

"It does," agreed Selina, and Catherine turned to show off the dress to her, then insisted on critiquing Selina's own latest ensemble, an evening gown in iris with matching satin shoes and a suite of jewelry in amethyst and diamonds on fine gold chain. She found it quite acceptable, to say the least.

"How are you enjoying London this time?" she asked. "I hear you're popular."

"I keep getting invitations. I can't possibly attend them all, and the pile just keeps growing!" said Selina. "Perhaps I should just decline them all."

"You mustn't do that. It would be social death," Catherine instructed her. "The art is knowing which invitations to accept, which to refuse, and whose events you can accept as a contingency but snub if a more prestigious one comes along."

"That's terrible!" exclaimed Selina.

Catherine laughed.

"Let me tell you…" she said.

She linked her arm in Selina's and urged her to take a turn around the perimeter of the ballroom.

"Men might discuss battle strategies and affairs of state and think we women have no idea," said Catherine, "but to be a success at court and in society, it is vital to know who your enemies and allies are, how far you can rely on them, what territory to cede, and when to stake your claim," she advised.

As they walked, Selina watched and made note of which among the guests Catherine greeted warmly with a smile and a word, those she favored with a nod, and those she ignored completely. It seemed the very fact that she and Catherine were now so publicly associated, as demonstrated by the promenade around the room, was sending a clear message.

"And we're allies?"

"Well, we wouldn't be normally. When we first met, I recall saying we'd hardly be friends."

"But marrying James changed that," said Selina flatly.

"If I must be frank, yes, to an extent. But…"

She seemed to be searching for the right words.

"Well, I just genuinely like you. I'd like to be friends with you."

"Not the kind of friends you are with Abigail, I hope."

Catherine laughed, ruefully.

"No, I am officially retired from that sport. I have to confess it was a thrill for longer than it should have been, but now I see now this endless pursuit of gossip and sport at other people's expense is pointless and destructive. Now I must reinvent myself."

"You're fortunate. After your honeymoon you can decide to never step foot in London again and retire to the country or the American wilderness. Or if James does decide to take advantage of his position, you can create your own social empire."

Catherine leaned in conspiratorially.

"And if you ever get bored with married life, there are always compensations…"

Selina was unimpressed at the suggestion and her expression plainly said so. Catherine laughed heartily.

"Oh don't mind me; I only said it to see the look on your face! It's obvious to everyone that you and James have eyes only for one another. In fact…"

Catherine stopped and looked at Selina with gentle seriousness. "It was seeing you two this summer made me really believe that love was more than just some poetic whimsy. Without your example, I may not have appreciated Martin. So thank you, Selina. I mean that most sincerely."

Selina smiled and thanked Catherine. She could scarcely believe that the new wife of Colonel Martin Pickering was the same brittle-humored woman she had met just a few months ago.

Then Selina's attention was captivated by the sight of her husband moving toward them and catching her eye with his; the look in them set her pulse racing. She knew that look. He wore it every time he made love to her.

"I've come to claim my wife," he told Catherine.

Selina squeezed Catherine's hand.

"I hope you and Martin enjoy your married life as much as James and I are enjoying ours," she said.

She kissed Catherine on the cheek, then accepted James's outstretched hand, and he led her to the dance floor for the beginning of a waltz.

"Remember our first dance like this?" said Selina, and they both smiled at the recollection.

This time, James held her closer, their bodies moving together in a unison learned only through intimacy of mind and body.

"Did you know that just about every man had his eyes on you and Catherine?" he whispered into her ear.

"Catherine is a very beautiful woman," Selina responded.

"Is she? I've never noticed," he answered, his left hand at the small of her back, rubbing imperceptible small circles.

"You, on the other hand, have made me the envy of every man here tonight."

"Is that so?" Selina smiled flirtatiously.

James answered the question with a light kiss on her ear. Selina offered a breathless moan and pressed herself closer.

"Indeed," he whispered. "They watch you looking at me like that and they know how this evening is going to end."

"It's late. Take me home," Selina murmured.

"More than happy to oblige the lady."

* * *

Selina was grateful for the empty carriage and the drawn blinds on the twenty-minute journey back to Mayfair.

No sooner had the door closed then she found herself on James's lap, his hand rising high under her skirts, while his lips took hers greedily.

She returned his kisses urgently; eager to experience those lips on her neck, her breast, and her sex, the potent memory of him having already touched her like that incredibly arousing.

In answer, James's hand slid across the front of her leg and his fingers tangled in the curls at the apex of her thighs where she was already slick with desire for him. With impassioned whispered words, she rose and assisted him in undoing the buttons of his breeches, then eased him free of their confines while his hands bunched her skirts around her waist and caressed her.

She came to him eagerly, intuitively knowing the moves of this particular dance, although it was new to her. Selina straddled his legs and slowly lowered herself onto him. The rapture on his face was the beginning of her own release.

At his instructions, she controlled the pace of their coupling, slow and teasing at first until her overwhelming need for him could be controlled no longer, plunging headlong into bliss a few scant seconds before James found his.

Five minutes later, the Penventen carriage rolled to a stop outside the door of their Mayfair townhouse.

Inside, the butler briskly informed James that Sir Percy Blakeney waited for him in the blue drawing room on a matter of importance.

Selina kissed James and told him that she'd wait for him in bed. She was about to ascend the stairs when the drawing room door, already ajar, swung open, and Sir Percy, who was dressed more soberly than James could ever remember seeing him, took a step into the hallway.

"Actually, James, this matter quite possibly concerns the lady as well," he suggested quietly.

Selina looked at James in surprise. His expression told her that he didn't expect the news to be good.

She took his hand and together they followed Sir Percy into the drawing room.

"What's this about, Percy?" James asked, closing the door.

The man sighed and helped himself to a whiskey from the decanter. James frowned—not at the liberty, but at Percy's apparent disquiet.

"We found where Henri Renauld was living this afternoon, and I sent two men to arrest him on suspicion," he began, and took a mouthful of the liquor.

"Well, that's good news," said Selina, hopefully.

Sir Percy smiled grimly at her.

"He killed one, seriously wounded the other, and escaped."

James and Selina were stunned into silence.

"At least his escape wasn't clean," Sir Percy continued, with another sip from his glass.

"He has been injured and was forced to leave behind his belongings. There are papers, maps, instructions, and more. I have men at the apartment examining them as we speak."

James opened his mouth to say something but Sir Percy preempted him.

"The reason why I'm here tonight relates to letters sent to Renauld that mention you both by name. I'm sorry, James. I promised you in Cornwall that this would be the end of your obligation to us. Now it looks like this is only the beginning."

Chapter Twenty-Eight

Percy handed the letter to James. It was in French and appeared to have been written in a rush. The ink had not had time to fully dry, nor had it been blotted before its author folded it in half to place in an envelope. The paper was not monogrammed but appeared to be of quality stock.

James read a few lines to himself, roughly translating them using the memory of his schoolboy French, then handed the letter to Selina.

"She will be much faster reading it than I," he explained to Percy.

Indeed Selina had already read the single page.

"Whoever wrote this was in a hurry and says as much," she told James. "He instructs Renauld to stay where he is and if there is a change to the program, it will come to him in a package at the usual rendezvous in Bourchier Street on Wednesday night. It says…"

She continued by reading directly from the letter.

Should the day pass without word from our mutual friend, we must presume that you are to continue with the original course which was set. I can help you no longer. I have been compromised by our acquaintance because of Sir James and his new bride. I have another friend who will take care of this problem, so Penventen should not trouble us. Take care with your appearance. Presume it is now known to authorities.

"It's not signed but it has to be Comte Alexandre," Selina concluded, handing the paper back to Percy.

James and Percy nodded their agreement with Selina's assessment. Percy turned to address her.

"Your French is certainly fluent, Lady Selina. I regret my remaining men are less so and I personally am not available for perusing paperwork. If my men bring paper they find to you, will you translate?"

"Of course."

"There's a treasure trove of documents and very few people we can entrust with our mission. We need to know as much as we can about their plans and know it quickly."

He turned to James.

"You and I should visit Newgate Prison tomorrow and speak to Morcombe directly; he may be more cooperative now. A month in jail has the habit of softening even a hard man.

"In the meantime, I will have agents discreetly patrol around your house, but do take care with your personal safety. The threat in the letter is oblique but should be taken seriously. But for it, I wouldn't have bothered you tonight."

Percy looked in his glass and found it contained a final mouthful. He knocked it back, placed the glass beside the decanter, and picked up his hat. He bowed to Selina and shook James's hand.

"Good night. I'll drop by at nine o'clock tomorrow morning."

Percy let himself out.

James offered Selina a sherry, but she declined. He poured himself a whiskey, looked at it, and set it down on the table untouched, his expression bleak.

A dozen scenarios had already played themselves in his mind—an assassination, a kidnapping, an accident on horseback. Any harm that befell Selina would kill him.

He cursed his selfishness. If he hadn't wanted her so badly, he could have walked away the night of the ball and not looked back. He should have done so because then she would be safe, but he didn't. He fell in love with her instead and as a result her very life was in danger because of him.

"It's all my fault," he groaned.

"Stop it," warned Selina softly, putting her arms around him, surrounding him with her warmth and the delicate scent of her perfume.

"No regrets," she continued. "Please don't ever regret us. For better or for worse, that's what our vows mean. We will face everything together."

James crushed her to him, raining kisses on the crown of her head, her brow, her cheeks, and her lips.

"How can I regret the better part of me?" he told her, stroking her cheek softly.

"But this is not how I wanted our married life to begin. I want to protect you."

"Then let me help you," she implored.

James held her beautiful face. Her stunning azure blue eyes met his gaze steadily. What a jewel he had married.

"For better or for worse, we'll do it together," he promised her.

* * *

Sir Percy Blakeney was as good as his word. He arrived just as the final stroke of the clock struck nine. At his shoulder were two men, each carrying a wooden box of approximately two feet by one foot by one foot.

James's butler ushered them into the blue drawing room where Selina and James waited.

Selina's eyes widened at the number of documents the boxes contained. Her expression didn't go unnoticed.

"You may regret your generous offer, Lady Selina." Sir Percy grinned. "Alas my wife is not in town to give you assistance; she is French."

"I should like to make her acquaintance one day," Selina responded absently, lifting out some of the contents of one of the boxes and starting to leaf through them on the desk.

On getting no reply, Selina looked up to find the four men watching her.

"Well, off you go," she said, dismissing them with the wave of her hand. "You have work to do. And so do I."

Uncaring of the company in the room, James kissed her swiftly and followed Sir Percy out the room.

The other two, the men who had carried the boxes, remained.

Selina looked at them quizzically. They were neatly but not expensively dressed. Aged possibly in their early thirties, one was ginger-headed and the other had a receding hairline of fine white hair. She would have said they were clerks, but their physiques looked more that of wrestlers.

"We are to stay with you, my lady," the ginger one offered in response to her expression.

"Ah," said Selina. Obviously these men were to be her protectors today.

"Do either of you read French?" she enquired.

The men looked at one another, then back to Selina, and shook their heads in unison.

Selina went to the bell ribbon and tugged it to summon the butler or a maid.

She regarded the men standing there. She had already begun to think of them as "Red" and "White," but that wouldn't do. She asked them their names and learned the ginger-headed man was Murphy and the white-haired was Webber.

"Do either of you read English?" she enquired of the men.

Mr. Murphy, obviously the informal spokesman of the duo, nodded at his associate.

"Mr. Webber reads a little, milady."

At that moment, the butler, a proud-looking man in his fifties with jet-black hair that Selina had suspected from the first day was not entirely natural, answered the bell call.

"Anderson, could you please ask Cook to keep us in refreshments? I fear that we will be here all day," she requested.

"And apart from Sir James and Sir Percy, I'm not at home to any callers. Also, please send Winifred to the stationers for a ream of inexpensive writing paper.

"Lastly, could you direct Mr. Webber and Mr. Murphy here to the dining room and add the two extra leaves to the table? I feel that we're going to need all the space we can get."

If Anderson thought her last request odd, he was too well trained to comment on it and instead waited for Murphy and Webber to pick up the boxes and follow him. Selina in turn gathered the papers she had already spread on the desk and took them through to the dining room, then decamped to the bedroom to retrieve her writing box.

She set up in a well-lit corner of the dining room and instructed Mr. Webber to examine each piece of paper methodically and direct Mr. Murphy as to where they be placed on the by-now extended dining table. Those sheets that looked like letters that had been dated were to be placed in one pile, letters that were not dated placed in another; then official-looking documents in English in another pile, official papers in French in yet another. Jotted notes, scraps of paper, and drafts were to make a fifth pile.

As they worked, Selina hovered, looked at papers, and fine-tuned the piles. After some time, over 300 documents in all had been methodically sorted, more or less.

Anderson arrived with the ream of writing paper; behind him, the maid with a tea tray and sandwiches.

Selina began her inventory with the official-looking documents first.

They were letters of credit on English, Swiss, and French banks, along with bank notes in all three currencies; there were also letters of transit and passports in different names, but where they described the bearer, they were all describing a man in the general appearance of Henri Renauld.

Selina made note of them all and placed her summary on top of that pile before picking up the letters, some of which were four and five pages in length, to start work on faithfully translating each one.

* * *

Newgate Prison was a bleak stone edifice with few windows to relieve its foreboding appearance. It had been deliberately designed that way by George Dance twenty years earlier, his intent to instill terror in those who would offend against the law.

Sir Percy and James entered the prison through a narrow door that seemed disproportionately small to the size of the imposing centre building placed between two wings eight hundred feet in length. The centre portion extended deep. The arcade opened onto a large quadrangle where manacled prisoners would be marched in file for an hour each day for daily exercise. A passage on the right led to the courtrooms while, either side of the quadrangle, a set of stairs led up to the chapel.

As male and female felons were separated with their own wards and quadrangles, so too were they separated in the chapel, where, each Sunday, the women would climb an extra set of stairs to listen to the sermon from a loft.

James and Percy made their way along a passageway under the chapel and waited in the arcade while one of the turnkeys went to find the prison keeper, his booted gait echoing loudly across the stone floor as he left.

As the two men waited, they observed a group of male prisoners herded toward the Sessions House passage. Sharply spoken guards yelled reprimands at those of their charges who dared turn to stare at these outsiders who were free to come and go.

After a few moments, the two visitors were instructed to follow the turnkey up a separate flight of stairs to the governor's office.

This room at least had a window to overlook the outside world or, at least, the Old Bailey Road.

Governor Rupert Lomax was a retired army officer—walrus-mustached, a waist showing evidence of living well without requisite exercise—who ran the prison on strict military lines.

Everything seemed brisk and impersonal. Even Governor Lomax's desk in expansive oak was devoid of papers save for three neat piles—

one at the end of his desk for his adjutant to take away, another for incoming correspondence, the third beside his blotter for his immediate attention.

Sitting before him, James could tell the man wasn't pleased with their interruption to his routine, even when the request to speak to a prisoner had come from the Prime Minister's office. His greeting to Sir Percy suggested they were acquainted, though not closely. James received nothing more than a passing glance, a nod, and "sir" in deference to his title as introduced.

"I understand that the prisoner in question has already been interrogated," Lomax said to Sir Percy.

"It's highly irregular that this should have been brought to the personal attention of the office of Prime Minister, I would have thought that you had other more pressing things to occupy your time."

Sir Percy was not the man to be intimidated by a semi-superannuated major.

"No, Mr. Lomax, nothing more pressing," he replied blandly, deliberately affording him the most basic title. "Certainly nothing that would concern you."

Lomax huffed.

"Well, I'm sorry. It's not convenient for you to see the prisoner today. I suggest you come back tomorrow with proper authority. One issued by the court."

At that, Lomax began reviewing his correspondence, effectively dismissing them.

James held his tongue. There had to be more behind the man's intractability than just an upset routine. He looked at Sir Percy, whose eyes glittered with ill-disguised contempt.

Calmly, Sir Percy stood, produced a paper from his inside coat pocket, and placed it under the governor's nose on top of the letter he was ostentatiously studying.

The expensive monogrammed paper bore a large dark green wax seal with the image of George III and an inscription, *Georgius Tertius*

*Dei Gratia Britanniarum Rex Fidei Defensor.*George the Third, by the grace of God, King of the Britains, Defender of the Faith.

Percy cleared his throat delicately.

"Now, as you can see, my good man, the authority to interview the prisoner comes from the Crown itself," he said, "and I should so hate to tell his Majesty that an investigation in defense of the realm was troubled by a fractious functionary."

Governor Lomax's face turned a dangerous shade of puce. His sudden, explosive roar for an aide was deafening.

A man burst into the room looking as pale as his boss was florid.

"Get Frederick Morcombe and put him in the spare cell on this floor," sputtered Lomax. "And take these…gentlemen down to speak with him."

The aide waited in the doorway for the visitors.

"Thank you," said Sir Percy.

"Conduct your business and get out," said the governor.

* * *

Selina had finished translating all of the dated letters. What she had read filled her with dread.

Glancing at the clock again, despite knowing very well that the noon hour had only just chimed, she wondered how long James would be. The importance of the particular letter she had just interpreted drew her attention again and she read it over:

> *R is dismayed that lightning did not strike twice and ruler of Olympus did not look favorably upon us.*
>
> *The loss of his bounty hurts us and our cause but not as much as the enemy within.*
>
> *Mirabeau should be considered our most immediate threat. He is too adept at politics and plays both sides.*
>
> *R demands a public and dramatic assassination and for the royalists to take the blame. Then we will have the revolution we desire.*

You have been the one chosen for this task. We acknowledge that this poses no small risk to you. There is compensation in gold and safe passage.

Seek out Club des Lumières when you arrive in Paris."

The letter ended with a flourishing letter "D" and no other identification.

Selina glanced at Sir Percy's two men now quietly playing cards, oblivious to the powder keg which sat in the room with them.

War inside France's borders would not be contained there for long, of that she was certain. She recalled Edmund Burke's pamphlet that she had read all those months ago.

France has always more or less influenced manners in England; and when your fountain is choked up and polluted, the stream will not run long, or not run clear, with us, or perhaps with any nation. This gives all Europe, in my opinion, but too close and connected a concern in what is done in France.

Violence, she knew, would spread like the plague, and revolutionaries in England, currently buoyed by the successful revolution in America and urging on that in France, would eagerly seize the chance to create a republican Commonwealth of England, Scotland, and Ireland, conveniently forgetting these countries had already fought against each other for hundreds of years.

And James recognized the possibility of revolution all those months ago, Selina realized. Now, despite everything, the engine of war was moving ever closer to their shores.

CHAPTER TWENTY-NINE

Sir Percy pulled out his pocket watch. It was ten after twelve o'clock. "How difficult can it be to extract a man from his cell and bring him up one flight of stairs?" he asked crossly, passing up and down the ten-foot width of the holding cell.

"We're wasting our time here. Would you like to accept a wager that we won't be seeing Morcombe at all?" asked James, standing by the wall with his arms crossed, watching his friend pace the floor.

Sir Percy narrowed his eyes.

"Your reputation at cards is only middling my friend, but you play a good enough game to hold firm on a bet," he observed. "What do you know that I do not?"

"Governor Lomax is hiding something," he answered. "No diligent man has a desk that well ordered—at the end of the day he might tidy a little, but I believe the desk was neatened for our benefit.

"Furthermore, Lomax didn't arrange his desk carefully enough. When he was thought he'd dismissed us, he lifted up a letter and the one beneath had Morcombe's name on it."

"How sharp-eyed of you, James," said Sir Percy. He tilted his head in consideration for a moment. "They might be official papers relating to his trial…"

"Possibly. But it looked like private correspondence to me. It wasn't letterhead from a solicitor, nor court documentation, but it was expensive paper."

"Hmm…Morcombe has no expensive friends, but someone is interested in his welfare," mused Sir Percy.

James nodded and was about to speak again when they heard hurried footsteps along the corridor.

James and Percy placed themselves in the doorway to see a guard rushing out of sight.

A moment later, a second guard grumbled along, ashen-faced. He looked at the two well-dressed gentlemen in passing and could not stop himself. "'E's dead. 'E weren't this morning but 'e is now."

"Who, man?" James asked sharply, trepidation settling in his chest.

"Morcombe, 'im from Cornwall we were supposed to be bringin' up. They've killed him."

In the background, an explosive and colorful set of expletives boomed from the direction of Governor Lomax's office. James supposed that he must have heard the news at the same time.

The governor appeared then, moving quickly for a man of his girth, following his two officers down the hall. Sir Percy spared a glance at James, who hung back in the crowded hall, then collared Lomax.

"Is it true my prisoner is dead?" he demanded.

"How the bloody hell should I know? I only just heard," the governor blustered.

"Well, don't dally man. I want to see for myself. Take me there now!"

Reluctantly, Lomax hurried the delegation of four along the hall and down to the cells. In the confusion, no one noticed the party was one short.

Now completely alone on the floor, James stepped into Lomax's now deserted office.

* * *

The Apartments of the Prime Minister, 10 Downing Street
7 pm

"Welcome to my vast and awkward house," said William Pitt, greeting Selina and James.

Although he was only thirty-one and just three years older than James, Selina could see the weight of responsibility was beginning to bear heavily around Pitt's eyes. Tonight he was impeccably dressed, but, in the comfort of his official residence, he eschewed the periwig he habitually wore in public.

Selina realized that Pitt's greeting was more than wry humor as they followed a footman along a convoluted set of passages and hallways. Despite architect William Kent's work nearly sixty years earlier, there was no disguising the fact that the residence of the Prime Minister of Great Britain was originally three homes.

Rather than being directed to offices as Selina had expected, they were ushered into a comfortable, informally decorated breakfast room.

At first she was concerned that she had misunderstood the invitation and that not changing her jade-green day dress for more formal evening attire was a mistake. She was reassured this was a business engagement when she saw Sir Percy was the only other guest.

They sat at the table with Sir Percy, but the Prime Minister remained standing by the fireplace.

"I've briefed the Prime Minister on the general nature of our work today, but I felt it was important that you share your revelations directly," he informed them.

Selina looked at James and he squeezed her hand in reassurance. He would start first.

"Governor Lomax's insistence that Morcombe's death was a result of misadventure with another prisoner is a manifest lie," James began baldly. "Morcombe was murdered."

Pitt, arms crossed, face calm, rocked ever so slightly on his heels in reaction to James's words. The passion of his assertion was the surprise, not the revelation itself.

"My proof is in a letter," James continued. "It's unsigned but addressed to Governor Lomax of Newgate Prison, asking him that 'special arrangements' be made for the prisoner should enquiries be made of him by the Prime Minister's office. It is dated one week after we returned to London.

"Morcombe had been in custody for nearly two months, so it cannot be a coincidence that this letter is sent so soon after Alexandre

Charlemont learns that we know of Henri Renauld. Morcombe only became a threat *afterward*."

"Was this among the documents left behind by Renauld?" asked Pitt.

"No."

"Do I want to know how and where you came by it?"

"Probably not."

"And its present location?"

"I have it," Sir Percy informed him. "It's been walked through the cabinet room. It is now part of the official secrets."

"But we have no clue as to the identity of the author?"

James looked at Selina. She glanced at him before addressing the Prime Minister.

"Not directly," she answered.

Pitt frowned and Selina hastened to give him a full answer.

"Whoever he is, we know he has a direct connection with Renauld," she explained.

"As you know, I have translated letters from Renauld's apartment. I have also seen the letter to Mr. Lomax. All three of us"—she indicated James and Sir Percy as she spoke—"are certain that it and several letters of instruction from the Renauld papers, including the order to kill the man Mirabeau, were written in the same hand and on the same paper.

"Sir Percy is trying to identify the paper's watermark in the hope of tracing the maker and the purchaser."

"Unfortunately time consuming, however," Sir Percy added.

"And time is a facility we don't have, my friends," sighed Pitt. "Mirabeau is France's last great hope.

"If he can persuade Louis to accept limits to his power and a Parliament like Britain's, it will be enough reform to satisfy most of the French revolutionaries, and the agitation to spread revolution to our shores will wither on the vine.

"But if he cannot, it means Louis's head on the chopping block and no turning back the tide of bloodshed. And if history is our guide, should France go to war with itself, it will also go to war with England."

Pitt paused, suddenly thoughtful.

"Where are Lady Selina's sketches of Renauld?" he asked.

Pinpricks of unease climbed their way up James's neck.

"They were dispatched the day Morcombe was transported to London," said James. "They were received, weren't they?"

Sir Percy and Pitt looked at one another.

"If they were, no one let me know," said Sir Percy. He rose and swiftly crossed to the door. With his hand on the doorknob, he turned back. "If they weren't, then we have a spy very close at hand."

The breakfast room door closed behind him with an affirmative thud.

Selina added the facts together.

"Only someone in government, in the cabinet, would have access, would they not?" she asked.

"Alas, dear lady, you are correct," Pitt replied soberly, sitting across the table from her and James. "So, until we know who our traitor is, it is imperative that not a word go beyond these four walls and beyond the four of us.

"Without those sketches as evidence to prove a connection between Morcombe and the plot against Mirabeau, the French authorities will not help us find the man."

Pitt's reverie was broken by Sir Percy reentering the room.

"The runner has returned," he said, jaw set. "The sketchbook is not to be found."

James quietly took Selina's hand.

"James…" Pitt began.

"William…no," said James softly.

Pitt leaned toward him across the table, his expression filled with regret. "If there were any other way, James, I would not ask. You know that."

Selina knew something significant had just passed between her husband and the Prime Minister. She couldn't fathom the communication, but it seemed to involve her in some way.

"How is it that I feel as though I am being talked about behind my back?" she asked them.

Later that night, Selina would sit at her dressing table, brushing out her hair in long, even strokes. As she did so, she would catch James's reflection as he lay on the bed. Well-muscled arms caught the even yellow glow of the lamplight, hands hidden as they supported his head. He was stripped to the waist, the bedding draped carelessly around his hips.

Her husband…she could scarcely believe that he was hers to touch.

He was incredibly handsome and, at that moment, still incredibly angry. Not at her, but that didn't stop Selina from feeling the furnace blast of his fury, which had been directed at no less a person than the Prime Minister of Great Britain himself only a few hours ago.

"France is in turmoil on the edge of bloody revolution and you want my wife to become a spy? To find a man who has proved quite capable of killing?"

What followed was invective such as Selina had not heard before.

Pitt stood against it with equanimity and waited for James's rage to exhaust itself. When it did, he offered a small smile of apology.

"I know what I'm asking, James," he said. "That's why I'm asking and not ordering. If you want to walk away from here tonight, then you do so with my blessing and with no harm to our friendship. I will not talk about your duty as an Englishman or love of your country.

"But remember that the threat to you and your wife at home is as pressing as a theoretical one in France. At least in France, you can take direct steps to cut the head off the hydra."

James said nothing in reply. His posture of tightly folded arms and eyes resolutely on the floor told Selina that his anger had reduced to a simmer, for now.

"Does my opinion count for anything?" she asked quietly.

James turned and regarded her bereft, already knowing what her opinion would be. His voice ached as he spoke.

"It does, my sweetheart. Of course it does."

He gazed into her eyes for a long time; silent communication seemed to flow between them, then, heedless of the company, James swept Selina into his arms and hugged her fiercely.

With his arms still around her, he turned to Pitt.

"It seems I am overruled," he said, resigned.

"But William, if we are to do this, I go too and I will not allow Selina out of my sight."

Now, hours later, they were at home and James had said less than a dozen words since.

Selina set her hairbrush down and walked over to the bed. She removed her pale blue satin wrapper and slipped into a white cotton nightdress before climbing into bed. James shifted position, supporting his head on one hand while stroking her shoulder and arm with the other. She settled in beside his warmth

"Don't ask me to be happy with this intrigue, Selina," he told her. "I have all manner of misgivings about this, not the least of which is the idea of you being anywhere near harm."

"But what else can we do?" she replied. "If by warning Mirabeau we play a part in a peaceful reform and keep England out of an inevitable war…"

"And that's exactly the point."

Selina frowned. "I don't understand."

"I think war with France is inevitable," James sighed. "I believe it's too late to bring revolution back from the brink. Nothing but the taste of royalist blood and complete overthrow of the social order will be enough to satisfy them."

"If you believe it's so hopeless, then why did you agree to help Pitt?"

"Because you asked?" he shrugged, half smiling at last.

Selina traced a finger from the centre of his chest, up his chin, and tapped him on the nose. The corners of her mouth raised in a smirk.

"Mmmm, I don't think so," she considered. "I don't believe that I have you so completely in thrall."

He raised himself up and positioned both arms on either side of hers to loom over her.

"You don't?" he enquired lightly. "You can be very persuasive."

Selina giggled and was treated to a cascade of butterfly-light touches from his lips across her face.

"Not that persuasive," she answered between kisses.

James momentarily stopped.

"You really want to know why I've agreed for us to go to Paris against my better judgment?"

Selina nodded.

"Because it's the right thing to do."

CHAPTER THIRTY

Paris

Just as the main artery of London was the Thames, so too did the Seine serve the city of Paris. The Seine snaked its way through the sprawling city, embracing as it did two islands, Ile de la Cite and Ile Saint-Louis, whose backs were crossed with numerous bridges to link the Rive Gauche to the Rive Droit.

The most magnificent of these bridges, which grazed the downstream edge of the Ile de la Cite, was the Pont Neuf, the most remarkable and elegant of all the Parisian bridges. Its impressive span of stone arches, decorated with elaborately formed corbels, spandrels, and cornices, glistened gold in the rays of the afternoon sun as the official English diplomatic delegation started its crossing over to the Left Bank.

Unlike London Bridge and indeed the other bridges of Paris, Pont Neuf contained no houses or superstructures, affording residents an unimpeded view across the Ile de la Cite to the Louvre.

The carriage crossing the bridge conveyed Earl George Granville Leveson-Gower, his wife Lady Elizabeth, their two young children, and their guests Lord and Lady Penventen. It attracted attention not just because of its size, but also because of its livery and crest. Displays of title had been outlawed in the new egalitarian France. That the crest denoted a diplomatic vehicle was of little interest to the people who watched it pass with scorn in their eyes.

Selina clasped James's hand in excitement as she gazed at the Louvre Palace, now home to the finest collection of art and jewelry belonging to the royal family. Also within the palace's walls was the Académie

Royale de Peinture et de Sculpture, which Selina ardently desired to visit. She had been delighted to learn their hostess, Lady Elizabeth, was an accomplished oil painter in her own right and hoped to visit the Académie with her.

Selina explained to her patient husband that the Pont Neuf had been constructed by Henry III and completed by his son Henry IV nearly two hundred years ago. She pointed out as they crossed the Ile de la Cite, that there, overlooking the bridge, stood a bronze statue of Henry IV on his warhorse as though still surveying his lasting creation.

The bridge was capacious, much wider than any crossing Selina had ever seen. It was quite capable of carrying traffic in both directions while still having plenty of room for stall holders to ply their wares. A carnival atmosphere reigned in the crisp late-October afternoon as purveyors of clothes and handcrafted jewelry competed with the fish, meat, and vegetable vendors for the attention of pedestrians.

The carriage left the smells and noise of the bridge and turned onto a pleasant tree-lined road.

Unlike London's mosaic of crooked, narrow streets, Paris spread her arms wide to boast expansive avenues and broad boulevards that took advantage of the flat topography on which the city stood. On one of these green leafy avenues was the new home of the British ambassador.

An efficient retinue of servants saw to luggage while maids prepared the evening toilette for the two ladies. James and Gower retired to the library.

At the age of thirty-two, Earl Gower was one of the young freshmen ambassadors in Paris, but his appointment came as a surprise to many with an interest in British politics. It had been widely tipped that the more highly experienced Randall Dobell, Earl of Canalissy, would reopen the embassy, which had been closed for the past year in response to the events of 1789.

"You have to credit Pitt's persuasive abilities," remarked Gower, who had discovered that the library was stocked with a particularly fine brandy and was now pouring some for them. "I had no idea I was to be ambassador to France until a month ago. I don't recall actually agreeing."

He handed James a balloon of the golden liquid.

"But now that I'm here, I rather think I'll enjoy it."

James lifted his glass in salute.

"Enjoy it while it lasts George. Paris is not going to be pleasant if the population decides to commit regicide," he commented.

"Well, let's see how long we can forestall that event, shall we?" Gower replied pleasantly, raising his glass in reply.

"I've applied to the National Assembly for leave to meet with Louis and Marie-Antoinette at the Palais des Tuileries. We've made it very clear to the Assembly that England would take a dim view should harm came to the French royal family. That appears to be the consensus policy of many of the ambassadors here.

"From my briefing with Pitt and my predecessor, Lord Sackville, I understand the Americans might also be persuaded to stay out of any war but only if they're convinced that we're not interfering in France's internal politics."

That earned a bitter laugh from James.

"I know, I know," said Gower, "but the Americans are very sensitive about such things, especially since they are debtors to France and consider themselves brother revolutionaries.

"I'm actually looking forward to meeting with the American ambassador. Short. William Short. He's been in Paris for a few years now. He was private secretary to Thomas Jefferson when he had the post. Was made ambassador earlier this year.

"Sackville says he's a very able man, but a lousy cricket player."

"He didn't make him play, did he?" James laughed.

"Absolutely! You know how obsessed Sackville is with the game. Cricket mad, him and his father. You must have heard about the ambassadorial cricket match he staged on the Champs-Elysees. Indeed!

"However, on a more serious note, Sackville says Short has formed an attachment with Rosalie, Duchess de la Rochefoucauld. As a member of the aristocracy, she and her family have a lot to lose if the rebellion becomes violent; I don't think he will get carried away with revolutionary zeal as long as she's in the picture."

Suddenly the sound of two small children shrilly protesting leaked through library door. The Gower youngsters, exhausted and fractious from their long journey, were being herded by their nanny to bed.

"Your Selina is getting on well with Elizabeth, isn't she?" smiled Gower fondly, thinking of his family.

"Yes, and I wanted to thank you and Elizabeth for your kindness," said James. "It's not been easy for Selina. Our courtship was a whirlwind affair and now this adventure…she's not had the opportunity to make many friends in her new world. But she's very fond of children. She misses her nephews and niece, so the opportunity to help Elizabeth with your two has been a blessing this past week."

"Well, she's a delightful young woman, James. Couldn't be happier for you. I can tell you this now. Elizabeth was very much looking forward to meeting your wife even before we knew about this appointment.

"Bess was somewhat delighted to see Abigail Houghall get her comeuppance this summer. She never did like the girl. Was firmly convinced she'd make life a misery for any man unfortunate enough to marry her."

"An insightful lady, I think," said James.

"Yes. Dodged a musket ball there, my friend."

* * *

Rain washed the city of the dust and smell of decaying autumn leaves and flushed the Seine of the acrid tang of detritus that assaulted the nostrils every time one crossed a bridge. Then, after several days of drizzle, a mild autumn sunshine chased away the clouds and a cool breeze promised a few fine days to come.

Selina wound her arm through James's as he assisted her from the carriage outside Notre Dame de Paris on the Ile de la Cite.

The cathedral, nearly twice as wide it was tall, dominated the landscape for miles around and stood imposing against the azure blue sky, its two square towers on the western side stretching 226 feet tall, but even then dwarfed by the magnificent 300-foot centre spire.

James and Selina strolled around its perimeter, stopping every so often for Selina to swiftly sketch a different view in a small notebook she carried in her purse.

As they walked around the curved apse, Selina asked James for the small telescope he had brought. He produced it from his coat pocket, and Selina peered up at the gargoyles.

The grotesque masks had fulfilled their duty as water spouts during the recent rains, and now only the occasional drip of water issued from their lips.

Glancing to see that they were unobserved, Selina kissed James on the cheek.

"Thank you, my love," she told him. "I cannot tell you how much it means to be here, just you and I."

In deference to their public location, James held her hands in his, stroking her fingers gently.

"You make me the happiest man in the world, Selina," James replied. "I can't think of any place I'd rather be than here with you."

Despite his initial misgivings about going to France, he was satisfied with the arrangements Pitt had put in place.

Sir Percy had men in his employ who would actively hunt for Renauld in the Parisian underworld using a sketch that Selina had drawn from memory. The likeness seemed good as far as James could recall of the original drawings, but Selina complained there was a lot about it that wasn't right.

Nonetheless, it was agreed it was sufficient for the present scheme, in which James would be contacted through an intermediary if a suspect was located, and, unbeknownst to the quarry, Selina would confirm the man's identity from a discreet distance.

At no time would Selina be in harm's way, and it was not to be an open-ended assignment.

If, after a month, Renauld could not be ferreted from his hole, James and Selina would leave for home, with the gratitude of the British Government.

As they crossed to the northern aspect of the cathedral, James smiled, utterly content for the first time in his life. He was fulfilled in a way he never thought possible just six months ago, and all because of this remarkable young woman by his side.

He never appreciated how jaded he had become until he experienced the uninhibited joy of making his bride happy. It seemed just the littlest things—a flower from the garden, an impromptu picnic, a moonlit stroll—brought delight to her and made her more beautiful to him every single day.

James wondered how he could ever have been so against marriage. It was joy to know that he would never be alone again.

Finally, at the entrance to the cathedral, Selina stopped to sketch the two towers built with magnificent symmetry, a testament to the artistry of the architect and the skill of the twelfth-century stonecutter.

After a moment, Selina stopped and put away her book.

"There are things missing," she said, "in the niches. I would have thought statues would be there." She pointed out the empty recesses.

"And look there," she added, drawing James's attention to the ledge above the entrance. "The statues have been beheaded."

"Comte Alexandre said the Assembly had nationalized the churches," he said grimly. "It looks like that wasn't all. They've issued scrip, assignats, against the value of church property."

"As currency?"

"I don't think it was meant that way to start with. I believe they were supposed to be bonds, but I know a number of people have paid a lot of money on them in speculation, and the way they've been traded in London, well, their value is going to collapse sooner rather than later."

Selina nodded at James's explanation.

"Which means the price of goods here is going to increase, putting further pressure on the government," she said. "But why would the

National Assembly allow people to vandalize the building? It would only serve to devalue its worth. It makes no sense…"

James and Selina walked into the cathedral, the sound of their footsteps echoing loudly in the deserted space. Candles that would have provided light in the rows and rows of chandeliers were long guttered and extinguished, their holders lying empty.

Pews were stacked untidily along one side of the nave, broken shards of pottery and glass scattered carelessly along the marble floor.

Light grey rectangular patches on the walls were ghostly impressions where icons had been hung, the art taken either by the faithful protecting the works or removed by revolutionaries to be stripped and sold for any value.

Metal plaques had been forcibly gouged from the walls; the scores in the wall marked the considerable effort of the looters. Bronze angels that had overlooked the aisle from their elevated pedestals on the nave were dismembered in the desperate acquisition for metal to sell as scrap, then to be smelted and turned into weaponry.

Selina clutched James's hand, staring wide-eyed as she catalogued the destruction in her mind. Although she was not a Catholic, indeed her ancestors fled Catholic persecution, the desecration of any church sat uncomfortably with her. A glance told her that her husband felt the same way.

A row of pierced crosses that formed the decoration on the railing of the oak choir loft had been hacked away to destroy the visible symbol of the Christian faith. Despite each sharing an increasing sense of foreboding, they walked farther into the gloomy desolation.

The destruction was even more pronounced as they approached the altar. Sacristy furniture that once housed the communion host had been ripped open, the thin layer of precious metal that had covered it now gone, along with the silver and gold communion cups.

The cross that would have dominated the altar was missing. Lying cracked and broken in a back corner of the apse lay a life-sized marble statue of Mary, cradling the battered body of Christ on her lap.

Selina looked at the rectangular plinth on which this statue once stood. On it was a phrase crudely daubed in paint:

Il n'ya pas de dieu mais la seule raison.

"'There is no god but reason alone,'" whispered Selina, quoting the graffiti.

"Go on, get out! There's nothing more for you here," a voice bellowed from behind in French.

James and Selina turned swiftly, James immediately on guard for a physical confrontation.

An old man, perhaps aged fifty she guessed, dressed in faded and tattered rags, was moving with surprising speed up the aisle toward them.

"We mean you no harm," James called out in French.

"Get away from there! It is still a holy place, no matter what you barbarians do."

They stepped away from the altar and met the man in the aisle.

"We mean no disrespect, sir," Selina pleaded. "It's our first time in Paris, and we wanted to see the cathedral."

"You're not from here," he stated, still eyeing them suspiciously.

"No monsieur, we're English."

"Anglais?"

All of a sudden the fight went out of the man. He stumbled sideways, bumping into a column before sliding down into a pew.

James looked at Selina with alarm. The old man was near to collapse. She rushed to the holy water stoup and wet her handkerchief in the small reservoir of water, then returned to where James and the man sat.

Taking the linen from her, James gently wiped the man's brow and grey-whiskered face.

"I am James Mitchell, and this is my wife, Selina." James felt it judicious not to use his title.

The man nodded, signaling his recovery.

"I am Robert Baird, one of the deacons of Notre Dame."

"What happened to the cathedral?"

Baird laughed bitterly.

"You do not know? It is no longer a place to worship the living God, maker of heaven and earth. It is now a temple to 'reason,'" he spat.

He saw the confusion on the young couple's face.

"Culte de la Raison," he explained impatiently, angrily even. "God does not exist, only reason.

"They've exchanged the worship of God for the worship of man's cleverness. Truth and knowledge are not God's to reveal, they say, but they are objects to be worshipped in their own right. But who is to say what is true? Who is to say what is rational?

"These cultists claim they are beyond superstition, but they have exchanged one religion for another. Did you know they hold fetes to venerate 'reason' and she is always a barely dressed woman draped in Greek robes?

"Without self-control they drink and fornicate in the street all for the glory of 'reason.'"

Selina surveyed the terrible damage that had been done to the magnificent building and wondered how such a thing could be considered reasonable.

Baird coughed. His chest sounded heavy and wet. He was not a well man.

He gathered himself together, and whispered, *"Pour Satan lui-même se déguise en ange de lumière."*

For Satan himself is transformed into an angel of light.

Realization spread across James's face at the mention of the word Lumière.

"Have you heard of Club des Lumières?" he asked.

"There are many clubs these days." The man shrugged. "Almost all of these groups want the end of Louis and the monarchy. 'In those days Israel had no king; all the people did whatever seemed right in their own eyes…'"

Baird coughed fitfully.

"If we wanted to find Club des Lumières, where would we go?" James pressed.

"How should I know?" yelled Baird abruptly. "Get out of here, you pagans! Go find your bacchanal somewhere else, those sans-culottes revolutionaries on the streets will be eager enough to tell you."

James and Selina glanced at one another and stood to leave. James reached into his pocket, then pressed several louis d'or coins into the old man's hand. He looked at them almost blankly.

"Que Dieu vous bénisse et vous garde en sécurité," Selina whispered to him. *May God bless and keep you safe.*

They left the man seated on the bench.

As the English couple disappeared into the sunshine, Deacon Robert Baird of Notre Dame de Paris started quietly sobbing.

CHAPTER THIRTY-ONE

Selina luxuriated in the hot bath that had been prepared for her. She had already washed and rinsed her hair, which now lay dark and damp around her pale shoulders. Through heavy lids she watched her husband undress, her artist's eye paying attention to the play of light across his flesh as he removed his shirt and then his breeches with an unhurried grace.

She would sketch him nude one day, Selina decided, his form the equal of the marble statues of King David or Adonis that she had seen on her visit to the Louvre with Lady Elizabeth.

The stir of air caused by his movement caused Selina's nipples to blush and pucker, adding to her growing desire. Her observation of him had not gone unnoticed either. This time her cheeks blushed.

Selina slid forward to allow James to join her bath. He settled himself behind her. The tickle from the hair on his legs as they slid on either side of hers stirred her more, and she let out a soft sigh of contentment.

She passed her cloth back to him and he washed himself, then drew it up and down and across her back before venturing down her left side and along her stomach. Encouraged by the stroke of his hand across her breasts, she leaned back against him, close enough for him to lightly kiss her ear and nape.

"You were quiet this afternoon," he murmured softly.

Selina nodded. Yes, she had been.

The destruction of Notre Dame's interior and the encounter with the Deacon had upset her more than she had realized.

Before James, Selina would have said nothing about her distress, withdrawing within so as not to concern others. She'd grown quite good at it over the years, masking her emotions not only from her family, but also from her father's servants, who relied on her for direction.

But now she wasn't alone. She was one half of a whole and James knew her. She was still learning to rely on his strength.

Knowing he was still waiting for her response, Selina turned her head to press her cheek against his chest, distilling her thoughts.

"I've read Edmund Burke and I understand the need for political reform, especially in France, which doesn't have a House of Commons and a House of Lords as we do," she began.

Behind her, James smiled. Somehow it seemed perfectly normal to be discussing politics with his wife in the bath.

"There is much we can improve on even back home," Selina continued. "A greater representation in government, the denouncement and abolition of slavery, but why the senseless destruction of churches, the…" She searched for the right word. "…de-Christianization of public life?

"'Politics and the pulpit are terms that have little agreement,'" James quoted from Burke.

"But the American revolutionaries didn't ban religion," Selina rejoined. "And as Burke also said, 'All other nations have begun the fabric of a new government, or the reformation of an old, by establishing originally or by enforcing with greater exactness some rites or other of religion.' France has not restored or reformed but abandoned Christianity completely."

James ran his hands down Selina's arms before sliding over her breasts to embrace her more closely to his chest.

"I agree, sweetheart. This experiment with atheism under the guise of rationalism will end in bloodshed and death before the decade is out," James predicted.

"The author Thomas Paine says 'his mind is his own church,' but if man is his own god, he has only his limited perspective and understanding. There is nothing stopping him from becoming entirely self-serving at the expense of his fellow man.

"The new adherents of Enlightenment believe that science and knowledge are ends in themselves, but they're not. They aren't guiding principles. They're just facts that can just as easily be pressed in the service of evil as good."

James ended his observation by drawing the tip of his tongue down the curve of Selina's ear. His hands moved freely across her breasts, stroking and fondling their silky smoothness. Her nipples became even more sensitive, and she gasped in pleasure as his damp fingers circled them.

James felt himself harden; he'd aroused himself by the unrestrained pleasure he was bringing his wife. As Selina's desire further stirred, she shifted against him, searching for satisfaction that only he could bring her.

Wordlessly he encouraged Selina to stand and he followed suit. The only sound was the dripping water from their bodies and the crackling of the blaze in the fireplace that replaced the warmth of the now-tepid bath.

They quickly dried, but Selina's hair was still damp. James led her by the fire, where they sat upon the rug and he first combed the warm, nut-brown strands with his fingers before obtaining an ivory comb from the dressing table.

As her hair dried, he kissed her languorously, drawing out each kiss from her lips for what seemed like an eternity before a new one began. Selina stretched herself full length across the rug, and yellow-orange fingers of light from the fire licked across her abdomen, inspiring him to do the same.

Selina stroked his hair and shoulders with her fingertips, raising goose bumps across his flesh. Provocatively he slid over her body so his face could meet hers.

He kissed her deeply as she held herself to him, sliding her legs up along the length of his, kneading his bottom with her heels, urging him to enter.

James did so slowly, inch by inch bringing pleasure, second by second bringing torment as he restrained himself from plunging into her heat. He lavished her neck and breasts with kisses as he unhurriedly thrust, nearly pulling out in full before returning with his full length.

Each stroke banked a fire of desire in her so achingly sweet and desperate for fulfillment.

Selina begged him faster with breathy moans and half words of encouragement, rocking her hips to prolong her pleasure on his momentary retreats.

Soon those moans became more urgent as her pleasure grew higher and higher before it cascaded through her whole being. She called his name over and over, fervently begging him to join her where utter pleasure eddied along every nerve.

He dove in after her, the peak of his release only a few seconds after hers.

James supported his weight on his arms as he remained in her; desire, love, passion renewed itself as he watched his wife surface from the bliss he had given her.

They scarcely needed say the words to express what they had shared, but they did anyway, renewing their vows of sacred love together.

* * *

Although Paris labored under strict austerity, its fashion houses were still busy producing dresses and gowns for the aristocracy and the well-to-do of the rest of Europe, as well as those still well-heeled women who remained in France.

A soiree to introduce the ambassador of Great Britain to the National Assembly was scheduled. Lord Gower had suggested that Lady Elizabeth should have a gown made by a Paris designer for the event, not because she especially needed to, but because it was thought diplomatic for the new ambassador's wife to be seen to support a local industry. She insisted Selina could not visit Paris without indulging herself in a locally produced gown also, and she suggested they visit the garment district of the eighth arrondissement, just off the Champs Elysees.

Lady Elizabeth, warming to her role as an ambassador's wife, made it clear to further flatter their new hosts' sense of egalitarianism by being seen to go to the dressmaker rather than having the dressmaker call on her.

But James was to attend a meeting with Lord Gower on the only morning available to them, and he was unwilling to allow Selina to travel out into the city without him. Gower supported James's security concerns, so it was arranged that a particular garment maker would visit the ladies at the embassy.

In the south-facing morning room, the furniture was rearranged to clear the centre of the room and allow the dressmaker and her two assistants space to show their wares. In one corner, a pair of screens was erected to enable the modeling of some sample outfits brought in a large traveling trunk.

Selina and Lady Elizabeth perused fabric swatches and fashion plates. It appeared that as philosophical fashion in France was harking back to the Greeks and Romans, so too was ladies' fashion.

Many of the fabrics were plain-colored cotton woven so thin it was almost transparent.

In the books, they saw square-cut necklines, V-pointed corseted waists, and bustles in silks and satins giving way to scandalously low scooped necks. There were ribbons tied beneath busts to emphasize their shape while the bodice of these new fashion dresses lightly skirted the torso, the wearer free from restrictive corsets, to drape fluidly to just above the ankle.

Both English women were startled as a young woman stepped out from behind the screen and modeled the latest style for them.

"You can see all her legs!" Elizabeth exclaimed.

"Not to mention her breasts," added Selina.

"But of course!" said the seamstress, dismissing their comments. "It is the latest style. You wet the dress like this..." She brushed a damp cloth across the décolleté and down the front of the dress.

"It reveals the natural silhouette, the magnificent form of la femme, and might I say that Mesdames would look glorious as such. You have outstanding figures!"

"Yes," said Lady Elizabeth, "figures that our husbands would not be happy to see on display for everyone to look at."

Selina noticed the model scowl almost imperceptibly and glance quickly to her coworker, who was watching from beside the screens. Believing herself to be unobserved, she mouthed two or three words silently. Selina made out one of them—"bourgeois."

Was it? Selina wondered. She knew what was inferred by the word. Was it somehow wrong to not want to wet one's clothing to see-through for people to ogle at them?

She considered how revealing her costume had been at the Boconnoc House affair. It seemed to Selina, as she watched the model disappear behind one of the screens to change, there was a difference between a costume ball, even one with a reputation such as that, and what one might wear at a diplomatic reception.

Three hours later, when she and Lady Elizabeth had made their choices, they were somewhat more conservative than the dressmaker had been urging. Selina selected a pale blue gown with a short tight sleeve, decorated over the shoulders and under the bust with cream lace, while Lady Elizabeth chose a dusky pink dress with white lace across the neckline and sky blue ribbon cascades, to be secured by a cameo brooch she already owned, sitting high on the waist.

The dressmaker was delighted to see gold coins as the deposit and promised their dresses would be a priority. As Lady Elizabeth was measured, Selina took the opportunity to ask of the dressmaker a question she'd wanted to all afternoon.

"Excuse me, *citoyenne*," said Selina, using the title that all Parisians had adopted in the year following the revolution. Liberty, equality, and brotherhood had come with the abolition of titles. They were all citizens now.

"That badge you wear, I understand the tricolor represents the flag, but who is the woman with the torch in the centre?"

"Marianne...Lady Liberty...something, I don't know." The seamstress shrugged.

"They give them out at the Quai de Montebello as well as food. We make do the best we can for the good of la Republique."

"Who gives them out?"

The woman shrugged again.

"Some club or other...there are many. They look to buy the favor of people and bolster their numbers."

"But that is a very striking symbol with the torch," pressed Selina. "I don't seem to recognize it. Is it the Club Jacobins? Or the Cordeliers? Or perhaps the Lumières?"

The woman's expression clouded. "Why are you interested in such things?" she demanded suspiciously.

Selina realized her misstep and, taking her cue from the woman, simply shrugged in response.

"Just curious, citoyenne, just curious."

* * *

In the coach as they rode into the city, Gower cleared his throat.

"Our appointment this morning may be a touch superfluous, James," he said.

"Really? How so?"

"There was a letter overnight. News from London. It concerns your mission. Pitt's men have uncovered the mastermind behind the embezzlement of the Exchequer gold. He's also implicated in the plot to kill Mirabeau."

"That ought to be cause for celebration, so why isn't it?" James frowned.

"It's Randall Dobell."

James swallowed bitterly. Lord Randall Dobell, Earl Canalissy, the man his mother claimed to be his real father, was, on top of everything else, a traitor to England.

"So, when does the bastard hang?"

"He won't," said Gower. "We can't afford a scandal, not with the government only just winning reelection.

"Dobell isn't a revolutionary, he's a financial opportunist. On top of purchasing and providing black-market arms for both the Americans and the French, he's been dabbling in currency speculation for some years. He plunged heavily in purchasing assignats here in France.

"Which, by the way, are almost valueless. The National Assembly has sold their value nearly twice over already. "But he's been playing a high-stakes financial game for years and was becoming desperate.

"According to the record of his interrogation, he hatched the wrecking plot for the gold from the *Zeus* as a last-ditch effort to restore his fortune."

"But what about Mirabeau?" asked James.

"Yes"—Gower smiled—"I was getting to that. You know Dobell was after my job? I mean this one, Ambassador to France? He'd been lobbying for some time. Seems he had it fixed in his head that from here he could supervise Mirabeau's assassination and put the match to the whole powder keg, not out of revolutionary zeal—I said he wasn't one of them—he just thought the mess would cover up his involvement."

"Dear God," said James angrily, "there are many good men dead because of him already, and he was willing to cause the deaths of a hundred thousand more to cover his tracks. And now he's got away with it, consequence-free."

"That's politics for you, my friend," Gower offered sympathetically. "If it's of any consolation, he's been made to retire from the House of Lords, and there are creditors by the score looking for him."

"It is not. That man needs to burn in hell. The sooner the better."

"Who knows? It may be sooner rather than later. It appears Dobell was intending to dupe the revolutionaries out of the larger part of the haul from the *Zeus*. And it was a large part."

"Sir Percy's agents report they're none too pleased with the old earl. They may claim him before the debtors' prison does."

They rode on in silence for a minute before Gower spoke again.

"Well at least you and Selina can leave France now at your leisure. With the earl out of the way, the threat to you and Selina is significantly diminished, and Mirabeau is safe."

James shook his head to disagree.

"Canalissy may not be a revolutionary, but Renauld is, judging by the correspondence found in his room," he reasoned. "Mirabeau won't be safe until Renauld is captured—this is a man who will carry his orders even if his original paymaster has gone. And there will be others just as happy to pay for the deed to be done."

"Like who?"

James thought for a moment, putting all of the pieces together.

"Members of the Club des Lumières whom Renauld was told to seek out by Earl Canalissy," he answered. "Mirabeau must be warned, and that has to be at your party."

Gower nodded.

"Then it's just as well I didn't cancel this meeting…"

The carriage stopped and James and Gower got out. Their destination was still a hundred yards away.

They strolled along the street and stopped to look in a window; Gower used the reflection to scan for anyone observing them. He indicated a cafe and said, loudly, "How about a coffee, James?"

Gower moved toward an empty booth at the back of the café. James followed. The owner himself came to serve them.

Mathieu was a short man and swarthy; his keen eyes missed nothing and his lips said less. He was one of Percy's contacts, James deduced, although it was never explicitly stated to him.

Gower asked for coffee and petit fours. A small nod was all Mathieu gave in reply.

He returned a few minutes later with the order.

"Percy says it's quiet here," said Gower, casually, as Mathieu put the coffee cups down.

"Not always, *citoyen,* but if you have business to conduct, then this table will afford you privacy."

He left and the men poured their coffee.

They sat for twenty minutes making meaningless small talk. James reflected that he was getting used to cloak and dagger work now.

Finally, Gower signaled Mathieu for their bill. As he drew out his money, he spoke quietly.

"What is the word on Renauld?"

"None, I'm afraid," the Frenchman replied softly.

"And the Club des Lumières?"

"Them too. They're not like the Jacobins and the others. They're secretive. But they occasionally meet at an address at the Quai de Montebello near Pont Neuf. And there's a Fete de la Raison tomorrow night on the bridge."

Mathieu accepted Gower's coins.

"Merci," he said. "I'll be just a moment with your change and your petit fours."

He returned a few moments later with a paper bag.

"I hope your wives enjoy the sweets," he said, handing Gower the bag, then, quietly, "This is going to be your best chance to find Renauld before your party. Dress plain and wear those."

CHAPTER THIRTY-TWO

To Selina, Paris during the day didn't seem that much different from London. That had surprised her. To be sure, one had to be on one's guard from cutpurses and the occasional street confidence trickster, but that would be true of any large city. Selina had read about the arrest of the French royal family and violent riots over the previous eighteen months, but during her three weeks in the capital, all she had seen were people going about their daily lives, trying to put bread on the table while the politicians gorged on rhetoric.

The cost of doing so was difficult. There didn't seem to be too many shortages of fresh meat and produce, but prices were quite high.

At night, who could tell what the difference was? When she and James traveled directly to and from their evening engagements by carriage, the curtains were drawn and the streets dark. They saw little of what became of them once the sun had disappeared over the horizon.

But tonight was different.

The order to dress plain had been for Selina and James. It was they who were to attend the Fete de la Raison at the Quai de Montebello in the hope of spotting Renauld. Selina wore one of her old grey household dresses and with her hand firmly held by James, they followed the crowds over the Pont Neuf.

She carried a shawl and her head was covered in a simple linen cap. The only adornment on her dress was the vivid tricolors of a rosette ribbon.

James was dressed in trousers, the attire of the working man as the sans-culottes identified themselves. The second rosette provided by Mathieu the cafe owner fluttered from his left breast pocket. To complete his appearance as one of the ordinary *citoyens*, he had not shaved that morning. Now a shadow of a beard darkened his features, giving him a dangerous air.

James pulled Selina closer as they crossed the bridge and were carried along by the press of people heading to the park along the riverbank by which the Quai de Montebello ran. The atmosphere was charged with both excitement and menace.

Children darted in and out of adults' legs as they made their way forward toward the light and music on the other side of the river. Young men treated the evening like a carnival, laughing and skylarking to impress their peers and the girls who openly flirted with them.

Yet there was an undercurrent of unease that permeated the assembly. Men and women, their jaws clenched, wore red scarves and walked with the determined gait of ones who were marching into battle.

Their fury with the aristocracy had not been sated by the house arrest of the royal family, and the object of their wrath could easily be their fellow man.

James carried on him a switchblade just in case.

The cacophonous sounds of drums and horns carried along by the wind reached their ears as they left the bridge. James swept Selina out of harm's way as a group of girls between the ages of twelve and sixteen rushed past them, boldly pushing past anyone who stood between them and the makeshift stage lit by dozens of lanterns.

"We're too late, we're too late!" one of them cried, pulled along by her sister.

"Don't be such a baby," the older girl scolded. "They won't choose the Goddess of Reason until nine o'clock; we still have time!"

As James and Selina reached where the crowd was assembled, a large man on the platform was quieting the makeshift orchestra. He then called on two men who emerged from the wings. Each hauled a large barrel.

He nodded to them and, with great theatricality, opened the lids. The crowd surged forward, arms outstretched, clamoring for the loaves of bread that were lobbed into the throng below.

"*Citoyens!*" bellowed the master of ceremonies. "Man does not live by bread alone! He lives by the beauty of reason!"

The crowd cheered and fought over the loaves that rained down.

"Against fanaticism! Against despotism! We swear to league ourselves," yelled the man, with ever-growing enthusiasm.

"Holy truth, holy liberty, swear we to make their laws triumph within these city walls or all to perish!

"Approach, young citizen maidens to celebrate Reason's Day. This festival is right for republicans...

"Elders, give us the name of the wisest one."

Another three men, one dressed in white, another in blue, and the third in red, walked the wooden treads up to the stage and paused as twelve young women filed onto the podium, including one of the group who had rushed past James and Selina earlier.

Each was dressed in a white cotton shift and wore her hair unbound but held back by garlands of paper laurel leaves.

"You, good mothers of families," announced the host to the crowd. "You see them! These are your daughters who, from here on, through their virtues will replace all your worm-eaten saints.

"Forget your past errors. To Reason finally raise your thoughts. Let all be as one!"

At that, the three men stepped forward; the first of them, the man in red, accepted a lighted torch handed up to him from the edge of the crowd. He walked along the line of the girls, illuminating them in turn, before doubling back to present the flame to a pretty brunette no older than sixteen, who was third from the end. The girl triumphantly held the torch aloft.

The horde roared its approval.

The band sluggishly started up a tune, taking several bars before all musicians were on the same passage. Selina found it difficult to hear the words until the crowd alongside them started to sing:

Divinity of all ages
You who we adore without blushing

Reason! You who our unwise ancestors
Made moan under the yoke of error for years
Be the guide of our fields,
Purge them of all abuse,
Inspire in the breast of our comrades,
The love of order and virtue
Make disappear from earth
All superstitions
Impress your holy character
Wherever the sun introduces its rays
Curse of tyrants and priests
You, sister of liberty,
Reason! On our country-style altars
Claim your rights and your pride.
The gifts of kind nature
Under your eyes are better assigned
The labor of the fields
Through you from routine has been freed.
It's you who makes happy homes,
Take our children as soon as they're in their cradles
May they all be wise republicans,
Intrepid and triumphant!

Selina mouthed the words a split second behind as she heard them, trying to make sense of the lyrics. She glanced at James, who remained silent, and appeared to be paying no attention to the spectacle in front of them, instead keeping a careful watch on the crowd. They had stopped their fight over the tossed bread—what hadn't been claimed was now just crumbs on the ground anyway—and they were singing lustily as they came to the end of the third verse.

With an arm around her shoulders, James urged her away from the spectacle.

"Come on, let's move," he breathed in her ear.

Selina gratefully left the noise and suffocation of pressing bodies, the madness of faces all wearing the visage of fanaticism. It was as though they'd been mesmerized, and, for the first time in Paris, Selina felt fear.

Now, some distance from the heart of the demonstration, she breathed the night air in deeply, wrapping her shawl tightly across her chest.

"What did we just witness?" she asked, keeping her voice low.

"It's as the deacon at Notre Dame told us, it's a religious ceremony. A cult," he answered.

"It's something I've had trouble understanding about this concept of worshipping reason," Selina continued. "It makes no more sense than worshipping a tree or worshipping a slide rule. They're just things, objects."

James sighed.

"You're right. It's as you describe with the slide rule. Reason is a process by which things becomes predictable through repetition and reproduction. But it is manifestly unfit for arriving at solutions for any moral or spiritual dilemmas.

"After that it is no longer reason. It's just opinion with no absolutes, and that's as useless and as dangerous as a compass without a lodestone.

"I've seen enough of the world to know that men can be persuaded to do the most evil things and be convinced that they are reasonable and right."

Suddenly, from close by, a man gave a low whistle to attract attention. James turned to see him, a short man with a cockade on his black cap. He beckoned James.

"Mon ami, we have a mutual acquaintance," he called.

"Have you found him?" James asked.

"Perhaps."

James moved off, certain Selina would follow his lead. He made sure that she stayed close.

The man never once looked back to see if they followed. He crossed the park to Quai de Montebello at a decent pace.

James and Selina rapidly crossed the road but made sure that they were never closer than ten yards from their quarry. Their contact made his way along the park, then crossed the road again to double back and come up behind a group of six or seven men warming themselves around a free-standing iron brazier.

The couple remained just beyond the edge of the light cast by the hungry, licking flames as the black-capped man abruptly fell into a half-stagger and lurched into the circle, belching loudly. He swayed to a halt and pulled a bottle from the pocket of his jacket, uncorked, and swigged from it.

Two men near him at the fire gave the drunk a wide berth, allowing him to bump into a third man who looked up and snarled abuse.

Selina gasped. "That's him. It's Renauld."

She watched their contact escalate his apparently drunken argument while all but the arguers and the two who had stepped aside at the beginning, started falling back to avoid the melee emerging before them.

"You're sure?"

Selina nodded and James signaled with a short sharp whistle.

Renauld looked up, alarmed, then swung a fist at the interloper, who ducked and, being short, was able to immediately drive his shoulder into the middle of his opponent's torso.

Renauld let out a winded *ouf*, doubled over, and fell to the ground, where he was subdued by the other two men at the brazier. The other men, innocent bystanders who sensed this was no simple brawl, took off for fear of being swept up into who knew what.

The "drunk" looked over at James and Selina and gave a salute.

* * *

Aged forty-one, Honoré Gabriel Riqueti, Comte de Mirabeau, was far from being a handsome man. A bout of childhood smallpox had left his face severely disfigured with scarring, but he made up for his disadvantage of appearance by being persuasively charming.

A shrewd individual, he was careful not to speak too long to any one man at the party held in honor of the new British ambassador, but he did not spare the women the benefit of his company.

This was how Selina found herself dancing ever more regularly with the notorious comte even as her husband watched intently from the sidelines.

It was the kind of setting Mirabeau could not resist—seducing a woman right before her husband's eyes.

As the dance ended, he whispered an improper suggestion in Selina's ear. She saw her chance. Taking a cue from Black Hat just three nights earlier, pretending to be tipsy and adding flirtatious giggles, she led Mirabeau away from the ballroom and toward a quiet drawing room.

"The reputation that the Englishwoman is a cold fish is dead for me now that I have met you, *ma cherie*," he said with an exaggerated gravity.

Selina walked into the middle of the dimly lit room as he closed the door.

"Perhaps there is still French blood in your veins," he lulled, crossing to her and taking her hand. "Let me see in the flesh what has only been hinted at under your gown as we danced."

"I can promise you an experience you'll never forget," she murmured huskily. She indicated a nearby studded gold velvet chaise longue. "Sit there and close your eyes while I prepare."

He released her hand and sat.

Selina backed away and lights in all four corners of the room were lit simultaneously.

"What the devil!" Mirabeau cursed, momentarily blinded.

As his eyes recovered, he saw not Selina but the English ambassador, Earl Gower, in front of him. To Gower's side, the delectable Lady Mitchell was in the arms of her husband.

"Brava madame, you would make an excellent spy," he said.

"And you would make an excellent corpse," said Gower, "but we need you alive and more cautious Mirabeau. France is dangerous these days and England does not want a war close to its shores."

"We bring you a message from His Majesty's Government that you would be wise to observe for your own safety," said James.

"We have foiled an attempt that was to be made on your life, but there may be others. In fact, you owe my wife a debt of gratitude. She was the one who identified your would-be assassin as a member of the revolutionary Club des Lumières. A stiletto between the ribs is not the most pleasant way to end a party such as this."

Mirabeau nodded and rose from his seat.

"And grateful I shall always be, despite your trickery," he told them.

He bowed to Selina and James, then to the ambassador.

"May I leave now?" He smiled.

"Of course," said Gower.

Mirabeau crossed to the door, then paused with his hand on the doorknob.

"What a strange world we live in when a friendly warning should come from an enemy, and the danger of an enemy should come from a friend," he mused without turning.

"Welcome to the Age of Reason," said James.

CHAPTER THIRTY-THREE

James watched Selina doze beside him, gently jostled by the motion of their private carriage as they entered the third day of their journey from Paris to Calais. By this time next week, they would be back in England.

He stroked a lock of her chestnut hair, feeling its silkiness through his fingers. It had been a late start this morning; Selina had more difficulty than usual in rising and her appetite had waxed and waned.

And for that James was anxious to leave France.

He stroked Selina's cheek tenderly before pulling a blanket up over her shoulders to ward off the November chill. Was it too early to know if she was expecting their child? he wondered. When would she know?

Despite Mirabeau's confidence in his certainty of being elected president of the National Assembly this month, James was still uneasy.

Winter was likely to bring further privation to the people of France, and the promise of a brighter tomorrow was hollow hope indeed on an empty stomach.

He and Selina would not travel to America before the New Year, so they would return to London and spend their first Christmas together there. The Christmas Eve Ball was a highlight of the Season, James reflected; Selina would enjoy that.

James's musings were interrupted by the sound of galloping horses catching up to the carriage.

He parted the back curtain slightly and counted four men, about fifty yards behind. They all wore long riding coats that flapped in the wind.

He frowned as he took in their features. The riders' hats were low across the brow and scarves covered their lower faces.

James redrew the curtain and turned to Selina.

"Wake up," he whispered urgently, shaking her shoulder.

She woke quickly. "What's amiss?" she asked, sitting up.

"Highwaymen, I'm afraid. Four of them," James told her tightly.

He banged on the roof of the carriage to attract the driver and his off-sider's attention and instructed him to pull up when it was demanded.

Alarm showed in Selina's eyes, but not in her voice. "What do you need me to do?" she asked.

For that, James loved her all the more. No panic, no hysterics; she was more self-possessed than most women he had met, and even some men. But she was his wife and worth more than his own life. He would not risk any harm coming to her.

"Put on your cloak," James told her as he reached under the seat for a small wooden box. As she dressed, James loaded a pistol.

"Have you ever used one of these?" he asked.

Selina shook her head as he pressed it into her hand.

"Grip it firmly but don't clutch it," he hastily instructed as the sound of the four horsemen drew nearer.

"If you can, support your wrist with your other hand because the recoil is fierce. Only put your finger on the trigger if you intend to shoot. Point where you intend to hit and squeeze the trigger."

Selina nodded her understanding.

James kissed her swiftly on the lips before sorting out some small, insignificant pieces of jewelry, coins, and a watch, whose chain could be seen dangling from his gloved hand.

"What are you doing?" Selina asked.

"If they're ordinary highwaymen, they'll take this to be a good enough haul."

"What do you mean, 'if they're ordinary'?"

James put a finger to his lips as he heard a shouted demand from outside the coach.

"Arrêtez vous!"

With that, the two coachmen slowed the vehicle to a stop on the quiet country road.

James whispered, "Stay here!" to his wife before cautiously opening the carriage door and stepping down.

All four men, dressed in long trousers in the sans-culotte peasant style, had dismounted.

To James it was not a good sign.

One was holding the reins of their horses; two held pistols aimed right at his heart. The fourth stood slightly forward of the rest, just three or four yards away. Silently, the man parted his coat with one hand to show a pistol tucked into his belt.

James held his hands up in the air, showing the sacrificial items he gripped in his left, drawing attention to them as they glittered in the sunshine before tossing them on the ground in front.

He let his hands fall in front of himself, the left loosely covering the right.

The man stepped forward and scooped up the loot, thrusting it in his coat pocket without so much as a second glance.

"I'm not so much of a pauper that I need your charity, Penventen," the man said in English from behind his scarf, his tone laden with disdain.

James placed the voice and his heart beat faster in dread.

"Then what *do* you want, Geoffrey?"

Geoffrey Dobell, the Viscount Canalissy, pulled his scarf down to uncover his face. He nodded to a point above and behind James, and the two coachmen dropped from their seat.

"Bring the woman out here," he told them in French.

Before they could carry out their order, Selina exited the coach herself to stand half behind her husband. The coachmen stood to one side.

Selina considered their situation.

A glance at the two coachmen told her that they were ready to flee at the very first opportunity and leave their passengers to their fate.

That left her and James facing four armed men, one of whom hated them with a passion.

She pointedly met Geoffrey's eyes and lifted her chin, determined to show more courage than she felt.

Provocatively his eyes raked up and down her form.

"Darling Selina, it's been so long. Have you missed me?"

A dozen angry words of abuse welled in Selina to hurl back at him, but she heard James whisper under his breath, "Don't respond."

Selina kept her mouth shut. Geoffrey was furious.

"You steal her from me and now you steal her voice too? No! I will not have it," he yelled. "Give me sweet words of love from your lips, my darling."

Ignoring the thudding of her heart in her ears, Selina shook her head slowly.

Geoffrey screamed in rage, venting his fury toward James.

"I have nothing left to lose! My title, my father, my fortune…you've stolen it all from me, but you'll not live another day to enjoy what is rightfully mine," he shouted, and stepped forward, drawing his fist back to strike.

James was faster, deflecting the blow with his left hand and jabbing hard in Geoffrey's middle with his right. As he doubled over, James swiftly kicked his shoulder and sent him tumbling into the dirt.

The two men with pistols drawn rushed at James. With determination born of nothing more than fear and instinct, Selina raised her right arm from beneath her cloak, revealing the pistol.

She fired and her aim was true.

To her dawning horror, one of the brigands staggered, dropping his pistol on the ground. He clawed briefly at his chest in silent agony, then fell to the ground and was still.

The harnessed horses panicked at the close report of the gun and bolted; so too did the coachmen.

Geoffrey's remaining two men leapt at James with flailing fists.

Without hesitation Selina grabbed the pistol dropped by the dead man. She lifted it and fired again, but her shot was wide this time.

James staggered from the raining blows.

Blinking back tears, Selina could see that her husband could not last long against the onslaught, so she turned the pistol in her hand and marshaled every ounce of strength she possessed to drive its butt down on the back of one man's head.

He staggered back, but as Selina prepared to deliver a second blow, her arm was pinned painfully behind her back and she cried out.

"Hold!" Geoffrey commanded loudly.

The melee died down, and there was silence but for the men panting from their desperate exertion. The man she had struck with the pistol hauled himself to his feet and rubbed the back of his head ruefully to find it was bleeding.

The click of Geoffrey's switchblade was disturbingly loud in her ears, and the sharp steel cold against her flesh.

Unbidden, a whimper of fear passed her lips, and she looked at James. A trickle of blood ran down his chin from a split lower lip; his cheek was red and swollen. He held her eyes, offering her courage and love, although there was fear for her there also.

"Tie him and get the horses!" barked Geoffrey. "You can leave him with me; he won't try anything…"

She watched as the two men bound James's hands behind his back with a leather thong that bit deep into his flesh before forcing him to his knees. Selina knew Geoffrey was right for once. James would not risk moving a muscle while the crazed Canalissy held a blade to her neck.

The two men quickly gathered in the skittish horses.

"Get Louis off the road. Hide him," Geoffrey grunted, nodding at the body of the dead man. "You know where to go. Take Penventen and wait for me. I'll join you tomorrow morning."

Geoffrey pulled her tight against him squeezing air from her lungs, and she could only whimper to give voice to her fear.

As he dragged her across to his horse, the two henchmen pulled James to his feet and forced him toward the horse of their deceased companion. Her husband yelled and struggled in the grip of the two men until one of them, fed up with the resistance and angry at the death of his partner in crime, punched James hard in the solar plexus. Searing agony flashed across his face before he sagged against his assailants and stilled.

"James!" Selina screamed, her breath leaving her entirely. Black spots danced in her vision as she gasped for air.

Selina was aware of being roughly hauled up onto a horse which, at its owner's urging, galloped off the road toward a wood.

She clutched her stomach in fear as the horse plunged through the wood into a hollow. They traveled for about half an hour in Selina's estimation, but not knowing the area and with the canopy of the spreading trees hiding much of the sky from view, she couldn't tell in which direction they had ridden.

Mercifully, Geoffrey had spoken not a word since the road, and she kept her silence also, feeling it wise not to speak even as he dismounted and signaled that she should do so as well.

Their destination was a small stone cottage with a thatched roof, and, with the knife now directed at her kidney, Geoffrey impelled her forward to open the door. It was just a single room, enough for a stove, a rough-hewn table, a stool, and a bed—the thought of which now terrified Selina. A single window was shuttered on the outside.

She slowly turned, wondering if Geoffrey was too far gone to reason with. She found his face now radiated a tranquility that was more frightening to her than his anger.

"You're here, at last you've come to me," he whispered in seeming awe.

"Why have you brought me here?" she asked, forcing calmness into her voice.

"You don't know?" he asked, clearly surprised.

Selina shook her head. "I'm sorry, I don't."

"You are too innocent and too lovely to know what kind of man he is," Geoffrey explained gently. "But you're free of him. I've rescued you."

"From whom?"

"From him," he said, becoming agitated. "From Penventen."

Selina continued to shake her head.

"I don't need rescuing from James."

"He won't steal another thing from me again," said Geoffrey, trying to ignore her words.

"You can't steal something that was never yours," she countered.

Geoffrey screamed in frustration and Selina jumped back in fright.

"He's bewitched you! That man lives a charmed life. He is evil!"

"That's not true Geoffrey," she told him. "He's my husband and I love him."

A sneer bloomed across Geoffrey's face.

"Too bad he's dead, or at least he will be tomorrow," Geoffrey told her. "I intend to watch him die…"

Selina was close to tears. Panic flooded through her, overwhelming her determination to remain calm and find escape.

"Don't hurt him please," she begged. "Let us go, and I'll promise not to say another word about this."

Selina felt sick at the thought of trying to bargain with the clearly insane man, but she didn't know what else to do. The eerie calmness he'd displayed when they first arrived at the cottage settled over Geoffrey's face again as he regarded her with a sickly parody of tenderness.

"You dear sweet thing, you've given your heart so readily to someone who isn't worthy of you."

He stroked her cheek and Selina forced herself not to flinch.

"I can show you what love is. An emotion Penventen knows nothing of."

His caress fell from her face and onto the hollow of her shoulder, then across to where her cloak was fastened. He tugged at the cord, releasing it.

"I will show you such passion and devotion…"

Her stomach roiled. Selina wondered how he might react if she vomited on him.

"No," she whispered as Geoffrey's hand slid under the cloak to her shoulder, causing the garment to dislodge and fall down her back. He drew his fingertip down her arm.

"No," Selina said more firmly. He didn't stop, so she slapped him hard across the face.

The hypnotic stare disappeared and the man shook with an unnatural fury. With a yell, he shoved her back toward the bed, but she stumbled on her dropped cloak and fell short of the mattress.

Geoffrey hauled her to her feet and she felt a deep fear course through her. Then she remembered there was more to protect than just herself.

"I'm pregnant," she said softly.

Geoffrey frowned as if not understanding her words, so she spoke again.

"I'm with child. James's child."

The man shook again, worse this time, as though he was having a seizure. Geoffrey raised his arm and slapped her hard across the face. She tumbled onto the bed.

Selina whimpered in fear, waiting for the inevitable assault.

It didn't come.

The sound of a slamming door and a bolt sliding shut drew Selina's eyes open. She was alone and wept with relief.

* * *

A number of hours must have passed since Selina cried herself to sleep.

The light that earlier filtered round the edges of the window shutters and doors had disappeared completely. The room was as black as pitch, but to her unutterable relief, she was still alone.

The pressure on her bladder suggested a great deal of time had passed. Feeling under the bed, she found a chamber pot and used it. A corked bottle on the table held watered wine and Selina drank deeply before dragging the table across to bar the front door.

Selina had no idea how long Geoffrey had been gone or whether he would return. If he did, she wanted forewarning.

Some time later, an hour, maybe two, a cockerel heralded the rising of the sun and was joined by the start of the dawn chorus. As rays of a new day turned the inside the cottage from black to grey, Selina looked around for anything she could use for a weapon. Nothing immediately presented itself, although the stool might do in a pinch. She tugged at the leg but it was too well made to give.

Selina sat on the bed in frustration, then suddenly leapt up and pulled up the corner of the thin mattress. The bed slats might be long enough to use as a bludgeon, and she cradled one in her hands as she waited.

As the morning sun rose higher, more light filled the cottage and she tried the window shutter, but it held firm. Tears filled her eyes at the thought of Geoffrey's return.

"Oh dear Lord, please help me," she whispered.

Her eyes returned to the little three-legged stool.

Ten minutes of work using it as a battering ram saw the window bar splinter and give way; the shutters groaned opened. The stool, still sturdy, provided a step for Selina to haul herself through the aperture.

She dropped to the ground outside and ran several yards from the building, then stopped to get her bearings before setting out in a direction she hoped would take her back to the road.

It was slow going through wooded undergrowth. Her heart pounded in fear and exertion in her ears like hoofbeats and raised panic every time she became of aware of it.

Then came the voice.

"Selina!"

She stopped.

She thought it wiser to say nothing and pressed on, trying to make as little noise as possible before emerging from the trees on a slight rise overlooking the road she and James had traveled the previous day.

Then Geoffrey shouted her name again and she ran.

Selina glanced behind her as she sprinted headlong across the open ground. A horse burst from the undergrowth in the tree line and plunged after her, Geoffrey whipping the animal on.

Closer and closer he came and Selina realized then it would be impossible to outrun him. Unsure of what to do next, another voice called her name from the left.

There was James, face swollen and bruised, running toward her, but she knew Geoffrey would be upon her before her beloved could cover half the distance. And now, for no reason she could begin to understand, Selina felt herself paralyzed, watching the horseman approach, feeling the ground shake with the thundering gallop of its hooves.

A loud crack rent the air and the vacuum behind it filled with a scream.

Two more from another direction and the scream stopped as Geoffrey tumbled from his stumbling horse.

Selina turned back, fascinated to see smoke apparently rising from James's hand. Then she realized he held a pistol and the first shot had been his.

But the world refused to stop shaking.

And time slowed too as she watched James drop the gun and run toward her while several other men, previously unseen, emerged from the trees.

James caught her, groaning from the pain of his cracked ribs, as she collapsed.

He soothed her with gentle touches and words and cradled her on the grass.

"You're safe, my love," he whispered. "You're safe."

But seeing other men approach made Selina tremble even more violently.

"They're our friends, sweetheart," James explained, sweeping away tears that now fell freely down her cheeks.

"They're Percy's men. I was freed yesterday afternoon, and we've been searching for you all night.

"When Pitt and Sir Percy realized it was Earl Canalissy leading the conspiracy, they thought he or his son might have been involved in the threat on our lives in London. They were on their way to meet us."

"Are you all right there?" one of the men asked James. He nodded and the man went to join the others in examining the body of Geoffrey Dobell and reining in his injured mount.

"And you, sweetheart. Are you unharmed? Did he hurt you?"

Selina shook her head in answer to both questions.

"I'm fine," she whispered, then smiled and rubbed her stomach tenderly. "*We're* fine."

"Thank God," James breathed as he held her. "Thank God."

EPILOGUE

The particularly briny smell unique to the North Atlantic coast filled the bright morning air. James strode up the gangplank to the deck of the *Marguerite*. The crew was readying the ship for sail. The departure tide was only one hour away.

He bounded two steps at a time down into a lower deck and straight to the cabin where Selina was introducing Edward Richard Mitchell to his uncle William for the very first time.

His son, with his mother; both of whom he loved immeasurably.

James's life was richer than he ever thought possible.

And now, with his family beside him, he was ready to build a life for them in a new world, far away from the threat of the war in the old one.

Rumors surrounded Mirabeau's premature death in April. Was it really a weakness of the heart or had assassins found a way to get to him? King Louis's ill-advised attempt to flee Paris a month later fomented only more hatred amongst the populace against the aristocracy.

But those were events very soon to be a whole ocean away, indeed a world away.

They were on their way to Pennsylvania, where good friend Toby Jackson was planning his own wedding, and Sarah Rosewall waited with her children, eager to introduce her new daughter, Margaret Ann, to her aunt and uncle.

James ducked through the low door as William handed back Edward to Selina. The baby shook his fist and shuddered from head to toe in the throes of a lusty wail.

"My children made that racket when they needed a feed," William said to James. "I'll go topside, we'll shove off shortly."

He closed the door, leaving the Mitchell family in the cabin that would be their home for the two-month sea voyage to America.

"Is everything all right?" Selina asked as she unlaced her shift with one hand and held Edward in the other. The infant latched onto her breast and drank greedily.

"A letter from London arrived this morning."

James sat on the bed.

Selina tilted her head in enquiry.

"Randall, Earl Canalissy, died three days ago. The letter confirmed that I am his heir and I am legally entitled to claim his title, otherwise it will be abolished and his lands will be forfeit to the crown."

"Do you want the title?"

James shook his head. He stood and kissed Selina and rubbed his little son's cheek as the lad fed.

"The only titles I care about are husband and father," he said. "We're free to start our lives on our own terms. I can't tell you how much that appeals to me, to be my own man with my family beside me."

Selina smiled.

"You're a good man, James, a man of honor, and I'm proud to be your wife."

She looked at him with eyes filled with love and admiration, and his heart swelled.

He remembered the words he spoke to her a year ago when he yearned for someone, for her, to look at him with love and respect, and to regard himself as a man worthy of both.

Now he felt that he was.

THE END

About The Author

Elizabeth Ellen Carter's first novel, *Moonstone Obsession*, was shortlisted for the Romance Writers' of Australia Emerald Award for Best Unpublished Manuscript prior to its publication in 2013.

Her next novel, *Warrior's Surrender* (2014), won the Readers and Writers Down Under 2015 Readers' Choice Award for Favourite Historical Fiction.

Carter has subsequently won praise and a wide readership for her highly researched historical romance adventures including a number of series and standalone novels.

Her titles *Dark Heart*, *Revenge of the Corsairs*, and *Live And Let Spy* were nominees for InD'tale Magazine's RONE Awards. The novella *Nocturne* was named one of the most anticipated titles of 2016 by Australian Romance Today.

Carter can be found online at www.eecarter.com

Moonstone Conspiracy
by Elizabeth Ellen Carter

Revolution in France, rebels in England, and
one woman caught in the crossfire...

The powerful sequel to Moonstone Obsession

For her unwitting participation in a plot to embezzle the Exchequer, Lady Abigail Houghall has spent the last two years exiled to the city of Bath. A card sharp, sometime mistress, and target of scandalous gossip by the London Beau Monde, Lady Abigail plots to escape her gilded cage as well as the prudish society that condemns her. But the times are not easy. France is in chaos, the King has been executed, and whispers of a similar revolution are stirring in England. And because of Abigail's participation in the robbery plot, the Spymaster of England is blackmailing her into passing him information about the members of London's upper crust.

When dashing English spy Daniel Ridgeway takes a seat at her card table and threatens to expose her for cheating, Abigail has no choice but to do as he demands: seduce the leader of the revolutionaries and learn what she can about their plot. As she's drawn deeper into Daniel's dangerous world—from the seedy backstreets of London to the claustrophobic catacombs of a war-torn Paris—she realizes an even more dangerous fact: she's falling in love with her seductive partner. And the stakes of this game might just be too high—even for her.

"...this romance is compelling with such vivid characters and adventure that it is quite easy to get wrapped up..." - *In D'Tale Magazine*

"When I heard the author was turning the female villain of the first book in the series into the heroine of this one, I found it hard to believe. Abigail deserved a nasty fate, not a happy ending - or so I thought. I'm delighted to admit I was mistaken - Ms Carter brilliantly persuaded me to take Abigail's side." - *Demelza Carlton* (author of the *Romance A Medieval Fairytale* and *Mel Goes to Hell* series)

In this series:

Moonstone Obsession (Moonstone Romances Book 1)
Moonstone Conspiracy (Moonstone Romances Book 2)
Available in ebook and print at your favourite online book retailer.
Moonstone Promise (Moonstone Romances Bonus Story)
is a free read from eecarter.com

WARRIOR'S SURRENDER
BY ELIZABETH ELLEN CARTER

A shared secret from their past could destroy their future...

Northumbria, 1077. In the years following William the Conqueror's harrying of the North, Lady Alfreya of Tyrswick returns to her family home after seven years in exile. But instead of returning victorious as her dead father had promised, she returns defeated by Baron Sebastian de la Croix, the Norman who rules her lands. To save her gravely ill brother's life, Alfreya offers herself hostage to her enemy.

When Alfreya gets to know her new husband, she finds he's not the monster she feared, and their marriage of convenience soon becomes a bond of passion. But Sebastian is a man with a secret – one that could destroy him.

As a series of brutal murders haunt their nights, the man who betrayed Alfreya's father returns, claiming to be her betrothed. He has learned Sebastian's secret and will use it and Sebastian's own family to further his own ambition – to destroy Sebastian, mark him a traitor, and plunge an unprepared England into war with the Scots...

"Plenty of action and even a touch of the supernatural which adds an interesting layer to the story. Ms Carter gathers together an interesting cast of secondary characters but the one who really stands out is the villainous, cunning and truly diabolical Drefan...a formidable enemy." – *Rakes & Rascals*

"Warrior's Surrender surpassed my expectations. The research and authenticity of settings, events, and characters was superb." – *Wordfrenzy*

"A complex, page-turning thriller that is also a story of resilience, rebuilding, and finding love. Without using any modern psycho-babble, Carter creates a terrifying villain who is quite obviously a psychopath." – *Lolly Russell*

"For those who like a generous but tasteful splash of hot and spicy in their romance, but also value a well-researched, historically accurate setting and an engaging story, Warrior's Surrender is a great find. Ms Carter's writing reminds me of Georgette Heyer." – *Story Enthusiast*

Available in ebook and print at your favourite online book retailer.

Captive of the Corsairs
by Elizabeth Ellen Carter

Book One in The Heart of the Corsairs Trilogy

Bluestocking Sophia Green's future is uncertain. Orphaned as a child and raised by the wealthy Cappleman family, she has become the companion to her attractive younger cousin, Laura, while harboring to her breast an unrequited love for Laura's diffident brother.

Sea captain Kit Hardacre's past is a mystery – even to him. Kidnapped by Barbary Coast pirates at the age of 10, he does not remember his parents or even his real name. All he recalls are things he would rather forget.

When Laura's reputation is threatened by a scandal, Sophia suggests weathering the storm in Sicily with their elderly uncle, a prominent archaeologist. Their passage to Palermo is aboard Hardacre's ship, but the Calliope, like its captain, is not all it seems. Both have only one mission – to rid the world of the evil pirate slaver Kaddouri or die in the attempt.

Initially disdainful of the captain's devil-may-care attitude, Sophia can't deny a growing attraction. And Kit begins to see in her a woman who could help him forget the horrors of his past.

Sophia allows herself to be drawn into the shallows of Kit's world, but when the naive misjudgment of her cousins sees Laura abducted, Sophia is dragged into dangerous depths that could cost her life or her sanity in a living hell.

"A thrill-packed read!" – *Romance Reviews Magazine*

"Elizabeth Ellen Carter knows how to write very believable characters and situations that keeps you wanting more." – *Marianne Bair*

Also in this series:
Revenge of the Corsairs (Heart of the Corsairs Book Two)
Shadow of the Corsairs (Heart of the Corsairs Book Three)

Available exclusively on Amazon from Dragonblade Publishing

LIVE AND LET SPY
BY ELIZABETH ELLEN CARTER

The King's Rogues Book One

England, 1804: Refused his rightful promotion, Adam Hardacre quits the Royal Navy in disgust and is quickly approached with an intriguing proposition to serve his country undercover.

His first assignment takes him home to Cornwall to expose traitors plotting a French invasion of England. There, he meets newly unemployed governess Olivia Collins, who has stumbled upon a hidden secret from Adam's past – his youthful summer love affair with the local squire's daughter. It is a tragic history that brings Adam and Olivia closer than is wise.

However, with the attraction deepening to something more, neither realize that Olivia unwittingly holds the key to his mission.

As Adam infiltrates the plot, Olivia finds out the shocking truth behind his lost love's death many years ago, and both their lives are in danger. But their growing relationship is clouded by suspicion. Who can and cannot be trusted – anyone or no one?

Or... even each other?

"Exciting and romantic. I couldn't put it down!" – *Kristin Nielsen*

"A lively account of mystery, hidden secrets, wonderful characters, romance, and, of course, spies. This is one you do not want to miss." – *Barbara Michael*

"Adventure and mystery and a love that overcomes tragedy." – *Beth Meador*

Also in this series:
Spyfall (The King's Rogues Book Two)
Spy Another Day (The King's Rogues Book Three)
Father's Day

Available exclusively on Amazon from Dragonblade Publishing